THE RULES of DATING

♥CHAPTER 1

Billie

"**S**hoot." My damn cell phone was dead again.

I looked around Kaiden's kitchen for a charger. He usually kept one on the counter, but it wasn't there today. So I headed to the bathroom, where he was currently showering, to ask him where it was. On my way, I noticed his phone charging on the nightstand. It was fully charged, so I unplugged it and stuck mine on the charger instead. Then his buzzed, and a Tinder notification popped up.

My heart sank.

Why would Kaiden be getting a notification from Tinder? Sure, we'd met on there a few months ago, and I had the app on my phone, too, but I'd stopped getting notifications right after I put my account into temporary deactivation. We were supposed to be exclusive.

Maybe someone he'd been talking to before we met had reached out? I wanted to ignore it and give him the benefit of the doubt in the worst way. But my dating history wouldn't let me. I had been burned before…*badly*. So rather than be the trusting girlfriend, I listened to make sure the shower was still running and then typed in his code—6969. I'd laughed when I noticed him typing it in once. But maybe I should have seen it as a red flag, representative of the dude's relationship maturity.

Inside the app, he had a shitload of messages, so I went to the one marked new and opened it.

Katrina: I can't wait to meet you, too.

Three obnoxious emojis followed: kissy lips, a heart, and a cocktail glass. Scanning back, they'd been talking for a while, and the last message had been sent by Kaiden only an hour ago. My heart started to pound. I felt like marching into the shower and drowning the bastard. But instead, I kept swiping. A sick feeling came over me as I read through the endless stream of conversations he'd been having. In the last week alone, the jerk had messaged with twelve women. One would have been bad enough, but *twelve?* Then I noticed his profile picture. Something about it looked familiar. I zoomed in for a closer inspection and realized why. I'd taken it! The asshole had cropped me out.

My face was so hot, it felt like steam might start billowing out of my ears. And today of all days. It was Kaiden's birthday, so I'd closed my shop early and rushed home to bake cupcakes before coming over.

First off, *I didn't bake.* And I certainly didn't close my shop early *ever*.

I'd also spent *two weeks* working on his gift—artwork for a custom tattoo he wanted to be surprised with. Do you know how stressful it is to design something for someone who gives you *no idea* what they want and doesn't want to see it until *after* it's permanently inked on their skin?

Grrrr. I wanted to scream.

But I didn't. Instead, I took a deep breath, closed my eyes, and slowly counted to ten. When I was done, I felt no better. I definitely still wanted to rip Kaiden's head off. But in that moment, it hit me that there was something other than yelling and screaming that *would* make me feel better. And that was *revenge.*

So I came up with a plan. First, I typed a message back to the last woman he'd been messaging with. Then I copied and pasted it to the eleven other unsuspecting women he was actively chatting up. When I was done, I plugged his phone back into the charger. But what if the ladies responded to my messages? That would inevitably cause a notification to pop up and tip him off about what was coming.

I couldn't have that happen, so I had to make a slight adjustment to my plans. Grabbing his cell, I wound my arm up and smashed the damn thing into the corner of his nightstand. After that, the phone no longer turned on, and I had to admit, the giant crack in his screen made me feel infinitesimally better.

When Kaiden walked out of the bathroom just two minutes later, my heart was still racing. Yet I knew what I had to do in order to pull this off. Sticking out my bottom lip, I hid the phone behind my back and offered my best puppy-dog pout.

"Sweetie, I'm so sorry. I accidentally broke something. I feel terrible."

He had a white towel wrapped around his waist and used a second one to dry his hair. "It's alright. What did you break?"

I held out his phone. "Your cell."

Kaiden's face fell. "Oh. Shit. How'd you do that? It looks like it was smashed against a rock."

Not quite. But close… "I'm such a klutz. I heard it ringing from the other room, so I ran in to grab it and bring it to you. I didn't want you to miss a call since it was probably birthday wishes. But on my way to the bathroom, I tripped and fell against the bed post. The phone took the brunt of it. I'm sorry. I'll get you a new screen after we're done at the shop later." *Or when hell freezes over…*

"I have AppleCare, so don't worry about it."

Yeah, I wasn't…

An hour later, we arrived at my tattoo shop. I'd blocked off all the appointment slots for the evening so I could work on Kaiden's birthday present without distractions. Sadly, the art I'd come up with—a sexy pin-up girl I was certain he'd love—might've been my best work ever. Normally, a Friday night would be pretty busy at Billie's Ink, with me and at least one other artist working until after midnight. But since I'd given everyone the evening off, it was only my receptionist, Justine, at the desk when we walked in.

"Hey, guys." She smiled. "Happy birthday, Kaiden."

"Thank you."

"So did Billie let you peek at your artwork yet?"

Kaiden shook his head. "Nope. I want it to be a surprise."

Justine rested her chin on her hands, looking starry-eyed. "There's something so romantic about letting your girlfriend give you a blind tattoo."

That sentiment made me snort-laugh, and I had to cover it with a fake cough. It was romantic alright, or in this case, *really fucking stupid. Tomayto—tomahto.*

I cleared my throat. "Justine, I know I said you could get out of here by six tonight, but do you think you can stay a little later? I have…" I smiled at Kaiden. "A surprise coming. Actually, *multiple* surprises."

The idiot beamed.

"Sure," Justine said. "Not a problem. I can stay as long as you need."

"Thanks. Let me just get the birthday boy settled in, and I'll come back out to tell you what's happening."

I led Kaiden into the back and told him to get comfy in my chair. Then I put on music—a little louder than usual—so he wouldn't be able to hear anything going on in reception, and smiled sweetly, telling him I'd be back in a few minutes to start.

I scurried to the front. "So…" I bit my lip as I spoke to Justine. "I hope you're in the mood for some trouble."

She grinned. "You know I'm always in the mood for trouble. What kind you got brewing?"

In hushed tones, I filled her in on what I'd found on Kaiden's phone. Her jaw was on the floor even before I got to the troublesome part. "And I invited them all out to drinks tonight."

Her forehead wrinkled. "Who?"

"The women he was talking to on Tinder."

"All of them?"

"*All* twelve of them. I have no idea how many are going to show up, but I told them to meet me here. Well, not me, considering I was pretending to be Kaiden, but you know what I mean."

Justine's eyes bulged. "Twelve women from Tinder are coming to meet Kaiden here?"

I nodded. "I told them he was getting a birthday tattoo tomorrow and wanted their help picking it out before they go for drinks at the bar down the block."

Justine covered her mouth. "Oh my God. What are you going to do when they get here?"

"I have a few hours, so I'm hoping I can finish his tattoo and bring him out to do the reveal for both him and the ladies at the same time."

Justine frowned. "That tattoo you drew is gorgeous. It's too good for that jerk's lying, cheating skin."

I smiled. "Oh, that's another thing—there's a little change of plans for the birthday tattoo. I actually need you to whip me up a stencil, if you can?"

Her eyes glinted. "Sure."

I pulled my phone out and typed into the search engine before I turned the cell to face Justine.

"I'd like a stencil of this, please."

Her brows dipped together, and then her eyes went wide. "You're going to tattoo *the Tinder logo* on Kaiden?"

I grinned. "He said anything I want..."

Justine cracked up. "You are *so fucking insane.* I love it! Can I video the entire thing, please? That shit will definitely go viral."

5

"Absolutely. I would consider posting that on social media as a public service. Maybe it will make other men think twice about cheating."

"What do I tell the women when they come in?"

"That's going to be a little tricky. We need to keep them from talking. Why don't you give them each a tattoo book? Tell them Kaiden called and said he would be a few minutes late, so they should look through and see if they find something they like. We must have a dozen portfolios between mine and Deek's. Though you'll have to talk quietly since the desk isn't too far from the waiting area."

"I'll figure it out." She shook her head and blew out two cheeks full of air. "This is going to be freaking epic."

I nodded. "Oh, it's going to be something, alright."

Kaiden fell *asleep*.

It was laughable, really. People did occasionally conk out in the chair, but usually it was a woman nervous about getting her first ink who'd popped a Xanax before coming into the shop. I never thought the fuckwad birthday boy would take a nap. Though I was grateful he did.

When I first started pressing the pedal, he'd rested his free hand on my thigh. I'd managed to remove it, telling him he needed to stay in the same position I'd put him in. But I worried that next time his hand would find its way to my ass, and I'd wind up punching him in the face. Not having him watch my every move also made the job so much easier. I didn't have to worry about him sneaking a peek of what I was doing in the mirror, and I was even able to bandage him up before he stirred.

For the last twenty minutes, Justine had been texting me from the lobby to keep me updated. Apparently *eight* women had showed up and were currently sitting just thirty feet away on the other side of my studio door, waiting to meet their handsome Tinder date. I swear, it felt like I had an electric current running through my body. I had to take a few deep breaths before waking Prince Charming.

"Hey." I plastered on my best fake smile and nudged Kaiden's shoulder. "Sleepyhead, it's time to get up."

His eyes blinked open. For a few heartbeats, he looked lost, but then he lifted his head and looked over at his arm. "Shit. I fell asleep?"

"You did indeed."

"How long was I out for?"

"Oh…hours."

He raked a hand through his hair. "You're finished already?"

"Yep. I can't wait for you to see it."

He sat up in the chair. "You shouldn't have bandaged it up."

"I want to keep it a surprise a little longer. Justine's still here, so I asked her to take a video of the big moment. *I want to be able to watch your mind-blown face over and over.*"

"Alright." He smiled. "Thanks, babe."

"It was my pleasure, *trust me.*"

My heart ricocheted as I walked toward the lobby. Kaiden followed. The moment I opened the door, Justine jumped up from her seat and blocked my path. "There's a customer here. A *real* customer," she hissed. "I was just trying to get rid of him."

I looked around her toward the front. Sure enough, a random guy was standing at the desk. He was dressed in a suit, with the knot of his tie loosened. He looked sort of like a cute narc. *God, please don't let him be a cop.* Beyond him, most of the chairs were filled with women, all of whom were now looking our way. One smiled and stood. There was no way I'd be able to stall the explosion about to happen, so this poor random dude was about to get a lot more than he'd bargained for.

Kaiden looked at the guy waiting at the counter and the people filling the lobby. "I thought you were closed tonight, babe?"

"I, uh, I invited some friends for the big reveal." Grabbing his hand, I took one last deep breath and pulled him out into the lobby. Once I was in the center of the room, with all eyes on me, my legs started to shake. Kaiden looked around at all the women, his gaze snagging on one particular blonde as he seemed to work to place her face. This thing was going to self-implode if I didn't detonate the bomb myself.

So I cleared my throat.

"Ladies, this is my boyfriend, Kaiden. Today is his birthday, and I wanted to do something special for him. Since he and I have such a wonderful relationship and share *so much trust*, he let me pick the tattoo that will forever grace his body. He hasn't seen it yet, but I think all of you will agree that it's the most fitting ink I could have given him."

My hands shook as I reached up and peeled the tape off Kaiden's bicep. Once the bandage was off, there was no going back. The giant pink flame symbol had to be six inches wide by six inches long—you couldn't miss it from down the block. Everything that came after that seemed to happen in slow motion.

Kaiden looked down. His face wrinkled in confusion. "What the hell is that?"

One of the Tinder ladies covered her mouth. "Oh my God. It's the Tinder logo. Holy shit! Did this really just happen?"

Kaiden pulled his arm forward to get a better look. "What the fuck, Billie?"

My hands flew to my hips. "Don't what the fuck me!" I waved my hands around the room. "Don't you even recognize any of these women?"

He scanned the lobby…the first face, then the second. When he got to the third woman, his eyes flared, and he blinked a few times. Then his eyes darted from person to person as everything seeped in. Kaiden closed his eyes. "What the fuck did you do?"

"What the fuck did *I* do?" I screeched. "Let's see. I made you dinner when you had to work late. I rubbed your back when you said you'd had a hard day on the job site. I even picked up your brother from the airport when he came to visit. But I guess what's most important here is that I believed you when you said you *wanted a relationship and were falling in love with me*."

Kaiden reached for me. I took two steps back and held my hands up. "Don't touch me."

"I can explain."

For some reason, that made me even more irate. As if there could be any explanation for his behavior. I lost it then. Pointing to the door, I screamed at the top of my lungs. "Get out! *Get the fuck out!*"

I'd been talking to Kaiden, yet one of the women bolted to the door and practically fell out onto the sidewalk.

"Good. Yes." I nodded. "Good idea. All of you, get the fuck out of my shop! *Noooow!*"

If I'd been in the right frame of mind, I might've appreciated the humor in the scene unfolding. A six-foot-two, two-hundred-and-thirty-pound tattooed man made a beeline for the door—running away from a five-foot-one lunatic who'd just tattooed a giant pink Tinder flame logo on his arm. He was so nervous he almost trampled a few of the Tinder bitches to get out the door.

Once the last of them was on the street, I closed the door, closed my eyes, and tried to calm down.

Then a man's voice sprung my eyes back open.

"Uh… I guess this isn't a good time," the cute narc said, the one person besides Justine and me remaining in my shop.

"Yeah, probably not," Justine murmured. "Maybe come back another day."

But I'd snapped, and it was going to take more than Kaiden leaving to glue me back together. I marched over to the counter with a deranged smile. "No, don't go. What would you like me to tattoo on you?" My voice went eerily flat. Also, for some reason, my eyes were no longer blinking.

He looked a little nervous. "Uhh… I'm not sure."

I tilted my head. "No? Then let me help you. Where do you get the women you fuck behind your girlfriend's back? How about the Bumble logo?" I lifted a finger into the air. "Or maybe Plenty of Fish in the Sea? That's kind of cute. A colorful little fish? Or maybe Hinge? I can probably knock an H out in fifteen, maybe twenty minutes."

The poor guy just kept staring at me.

I put my hands on my hips. "Well, what's it going to be? I don't have all day."

I noticed he had a piece of paper in his hand. It looked like there was a picture on it. I snatched it and started to laugh maniacally. "A rose? *A fucking rose.* How cliché can you be? You must already have an infinity symbol, huh?" I tossed the paper at the guy. He made no attempt to catch it.

"You know what?" He thumbed toward the door. "I'm just going to go…"

"Good! You're probably an asshole too! You know how I know? *Because you're all assholes.*"

The guy smiled sadly at Justine. "Thanks for your help." He pulled open the door, but stopped before walking through. "I'm guessing you must be Billie?"

When I didn't answer, he shook his head. "Okay then. It was nice to meet you. By the way, I'm Colby Lennon, your new landlord."

❤CHAPTER 2

Colby

Holden came over bright and early the next morning to fix the leaky sink in my kitchen. I could've done it myself, but he knew how important weekends were for me—the only full days when I could spend quality time with my daughter, Saylor. Holden wasn't just the handyman around here, though. He was now part owner of the building, along with me and two of our other good friends. As a career musician, Holden didn't technically have a day job, so when he wasn't touring, he handled repairs around the building. He'd grown up helping his dad, who was a contractor, so he knew how to fix pretty much anything. He'd held many odd jobs before becoming our permanent handyman.

Saylor sat next to me at the table, drawing while I drank my morning coffee and watched Holden mess around under the sink. He came up for air and looked over at the paper my daughter was sketching on.

"Did she just draw what I think she did?" he asked.

I looked over to find my three-year-old had doodled something that looked suspiciously like a penis with eyes…and tentacles.

"What is that, Saylor?" I asked.

"That's you, Daddy," she proclaimed.

"Sounds about right." Holden laughed.

Saylor loved to draw, loved art in general. Even at the young age of three, it was evident. Her appreciation of art was one of the reasons I'd wanted to surprise her with a tattoo in her honor. That plan had certainly gone to hell. *Which reminds me…*

I turned to Holden. "Hey, what do you know about the girl who rents the tattoo shop space downstairs? Billie?"

"You haven't met her?"

I shook my head. "Oh, I met her alright."

"What happened?"

I gave Holden the CliffsNotes version of what I'd witnessed at the shop last night—or at least what I'd been able to decipher from the circus happening around me before I left.

"Shit. I can't blame her for going apeshit on the guy. Pretty brilliant set-up."

I chuckled. "I have to admit, it was—even if I got caught in the crossfire."

"But I'm telling you…" He pointed a wrench toward me. "She's cool as shit. You most definitely caught her at a bad time."

"Yeah, well, she should've treated a customer with respect, even if she was having a bad day."

"What was her reaction after you told her you owned the building?"

"She looked shocked, but not enough to apologize. Anyway, I bolted out of there before she had the chance to say much else."

"I wanna go to Mommy class!" Saylor interrupted.

"Mommy class" was a Mommy and Me class I took her to once a week. I was the only adult male participant, but thankfully they welcomed us with open arms, despite the fact that there was no *Mommy* in the picture. Saylor was old enough to know it was odd she didn't have a mother around, but not quite old enough to have any hang-ups about it. I knew it was only a matter of time, but for now, I was enough. "*Daddy is my mommy*," she would say. I dreaded the day she started grilling me for answers about why her mother didn't want to be a part of her life. Until then, I was thankful she never asked to know more. She accepted my generic explanations like, "*Your mother is not able to be with us. She has some things she has to work on in life that we're not meant to understand right now.*"

I looked down at my phone. "We still have some time before class. We gotta get you cleaned up first. You have donut frosting all over your face. No wonder you love Uncle Holden. He's always bringing you sugary crap."

He shrugged. "I know she loves donuts. I can't resist."

"Yeah, but you don't have to bring them *every* time you come. I'm trying to teach her healthy habits."

"Oh, healthy like we were?" He scoffed. "Do you not remember all those damn trips to the corner store for candy? We're lucky we still have teeth."

Saylor flashed a big smile, displaying her little teeth. I was already bracing for the day they started falling out. I knew I wasn't gonna handle her growing up very well.

Holden patted my daughter's head. "If Uncle Holden ever gets his big break, I'm gonna buy a whole donut shop and name it after you."

I stood and carried my coffee cup to the sink. "We've got to start getting ready. You sticking around while we're out?"

"Yeah, it's gonna take me a while to fix this."

"Alright, don't kill yourself. It's not a big deal if you have to come back tomorrow. It's just a leaky faucet."

"It's gonna drive me nuts if I can't figure this shit out. You know that."

"Well, better you than me." I laughed.

We were fifteen minutes late to the "Manhattan Moms of Girls" weekly meetup. Half of the heads in the room turned our direction when we walked in, but their faces were friendly. Everyone treated me like one of the girls here. Except for the fact that occasionally, the women would flirt with me. Even the married ones.

"Hey, Colby," one of them shouted from across the room.

I smiled over at Lara Nicholson, a single mother in the bunch. She was separated from her husband, and they shared custody of their daughter, Maddie. Lara had often suggested we get our daughters together for a playdate. I got the impression it was really me she wanted to play with, given how persistent she was. I wasn't feeling it, though. I hadn't really been *feeling* much of anything lately. I went on the occasional date, but I was way more selective now that I was a father. I sure as hell didn't want to bring a woman around my daughter unless that person turned out to be exceptional. And given that Saylor had come into this world through an accidental pregnancy, I was now paranoid of history repeating itself.

The theme for this week's Mommy class was "spa day," and there were various stations set up for the girls—one where they could get their hair done up in a bun like a princess, another where they could play dress up, and another where they could get their fingernails painted. It was a great opportunity for Saylor to interact with other kids outside of preschool. And I was grateful for a nice air-conditioned place to take her to socialize, considering it had been hot as balls in the city lately, so the playground sucked.

A lot of the mothers were getting their nails painted, too. My daughter took notice and announced, "Daddy, paint your nails!"

"No, honey. I don't think that's for me."

"Come on over, Colby. I'll take care of you," said Amanda McNeeley in a suggestive voice. Amanda was another of the single ones.

Seeing no way out, I walked over and sat down. "What color should I get?" I asked my daughter.

"Pink!"

I looked over at Amanda and smiled. "Might as well go all in, right?"

Saylor picked the brightest fluorescent color, and Amanda shook the bottle. As she painted my nails, I looked over at my kid's smiling face. She watched the process intently. There really was nothing I wouldn't do for her. This proved it.

On the walk home, I noticed a mane of long, dark hair blowing in the summer breeze and coming down the sidewalk toward us. It was Billie, the angry tattoo artist, walking toward her shop from the opposite direction. *Damn.* Seemed I was so distracted by her miserable demeanor last night, I didn't properly notice what a smokeshow she was. Billie was a petite little thing, short even in the sky-high heels she wore. Her black hair was a stark contrast to her porcelain skin. And she had one full-sleeve tattoo.

Her mouth curved into a smile when she spotted me. Although, I soon realized the smile wasn't for me at all. "Who do we have here?" she asked as she stopped in front of us.

"This is my daughter, Saylor. Saylor, this is Billie, the *nice* lady who owns the tattoo shop."

Billie knelt. "Your daddy actually thinks I'm a crazy person, and with good reason, but I swear I *am* a nice lady." She adjusted the collar on Saylor's dress. "How old are you?"

My daughter held up three little fingers. "Free. But almost *four.*"

"Three. Wow! You're a big girl."

"Look at my nails, Billie!"

"They're so pretty!" Billie held out her hand. "I have blue nails, too."

I showed off my own fingers. "And I have pink."

Billie's eyes widened. "Yes, you do." She laughed. "That's rad, Mr. Landlord."

"Please call me Colby."

She nodded. "Colby."

Pretty sure she had me pegged as an uptight dickwad after last night. At least the pink nails might have earned me a coolness point in the other direction.

She stood up. "Look…I want to apologize for my rudeness. That was just a really bad night for me."

"Yeah. I overheard it all."

"Figured you did."

When she looked down at the ground, my eyes briefly fell to her chest. It was hard not to look, considering she was wearing a *corset*, with two milky white mounds playing peekaboo—a black corset under a red-and-black plaid shirt rolled up at the sleeves.

My daughter reached out and touched Billie's arm, tracing the designs on her sleeve tat.

"She's always been mesmerized by body art," I explained. I patted Saylor's back. "Would you like Daddy to get a tattoo someday?"

She nodded, not taking her eyes off of Billie.

"I wanted to surprise her." I winked. "But you know, that plan went to hell."

"Thank God it did." She snorted. "What were you thinking? I mean, maybe if her name was Rose, I would let you tattoo a rose on your body. Other than that, it's lame. I'm not tattooing anything boring and generic on you." Billie looked down at Saylor. "You wanna pick out a tattoo for your dad?"

Saylor jumped. "Yes!"

"You want to come into the shop for a bit?"

I placed my hand on Saylor's shoulder. "I wouldn't want to impose."

16

Her eyes met mine. "I don't have a client until four."

My daughter made the decision for me when she took Billie's hand, and they walked toward the shop together. I took the opportunity to admire my beautiful tenant's backside, which was just as attractive as the front. She wore black leggings that had a bit of a shimmer to them and left little to the imagination. No wonder this shop always seemed busy. *Goddamn.*

A bell chimed as she opened the door.

"Children aren't normally allowed in here for safety reasons," Billie explained. "But as long as I'm not working on anyone, it's fine."

I scratched my chin. "Ah… I'd never thought about that. Glad I never promised Saylor she could watch me get the tattoo."

"Yeah. Most legit shops have that rule." She walked over to a shelf, pulled out a big black binder with laminated pages, and handed it to Saylor. "There are lots of pretty ones in here. Take a look and let me know what you like for your dad. Or I can make something new from scratch." She smiled.

Saylor sat and placed the binder on her lap. "Butterflies!" My daughter pointed after flipping through the first few pages.

They weren't just butterflies, but butterflies intertwined with other things I couldn't fully make out. Not a single design was what one would consider, as Billie put it, *generic.*

I wrapped my arm around Saylor as she turned the pages. "Amazing, huh?"

She nodded and continued to eagerly flip through.

"Would you like a snack, Saylor?" Billie asked.

She nodded without looking up from the book.

"Do you like Goldfish?"

Saylor beamed. "Yummy! Goldfish!"

"She *loves* Goldfish." I narrowed my eyes. "But why do *you* have Goldfish?"

Billie shrugged. "I like them, too. They're small, easy to pop into your mouth without getting crumbs all over the shop.

So sue me. You know what else I like? Juice boxes. They're more environmentally friendly than plastic bottles." She smiled. "You wanna juice box, too, Saylor?"

My daughter nodded. "Yes!"

"Yes, what?" I asked.

"Yes, *please*," Saylor clarified.

"Wow, Goldfish and juice boxes, Billie. Remind me to bring you some Lunchables the next time I stop in," I teased.

Billie chuckled and went to grab my daughter her snack. Once again, my eyes were glued to this sexy woman's backside, which was taut yet round. *Fucking gorgeous.*

She returned with a snack-sized package of pizza-flavored Goldfish and a mini box of apple juice. She opened both items and placed them on a small table next to my daughter, who finally took a break from the book to enjoy her snack.

"That was really nice of you. Thank you," I said.

"It's my pleasure." Billie took a seat on the opposite side of me.

"Listen…" I lowered my voice. "Apologies if I came off as threatening in any way last night. Throwing the landlord thing in your face like that—"

"I didn't take it that way. I mean, you *are* my landlord, so…" She sighed. "Anyway, I'm the one who should be apologizing for refusing to accommodate a paying customer who'd waited patiently, landlord or not. What you experienced last night is not a normal reflection of how I do business."

I nodded. "Don't worry about it. You had every right to be pissed." I paused. "If you don't mind me asking, how the hell does something like that happen?"

"You mean besides the fact that he's a prick?" She immediately covered her mouth and looked over at Saylor, who was oblivious. "Sorry. I wasn't thinking."

"No worries. She's too into her snack and your book."

18

She shook her head. "I didn't see last night coming. The only consolation is that I'd only invested a few months in the relationship, which I consider a godsend."

I nodded. "I'm glad to hear that, but what I really mean is how the heck did you orchestrate that?"

"He left his phone out, and I saw a Tinder notification pop up. That wasn't supposed to be happening, so I had to investigate. I knew his access code, and once I realized what he was up to, I decided to set up dates with all of the women he'd been chatting with—at the same time. And you know the rest."

"That was freaking epic."

"Thanks." She smiled proudly. "I thought so, too."

"It takes a lot of strength to execute something like that when you're hurting."

"I think the hurt is what gave me the strength, oddly."

I nodded. "I get that."

Billie impressed me. Not only was she extremely talented, she was tough—with a hint of crazy. I became more curious about her by the second. I looked into her eyes for a moment, but that was cut short when she got up to fetch a napkin for Saylor.

She then returned to her spot next to me. "Do you live in the building, or are you just the new owner?"

"I live upstairs, too, yeah."

"And you're the only owner, or…"

"No." I shook my head. "You know Holden, right?"

"The musician-slash-handyman? Yeah. He's cool."

"Yup. He's part owner, too. Along with two of our other friends."

Her eyes widened. "Wow. So the four of you own the building together?"

"Yeah. Well, the company we formed together owns the building. One of the guys, Owen, works in commercial real estate and brokered the deal. And then there's Brayden."

"You guys must really trust each other to go in together like that."

"We do. They're the only three people I can say that about."

"So you must have gone upstairs last night and told your wife all about the nutty tattoo shop owner, huh?"

Oh. Everyone assumes I'm married because of Saylor. "There is no wife."

"Oh." Billie's lips parted. "Divorced?"

"No. Saylor's mother was never in the picture." My voice dwindled to barely a whisper. "She didn't want to be."

The color drained from her face. "I see."

I stood and motioned for her to walk to the other side of the room with me, away from Saylor.

"The pregnancy was a…surprise to say the least," I murmured, looking out the window. "The last thing I ever expected. The woman and I didn't exactly know each other. But Saylor's the best thing that ever happened to me."

Billie looked over at my daughter. "She's beautiful."

So are you, I wanted to say. She really was, uniquely beautiful. Though she wore heavy makeup, I somehow knew she'd be even more beautiful without it.

"But it must be challenging raising her on your own," she said.

"Thank you. And yes, I hadn't ever held a baby before my own."

"That's wild." Billie looked at me like she expected me to elaborate. But this wasn't the time. I didn't want Saylor to overhear.

I got lost in Billie's eyes for a few moments. They were a deep brown, like the color of coffee beans. Then Saylor slurped on the last of her apple juice and broke me out of my trance.

"Did you choose a design?" Billie asked as we walked back over to her.

"This one!" She pointed to the most ostentatious rainbow unicorn.

Billie cracked up. "Well, I'm happy to ink that on him, if your dad's okay with it."

"I might have to think on that one. I always say there's nothing I wouldn't do for my daughter." I waggled my pink fingernails. "But that crazy-looking unicorn might be the first exception."

"Well, if you reconsider, just say the word. Or if you want anything else, I'll do that, too." She winked. "Unless it's a rose."

I nodded. "I think I need a bit more time. If last night taught me anything, it's not to rush into such an important decision."

"I definitely agree." She smiled.

There wasn't much reason for us to stay, and I didn't want Billie to have to kick us out, so I turned and patted Saylor on the back. "Say thank you, Saylor. We have to go upstairs."

"Thank you!" My daughter reached out and hugged Billie.

Billie closed her eyes as she received the embrace. "You are so welcome, pretty girl. Come back and visit again soon. I always have Goldfish and juice boxes."

She walked us to the door.

Before we left, I turned around one last time. "Hey, Billie?"

"Yeah?"

"That ex of yours is an idiot."

Her cheeks reddened. Maybe it was because of what I said. Or maybe it was because I'd just sneaked one more look at the cleavage peeking out of her corset.

❤️CHAPTER 3

Colby

Tuesday after I left the office, I slowed on the sidewalk as I passed the tattoo parlor, hoping to catch a glimpse of the owner—otherwise known as the woman who had been haunting my dreams the last few nights. It was fucked up. I very rarely dreamed—or at least I very rarely remembered my dreams—but three nights in a row now, I'd had the same goddamn one. I was in Billie's shop, lying in her tattoo chair while she inked a black-and-white picture of a bridge onto the skin over my right pectoral muscle. It would have been innocent enough if it stopped there, but of course it didn't. Halfway through my tat, she pressed the pedal on the floor and lowered the chair. Then she leaned over and licked her way up my abs… It always ended the same way: Billie in the chair with her legs over my shoulders as I drilled the shit out of her.

Lovely, isn't it? The woman is sweet to my daughter, and I repay that kindness by having a recurring erotic fantasy and jerking off to the memory every morning. Just thinking about it made me feel like a dirtbag, so even though I wanted to pop in and spend a few minutes with Billie, I didn't really deserve to.

So, I decided to leave it up to fate. If I happened to see her in the window, I'd stop. If not, I wouldn't. Unfortunately, luck wasn't

22

on my side tonight, and the only person I saw was the receptionist. Oh well. It was probably for the best. Billie had obviously just come off a bad breakup, which meant the timing wasn't right—not that she would likely go out with me even if the timing were perfect.

I passed her door and continued to the main entrance for the apartments, walking straight to the elevator. When the doors slid open, my buddy Owen stepped out.

"Hey," I said. We did a quick fist bump and one-arm-shoulder-hug thing. "What's going on? I haven't seen you in a while."

"Yeah, I've been really busy. My assistant left to go on maternity leave, and one of my agents quit without giving any notice, so I'm shorthanded."

I looked down at what Owen had in his hand and grinned. "A toolbox? Are you going to a costume party or something? Because I *know* you don't have a damn clue how to use one thing in that box, dude."

"Bite me, asshole. I'm not incompetent. I just prefer not to get my hands dirty."

I chuckled. "Yeah, I heard your manicurist gets upset if you develop a callus."

I was busting balls, of course, though Owen really did get manicures. Out of my crew of four, he was definitely the one who called people to fix shit, rather than having people call him.

"Seriously, though," I added. "Where are you going with a toolbox?"

"Holden got a last-minute gig. He didn't want to pass it up because some music bigwig was going to be there, so he asked me to cover for him as the super for a few days. Trust me, I tried to say no, but he seemed pretty desperate. Now *you* could be a good friend and cover for me, though…"

I grinned. "No can do. I have a sweet girl waiting for me upstairs."

"Come on. It won't take too long. Uncle Owen can take her out for ice cream while you're doing this maintenance call."

"Why do you assholes always want to feed my kid sugar?"

Owen smirked. "That's how we get all the girls to like us."

I laughed as I stepped into the elevator and pushed the button. "You're an idiot. Have fun sticking your hands in a toilet or whatever shitty thing you wind up doing."

"Yeah, fun—fixing air conditioning. Maybe I'll get a tattoo after, because the thought of someone continually poking me with a needle sounds almost as fun."

The elevator doors started to slide shut, but my ears had perked up at the word *tattoo*. Reaching forward, I stopped the doors from closing. "The air isn't working in the tattoo parlor?"

"Nope. The owner called it in a little while ago."

Well, well, well. Maybe fate had other plans for me. "On second thought, you have no idea how to fix an air-conditioning unit. Why don't I go check it out? My sitter has Saylor at the park right now, but they'll be back in about an hour. You'd just have to be around to relieve her if I'm not done in time."

"Really?"

I stepped out of the elevator and plucked the toolbox from his hand. "Really. But you owe me one."

"You got it. Thanks. If I have an hour, I'm going to run to my office to get a file I need for the morning. But I'll make sure I'm back before Saylor and the sitter return."

"Alright. Just don't be late."

"I won't. Thanks again, buddy."

I *almost* felt a little bad. Although not bad enough to admit I would've used any excuse to go to Billie's, and definitely not bad enough that I wouldn't be collecting on Owen's IOU one day.

"Hey," I said to the receptionist. "I'm here to look at the AC unit?"

She squinted at me. "Aren't you the guy from the other night? The one who fell into the middle of the Tinder reunion?"

"One and the same." I smiled and extended my hand. "Colby Lennon. I'm one of the owners of the building. We try to handle the repairs ourselves, if it's possible."

She smiled and shook my hand. "Justine Russo. If you're going to fix this AC, I'm pretty sure you'll get a sunnier reception from Billie this time. It's blowing hot air. I think it's up to eighty-five in the back already."

"I'll see what I can do. Where is the unit?"

"It's in the rear of the studio. Help yourself. Billie's back there."

I headed back, feeling a little too excited about fixing a damn air conditioner. But that excitement quickly deflated when I opened the door to the studio and found Billie lying in a tattoo chair while some big, tatted dude rubbed her shoulders. She was wearing what I was starting to consider her signature work outfit—a corset, but without the flannel over it now.

Neither of them seemed to have heard me walk in, and it felt like I was interrupting a private moment, so I cleared my throat before fully entering. The big guy lifted his chin, but never took his hands off of Billie. "Can I help you?"

"Yeah, I'm, uh, here to look at the AC."

Billie sat up from the chair. The big smile that spread across her face made me feel a tiny bit better about what I'd walked in on.

"Hey, what's up, big daddy?" She winked.

Fuck. My cock twitched. Was it her calling me daddy or the wink? Maybe both. I tried to play it cool and lifted my chin. "Hey. What's up?"

She turned to the tatted guy. "This is the new landlord I was telling you about—the one I'm *not* tattooing a rose on. Deek, this is Colby. Colby, this is Deek."

Billie swung her legs in the air and jumped down from the chair. It was impossible not to notice her tits jiggling in that little corset. Today's was black lace, and I found myself wondering if she had on matching lace panties under her jeans. I bet she did. The flannel she usually wore was tied around her waist. I couldn't blame her; it was fucking hot as hell in here.

Billie tilted her head toward the back of the room. "Follow me."

I did my best not to stare at her ass as we walked, though it wasn't easy. Her jeans were tight, and today's corset didn't meet the top of her pants, so she had an inch of skin exposed, too—it was so damn creamy.

Fuck. What was with me and this woman? I wasn't usually such a damn horn dog.

Billie waved her hands Vanna White-style when she reached the big condenser in the back of the room. "Here's the offending equipment. I've named him Kaiden since it's useless and blowing hot air."

I laughed. "Good to know. And where's your thermostat?"

She pointed to a wall ten feet away, then hooked her thumbs into her belt loops. "Well, I won't stand on top of you while you work. Just yell if you need anything."

"Sounds good."

After I checked the basics in the air handler, making sure nothing was frozen and the filters were clean, I walked over to the thermostat. While I unscrewed the cover, I listened to the conversation going on behind me between Billie and Deek.

"It would be good for you," he said. "I think you should do it. Just ignore her."

"You've met Renee. She's not someone who's easily ignored."

"You know what I think your real issue is?"

"No, but I'm sure you're going to enlighten me."

"You suck at taking help from anyone."

"I do not."

I glanced over. The big guy frowned at Billie. "Do I need to remind you of the ridiculous interest rate you paid on your loan to open this place?"

"No, I think the other six-hundred-and-thirty-seven times you've reminded me so far is more than sufficient."

"Could have been interest free from me."

"I didn't want to risk your money."

"You're one of the most sought-after artists in a city of eight-million people, and it's trendy for people from all walks of life to get ink these days. It wasn't a risk."

Billie shrugged. "Whatever. There's nothing wrong with doing things for yourself."

"I agree. But there's also nothing wrong with taking a little help from people who love you once in a while."

"I'll think about it. Now rub my neck more."

I lost track of their conversation after that, probably because it was driving me nuts that some dude was touching her, so I needed to drown them out altogether. Twenty minutes later, I was pretty sure I'd found the culprit of the AC break down. Two old, yellow wires in the thermostat were practically shredded and no longer connected. Since those were usually the wires for the cooling, I hoped a quick rewire might solve the problem. Luckily the toolbox had a spool with some copper wire, so after I stripped back the rubber casing with a wire stripper, I figured I'd let Billie know what was going on.

Another guy had just come into the shop. He walked right over to Billie, grabbed both of her cheeks, and planted a big kiss on her lips. My jaw flexed. But then the dude strolled to Deek and kissed him on the lips, too. He also rubbed Deek's arm. "Are you ready to go? I'm not paying the late charge for doggy daycare anymore because you have to stick around work and gossip like a bitch."

Deek rolled his eyes. "It's ten bucks."

The guy put his hands on his hips. "It's ten dollars I could be putting in the Botox-fund jar."

Billie chuckled. "Goodnight, boys." She yelled toward the lobby, "You go home, too, Justine! Lock up on your way out, okay, babe?"

"Will do! 'Night, Billie!"

The two men bickered some more as they walked out of the shop. Billie watched with a smile on her face before turning back to me. "What's going on, Daddy-O? Did you fix Kaiden? Actually, maybe we need another name for that unit. Because Kaiden isn't fixable."

I smiled and held up the wires. "I think I might've found the problem. Won't know until I rewire the thermostat, but these don't look too good."

"Alright, awesome. Because if it's not fixed very soon, I might be peeling these jeans off and walking around in my underwear. They're stuck to my legs." She fanned herself. "I can't take the heat."

"Well, on second thought, maybe I don't know how to fix it." I smiled. "You want a hand with those pants?"

She laughed. "I'm an angry person when I'm hot. That first night you were here, I wasn't even warm. So you might want to get that repair done."

My mood had definitely improved after finding out Deek wasn't interested in Billie. Now that it was just the two of us, she followed me to the back and sat down on the floor next to my toolbox.

"So what do you do all day, Mr. Landlord? You wear a suit. Are you in real estate as your full-time job?"

I started to twist the new wires to connect them to the old as we talked. "Nope. I'm an architect."

"Really?"

"Yep."

"I don't think I've ever met anyone who's an architect."

I grinned. "Is it as exciting as you imagined?"

Billie laughed. "Definitely more."

After the first wire was connected, I started to twist the second one, but when I touched the ends together, they sparked, and I got a little shock. Then all the lights went off. "Crap," I groaned. "I blew a circuit."

There were no windows in the back of the studio, so it was pitch dark. I couldn't even see Billie.

"What can I do?" she said.

"Nothing. Hang on. I think there's a flashlight in the toolbox." Kneeling, I reached over to where I *thought* the toolbox was sitting.

"Ummm…" came her voice in the dark. "That's not a flashlight. That's a boob."

"Shit. Sorry."

She laughed. "Why do I have a feeling you're really not?"

"Is someone projecting her fantasies on me?" I teased. "You know, when someone jumps the gun to accuse someone else, it's probably because they're guilty themselves."

"So it's *me* who isn't sorry you just felt me up?"

"Look, I get it," I continued. "I'm a good-looking guy, and you have needs. No judgment here. If you want, I'll do it again—for your benefit, of course."

"I think that little shock you took before the lights went out short-circuited your brain, Mr. Landlord."

"The lady doth protest too much, methinks."

Billie cracked up. "Did you just quote *Hamlet* to justify touching my boob?"

I finally pulled the flashlight from my box and held it up to my chin to light my face. "I took Saylor to Shakespeare in the Park last month. We both fell asleep on the grass. I think that might be one of the few lines I heard."

"I think I have some candles in my supply drawer," Billie said, struggling to her feet. "Can you walk with me to light the way?"

I followed her with the flashlight as Billie dug three candles out and placed them all around the studio. While she was lighting the last one, I couldn't help but notice how beautiful she looked in the soft glow. I wasn't sure when I'd turned into such a wuss, but I wanted to take her out to a nice dinner with candles in the worst way.

She caught me staring and gave me a look. "What?"

"Nothing." I shook my head. "Where's your electric panel? We obviously need a reset."

"It's in the bathroom. Don't ask me why they put it there."

When I opened the panel, I was surprised to find actual fuses. I was able to reset the front lights in the reception area, but the ones in the back wouldn't go on. I unscrewed one of the corresponding fuses and checked it out. "It's blown. You wouldn't happen to have any, would you?"

Billie shook her head. "Umm…no. Half the time I don't have lightbulbs, and I've run a few doors down to Chipotle more than once to steal napkins when we ran out of toilet paper."

I dug my phone out of my pocket. "Let me call Owen. His office is next to the new Home Depot that just opened. If he's still there, he can pick one up on his way home."

When I reached him, Owen had just walked into his office, so I'd caught him in time. That left Billie and me with nothing to do but sit around in the dark and wait for him to get back. But I was melting in these work clothes. "Owen should be here with the part in about twenty minutes. In the meantime, I have to take off this dress shirt. I'm roasting."

"I have no idea how you've worn it this long," Billie said.

After I shed a layer, Billie went to sit in her tattoo chair. I sat in the one across from her. "So, how did you get into tattooing?" I asked.

"I was showing a few pieces of my art at a gallery when I was eighteen, and a tatted guy bought one of my pieces. He asked me about my plans for the future, and when I said I wasn't sure, he asked if I was squeamish. I said no, and he gave me his business card and told me to drop by. He said he would let me shadow him, if I wanted, to see if tattooing might be something I was interested in."

She smiled. "My mother was so pissed. She owns the gallery and was trying to push me to go to college to be a curator like her. Honestly, that's probably why I stopped by the guy's tattoo parlor the next day. My favorite pastime as a teenager was riling up my mother. I still kind of enjoy it, actually… Anyway, I was mesmerized by the colorful work Devin did, and within a month, I'd started working as a receptionist for him so I could learn the business. Eventually he let me train under him as an apprentice."

"That's pretty cool. So you were basically discovered?"

"I never thought of it that way." She laughed and shrugged. "But I guess so. Although my mother would say Devin hired me to look at my ass, not because I had any talent."

I frowned. "That's not very encouraging. Was there a reason she thought that? Like, did the guy ever hit on you?"

Billie shook her head. "Absolutely not. Devin's like a father to me. And he's been happily married as many years as I've been alive. My mother just hates what I do for a living."

"Why?"

"Because she doesn't consider it art. Only paintings that hang in a gallery and sell for six figures are worthy of Renee Holland's time. She calls my work '*a waste of talent drawing obscenities*'."

"Well, for what it's worth, I'd rather look at your art book than walk around MOMA any day of the week."

She smiled. "Thank you. She's been bugging me to show some of my art at an exhibit she's planning. It's sort of a good opportunity, because there will be a lot of reviewers from magazines that people who like my kind of art read. But I'm not sure I want to do it, because I hate the thought of owing her anything."

"You know the old saying, 'don't cut off your nose to spite your face'? Sometimes in life you just need to suck it up if it helps you get where you want to be."

Billie was quiet a minute. "Yeah, I guess. Maybe I'll think about it some more."

Eventually, Owen showed up with the part I needed, but since he had to relieve my sitter in a few minutes, he couldn't stay. Billie and I were once again alone.

"Alright. I'm going to go plug this baby in, and hopefully we'll get the lights back on," I told her.

"You go ahead." Billie groaned. "I'm too hot to move."

Ten minutes later, the lights flickered back on. When I turned around, Billie was lying back in her tattoo chair. Her skin glistened with a sheen of sweat, exactly the way I'd pictured her in my dreams. And that sent my mind reeling about fucking her on the chair. I couldn't stop staring at her.

"Umm…check me out much?" Billie laughed as she sat up.

"No, I wasn't… I was just thinking about the wiring."

She swung her legs up and hopped down. Smiling, she strutted toward me. "You are *so full of shit.*"

"I am not."

She stood right in front of me and raised a brow. "Look into my eyes and tell me you weren't just thinking some dirty thought about me."

My gaze shifted back and forth between her eyes. I opened my mouth, and then closed it. Then I opened my mouth once again, but nothing came out.

Billie laughed. "It's okay. You just have to own it when you get caught." She ran a fingernail down my arm. "I mean, you didn't notice me noticing all these muscles while you were busy looking at me. To be honest, I didn't think you'd look like this under your stuffy dress shirts. But if you *had* caught me looking, I'd have owned it. There's nothing wrong with appreciating someone's physique. It's just creepy when you lie about it."

Well, if that's how she feels… I looked down. Since she was so short and standing so close, I had a straight view of her phenomenal cleavage. I grinned. "In case you're wondering, I'm looking. I admit it."

Billie laughed again and shoved at my chest. "You're such a dork. Now fix my AC before I die of heat exhaustion, Mr. Landlord."

"Yes, ma'am."

A half hour later, I finally got the AC blowing cold air. I hated to leave, but I really needed to go make my daughter dinner. So I collected the tools and packed them into the toolbox. "I have to get upstairs and feed Saylor."

"Oh, yeah, of course. Thank you for coming to my rescue. The old landlord would've taken four days to return my call. I appreciate the fast response."

"No problem. Why don't I give you my cell number, just in case it gives you any more problems?"

"That would be great, thank you."

Billie handed me her phone, and I punched in my number and handed it back to her. "Well, have a good night."

"You too, Colby."

It had been a good couple of hours together, some flirting even. So while I knew she'd just come out of a relationship, I said *fuck it.* "Hey, would you want to have dinner sometime?"

Billie smiled sadly and shook her head. "I don't think so. I'm sorry."

Ugh. Talk about a kick in the gut. But like she'd told me to, I owned it. I forced a smile. "Well, that sucks."

She smiled back. "I'm sorry. It's not you."

"It's not?"

She shook her head.

"Well, if it's not me, I guess it would be okay if I tried again another time?"

She laughed. "Goodnight, Colby."

"See you soon, Billie."

❤CHAPTER 4

Billie

Deek kicked his feet up. "Why the hell would you tell him no? That dude is smoking hot, successful—he has everything going for him. Well, except that he doesn't have tats. That I don't like."

It was Thursday afternoon, and I'd gone upstairs to Deek's apartment in between clients. He and his boyfriend lived just above the shop. He was burning incense, probably because he'd smoked weed before I got here. Aside from working full time for me, he also did some freelance web design on his days off. He was good at it, but unlike when he tattooed, he usually got stoned to work on a website.

Deek had spent nearly all of this particular coffee chat giving me shit for turning Colby's dinner offer down. Now I wished I'd never told him about it.

"Colby might seem like a catch, but there are other things to consider, Deek. Especially after the shit I've been through lately. I'm not gonna waste my time with anyone who has the potential to hurt me."

"Uh, anyone you're remotely interested in has the potential to hurt you," he pointed out, raising an eyebrow. "But you're going to write him off because of Tinder-swindler Kaiden? There's no evidence Colby is anything like that. Name one thing wrong with him. I bet you can't."

I struggled to come up with something. Finally, I sighed. "There's nothing *wrong* with him. But he has a kid. As stinkin' adorable as she is, I can't get involved. He has his hands full, so I'm not sure a relationship is his priority, either. Not to mention, I don't know if I want to have kids *myself*, let alone raise someone else's." I took a long sip of my coffee. "So, it's not about what's wrong with *him*. It's about what would be wrong with the whole situation."

"Aren't you jumping the gun a little?"

"No! When there's a kid in the picture, there's no such thing as jumping the gun. You have to decide from the get-go whether you're in or out, whether you'd be okay with being a part of their life. If the answer is no or you're not sure, you can't start anything at all. Plain and simple. That's not fair. All or nothing."

He scratched his chin. "Alright. I guess I can understand that point of view. But maybe keep an open mind. It's not like there's an ex-wife in the picture. That's a rarity. I hate to say it, but it makes things easier that the kid's mother is MIA. At least you wouldn't have that additional complication." He drank the last drop of his coffee. "What's the deal with that anyway? Why did she leave?"

"I don't know the full story, just that the woman didn't want to be a part of her baby's life, so Colby is raising her himself."

I'd thought a lot about Saylor's "mother" recently. What kind of person would leave her kid and disappear? I'd wanted to ask Colby for more details the last time we were together, but I was almost afraid of the answer. Like, did *he* do something to scare her away? I doubted that, but I was damn curious, even if it wasn't any of my business. Would he have married her if she'd stayed?

Either way, the whole thing was heartbreaking. Saylor was too young to understand the decision her mother had made. That shit would hit her like a ton of bricks someday. I'd thought I had it bad with a mother who was sometimes verbally abusive. But at least she was around, I guess.

Then I thought of something else to help my case. "You're also forgetting that he's the freaking landlord now, Deek. That's a good way to have to pack up and move when things go sour."

He wriggled his eyebrows. "It's also a good way to get free rent."

"For a whore, maybe."

"I'm teasing." He laughed. "It's not just him who owns the building. You know that, right? There are four of them. It's like they all grew from the same tree of fineness, too."

"Yeah. They're all friends. The only other one I really know is Holden, though I saw Owen two days ago when he dropped off a part for the AC."

"Pretty crazy story how they ended up with this place," he said. "A wealthy friend of theirs passed away from leukemia and left the four of them a huge inheritance. They kept it in the bank for a while, and they finally decided to buy this building. Pretty good investment, if you ask me. They all live here, so none of them has to pay rent, and they're making money every month."

I narrowed my eyes. "Where'd you hear about how they inherited the money?"

"Holden's my buddy. We talk. Dude's a talented drummer. Have you heard him play?"

"No." I fiddled with the lid on my coffee. "Holden is cool, though. Owen seems like a stuck-up suit."

"I would've thought that about Colby, too," he said. "But you can't judge a book by its cover."

That was for damn sure. The first night I met Colby, I never imagined he had a little kid and was such a good dad. He looked like your typical hot player on the surface.

"Who's the other one I haven't met?" I asked. "What's his deal?"

"Name's Brayden. He's some kind of business hot shot. Holden is the one who sticks out like a sore thumb—you know, the artsy, creative type. Kind of like someone else I know." He winked. "But seriously, there had to be something in the water where they grew up, because the four of them are smoking hot and all successful in their own way."

"Well, thanks for the insider info."

"You can always count on me for that." He grinned. "And my two cents."

"That's why I love you." I stood up, stretched, and walked toward the door.

"So, I haven't changed your mind about going out with the guy?"

"Afraid not." I laughed. "Anyway, I'm gonna get going. I want to organize some stuff in the shop before my client this afternoon."

After I hugged my friend goodbye, I took the stairs down since Deek's apartment was just on the third floor. When I got to the bottom of the stairwell at the second level, my heel got stuck in a big crack in the cement, and I nearly fell flat on my face. I did skin my knee.

"What the fuck?" My voice echoed. "Who the hell is in charge of maintaining the floors around here? They should be fired! Crack's bigger than the one on my ass!" I rubbed my leg. "Ow!"

The door to the stairwell opened. "Is everything o—" He paused. "Oh my God, Billie? Are you okay?"

I looked up to find Colby with his eyes wide as I lay on the ground. *Shit.* He reached his hand out to help me up.

"Yeah." I shook my head, feeling kind of bad for yelling like that, considering the look of concern on his face. "I'm fine. But your building isn't. There's a big crack in the cement right here."

"Yeah, I heard. Bigger than the one on your ass. I'm intrigued."

I rolled my eyes. "Sorry. I was a little worked up. My heel got stuck, and I nearly face planted." I bent to pick up my heel, which had broken off of my studded, black stiletto.

"Shit." He looked down at my knee. "You're bleeding."

"You don't say? It was either my knee or my face. The knee saved my teeth."

"My apartment is right over there. Let me help you clean up."

Feeling a bit frazzled, I nodded as he took my arm and led me down the hall. I had a first-aid kit down at the shop, but I guess I was curious about his apartment. Well, that's what I told myself. Curious about the *apartment*.

Colby's apartment looked surprisingly neat for someone who had a kid. Were it not for the plastic cup on the counter featuring Elsa from *Frozen*, I would have never known a child lived here. Brown leather furniture and sleek, modern décor made it look more like a bachelor pad, fit for the wild bachelor I was sure Colby used to be.

I looked around. "Nice place."

"Well, the cleaning lady came this morning. Otherwise, you would've been greeted by an explosion of Lalaloopsy dolls in every corner of the room. So, things are deceiving today."

"Lalaloopsy… Are those the freaky-looking dolls with the button eyes?"

"Yeah, I'm surprised you know them."

"I had to tattoo one on someone once. And my friend's daughter collects them."

"I should introduce her to Saylor." He laughed.

"Where *is* Saylor?"

"Preschool," he answered as he rummaged through some cabinets. "She goes to a full-day program. I have a nanny who watches her after while I'm at work, but two days a week I come home early so I can be here when she gets home. I just work the remainder of the day from here on days like today."

Such a good dad. "Oh, that's cool." I sighed, limping with my broken shoe over to the open kitchen area. "It must be tough juggling it all, huh?"

"Yeah. But it's worth it." He smiled as he lifted a plastic container out of one of the cabinets and shook it. "Bingo! Found the first-aid kit."

He carried it over to where I was sitting on the stool. He sat down next to me and inched closer. His spicy cologne drifted toward me, and my body was all too aware of his proximity as he opened a bottle of peroxide, dabbing it onto a cotton ball before he began gently cleaning my knee.

"I'm really sorry you fell," he said in a low voice.

"No worries. I'm sorry I yelled."

"You had every right to. And I'll make sure to get that ass crack in the floor repaired. I'll reimburse you for your shoes, too. Although, I'm pretty happy for the excuse to spend a little time with you, even if it's under the wrong circumstances." He smiled. "Because, you know, someone didn't want to go out with me. So this is the next best thing."

"You can always come to the shop to say hello. I don't need to be injured so you can see me."

He looked up briefly. "Well, I don't want to disturb you when you're working." Then…he blew on my knee.

Oh. His hot breath against my skin felt like it permeated my entire body. *Damn.* Who knew a guy blowing on my knee could turn me on? I wonder if that's a thing, if they have porn for that. Erotic skin-blowing. I swore I felt it in my damn vagina. I needed to get laid. *Just not by Colby.* Nope. I couldn't fall for this amazingly gorgeous man in front of me who, based on his actions right now, clearly knew how to take care of a woman.

"Let's let your wound air out a little before I put a bandage on it."

Or you could blow on it again. I placed some hair behind my ear. "Thanks."

There was something so sexy about the way he'd taken care of me. Being a father probably made him a natural caretaker. I

40

supposed that would be one benefit of dating a single dad. It felt nice playing *daddy's girl* for a minute. I'm apparently all sorts of kinky up in my head today.

I cleared my throat. "So what does your nanny do for you besides watch Saylor when you're working?"

"She's older and unattractive if you're…insinuating something?"

"Actually, I wasn't. But it's interesting how quickly you went there. Dirty mind." *I'm one to talk.*

"You have no idea." His eyes twinkled. "But definitely *not* when it comes to my nanny." He laughed. "Kay is in her fifties, actually. She's great. Her job is to watch Saylor and nothing more. I don't expect her to pick up the house or cook or anything like that. I also don't like having people in my house, you know? I don't want my daughter to have all of her important memories with someone other than me. So, the second I'm home, the nanny is gone."

"You cook dinner every night?" I asked.

"I try. I limit takeout to once or twice a week." He chuckled. "Saylor loves sugary crap. I can't control what they give her at preschool, and everyone is always giving her candy left and right. So I try to cook as healthy as possible. I have to sneak a lot of things into her food because she won't eat vegetables—sweet potato into spaghetti sauce and greens into various things. It's like a science experiment sometimes, putting just the right amount in—not so much that the taste is overpowering."

I scrunched my nose. "I'm not a fan of veggies, either. Can you teach me your tricks?"

"Hang on." He went over to the fridge and took out something wrapped in foil. When he unwrapped it, it looked like a dessert. He offered it to me. "Take a bite."

"What is it?"

"Brownie. I want you to taste it." He held it to my mouth. His fingers grazed my lips as I opened.

As I chewed, it tasted like any other brownie—chocolatey, moist in the middle, a bit of frosting on top.

"It's good," I said with my mouth full.

"Yeah?" He raised his brow. "Well, there's a load of spinach in that thing."

"Really? I wouldn't have known." I swallowed. "You're sneaky, Colby. What else are you sneaky about?"

"Don't use my brownies against me. That's being sneaky for a good cause."

"Seriously…" I laughed. "That's a brilliant idea."

He reached out and swiped just under my bottom lip. "Sorry. You had some chocolate there."

Damn, I felt that, too. Just like every other bit of contact with him today. I needed to get out of here before my freaking panties melted. "Thanks." I licked my lips and noticed the way his eyes seemed glued to them. "What else do you have up your sleeve?"

"I might have a few other tricks I could show you." His eyes sparkled.

His gaze burned into mine, and that left no doubt what he was referring to. And given the state of my panties, my body, if not my mind, heard it loud and clear. He reached into the first-aid container and took out a Band-Aid, which he placed over the cut on my knee. He lightly rubbed over the area with his thumb, once again lighting a small fire inside me.

He watched as I devoured the rest of the brownie. His piercing blue eyes then fell to my breasts, and rather than call him out on it, I took a few moments to enjoy his lusty stare. When he looked up at me, our eyes locked, and I could've sworn he leaned in a little. Was he looking for silent permission to kiss me? My heart sped up. *Jesus.* I wanted that so badly.

Then the door opened, and I instinctively moved back.

Colby ran a hand through his thick mane of light brown hair and tried to act casual. "Hi," he said to the woman coming in.

"Oh, you're here already." She smiled.

"Daddy!" Saylor ran straight to her father. He lifted her up and showered her face with kisses before tickling under her neck, causing her to squeal in delight. It was a heartwarming sight, even for my cold, black heart.

He put her down, and the little girl's cheeks were rosy from laughter.

"Hi, Saylor!" I waved.

"Hi, Billie!"

It was cute that she remembered my name. It had taken a bit for her to notice me, though, because she'd only had eyes for her father from the moment she walked in the door. The nanny, meanwhile, gave me a once-over. I was sure her imagination was running wild about me and my broken shoe. I suppose there were all sorts of ways I could've broken a shoe with Colby.

"Thanks again for dressing my wound, Colby. I'm gonna let you guys get back to your afternoon."

"You don't have to leave," he urged. "I can make some coffee or something…"

I pointed my thumb toward the door. "Already had some caffeine upstairs with Deek." Looking down at my phone, I added, "I also have a client in twenty minutes."

"Ah. I should've known you had to get back to work."

"Yeah. Thanks for the brownie, too."

He nodded. "You need to let me know how much those shoes cost."

"Don't worry about it. They were on clearance when I bought them."

"Well, I have to pay you back somehow." He slipped his hands in his pockets. "Dinner would be one way, if that weren't off the table."

"Make me more brownies." I winked, then bent down and pinched Saylor's cheek. "See ya around, cutie. Enjoy your afternoon with Daddy." *Your hot freaking daddy I currently want to ride the shit out of.*

I smiled at her, trying to rid my mind of those dirty thoughts. I nodded toward the nanny and booked it out of there, feeling flushed and second-guessing my vow of resilience because I hadn't had the hots for someone like this in as long as I could remember.

I might have been saved by the bell when it came to that almost-kiss, but thoughts of the hot single dad upstairs continued to consume my mind for the rest of the afternoon.

❤CHAPTER 5

Colby

I hadn't seen Billie in seven days.

Though not for lack of wanting to. Every night when I got off the subway down the block from my apartment, I gave myself a pep talk:

Keep walking. One foot in front of the other.

Don't even look in her window as you pass.

You can do it.

She doesn't want to see you anyway.

You asked her out. She said no.

Take a goddamn hint, dumbass.

Four buildings down from her shop, I got ready to start my nightly mantra, but I only made it as far as *Keep walking. One foot in front of the*—when I stopped abruptly.

What the fuck?

The front glass window of Billie's tattoo shop was gone, replaced by a sheet of plywood. Now I had no choice but to stop in.

Justine was at the front desk. I pointed over my shoulder to the window. "What happened to the glass?"

She frowned. "It was like that when Billie got here this morning." Before she could say any more, the shop's phone rang.

Justine thumbed toward the studio as she reached for the receiver. "Why don't you go on back and talk to Billie? She's between customers and can fill you in."

I nodded. "Thanks."

I knocked, and when I opened the door to the studio, Billie's back was to me. Apparently she hadn't heard me, because when she turned around she jumped and clutched her chest.

"Shit." She plucked an AirPod from one ear. "I didn't see you come in."

"Sorry. Justine said it was okay, and I knocked before opening the door."

Billie shook her head. "It's fine. I'm just jumpy today, that's all."

"What happened to the window?"

"I don't know. When I got here this morning it was smashed, and there was a brick inside on the floor."

"A brick? Were you robbed?"

She shook her head again. "No, that's the strange thing. Nothing seems to be missing. There was even some cash left in the front register from the night before. The police said it could have been kids randomly vandalizing, but they also asked if I'd had any unhappy customers lately—or any relationships that had recently ended badly." She grimaced.

"Gee, Billie, I don't know why an ex would want to get even. It couldn't be the giant pink Tinder logo you inked onto his arm..."

She tried not to smile as she picked up a roll of paper towels and chucked them at my head.

I caught them. "I'm just teasing."

"I know. But you're also not wrong. In hindsight, I might've taken things a little too far with Kaiden."

I shrugged. "Nah. Guy was a piece of crap. He got what was coming to him."

"Thanks for saying that, even if it's not true." She opened a cabinet. "I just canceled my last appointment for the day. Having that window smashed this morning really freaked me out. I'm going to make myself a Honey Jack and Coke. You want one?"

I shrugged. "Sure."

Billie mixed two drinks in plastic cups. Hopping up on her tattoo chair, she motioned to the seat across from her. "Pop a squat. Deek is on dinner break for an hour. Oh, wait—do you need to get home to Saylor?"

I checked the time. "I have a little while before I have to relieve the nanny." Even if I hadn't, I got the feeling Billie needed some company, so I would've texted and asked the nanny to stay later, though I rarely did that. I sucked back some of my drink. "So are the cops going to visit your ex and question him about the window?"

Billie shook her head. "I didn't tell them about Kaiden."

"Why not?"

"I don't know. Guilt, I guess. I don't think I was wrong for inviting all the Tinder women here, but maybe I was a tad aggressive with his tattoo. It's just…" Billie shook her head and sighed. "I guess you could say I'm not very lucky in love. I've been burned a few times, and I let it all come to a boiling point on Kaiden."

I nodded. "I get it. I don't have the best track record with relationships myself."

"Oh yeah? You want to go toe to toe? See who has the worst relationship story?"

"Sure." I smiled and lifted my chin. "Ladies first."

"Welp, I guess my worst relationship would be Lucas. We met when I was twenty and backpacking through Australia. I'd just finished my tattoo apprenticeship and decided to take a month off before I began working full time as an artist. I love to travel—that's probably the one thing my mother and I have in common—so I flew to Melbourne and started to work my way up the Great Ocean Road. I met Lucas at Bells Beach, the place where they have the big annual surfing contest. I was there early one morning, watching the sun come up, and he walked up with his board and offered to teach me to surf. Long story short, we spent the next five weeks together, traveling all over Australia. Lucas was from California, he worked in Silicon Valley, and he told me he'd recently sold an app for twenty-million dollars, so he was taking a break to figure out what he should do next. When it was time for me to return to New York and start my new position as a full-fledged tattoo artist, Lucas came home with me. I was head over heels, and I thought he was, too."

I nodded. This story already made my stomach turn.

"Anyway," she said, "Lucas and I moved in together. We soon realized my apartment was too small for two, so we signed a lease for a great place I could never have afforded on my own, got a joint bank account where he parked his spending money—over two-hundred-thousand dollars—and I was happier than I'd ever been. I had the guy of my dreams and had just started a job I absolutely loved. I even introduced him to my mother, and we were planning a trip out to California so I could meet his family. While we were there, he was going to pack up and bring the rest of his things to New York. Things were going great…until I came home from work one day and everything of value was gone from my apartment. And our joint bank account, which had also held sixty-thousand dollars of an inheritance I received when my grandmother died— was empty too."

I raked a hand through my hair. "Jesus Christ. I'm sorry, Billie. What happened after that?"

She shrugged. "I went to the police. Turned out the guy was a known scammer and had done it to others. But he hops around from country to country, so he hasn't gotten caught. Not that I would expect him to have any of my money left. He spent cash as if he actually *had* twenty million in the bank."

Billie gulped down the rest of her drink and pointed to me. "Your turn. I'm guessing this is one contest I'll win. I haven't even known you that long, and I know you wouldn't do something so stupid."

I shook my finger back and forth. "I wouldn't be so sure. Don't assume this pretty face has a matching set of brains. I've done my share of dumb shit."

Billie leaned back in her chair and folded her hands behind her head. "Oh, I can't wait to hear this."

"Well, in the end, my outcome is better. But I've definitely led with my head in the past." I pointed to the one on top of my shoulders. "Just not always this one."

Telling this story required some liquid courage, so now I emptied my cup. "Almost five years ago, I met a woman named Raven. Because I'm apparently cliché as fuck with more than just my choice of tattoos, Raven was a stripper, and I met her at a strip club—on Halloween of all days. I was out with my buddies, got to talking with one of the women after the show, and wound up taking Raven home with me. She left the next morning, and I never heard from her again—until August of the next year, when she showed up on my doorstep with a five-week-old baby."

Billie's eyes grew as wide as saucers. "No way!"

I nodded. "Yep. She told me it was my kid, and that she had a job interview she couldn't miss and no one to watch the baby. She pretty much said three sentences, set the baby carrier and a diaper bag down in the doorway, and turned around and took off. I stood there shell-shocked for a minute, but then ran after her. Two buildings down, I realized I'd just left a baby alone in my apartment, so I ran back."

"What did you do when she came back?"

I looked Billie in the eyes. "I'll let you know when that happens."

"Oh my God, Colby. Are you saying Saylor's mother left her on your doorstep and you never saw her again?"

I nodded. "To be honest, I wasn't even sure the baby was mine at first. I had no idea what to do. I'd never changed a diaper in my life."

"Did you try to find her?"

I nodded again. "For a long time. But the only thing I knew about her was that she worked at the strip club. Of course I went back there, but the manager said she hadn't worked there in six months. I went as far as hiring a private investigator to track her down, but she was nowhere to be found. Turned out Raven wasn't even her name, it was Maya, and she wasn't in the country legally, so the paper trail was pretty scarce."

Billie shook her head. "Holy crap. That's crazy."

"Do I win?"

She laughed. "I think you might."

"Then I guess I win twice. Because Saylor turned out to be the best thing that's ever happened to me. My crazy story might beat your crazy story, but in the end, I got the love of my life."

Billie's face went soft. "That's really beautiful, Colby."

A few minutes later, Deek walked in. He surveyed the scene and smirked at Billie. "Am I interrupting something, boss?"

Billie rolled her eyes. "No, Deek. Colby and I were just talking."

"Uh-huh." He lifted his chin to me. "How you doin', man?"

I hopped out of his tattoo chair and extended a hand. "Not bad. You think her ex, Kaiden, did this to her window? Maybe you and I should go have a talk with him."

Deek smiled. "I like the way you think."

"Uh, no one is going to talk to Kaiden," Billie said. "We're just going to chalk this up to some kids being jerks and put it behind us."

I looked at Deek, and he shrugged. "She's my boss. She might be short, but I'm afraid of her crazy ass."

I chuckled. "Alright. But if you change your mind, you know where to find me."

Billie shook her head. "I think I'm going to get out of here. Do you need anything from me before I leave, Deek?"

"Nope. All good."

"Okay, I'm going to head out. Justine leaves now, too, so I'm locking the door behind us, just to be safe. You'll need to keep an eye out for when your appointment knocks."

"Yes, boss."

Billie looked at me and tilted her head toward the door. "Come on. I know you have to get to your daughter. I'll walk out with you."

Out on the sidewalk, Billie and I stood for a minute, looking at the plywood sheet.

"Is there anything I can do?" I asked. "Call a glass company or something?"

"Thanks, but I already scheduled a company to come install new glass tomorrow morning. And I'm also having an alarm installed on Saturday—with cameras. If there's a next time something like this happens, I'm going to know who it was."

I nodded. Billie was tough, but she had to be shaken up from the day. "Good. Can I walk you home at least?"

She smiled. "I appreciate the offer, but I'm going to grab an Uber tonight. I'm too lazy to do the mile-and-a-half-long trek, nor do I feel like riding two subways. It's been a really long day, and I just want to get home and soak in a hot bath with some wine."

I grinned. "If you need someone to wash your back…"

She play-slapped my abs. "Goodnight, Colby. Thanks for checking in on me."

"Anytime, sweetheart." Just as I was about to walk away, I turned back. "I almost forgot. Saylor asked me to invite you to her birthday party on Saturday."

"Really?"

I nodded. "You don't have to come, but I don't want her to find out I didn't extend the invitation. Like Deek said, sometimes it's the little ones we're most afraid of. My boss just happens to be only three-feet tall."

Billie smiled. "What time is the party and where is it?"

"It's at three. Her actual birthday isn't until Monday, but I'm having a few of my friends, a girl Saylor plays with from preschool, and my parents over. It's just in our apartment, nothing too fancy."

"I'll try to stop by. The alarm company is calling me in the morning to give me a four-hour window that day, so I'm not positive I'll make it, but I'll try."

I rubbed my chin. "So when my daughter invites you, you'll come. But not when I invite you to do something with me?"

"Don't be offended, Big Daddy. Saylor doesn't have that thing I've recently determined I'm allergic to."

I shook my head. "What thing?"

"A penis." She winked. "Nighty-night, Colby."

Saturday afternoon, I got excited every time someone knocked at my apartment door. But by seven thirty, it had become apparent that Billie wasn't going to make it. Most of the guests who had come to help Saylor celebrate her fourth birthday had already left, and it was only Owen, Holden, and me still sitting around drinking beer when there was a knock at the door. I hadn't told the guys I'd invited Billie, because once they caught on that you liked a woman, the ball busting never stopped.

So I pretended to be surprised when I opened the door and Billie was on the other side. She held a couple of wrapped gifts in her hands.

"Hey. It's good to see you," I said.

She looked around me and into my apartment. "Am I too late? The alarm company took *hours* to install the system. I locked up as soon as they left."

Saylor came running from behind me. "Billie! You came!"

Billie bent down, and my daughter threw her arms around her neck.

"I'm sorry I'm late. I came as soon as I could."

"It's okay. You got here just in time. Uncle Holden is going to sing me a special song. He wrote it just for my birthday."

"Did he? Wow, no one has ever written a song for me." Billie tapped Saylor's little nose with her pointer. "You must be super special."

We were still in the doorway, so I nodded toward the inside of my apartment. "Come on in. I still have a ton of food, and there's cake, too."

The guys said hello, shooting me questioning looks. I ignored them.

"Are you hungry?" I asked Billie. "It'll take two seconds to heat something up. We had all of Saylor's favorites: baked ziti, chicken fingers, and peanut butter and banana sandwiches."

"Oooh…peanut butter and banana sandwiches sound delicious. But I just ate at the shop a little while ago. I ordered in while they were working. I thought I might starve to death if I didn't."

"How about some cake then?"

Saylor jumped up and down. "Daddy made it himself."

Billie raised her eyebrows. "You baked a cake?"

"Don't get too excited. It's from a box, lopsided, and I didn't wait long enough for it to cool before frosting it, so the top is sort of icing mixed with cake bits. But if you close your eyes, it tastes pretty damn good."

She smiled. "Maybe just a little piece."

"You got it."

While I cut a slice of cake, Billie gave Saylor the gifts she'd brought.

"Daddy, can I open them, *pleeeeeaaassseeeee*." She said it like I was physically capable of denying her anything in this world.

"Sure, sweetheart. Go ahead."

The first present she unwrapped was an art set. It looked like a pretty nice one, too—not a typical kids' set. Billie pointed to it. "This was the first set of paint markers I ever had. I was about your age when I got them. Once I started to draw with those, no one could stop me. I fell in love with art."

Saylor held them to her chest. "I can't wait to draw with them!"

Billie held out a second gift. "And this is something I made just for you." She looked over at Holden. "I can't sing like your Uncle Holden, but I hope you like what I drew."

Saylor ripped open the wrapping paper. Inside was a framed photo of a fairy. When I took a closer look, I realized the fairy's face was Saylor's.

"Holy crap. You drew that from memory?"

Billie nodded. "It wasn't hard. This little girl doesn't have a face you easily forget."

"Daddy! I'm a fairy! I'm a fairy!"

"I see that. Those are some pretty amazing gifts, Saylor. What do you say?"

Saylor wrapped her arms around Billie's waist. "Thank you, Billie. I'm going to draw you a picture with my new markers!"

"You're so welcome. I can't wait to see what you create."

Saylor ran over to Holden and Owen to show them her new Saylor Fairy.

"You didn't have to go to all that trouble," I whispered to Billie.

"I wanted to. Plus, that reaction just made my entire day— my week, even. I might start drawing her something on the regular just to have someone look at me like that."

I smiled. "Tell me about it. Why do you think she has four-hundred elephant stuffed animals? She loves them, and I'm addicted to the way her eyes light up when I bring one home."

A little while later, Owen left. Then Holden said he needed to get going, so he told the birthday girl to take a seat so he could serenade her. It didn't matter if they were four or thirty, women could not resist when Holden sang. He'd written a sweet little lullaby, and my daughter wore a toothy smile from ear to ear the entire time he sang it. I'd been enjoying it, too, until I glanced over and saw the way Billie was looking at Mr. Rockstar.

Fuck. A lot of women loved Holden and his scraggly I-don't-give-two-shits look. But they *all* wanted to jump his bones once he broke out an instrument or started crooning. I wasn't even sure why he was the drummer in his band. The dude could've fronted any group he wanted as a singer. Even I had to admit his voice was damn sexy.

When it was over, Billie blinked a few times. "Wow. That was amazing."

Holden flashed his signature *aww, shucks* smile, and I couldn't get the fucker out of my apartment fast enough. I might've actually shoved him through the door. Though I thought I'd done it discreetly.

"Do you want me to go, too?" Billie asked when I turned back toward her. "You sort of rushed your friends out."

"I did?"

She lifted a knowing brow.

So I came clean. "Women can't help but fall for Holden, whether he's singing or playing the drums. It was only a matter of time until you tossed your panties at him if I let him stay."

Billie chuckled. "Do I seem like the panty-tossing type to you?"

I sighed. "Owen's *grandmother* hit on Holden after she saw him play the drums once."

"His voice is beautiful, and I'm sure he's a very talented musician. But I'm not interested in Holden."

"No?"

She shook her head.

"How about any of his friends? Because I've heard dudes who can bake a cake are way better in bed than the ones who can sing."

Billie's eyes sparkled. "That cake *was* pretty delicious."

Luckily, my daughter ran back out to the kitchen before I pushed things too far—like suggesting I smear the rest of the cake all over her body and lick it off.

"Daddy, can we go to the bridge now?"

"In a few minutes, sweetheart. Why don't you go get a sweatshirt?"

"Okay!"

Saylor ran back toward her bedroom, and I realized what I'd done.

"Hey, kiddo, don't take everything out of your dresser to find one sweatshirt. Just pick something on top."

Billie laughed. "You know your daughter."

"Last week I told her to grab a pair of shorts. I was finishing up a project for work on my laptop. When I went into her room, it looked like a bomb had exploded in a kid's clothing store."

"That's what my apartment looks like most of the time."

I chuckled. "Women."

"So where are you two off to? Saylor said a bridge?"

"Oh yeah. We're going to check out the Ward's Island Bridge. It's a tradition my dad started when I was born. He's an architect, too, and he loved to show me different structures around the city. Every year on my birthday, he took me to a different bridge. We actually haven't missed one yet, and I'm twenty-nine."

"Really?"

I nodded.

"How long until you run out of bridges? What are there, like thirty in the city?"

"Close." I smiled. "There are two thousand and twenty-seven of them in the five boroughs."

Billie's face wrinkled up. "You're kidding, right?"

I laughed. "Nope."

"Oh my God. You must think I'm an idiot."

"Not at all. Honestly, most people would guess the same. Everyone knows the main ones—Brooklyn, Verrazano, GW, Queensboro..."

"Where's the one you're going to see tonight?"

"It's up on a Hundred and Third. It's a footbridge that crosses over the Harlem River to get to Ward's Island. Why don't you come?"

Billie hesitated. "It's your tradition with your daughter. I don't want to intrude on your time together."

"Trust me, Saylor would be thrilled. It's always just us two."

"I don't know..." She still wasn't sold.

"Do I need to have my daughter ask you so you'll say yes? You act like I'm asking you to go to the gas chamber."

Billie laughed. "I do not."

"Prove me wrong, then, and come. I'm not asking you on a date this time. We can be friends, can't we?"

She bit her lip. "Fine. Yes, we can be friends."

"Great." I winked. "But just to clarify, I sometimes look at my friends' asses."

♥CHAPTER 6

Billie

It was my favorite part of the day—the quiet time in the morning at the shop before any of my staff arrived. I'd come in early to organize some of my equipment and straighten up the place. The only problem was now I had way too much time to think without people here. And all I could seem to think about lately was Colby Lennon.

After our trip to the Ward's Island Bridge the other night, I'd thought he might've called or texted. But it had been three days, and nothing. Not a word. The question was, why the hell was I expecting a call or visit when I'd made it clear I only wanted to be friends? He was giving me what I supposedly wanted: space. *Friends* shouldn't be expected to call so soon.

The trip to the bridge had been pretty chill. It was cute how into the whole thing he was, explaining the architecture and history. And Saylor seemed to eat up every word her dad said, even if she probably couldn't understand half of it. As if a four-year-old cared about a sixteen-million-dollar renovation project. Or the fact that the bridge had been covered in yellow and featured in *The Wiz* back in 1978, in the scene where Diana Ross and Michael Jackson sang "Ease on Down the Road."

You'd think Saylor did understand and appreciate it all, though. She'd smiled at everything. I hadn't wanted to crush Colby and tell him I didn't care all that much about bridge history. But I *did* enjoy the passion in his eyes when he spoke. That I could've watched all day. And honestly, I enjoyed spending time with him and Saylor, regardless of what we were doing.

I was apparently smitten with him, whether I was willing to admit it or not. Thus, my current situation: checking my phone and looking out the shop window for any sign of Colby.

With only ten minutes until I had to open, I decided to visit the truck outside and grab a coffee. It was one of those rare dry, breezy mornings in the city when the humidity had taken the day off. I waited in line and ordered my usual, a small coffee with one cream and one sugar. When I turned around with the little blue cup in hand, I spotted him walking toward me.

Colby was headed to work, dressed in a three-piece navy suit and looking all…rich and shit. Damn, he could rock a suit. Seeing him dressed to the nines made me want to jump him.

Instead, I lifted my cup in a salute. "Hey, you."

"Hi." He smiled. "Long time no see."

"Yeah. I should be saying that to *you*." *What does that even mean? That I've been waiting for him to call? Ugh.*

"The past couple of days have been a literal shitshow."

"Uh-oh." I frowned. "Why?"

"Stomach bug. Not me. Saylor. We've never been through anything like it. And on her actual birthday, no less."

"Oh no. I'm sorry."

"Yeah. She might have gotten it from someone at the party. I got lucky. It's so far evaded me." He sighed. "You're not sick, are you?"

"No."

"Good. I would've felt crappy if you'd gotten it."

"Is she okay now?"

"Yeah. We waited a full twenty-four hours on day three to make sure she was over it. But she went back to preschool today."

"Thank goodness. I can't imagine how horrible that must've been."

"Yeah. Real sexy to be covered in vomit for two days straight, right? That'll make you change your mind about dating me."

"Actually, the fact that you're such a good, hands-on dad is one of the sexiest things about you." *Agh. Speaking without thinking again.* Given that I had no desire to date someone with a kid, I didn't quite understand why him being a good father was such a turn-on. But it was. *Still didn't need to share it, Billie.*

"Well, that's a great note to head to work on. I'll take that compliment and run with it. Unfortunately, I'm running a bit late, so…"

I waved him off. "Go! Go."

Colby looked over my shoulder, and I turned to find his friend Holden had suddenly appeared. I'd almost forgotten he'd booked the first appointment of the day.

"Whaddup?" Holden said.

"What are you doing?" Colby asked.

"I'm actually headed over to Billie's."

Colby's eyes narrowed. "What are you doing there?"

"You know that tat I have of Hailey's name?"

Colby's brow lifted. "Yeah?"

"I'm finally getting rid of it. Billie is going to cover it up for me."

When Holden booked the appointment, he'd mentioned he wanted to remove an ex-girlfriend's name from his lower abdomen. We'd decided to have him look through some of my designs first since he didn't have a clue what he wanted.

"Isn't that practically down by your dick?" Colby groaned. "The one you said you got so she'd see her name when she was going down on you?"

"That's the one. Down by the V…not the dick, though." Holden laughed.

"Trust me," I said. "There's a big difference between 'practically down' by someone's dick and *actually* on someone's dick. I've tattooed both, so I should know."

Colby's eyes widened. "You've tattooed someone's dick before?"

"I have."

"That's awesome." Holden laughed. "I wanna see pics, if you have them."

I'd expected Colby to laugh, too, but his face was stone cold. He didn't look happy about any of this. Not the V nor the dick.

Colby cleared his throat. "Well, you two have fun. I've got to get to work."

Holden and I watched him walk away for a few seconds before he followed me into the shop. Once the door closed behind us, he turned to me. "What the hell was that all about?"

I played dumb. "What do you mean?"

"Colby looking like he wanted to murder me."

"Really?"

"You didn't notice?"

"Notice what?" I blinked.

"The look on his face when he found out what you were helping me with!"

"I wasn't paying attention to his face," I lied.

"Well, I was. I know my friend. He did *not* like the fact that you'd be touching me. He must like you, Billie. Colby hasn't been into anyone in a long while."

"Don't be ridiculous. It must be your imagination."

"He *likes* you," he repeated. "He mentioned that you guys hung out the other night, too, right? So don't tell me I'm imagining things."

Feeling my face heat, I pointed. "Mind your beeswax, and get in the chair. We got work to do. I have a fully booked day."

Holden dropped the subject of Colby as we looked through the drawings I'd put together based on our last consultation. He settled on a series of musical notes intertwined together as they flowed from the mouth of a bird and wrapped around two drumsticks. It would be a little challenging to fully cover the name with the art he wanted, but I knew I could figure it out. I hadn't screwed up a tattoo yet and wasn't planning on starting today.

Holden settled into the seat, and I got going on his ink. I usually didn't like to talk while I was working, but Holden was chatty. I'd been sort of half-listening to the stuff he said about the music scene. But when he changed the subject to Colby, my ears perked up.

"You know, Colby used to be the biggest player of all of us," he noted.

I pretended like I wasn't fully invested in this particular topic of conversation, careful not to look up from what I was doing. "Is that right?"

"Yeah. Well, not in high school. But pretty much the second half of college until…well, until Saylor."

"What was the deal in high school?" I asked.

"Colby was in love with his high-school girlfriend, Bethany. But she decided it would be better if they went their separate ways after graduation since they were going to different schools. It wasn't exactly his choice, so that first year, he was obsessed with finding out what she was doing—and with whom—while she was away."

I struggled to gobble up every word through the sound of my needle.

"When he discovered through the grapevine that she'd fucked a couple of guys, he decided he wanted to get back at her. He went balls-to-the-wall wild his sophomore year—screwed everyone in sight. It started out to spite Bethany, but I think he decided he liked it. Bethany and he never got together again after that. But I'm pretty sure he still cared about her and was holding out hope."

"Well, that sucks. You saw all this firsthand? Did you go to the same college as Colby?"

His body shifted as he shook his head. "No. I went to a different school. But I'd visit him all the time because we were only an hour away from each other." He sighed. "Anyway…there's more to the story as far as Bethany goes."

I finally looked up. "Why? What happened?"

"She moved to New York after grad school and went to find him at his parents' house one Christmas. She told him she was still in love with him, after all those years apart, and wanted to know if he was interested in dating her again. She said they could have a fresh start."

"What did he say?"

"Well, you see, this was like four years ago—right after he found out about Saylor."

"Oh…" My heart sank a little for Colby, even if I didn't like this Bethany. And I could see where this was headed. "What was her reaction?"

"She was totally shocked. Couldn't handle it. That was the last thing she ever expected. Heck, it was the last thing any of us expected. She bolted after that. So he never got a second chance with her."

For the first time since this conversation started, I stopped working on him altogether to concentrate. "Was he devastated?"

"At that time, his focus was solely on Saylor. Everything was still so new. So while Bethany coming back was a bit of a mind fuck, nothing really fazed him at that point. It wasn't the same as if she'd come back a year earlier." Holden stared off. "But you know…I can't imagine what his life would be like if he'd settled down with Bethany and never had Saylor. I can't picture him without that little girl now."

"I totally agree."

He sighed. "But yeah, Bethany is definitely the one who got away."

I gulped. "Do you think he still loves her?"

"I can't be sure he doesn't still harbor feelings for her, but I do recall him saying she couldn't have loved him that much if she wouldn't even consider accepting his daughter. He understood her reaction to a point, but I think the fact that she left so fast really turned him off. I do think if she'd accepted it from the get-go they'd be married right now. Instead, she's married to someone else."

"Oh yeah?" I licked my lips. *Bethany is married. Why does that make me incredibly relieved?*

"Yup."

The fact that Colby was in love with this girl who apparently didn't even deserve him irked me and made me jealous at the same time. If she knew what a great father he'd turned out to be, I bet she'd regret her decision.

"Anyway…" Holden said, "I guess the point of me telling you all my boy's business is that it was nice to see him riled up out there. He's been so out of it the past few years—and with good reason—but he needs to get back in the game. I might have to fuck with him a bit more, light more fires under his ass. Maybe I'll tell him I had a little fun with you today, see how he reacts. Then call him out when he freaks out on me again."

"Why would you do that?"

"Because I'm a dick, and he and I love to mess with each other. I'm also pissed at him for not telling me sooner that he had it bad for you."

"That's your theory. He's never said that to you, right?"

"Believe me, he doesn't have to say it. Looks like the one he gave me out there this morning don't lie. It was actually more of a warning. And it told me everything I need to know."

I went back to work, my thoughts no clearer than when I'd arrived this morning, and a little while later Holden's design was finished. I bandaged him up and sent him on his merry way. If only everything he'd told me had gone out the door with him.

Instead, Colby, Bethany, and where things stood with him and me ran through my head all afternoon.

At the end of the day, I was closing up the shop when Colby surprised me with a visit on his way home from work. He looked just as hot as he had this morning, only now his tie was loosened and his hair a bit disheveled. The only thing sexier than put-together Colby Lennon in a suit was mussed-up Colby Lennon in a suit. Any version of him *suited* me just fine.

"Hey, Billie." He smiled. "How's it goin'?"

"Hey! How was your day?" I asked.

"Good." He nodded. "How was yours? Did that ass Holden get what he wanted on his V?"

"He did. It came out awesome, actually."

"I have to confess…I know it did. He sent me a text of it to fuck with me."

"He seemed to think you were…" I cleared my throat. "Jealous."

"Why *wouldn't* I be?" His eyes bore into mine.

"Because I don't fraternize with my clients, so there's nothing to be jealous about."

He let out a long breath. "It's not that I thought you had a thing for Holden. It just irked me that he got to spend time with you when I didn't. And he's a good-looking motherfucker, so I suppose you touching him *down there* made me a bit uneasy." He shrugged. "What can I say? I'm a jealous bastard and am apparently terrible at hiding it."

For the third time today, I let my inner thoughts slip with Colby. "I actually think you're hotter."

His eyes lifted to meet mine. "Well, that's interesting information."

"Yes."

Holden's type used to be more my speed—until Colby. Who would've thought I'd choose the straightlaced suit? Now, all I seemed to want to do was pull on this dude's tie and bring him to my mouth.

"So what do we do about this?" he asked. "Your attraction to me."

I swallowed. "Nothing. We do nothing. You know you're an attractive man. That's not news. It doesn't change the fact that I'm not interested in starting anything right now."

He nodded slowly. "I think I have a solution for that, actually."

"What solution?"

"Hear me out." He moved in closer. "We don't have to date, Billie. We can…undate."

"*Undate*? What exactly is that?" I asked, all too aware of his proximity—just a few inches from me now.

"It's more of what we did the other night, when we went to see the bridge. It wasn't a date, right? It was like just the opposite. An undate. So that's what I propose we do."

I crossed my arms. "What would this entail?"

"We'd spend time together, but only under the most unromantic and mundane of circumstances." He scratched his chin. "I'll give you an example. Say I'm working on something around the apartment and realize I need to run to Home Depot. There's nothing remotely sexy or suggestive about that. Boom. You'll be the first person I think of. I'll call and ask if you want to tag along, if you're available. No pressure. No temptation. Undate."

"What's the point of that?" I chuckled.

"The point is, we can be friends and hang out without any of the other pressures. The point is, I'll still get to see you, which makes me happy."

Our eyes locked, and I wondered how obvious it was: that just being around him made me happy, too. "I guess this sounds harmless enough," I conceded. I was sure those would be famous last words, though. Because as harmless as he made this undate thing sound, I could hear virtual alarm bells going off.

"Yeah?" He beamed.

"If this is what you really want, I can play along."

An intensity filled his eyes. "What I really want?" He shook his head slowly and laughed. "This is not what I *really* want."

A chill ran down my spine. "Tell me what you really want, then." I was a glutton for punishment, apparently.

"I don't think you want to know," he said.

"I do, actually. It's like morbid curiosity."

After a long pause he said, "Okay then. What I really want to do is untie that fucking corset one lace at a time and bury my face in your beautiful tits while you straddle me on that chair over there. *Right now.* So maybe phrase your questions more carefully. Because the truthful answer to what I *want* is never gonna be PG or gentlemanlike when it comes to you." He smiled and turned toward the door. "I'll call you soon," he said before disappearing.

Dazed and horny, I stood staring out the window for an indeterminate amount of time. I then locked the door to the shop and retreated to the bathroom where I promptly leaned against the door, pulled my panties down, and replayed his words while massaging my clit.

HAPTER 7

Colby

Now for the moment of truth. With Saylor occupied for a rare Saturday, I picked up my phone and tapped out a text to Billie.

Colby: Up for our first undate today?

She texted back almost immediately.

Billie: What did you have in mind?

I chuckled as I responded.

Colby: I thought we established the other day that it was dangerous to ask what's on my mind... But if you're referring to my plans, I'm heading to IKEA and wanted to know if you'd like to join. We have an empty apartment we just renovated, and we're experimenting with leasing it furnished as an Airbnb. I'm in charge of getting it ready. So I need to pick up a bunch of housewares, stuff like glasses and utensils.

Billie: Mmm...I do love the Swedish meatballs from IKEA. When are you going? I made plans to take a kickboxing class at one o'clock. A friend of mine is holding a free trial group lesson to drum up some new clients.

I'd taken boxing classes growing up and was pretty good at it. I thought there might be an opportunity to show off a little, so I extended an invitation to myself.

Colby: Mind if I join you? I've been looking for a fun way to get some exercise. Running and lifting weights is pretty boring. Maybe we could do a double undate and hit IKEA after?

Billie: Sure. Taylor would love that. The more the merrier. Can you meet me at the gym? I have some errands to run beforehand. I can send you a link to the address.

Colby: Sounds good. Looking forward to it.

I'd never admit it to anyone, especially not my buddies, but I worked out before I left for the kickboxing class. If there was a chance to take off my shirt, I wanted to look as cut as possible. I did a hundred sit-ups and almost as many curls to pump up my biceps before heading to the address she'd sent me.

I'd thought I was looking pretty good…until I got a glimpse of the guy setting up mats at the front of the room when I walked in. He had on baggy white pants like you wear for karate and no shirt. I was fit, but this dude made me look frail. I have no fucking idea why, but somehow I knew he could make his pecs dance to the rhythm of music as a party trick. That thought made me frown, as did remembering the forty minutes I'd wasted exercising before coming here. There was no way in hell I was taking off my shirt anywhere in the vicinity of Mr. Universe.

But I found a reason to smile anyway when I saw Billie waving. She had on a cropped top and a pair of shorts, and although I loved those corsets, I wasn't missing them at all at the moment.

"Hey. You made it," she said.

"Yeah, the location actually worked out well. I borrowed Owen's car and drove so we'd have a way to get the stuff from IKEA home after we're done. And my parents only live a few blocks away, so I dropped Saylor there. They usually come by our place one or two Saturdays a month to spend time with her while I catch up on errands and stuff. She was excited to go to their place for a change."

"Oh, that's great." She motioned to the other side of the room. "Come on, I'm over here."

I followed and dropped the duffle bag I'd brought on the ground next to hers.

"It's great that Saylor's grandparents are so involved in her life," she said as she stretched a little.

"Yeah, my parents are pretty amazing with her. They moved from Pennsylvania, where I grew up, to New York to be closer to me after Saylor was born. My mom would babysit all weekend, every weekend, if I let her. But since I'm not around ten hours a day for work, I try to put in quality time on Saturdays and Sundays. I usually take her out to see different things in the city on at least one day, unless the weather is bad. Believe it or not, she loves checking out libraries the most."

Billie smiled. "Saylor's growing up with such a healthy male role model. Being a woman, I can't express how important that is. My mom was only nineteen when she had me. My dad was twenty-five and married to another woman when Mom found out she was pregnant."

"No shit?"

She nodded. "Even more fun than that, his wife was already two months pregnant when my mom got pregnant. So I have a half-sister who's only eight weeks older than me."

"Wow. How did that play out growing up?"

"Welp, my dad had no real interest in getting to know me. When he'd first gotten together with my mom, he'd told her he was in the middle of a divorce, and she believed him. But as far as I know, he's still married to the same woman all these years later."

"Damn." I shook my head.

"Yeah, it really changed the course of Mom's life. After that, she dated once in a while, but I don't think she ever trusted a man enough to get into a serious relationship. It's funny, I pride myself on being nothing like her, yet I pretty much did the same thing—fell for a guy who screwed me over and lost all trust in men."

I tapped my chest. "Present company excluded, I hope."

"I think the jury is still out on that. I've heard about your playboy ways, you know."

My eyes narrowed. "What are you talking about?"

"Holden likes to gossip while getting tattooed."

Seriously? What the fuck. Why the hell would Holden tell her shit like that, true or not? I was going to kill his grungy ass when I got home. I frowned. "I'm not like that anymore, Billie. Having Saylor brought me a whole new perspective. Now I think to myself, *would I want some dude treating my girl that way?*"

"I do believe you've changed a lot. I didn't mean to put you down. I was mostly teasing, anyway."

Mostly. Great.

Our conversation paused when the buff guy walked over. He opened his arms and smiled at Billie. "You made it!"

She stepped into a hug, and the dude lifted her into the air and spun her around. Clearly, he did not feel intimidated by the man standing next to her.

"You're squishing me, Taylor!" Billie squealed while laughing.

Great, *this guy* is Taylor. By the name, I'd assumed the instructor wasn't a man. Now I had to endure a whole hour of the woman I came to impress looking at that. Today's date, or rather *undate*, had not started off as planned. In the first three minutes, Billie had told me she'd heard I was a playboy, and now Mr. Universe had her tits squished up against his ginormous pecs. *Awesome. Just awesome.*

The instructor set her back on her feet, but he kept his arm wrapped around her waist. "How are you, beautiful?"

"I'm good," Billie said, motioning to me. "This is my friend, Colby."

The guy extended his hand. "How you doing, Colby? Thanks for coming down today."

I forced a smile. "Happy to be here."

Taylor looked at his watch and thumbed toward the front of the room. "I gotta start class. I'll talk to you more after, okay?"

Billie nodded. "Sounds good."

After we did some stretches and warmed up, Taylor showed us some kickboxing moves. We practiced foot jabs and sidekicks, and then he told the class to pair up for some light sparring. I looked over at Billie. "Should we pair up with someone more our sizes?"

Billie put her hands on her hips. "Are you saying you don't think I'm a match for you because you're a foot taller than me?"

I chuckled and shrugged. "Kinda makes sense, doesn't it?"

The instructor walked around the room, talking to all the pairs, and when he got to us, he put his arm around Billie's shoulders again.

"I'll take this little troublemaker." He pointed to a guy in the back of the room. "Colby, why don't you spar with that guy? It doesn't look like he has a partner yet."

Yeah, like I was letting *him* put his hands all over Billie. I shook my head. "It's fine. I'll stick with Billie. Don't worry. I'll go easy on her."

Billie and Taylor looked at each other and burst out laughing. "You're going to go easy on Billie?" he asked. "Tell me, does that mean Billie has to go easy on you?"

I shrugged. "Nah. She can take her best shot."

Taylor patted my shoulder with a chuckle as he walked away. "Don't say I didn't warn you, friend."

My brows drew together as I looked at Billie. "What was that all about?"

She held up her hands in the kickboxing stance the instructor had taught us. "Are you ready to fight, Lennon?"

The gleam in her eye should've told me I had no damn clue what I was in for. But I shrugged like an arrogant idiot. "I'm always ready."

I rubbed my lower back as I killed the car's engine in the IKEA parking lot. There was definitely going to be a bruise there. "I still can't believe you didn't tell me you had a damn black belt."

Billie chuckled. "We tried to warn you, but you were too busy assuring me you wouldn't hurt me. You know, because I'm so small and helpless."

"I never said helpless."

Billie opened the passenger door. "Come on, Wussy."

I shook my head as I got out. Not only had I not landed a single shot on her, but Billie had flipped me over her shoulder like I was a damn rag doll. I'd gone from thinking I was going to impress her with my six-pack to being completely emasculated.

As we walked from the parking lot to the entrance, Billie couldn't stop laughing. "I'll tell you what," she said. "You can push the cart. That's a tough-guy job. It'll make you feel more manly."

"You know what will make me feel more manly? If you could reach up and pull my *balls* back down out of my body cavity. I'm pretty sure that's where they've been hiding all afternoon."

Billie yanked a shopping cart from a row of them and pushed it in my direction. "If you keep whining, I'm going to change your name from Wussy to something that rhymes with it and starts with a P."

Crash!

Shit. Billie and I looked at each other. A devilish smirk spread across her face…and then she turned and bolted.

I looked around. The coast seemed clear, so I ran as fast as I could while pushing a heaping cart full of crap. For the last hour and a half, Billie had been picking things out and holding them up to show me. If I agreed, she chucked them over her shoulder for me to catch with the cart. I'd been zigging and zagging, trying to scoop up all the merchandise she threw as I followed her around— both of us laughing like school kids the entire time. That is, until I missed that last toss and a glass bowl shattered on the floor.

IKEA was a giant maze, and both of us kept running, turning left and then right, until we finally arrived in the warehouse portion of the store, which was right before the checkout line. Billie leaned over with her hands on her knees, huffing and puffing.

"I think we're in the clear," she said.

"Pretty sure I would've rather paid for the twelve-dollar bowl than make a run for it. This cart is so full, it almost tipped like ten times."

She laughed. "Did we get everything we need?"

"I'm not sure. But we definitely bought a lot of shit we *don't* need. Like I think we could have done without the motorized ice cream cone spinners. The tenant can lick their own ice cream."

Billie grinned. "Those are for me and Saylor. They light up, too!"

I snorted. "Come on, let's check out before I'm completely broke."

While we loaded everything onto the conveyor belt, I lifted my chin toward the in-store restaurant located just after the cashier stations. "You still up for meatballs?"

"Uh…hello? It's the only reason I came."

I clutched my hand over my heart. "Oww, that hurts. And here I thought you came for the company."

After we were all checked out, I wheeled the cart over to a table for two in the corner of the restaurant. "Why don't you stay here with the stuff, and I'll go get us some meatballs."

"Okay. But can you get me a drink, too, please? I'm so thirsty."

When I came back, I set two big plates of meatballs on the table.

"Did you forget the drinks?" Billie asked.

I grinned and lifted a finger. "Actually, I didn't. I brought them." My gym bag from earlier had been lying on the bottom shelf underneath the cart since we walked in. Taking it out, I unzipped and started to unpack. "Wine, madame?" I held a bottle of merlot over one arm, showing the label like a maître d'.

Billie cracked up. "You brought wine with you? I thought it was strange when you took your duffle bag into the store. But I figured maybe your wallet was in it and stuff."

I shrugged. "What choice did I have? You won't go out with me, so I have to make the best out of our undate at IKEA." I unloaded two plastic wine glasses, white cloth napkins, and a candleholder with a red candle.

Billie picked up the candle and examined it before raising a brow. "A winter village scene?"

I shrugged. "They're Christmas candles. I only had an hour to get out of the house with a four-year-old. Don't judge."

The looks we got from the people around us as we ate meatballs by candlelight were pretty comical. I was also pretty sure it was against the rules to have an open flame in IKEA, let alone an open bottle of wine, but evidently the people behind the counter hadn't read the employee rule book to be certain. Either way, the smile on Billie's face made it all worthwhile. After we were done eating, I blew out the candle and started to pack up.

"You know…" Billie shook her head. "I think you just snuck a date into our undate."

I shoved the cork back into the top of the wine bottle and zippered it into my duffle. "I did not."

She squinted at me. "I'm pretty sure you did. What's the difference between what we just did and a date? We shared a candlelight meal with wine and cloth napkins."

I leaned down and whispered in her ear. "The difference is, you don't get to come at the end."

When I pulled back, Billie's jaw was hanging open. I freaking loved that she looked so affected. She swallowed. "Is that the way all your dates end?"

I shook my head back and forth slowly. "No, but it's damn straight the way ours would."

"Do you want me to drop you off at home?" I asked as we stopped at the first light.

Billie shook her head. "I have an appointment at the shop tonight. I don't usually work Saturday evenings—that's why I was off today—but one of my regulars moved to Florida and is only in town for the weekend. He asked if I could add something to the sleeve I did for him a while back. So if you're going to your apartment, that works out great. If not, no biggie. You can leave me wherever. I'm sure you have to pick up Saylor."

"I'm actually going to unload everything we bought at the apartment it's going into before I pick her up. She'll probably fall asleep on the drive back from my parents', and I don't want to have to wake her to do it later."

She smiled. "So thoughtful. I don't know too many men who put that much effort into planning ahead, and not just with Saylor—even today, for example. Our undate was really cute."

I leaned toward her a little. "Any chance it earned me a *real* date?"

I'd been teasing, at least half teasing, but Billie's face fell. "I'm sorry, Colby. Maybe doing this undate thing wasn't a good idea. I'm laughing and having a good time with you while drinking wine and sharing a meal. It's not fair of me to lead you on."

I panicked. "I was joking, Billie."

She didn't look like she believed me. "Are you sure?"

"Positive. If my choices are being friends with you or nothing, I'll take friends. You don't have to worry about leading me on. I'm a big boy." Though inside I felt pretty crushed. I guess all the fun today *had* gotten my hopes up a little. But I wasn't about to let her know that because I didn't want her to cut me off altogether. "You know what?" I said. "I don't think I even *want* to go out with you anymore."

"Oh really?"

I shrugged. "I mean, you can't throw for shit, and I noticed those little drops of brown sauce from the meatballs you dribbled onto your shirt. You're kinda not my type anyway."

Billie smiled. "Yeah? So what exactly is your type?"

I looked over at her before returning my eyes to the road. "I like blondes. *Really* tall ones, at least six feet. And flat-chested, too. I can't forget that."

Billie chuckled. "Flat-chested, huh?"

I nodded. "Yup. The flatter the better. Give me a girl who looks like an ironing board any day of the week."

"Well, I guess I'm really not your type then…"

"Nope." I drummed my fingers on the steering wheel. "So you don't have to worry about leading me on one bit. Actually, when you come too close, I kind of feel like I might catch the cooties."

The ear-to-ear smile on Billie's face made it worth lying through my teeth.

Too soon, we pulled up at the apartment. I double parked, and my platonic, *not flat-chested* friend helped me take all of the bags to the empty unit. After the last trip, Billie looked at the time on her phone. "I need to go get ready for my appointment, but I had a lot of fun today."

I shoved my hands into my pockets. "Me, too. Let's do it again soon."

Billie nodded and pushed up on her toes to kiss my cheek. "Goodnight, Colby."

I stayed firmly rooted in place as she walked to her store. When she got to the door, she stopped, but didn't look back.

"Hey, Lennon?"

"Yeah?"

"Why are you watching my ass if I'm not your type?"

I chuckled as she swung the door open and disappeared inside.

Billie Holland was *definitely* not my type anymore. Because *type* referred to a group or variety of something you like. And these days, I didn't want a variety. I only wanted *one woman*.

♥CHAPTER 8

Billie

The following day, I paced through the living room of Deek's apartment. "You're supposed to be knocking some sense into me, not encouraging this!"

I'd gone back to his place after we got ramen for dinner and decided to fill him in on my time at IKEA with Colby. I worried I was starting to weaken to the guy's charms. Based on my last conversation with Deek about this subject, I should've known he would only encourage my inevitable dissent into falling for Colby.

"Why are you still so damn hesitant?" he asked. "That guy is a catch, from everything I can see. Heck, if he swung both ways, I'd tell you to go for it or else I would."

"It's more than one thing."

"Like…"

"He used to be a playboy, for one. Holden said Colby was the worst out of all those guys—had something to do with a high-school girlfriend who wronged him. He was never the same after that and went wild. Total manwhore, apparently. Until Saylor. She tamed him. But probably only because he no longer had time to play the field."

"Okay, so he has a playboy past. Like half the other men out there. Myself included. *Yet*…he's apparently not like that anymore. Probably got it out of his system. So, what's your other excuse?"

I rolled my eyes. "As we've discussed, he has a kid. He doesn't even have time to focus on a relationship."

Deek chuckled. "You realize you're contradicting yourself, right? First the guy is a playboy, now he's too responsible and a devoted father? God forbid!"

I sighed. My arguments were weakening pretty fast.

"You know what I think?" he asked.

I crossed my arms. "What?"

"You're making excuses out of fear. Take away those two factors you just mentioned and think about whether you genuinely like the guy. I bet if you made a list of the pros, they would greatly outnumber the cons."

If I thought about how Colby made me feel and my attraction to him, my feelings were undeniable. "Okay. Truth. When I'm around him, I'm happier than I've been in a very long time. There's nothing not to like if I remove the child aspect and the fear about his past. The list of things I like would fill that entire paper. But I can't just ignore the other stuff."

Deek shrugged. "Sure, you can."

"How can I even trust my own judgment? Look at my track record! I didn't see any of that coming with Kaiden."

"Sounds to me like you're due for a good one, then. The universe is trying to shove it in your face, and you're being too damn stubborn. Pretty soon the universe is gonna get downright pissed and give up on you."

I rolled my eyes. *Note to self: if I want someone to convince me I should steer clear of Colby, Deek is not that person.* I should probably be talking to my mother about this. She'd have no problem convincing me that a guy like Colby would never be interested in a girl like me.

After I left Deek's, I took the stairwell down so I had to pass by a certain someone's apartment on the way out. My brain told me I needed to flee the premises, but apparently my feet were listening to some other part of me, because rather than do what they should've and continue out the door, they stopped right in front of Colby's place.

Should I knock?

There were so many reasons knocking would be a bad idea. For one, it was on the later side. Saylor was probably sleeping, and I'd wake her up. *But it would be nice to see him. To say hello.* Ugh. Why couldn't I just lift my damn hand and knock? I looked up at the ceiling and let out a long breath. Then I began to pace as I continued to debate whether to knock or leave. A woman exiting her apartment smiled at me, and I waved at her awkwardly.

It must have been about ten minutes that I loitered there like an idiot, talking to myself and continuing to pace.

Then Colby's door opened. He scratched his head. "Billie?"

"Oh!" I feigned laughter and ignored my pounding heart. "Hey, Colby."

He was dressed casually in jeans and a black hoodie. He looked hot. *But when does he not look hot?*

Concern crossed his face. "Is everything okay?"

Running my hand through my hair, I exhaled. "Sure. Yeah, why wouldn't it be?"

"Well, for one, my neighbor called and said there was a strange woman standing outside my door talking to herself. So I looked out the peephole, and here you were. That was several minutes ago. I didn't want to interrupt whatever you were working through. But then it got to a point where I couldn't help myself." He tilted his head. "What *are* you doing?"

81

My mouth opened and closed a few times. "Honestly…I was debating whether or not to knock."

"I figured as much. But why?"

I exhaled. "Would you believe me if I said I didn't want to wake Saylor?"

"Probably not." He smiled. "But you know what? I'm glad you're here, and after all the time you've invested out here, I think you should come in." He looked over his shoulder. "Also, you'll be very happy to know I'm doing the most *unsexy, undatelike* thing ever, so you won't have to worry about things getting too wild up in here."

As I stepped inside, I immediately noticed the mountain of laundry in the middle of the room. It was practically five-feet high, an explosion of pastel colors mixed with masculine ones, dresses mixed with collared shirts, pink towels mixed with black.

"I interrupted your laundry night. I should go…"

"Are you kidding? Best interruption ever, trust me."

I plopped myself down next to the pile and began to fold.

He held out his hand. "Whoa. What are you doing? You don't need to do that."

I looked up. "I actually love folding laundry. I find it so relaxing, placing the warm material against my face, stopping to smell the fresh scent, focusing on folding it just right. It's like sensory meditation." I grabbed a random item and took a long whiff.

"You know that's my underwear, right?"

I froze. *Shit.*

"But by all means, continue doing that. It's hot. And relax away if you like folding and smelling. I'll take an impromptu meditation session with you any day."

I felt my face heat. "Anyway, they smell good." I folded the boxer briefs and set them aside.

He laughed, joining me on the floor across from the pile.

"This is a nice change of pace. I normally put the TV on low volume to pass the time, but I'd much rather look at you."

"How often do you do your laundry exactly, because this is… quite a lot."

"Once a month, maybe?"

"Yeah, I can tell."

He might have been a dad, but he was also a typical bachelor in many ways.

We sat together folding laundry for several minutes when I noticed him staring at the inside of my right forearm. While my entire left arm was an ink sleeve, I only had one tattoo on the other. It was a Victorian key.

"Does that one have special meaning?" he asked. "I noticed it's all by itself."

I smiled and held my arm out. "It does. My grandmother wore this key around her neck every day after my grandfather died. He was in the military, and they met while he was home on leave once. This key opened his footlocker, where he kept everything important to him. At the end of their first date, he told her he didn't need it anymore because the most important thing he could have was right in front of him. They'd been married for fifty-one years when he died. And when my grandmother passed two years ago, we buried her with the key."

"Wow. That sounds like something Rose would do, from *Titanic*."

I laughed. "I'm surprised you know who Rose from *Titanic* is. But yeah, it does."

Colby went quiet for a few minutes. He seemed lost in thought. So I tucked a pair of socks into a ball and chucked it at him. "What are you thinking about over there?"

"Nothing."

"*Liar.*"

He smiled. "I guess I was just thinking about how the woman who is the president of the All Men Suck Club is actually a romantic at heart."

"I am not. It's just a tattoo."

He caught my eyes and grinned. "Uh-huh."

He surprised me by letting the subject drop. "Have you eaten?" he asked instead.

I placed a neatly folded pair of pants to my right. "Actually, I had dinner with Deek a couple of hours ago."

"A couple of hours ago? Well, you must be getting a little hungry again. Let me get you a snack."

"I'm not a three-year-old. That's not necessary."

"You're a guest in my house." He stood up. "It *is* necessary for me to offer you something. Want some wine?"

"No, thank you. I drank with dinner."

Colby went to the kitchen before returning with a couple of things that made me smile.

"In these parts, there is no lack of kiddie snacks. I figured if you like Goldfish, you might like these."

He placed a small Lunchable container in front of me, along with a box of grape juice.

"You know me so well. This is perfect, actually." I laughed. "Don't mind if I do." I opened the package and placed one of the small slices of cheese atop a cracker and took a bite. "I thought maybe you were going to grab me a spinach brownie."

He hopped back up. "I have some of those. Want one?"

I chuckled. "No. Sit. This is more than enough."

Colby returned to the floor and watched intently as I devoured my snack, as if watching me eat was some kind of spectator sport.

"What?" I finally asked with my mouth full.

"Sorry. I like watching you—the way you lick the corner of your mouth every once in a while. Even the way you eat is unique. It's cute."

84

"Well, you haven't watched me eat a rack of ribs. Because there is *nothing* cute about that." I took a sip from the juice box.

"Note to self: figure out a way to get Billie to a steakhouse, just so I can witness this."

"Make sure you pack wipes, then."

After I finished my snack, I got up to discard the rubbish. Then I resumed folding. We were finally starting to make a dent. "I'm not gonna find any random women's panties in this pile, am I?"

He shook his head. "No panties to be found in here unless they have Disney characters on them in toddler size three." He grinned as he fished through socks for matching pairs. "On the subject of undergarments, though, I have to ask you a serious question."

"Okay…" I said, shaking out one of Colby's shirts to smooth the wrinkles.

"What's with the corset thing?" he asked, his eyes dropping to my chest.

I looked down at my open plaid shirt. "Why do I wear them all the time?"

"Yeah."

"I just think they're flattering. They suck everything in in all the right places and push the right things out. It's my signature style, I guess." My brow lifted. "Why? Do you have a problem with them?"

He bit his bottom lip and nodded. "I do."

"Really…"

"My problem is they make it *really* hard not to stare. Your corsets are becoming my weakness. Sort of like how *you* are becoming my weakness." He lowered his voice. "But pretend you didn't hear that, because this is supposed to be a boring undate of laundry folding and nothing more."

Even doing the most mundane things with Colby felt like… more. Hardly boring. And now I was thinking about what he'd just said about my corsets. I shook my head to bring myself back to the task at hand. "There is definitely something even more enjoyable about folding someone else's laundry."

"Well, you have an open invitation to come over and do ours anytime. Just don't stand outside for fifteen minutes first."

I chuckled. "You're not going to let me live that down, are you?"

"Do you know how many babies were born in this world in the time you stood at my door contemplating whether or not to come in?"

"Your neighbor must have thought I was a solicitor or something."

"She didn't know what to think."

"I guess it's nice to have neighbors who look out for you. You know, in case some crazy broad shows up at your door." I shook out a towel. "What did you tell her?"

"Well, once I looked out the peephole and realized it was you, I walked over to the other side of the apartment so you wouldn't hear me tell her the girl standing at my door was actually someone I have a very big crush on, and that you were the furthest thing from a crazy person. I told her you were probably just apprehensive about knocking because of what that might lead to—because it was so much more than just knocking on a door. It was a figurative knocking of sorts, knocking on a world of possibilities that are both scary and exciting."

"You really told your neighbor all that?"

"No." He winked. "I said, 'Thank you for letting me know. I'll take care of it.'"

I threw a pair of his underwear at his head. Then, I looked more closely. That particular pair of red briefs seemed awfully... small.

I snickered. "Aren't those a little small for you?"

He bent his head back in laughter. "They're *a lot* small for me."

"Then why do you wear them?"

He lifted them up with both hands. "My mother brought this pack of underwear back from Brazil for me. She took a trip there last summer. She bought a men's size medium-large, but they shrink to like an extra small after I dry them. So they're basically disposable. I can't wear them more than once. Now I'll donate 'em or something. I think that might be the last one in the pack."

"You had me scared there for a minute," I teased.

His eyes widened. "Believe me, there's nothing extra small about me. I feel the need to clarify that, since according to your boundaries, that's not something I'll ever be able to prove."

The wicked smile he flashed made my insides quiver. This man had an unnerving effect on me. And with each moment that passed, it became harder and harder to pretend that didn't mean anything.

"All kidding about my shrunken underwear aside, Billie, I don't blame you for your hesitation with me. I hope you know that. I think if I were in your position, I might hesitate, too." He threw the red boxers aside. "And you know what? There's nothing wrong with being cautious. Especially when there are more than two people involved in the scenario. I get it. I really do." His eyes lingered on mine, his expression serious. He cleared his throat. "Anyway, this has got to be the most boring evening you've ever had with a guy, huh?"

"Actually…this is the best undate I've ever had," I told him.

His eyes sparkled. "Me, too. I like our undates."

After another half hour, we finally got to the bottom of the pile. Everything was now folded nicely, and we put the stacks of categorized clothing back into the baskets he had out. There were now four of them filled with clothes.

I looked around the room. "Is that it? Nothing more to fold?"

"I wish." He chuckled. "As I said, I tend to put off laundry until the very last minute. In fact, one of the reasons my daughter has underwear of every Disney Princess ever in existence is because I've been known to buy her more underwear just so I don't have to do laundry. It doesn't help that Saylor spills stuff on both her and me, so we go through multiple outfits a day sometimes. I've still got another load in the dryer waiting to come out and another load that has to go in."

"Well, lead the way. Let's tackle it all tonight. I'm no quitter."

I stood and followed him into the laundry room, which was a tiny, narrow area just off his kitchen. After squeezing into the tight space, our bodies were so close that I could practically feel him without even touching him. My breathing became rapid, and I knew why. I wanted him to kiss me. His eyes lowered to my lips, and it seemed there was no going back now.

A second later, a loud buzzing sound broke me out of my trance. The dryer had gone off.

"Shit." He closed his eyes. "I usually try to stop it before that happens."

"Will she wake up now?" I asked, slightly out of breath.

"She's a pretty deep sleeper, so probably not."

Feeling a bit rattled, not only by the buzzer, but by the fact that I'd lost my resolve, I made an impulsive decision. "You know what? I didn't realize the time. It's getting a bit late, and I have an early client tomorrow. I should probably head home. You think you can handle the rest yourself?"

"Absolutely." He nodded, probably reading between the lines. "Let me call you a car."

"You don't have to do that."

He pulled out his phone. "I insist."

My ride got here in two minutes, less than the amount of time it took to carry the unfolded laundry from the dryer out to the living room.

Colby hugged me goodbye, the hard muscles of his chest pressing against my breasts and reminding me of exactly *why* I'd decided to leave early.

The ride home was anything but uneventful, though. Because five minutes into it, my phone chimed. Colby had sent me a photo, along with this message:

Just in case you still had any doubt about the underwear situation.

My jaw dropped. It could've been a Calvin Klein ad. Colby stood in front of a full-length mirror in nothing but gray boxer briefs. His beautiful, hard chest and taut abs were on full display, as was the thin line of hair trailing down into his underwear. And let's just say the prominent bulge staring me in the face most definitely could *not* have fit into those tiny red Brazilian briefs. *Christ on a Lunchables cracker.* He was hotter than I'd ever imagined.

And now I was back to thinking maybe he wasn't such a good guy after all—because he was clearly trying to kill me.

❤CHAPTER 9

Colby

"**A**lright, are we all in agreement?" Owen looked around the table. "We're going to upgrade the HVAC system with the money we have in the account, and put off doing the roof until next year?"

I raised my beer. "Agreed."

Owen turned to Holden and Brayden. "What about you guys?"

They both shrugged, as was typical. They tended to go along with the group consensus.

"Works for me," Holden said.

"Same," Brayden added.

Owen leaned forward and held his beer over the middle of the table in a toast. "Then this month's board meeting is officially over. Let the real drinking begin."

We all clanked beer bottles.

On the second Friday of every month, the four of us got together to discuss the building and make decisions. Technically, our meetings were considered shareholder board meetings since we were a corporation, but considering we held them in a bar and had to yell over the band playing, it was more like a night out with the guys.

Holden stood. He cupped his hands around his mouth to talk over the music. "What are we doing tonight, boys? Tequila or whiskey?"

I preferred beer, but it wasn't worth the ball-busting I'd get if I didn't participate. The other guys all said tequila, so I shrugged. "Tequila it is."

As usual, we took turns going up to the bar for a round of shots and picking up the tab. By the fourth one, I was glad there weren't five of us, because I was already feeling no pain.

Holden pointed to the band. "I'm friends with these guys. When I talked to them earlier, they invited me to sit in with them for a song. I think I'm gonna take them up on it." He motioned to a table of four women who had come in a little while ago and were sitting near the stage. "I'll make us some friends, too."

Making friends with women was never a problem for Holden. On his way up to join the band, he stopped by the ladies' table, and within a minute, he had them all smiling and laughing.

When he finally left their table, he spoke to the band, and then the drummer got up. Holden took a seat at the drum set and grabbed the microphone. He twirled a stick in his other hand before pointing it at the ladies he'd just chatted with and flashing his signature lazy smile. "This next song is dedicated to my new friend, Nikki."

I chuckled when they started playing the old Van Halen song "Hot for Teacher" and leaned over to Owen. "I guess we know what Nikki does for a living."

"Yeah, no shit." He shook his head. "Dude's got a song to get in any girl's pants."

A minute later, Owen's phone buzzed. He looked down at it and frowned. "It's the office. I'm going outside so I can hear."

"Alright." I nodded.

Owen came back ten minutes later, just as Holden returned to the table.

"Sorry, guys, I gotta run. I have an emergency at the office," Owen said.

"What? We just got here." Holden pointed to the table of four women. "Those ladies just asked us to join them and bought us all a round of shots. There're four of them. You can't go, dude."

Owen patted Holden's shoulder. "I have faith that you can handle two, buddy."

I wasn't really in the mood to hang out with the ladies, but I didn't want to be a drag, so I walked over with the guys. I'd just have a beer and call it a night.

But then it turned out the women were all super nice—a few years younger than us, but pretty and outgoing. Oddly, the four of them had been friends since they were kids like we had, which was kind of cool. Nikki, the blonde Holden was cozying up to, was a teacher and had received tenure today, so they were out celebrating. After a half hour or so, Brayden said he had to get going, and so did one of the ladies, so I figured it was the perfect time to make my exit, too. But just as I was about to do that, Nikki suggested the remaining five of us go back to her place.

"I think I'm just going to call it a night," I said. "I have a daughter. She's with my parents tonight, but I gotta get up early tomorrow and get her."

"You told your parents ten o'clock. I was there when they picked her up, remember?" Holden said. "And they told you to take your time. Come on…don't be such a wuss."

"My apartment is just around the corner," Nikki said. She tilted her head. "Come for one drink."

Four years ago, I would have been the one begging my wingman not to ditch. And the only reason I didn't feel like going was because of some sort of loyalty to Billie—a woman who didn't want to date me. Though, lately, I got the feeling she was starting to come around, and I didn't want to fuck that up.

Holden put his arm around my shoulder. "One drink. She lives around the corner."

I gave in. "Alright, just one drink."

This scene was starting to look too much like my college days, at least the parts I didn't see in double right now. Nikki lived in a typical, small New York City apartment, where the kitchen was only five feet from the living room couch. She and Holden were currently sucking face at the kitchen counter, her legs wrapped around his waist. Meanwhile, the other two ladies and I were on the couch, awkwardly trying not to notice him rounding to second base. At least I thought it was awkward.

I slapped my knees. "Welp. I should get going."

Erika, the redhead sitting on my right, laid her hand on the inside of my thigh. "Don't go." She looked at her friend and smiled. "Melissa and I don't mind…sharing, if you're cool with that."

Melissa put her hand high on my other thigh and rubbed back and forth.

Fuck. I closed my eyes. This shit never happened to me anymore.

I looked at Erika, then Melissa. Both were attractive with great figures, and it had been a while since I'd been with anyone. Not to mention, how many offers of a threesome did a man get in life, particularly with women who looked like these two? Not very many. Yet I had a nagging feeling in my gut.

"I think I might've had too much to drink," I said. "Would you excuse me a minute? I'm going to hit the head and splash some cold water on my face."

"Sure, of course," Erika said. "Take your time."

I needed to remove myself from the situation in order to think clearly. But after locking the bathroom door, I really did splash some water on my face. Then I had a heart to heart with the guy in the mirror.

"Two beautiful women—why aren't you jumping at this opportunity, Lennon?"

I hung my head. *Because neither one of them is Billie, that's fucking why.*

I looked up again. "It's just sex. A threesome, for Christ's sake. They don't want to marry you, jackass."

I shut my eyes. *But how will you look Billie in the eyes after that?*

Then again…Billie had told me flat out that she wasn't interested, on more than one occasion.

She's.

Not.

Interested.

In.

You.

Get that shit through your thick skull already, Lennon.

I spent the next five minutes alternating between looking in the mirror and talking myself into a threesome, and hanging my head in shame for even considering it. But all I managed to accomplish was making myself feel nauseous from the motion of my head going up and down. When the room started to spin, I sat down on the floor next to the toilet bowl. That turned out to be a good thing, because thirty seconds later, my head was in it as I retched up every last drink I'd had in my stomach.

Ugh. Light from a window beamed in and landed straight in my eyes. I lifted my head and tried to get some spit in my mouth so

94

I could swallow, but all my tongue found was more of the same horrible taste. Did something die in my mouth last night? I looked around. *And where the hell am I?*

This was definitely not my bathroom.

I stared at the closed door until bits and pieces came back to me.

The ladies from last night.

That's right… We'd gone back to someone's apartment after the bar. It was supposed to be for one drink, but there had been several more rounds of shots. I was a little fuzzy about what happened after that. While I gave my brain a chance to fire up, I dug my phone out of my pocket to check the time. *Shit*. It was already eight thirty, and I'd missed a bunch of messages. I scrolled to the first unread one, which had come in at one in the morning.

Holden: Dude, what are you doing in there? Come join the party.

The next one had come in at a few minutes before eight this morning.

Billie: Hey. I have a ten o'clock appointment today. If you have time, stop in. I should be there in a little while. I want to talk to you about something.

I closed my eyes and shook my head. *Fuck.*

The next message had come in ten minutes ago from my mother. When I opened it, a photo popped up. My daughter was sitting at my parents' kitchen table, her little tongue peeking out the side like she was concentrating. On the tray in front of her, she had formed the letter D out of Cheerios.

Mom: She told me D was for Dad and did that all on her own!

I smiled, but moving my face actually hurt. Right now, that D stood for *dickhead*. I needed two aspirin, a toothbrush, and a shower, pronto. And I needed someone to bring them to me while I sat on the floor. I absolutely did not feel like moving at the moment, but I didn't have much of a choice since I couldn't pick up my daughter in this condition. She was only four, but she was observant and would definitely notice me still wearing the clothes I'd had on last night. So I dragged myself up and rummaged through the medicine cabinet for some toothpaste, then used my finger to do a quick brush before bending over and guzzling a full glass of water straight from the faucet.

That would have to hold me until I got home. I took a quick look in the mirror. My hair was sticking up all over the place, and dried drool was pasted to the side of my cheek.

Fuck it. I'll fix it later.

I had no idea what was waiting for me on the other side of the door. For all I knew, the women might not even remember I was in the bathroom, and I'd wake them and scare the shit out of them. So I creaked the door open as quietly as I could and tiptoed out.

The place was quiet, with no bodies in sight, so I made my way toward the door. But when I reached the hallway, I made the mistake of looking into the bedroom.

Holden was face up, spread eagle across the bed, his junk on full display. And he wasn't alone. All *three* of the women from last night were naked, too. One was curled up on his right side with her head resting on his chest, and the other two were on his left side spooning together while snuggled up against him. I shook my head before walking out.

Only fucking Holden.

Outside on the street, the sun was way too bright. I squinted as I started to walk. Luckily our building was only a few blocks away. People were coming and going on the sidewalk, all clean and dressed for the day, while I kept my head down during my walk of shame.

Which is exactly the position I was in when I turned the corner onto our block and walked straight into someone.

"Shit, sorr—" My words got caught in my throat when I looked up at the person I'd crashed into.

"Colby?"

"Billie, what are you doing here?"

She smiled. "Ummm...I work here, remember? A few buildings down. I was just heading to the deli to get my coffee."

"Yeah, uh, of course. Sorry. Not sure what I was thinking."

Her smile wilted as she looked me up and down. "Are you... just getting home from last night?"

My first inclination was to lie and say no, I'd run out for something. But she looked into my eyes, waiting for an answer, and I couldn't bring myself to do it. "Yeah, I, uh, went out with the guys last night. I had a little too much to drink and, uh, fell asleep, I guess."

"At one of the guys' apartments?"

I frowned, and the look of disappointment on Billie's face felt like a kick in the stomach. She shook her head and put up two hands. "Sorry. I don't want to know the details. I have to go anyway."

She started around me, but I stopped her.

"Billie, wait..."

She wouldn't even look at me. "It's fine, Colby. You don't owe me any explanation. You're a single guy. I get it."

I shook my head. "It's not what it looks like."

"No? So you didn't just leave a woman's apartment after spending the night?"

"I did, but nothing happened."

She pursed her lips. "It's none of my business. And I really need to go get my coffee before my client gets here."

"Just give me one minute so I can explain."

She took a deep breath and exhaled without saying anything. But she wasn't walking away anymore, so I figured I should get talking.

"The guys and I went out for our monthly meeting about the building, and then we had a couple of drinks. There were these four women, and Holden wanted to go back to their apartment. He gave me shit about being his wingman, so I went."

She nodded. "Oh, I see. That clears it all up."

"Really?"

"Yeah. So you spent the night to make your friend happy."

"Exactly."

"Well, I hope you used a condom at least."

She tried to walk away again, but I stopped her. "I didn't need to."

She rolled her eyes. "Great."

"I mean because I didn't sleep with anyone. In fact, I slept alone in the bathroom, even though I could have had a threesome."

The minute the word *threesome* came out of my mouth, I knew it was dumb.

Billie's cheeks heated. "You should've stopped talking while you were ahead, Colby." She started walking again.

This time I grabbed her arm. "Wait. I don't want to leave you upset."

She frowned as she stared down at the cement. "I'm not."

"Billie, look at me."

Taking a deep breath, she lifted her eyes to meet mine. What I saw made my chest tight. She looked so damn hurt.

"Nothing happened. I swear."

She looked at my hand on her arm and then back up to me. Her eyes filled with tears. "Please let go of me."

I immediately released her and stepped back, raising my hands. "Sorry. I'll call you later?"

"Sure."

She walked away and never looked back.

Fuck. This is not good.

"Daddy, look what I made!" Back at our place, Saylor removed drawing after drawing from her backpack.

"Wow, that's beautiful, baby. Is it a giraffe?"

My daughter giggled. "No, Daddy. It's you!"

I squinted at the paper. "What are those things on my head?"

"It's the party hats you wore on my birthday."

"Oooohhh." I nodded. That made sense now. When we sang happy birthday to her, I'd been wearing two of those cardboard hats with elastic strings on top of my head.

Saylor clasped her hands behind her back and rocked back and forth. "I made it with the markers Billie gave me for my birthday."

Hearing that name from my daughter's mouth made my heart sink. I'd called Billie three times today. The first two times it rang and rang before going to voicemail. The third time it rang once and went to the recording immediately—like she'd hit ignore on her phone. Which gave me an idea. I looked at the time on my cell. It was only about five. She might still be working.

"How would you like to stop by Billie's shop downstairs and show her what you made?"

Saylor jumped up and down. "Yes! Yes!"

I smiled. "Go grab your shoes."

Justine was at the desk when we walked in. She smiled. "Hey, Saylor. How are you?"

"Good."

I motioned toward the back. "Is Billie still here?"

"Yep. She just finished up her last customer. You can go on back. It's just her and Deek cleaning up for the day."

"Thanks."

Billie was washing the mirror at her workstation. Her face fell when she saw me in the reflection.

Shit. It's even worse than I thought. Like a coward, I nudged my daughter to walk into the room first. "Hey. We just stopped by to show you the picture Saylor made with the markers you got her."

Deek looked over at me and folded his arms across his chest.

Damn…she told him, too. I lifted my chin anyway. "What's up, Deek?"

His answer was to shoot daggers at me. After an awkward couple of seconds, Billie and Deek exchanged glances before she took a deep breath and walked over to us. She knelt in front of Saylor and put on a smile. "Let me see what you made, honey."

Saylor handed her the construction paper.

"Wow, good job. It looks just like your dad."

My brows shot up. "How did you know it was me?"

She pointed to the paper. "The party hats."

I smiled. "Guess that's why I'm an architect and not an artist." Shoving my hands into my pockets, I rocked back and forth on my heels. "How was your day?"

She glanced up at me and pursed her lips. "Saylor, sweetheart, why don't you show your beautiful artwork to Deek." Turning to her employee, her tone didn't leave much room for options. "Deek, would you mind taking Saylor up front to look at her drawing? I think Amazon delivered a few cases of snacks earlier. I'm sure you can find one she'd like."

He nodded. "No problem, boss."

When he walked past, he hit me with a warning glare. "I'll be right out there."

As soon as Deek closed the door behind them, Billie poked her finger into my chest. "Don't you *ever* do that again."

I raised both my hands in question. "Do what?"

"Use your sweet, innocent daughter to try to get back into my good graces."

I sighed. "How else was I supposed to talk to you? I tried to call you three times."

"Do you not know how to take a hint? I didn't feel like talking to you, Colby."

"Today or forever?"

"I don't know."

She wasn't looking at me, so I crouched down so our eyes were aligned. "I swear to God, Billie, nothing happened. I went as Holden's wingman. There were three women. Holden was hooking up with one, and I had too much to drink and passed out in the bathroom after puking. When I got up this morning, all four of them were in bed naked."

Billie's lip curled in disgust. "Please don't tell me any more."

"I'm sorry. But it's the truth. Nothing happened with me and any of the women. Do you believe me?"

She took a deep breath and sighed. "It doesn't matter, Colby."

"Of course it does."

"No, it doesn't. In fact, you don't owe me any explanation, and there's nothing to apologize about since there's nothing going on between us."

"Give me a break, Billie. Of course there is. We might not be having sex or dating, but there's something going on between us."

She looked away. "There isn't. I'm sorry if I led you to believe there was."

I could handle her being mad at me. I could even handle if she didn't believe what I said. But I couldn't handle her pretending nothing was going on between us anymore. Because I *knew* what I felt wasn't one-sided. At least I had before I'd gone and fucked everything up.

I crossed my arms. "You know what? Keep telling yourself that. Maybe eventually, you'll start to believe it." I shook my head. "And you're right. I shouldn't have come with my daughter. Not once in four years have I used her like that, not for anything. It may have been wrong, but that should tell you that what's going on between us is pretty damn real…at least for me." I paused. "I'll see you around."

❤CHAPTER 10

Billie

Holden had booked another appointment with me for Monday morning. He'd said he wanted a small addition to his tattoo. I'd been anxious to see him, mostly because I knew I wouldn't be able to resist digging for information on *Threesomegate*.

"Hey, Billie. Looking beautiful as always," Holden said as he made his way into the shop.

After Deek and he clasped hands, Holden headed over to my station.

"So what are we doing today?" I asked.

He lifted his shirt and slid down his pants a couple of inches to display the design I'd previously inked on him. "I decided I wanted to add this ribbon in the middle."

He pulled up an image on his phone and faced it toward me. It was a little orange awareness ribbon.

"That's easy enough." I tapped the chair. "Take a seat."

"Thank you, ma'am." He settled in and leaned back.

"So…I heard you guys had a lot of fun the other night." I cringed internally. I couldn't even wait until I had my equipment together. I did my best to seem casual despite the fact that my heart was pounding.

"You heard this from whom?" He smiled.

"From Colby. He told me *everything* about what happened. You know, your wild and crazy night at some girl's house. Sounds like a good time was had by all."

I kept it vague, hoping Holden would spill the beans, even if I wasn't sure I wanted to know the whole truth. I felt like I was dying. Trying to remain calm and collected when you're really jealous and anxious as shit is an art form.

"You mean Colby admitted how fucking lame he is?"

"*Threesomes* are lame?" I said, opening my eyes wide.

"I don't know who told you threesome; it was a foursome. And Colby didn't have anything. He freaking passed out in the bathroom."

My pulse slowed a bit. This matched Colby's story. "Well, that's too bad."

"It wasn't bad for me. I reaped the benefits. Those girls were hot and horny as all hell. Who knew teachers were so freaky? It's like, were my teachers like that back in the day, and I just never knew? Goddamn." He laughed.

My stomach churned as I rationalized one more question. "So Colby didn't even kiss one of them?" I had no right to that information, but I just *had* to know.

He shook his head. "I don't think so. I mean, I wasn't watching him every second before he passed out. But I'm pretty sure he didn't."

I felt terrible about giving Colby shit. Still, if he hung out with Holden enough, it was only a matter of time before the old gigolo ways came out to play. I activated my needle and got to work on Holden's ribbon. Speaking over the noise, I asked, "Why do guys like threesomes—or foursomes—anyway? Isn't it a lot to juggle?"

"It can be, yeah. But I'm always up for a challenge." He winked. "It reminds me of a one-man band. You have your mouth on one instrument, your hand on another, and all the while someone else is…blowing your horn, for lack of a better word."

I rolled my eyes. "I hope you're being safe with all of your instrumental maneuvering in the orchestra."

"Always," he said matter-of-factly. "If I've learned anything from my boy Colby, it's that it only takes one time to change your life."

I cleared my throat. "So, did Colby not *want* to participate, or did he not do it because he was too drunk to be up for the challenge?" I was a runaway train at this point.

"I don't think he would've been into it, even if he were more sober. I had to force him to come with me in the first place to be my wingman. He didn't want to go."

"Well, he has free will. On some level, he must have wanted to. He probably just chickened out. I would imagine having a kid makes you think twice about your decisions."

"Maybe. He *is* more responsible than he used to be." He looked over at me. "Any reason you're particularly vested in Colby's intentions the other night, Billie?"

I hesitated. "No. I'm just curious about it all."

"Come on. I'm not dumb. I know there's some shit going on between you two. He hasn't talked to me about it, though— probably because he knows I come here, and he doesn't trust my big mouth."

"Can you blame him?" I asked.

"Not at all."

"Anyway… There's nothing going on between Colby and me."

"Really? Because you've been grilling me about him since the second I walked in, and you're turning all red right now."

I was sweating. "Shut up and let me finish this in peace."

He chuckled. "You're the one asking me questions."

"Seriously. I have another client soon. No more talking."

He rested his head back. "Alright."

Holden dropped the subject and stayed quiet as I continued working. Beads of sweat formed on my forehead.

After forty-five minutes, I finally finished. "You're all set. It looks good. The orange color really pops."

I'd been so preoccupied with digging for information earlier, I hadn't thought to ask about the meaning of the ribbon. That was very unlike me. I'd tattooed dozens of pink ribbons for breast cancer, but this was the first orange one I'd done.

"What's the orange ribbon stand for?"

"Leukemia awareness."

I should've known. Their friend who died and left the inheritance. "Ryan…" I said.

"Yup." He nodded. "You know about him, right?"

"Yeah. Colby's told me the story. I'm very sorry for your loss."

"Thank you. I miss him every day." He sighed as he got up from the chair. "If there's one thing Ryan's death has taught me, it's that life is too short. I think everyone reacted to losing him differently. Me? I've continued to live it up the only way I know how, which is to have fun anytime I can. But the four of us didn't all change for the better."

"How so?"

"Owen buries himself in his work. Brayden seems mad at life sometimes. I think he lost faith when even God couldn't save Ryan. Like I said, I party and focus even more on my music. And Colby…" He paused. "Well, Colby's life changed with Saylor soon after Ryan's death, so it's hard to know what he'd be up to if she hadn't come along. Who knows… Maybe she saved him. But he's often said one of the reasons he tries so hard to be a good dad is because he knows it's an opportunity he shouldn't take for granted. I think out of all of us, Ryan was the only one who knew he wanted kids. He always used to say he couldn't wait to grow up and start a family. That was probably because he knew he might not have the chance."

My stomach tightened. "That's heartbreaking."

"Want to hear something freaky?" he said.

"I've never been one to shy from freaky info. Shoot."

"Ryan's mom went to one of those mediums after he died. And Ryan supposedly came through and said he's already back here with us."

I narrowed my eyes. "What does that mean?"

"Well, that's what she asked the medium! And the medium dug for more info and said Ryan reincarnated and came back to Earth." He paused. "As a little girl." He moved his eyes from side to side. "Take from that what you will."

"Jesus Christ," I muttered.

"Right?" He laughed. "Anyway, not to leave you on a weird note, but I gotta run. Thanks again for adding this for me."

"No charge, okay?"

His eyes widened. "Are you serious?"

"Yes. This one's on Ryan." I smiled.

"Thanks." He leaned in and kissed me on the cheek. "You're the best." He turned around again before he left. "You know what, Billie? Take Ryan's story as a lesson to grab life by the balls—or in this case, Colby's balls." He winked. "If that's what you want. Something tells me he'd *love* it if you did."

I rolled my eyes as he disappeared out the door.

After Holden left, I remained with thoughts of Colby. I'd given him shit when he hadn't actually messed around with anyone the other night. I should've been over the whole thing, yet I was still mad. But now? I was mad at myself. I also missed him and didn't know what to do with that feeling. Things were better off the way they were now, weren't they? I'd been weakening to his charms recently, and I'd already decided I wasn't going to get serious with someone who had a kid. So now maybe with him mad at me, I needed to leave well enough alone, let him be pissed so we could stop this game we'd been playing. As my conversation with Holden proved, life *was* too short to waste anyone's time.

I had to put my ruminations aside to deal with my next customer, a repeat client named Eddie Stark, AKA Eddie Muscle. Eddie was a good-looking dude, although not my type. He was a bit older, divorced, and massively built—a real musclehead and gym rat. I liked muscles on guys, but there was such a thing as too much, and Eddie fit that criteria. Every time he came in, he asked me out. And every single time, I shot him down. He'd always ask: "Is today going to be my lucky day?" And I'd usually respond with: "Afraid not." I always used the excuse that I didn't date clients. I'd planned for today to be no different.

After I finished up his latest design, he asked, "Have you heard about the new bar that just opened in this neighborhood? They have really good tapas."

Eddie was nothing if not persistent.

I nodded. "I have, yeah."

"We should check it out. And before you tell me again that you don't fraternize with clients, I should add that I won't be coming in anymore since I'm gonna be all set for a while after this one. So, if I'm taking a long break from any more ink…technically, I won't be your client."

The word *no* was at the tip of my tongue. But then I wondered if going out with someone other than Colby was exactly what I needed. I shrugged and forced out the words before I could change my mind. "You know what, Eddie? Sure. Yeah. Why not?"

His eyes widened, and he smiled like a Cheshire cat. He certainly hadn't been expecting me to say yes.

Then I looked over at Deek, who'd overheard the entire exchange. He looked at me like I had ten heads. Justine smirked from the doorway. She'd apparently heard everything, too. No one in the room had expected me to agree to a date with Eddie Stark— least of all me. I'd never once accepted a client's advances. And I'd gotten hit on quite a bit. Guess there was a first time for everything.

"Well, that's about the best news I've gotten all year." Eddie beamed. "What night works for you?"

I picked a night at random. "Wednesday?"

"Okay, sounds good. Shall we meet there or…"

"Yeah."

"Say seven PM?"

"Sounds great." I smiled.

After Eddie left, Deek wasted no time. "What the hell was that all about?"

"What do you mean?"

"You don't even like that guy."

"He's nice. And he deserves points for his persistence."

Deek arched his brow. "So he deserves points for persistence, but Colby doesn't?"

Damn, was that a good point. I crossed my arms. "That's a different situation."

"Exactly. Colby scares you, and this guy doesn't because you don't really like him."

I sighed, unable to even deny it.

Justine chimed in. "I've always had a crush on Eddie myself. If I weren't already married, I would've tapped that before Billie had a chance. I like 'em big and wide like that."

"Seriously, Billie?" Deek said, ignoring Justine's comment. "It's so obvious what you're doing." He shook his head. "Look, I'll admit, I was a little suspicious about that threesome shit with Colby, too. But you've got to give him credit for telling you the truth about that night, even if it sounded shady. And his story matched Holden's. Sounds to me like he just got wrapped up in his friend's antics. If I got blamed for everything my friends did or roped into witnessing…" He shook his head. "Heck, I'd probably be in jail."

"Colby is pissed at me now anyway. So maybe I should just leave well enough alone."

"He's pissed because he likes you," Deek said. "And all you keep doing is sabotaging things."

The truth hurt. I couldn't even conjure a response.

"Okay." He walked away in a huff, but then came back. "I'm just gonna say one more thing. You're blind if you can't see that your knee-jerk reaction right now is all the proof you need that you have true feelings for Colby. You can't even bear to talk about it because you know damn well you can't hide it. So, whatever. Go out with Eddie Muscle. Pretend like it's not just a front. But you're only wasting time."

Wednesday night arrived, and though I hadn't been excited about my date with Eddie, once we got to the bar, I found myself enjoying his company. I wasn't attracted to him the way I was attracted to Colby, and I knew this wouldn't go anywhere, but overall, I didn't regret coming out tonight. Not to mention, the tapas *were* really good.

Eddie dipped a piece of shrimp in some cilantro-lime sauce. "It's amazing how far the shop has come in the past couple of years. I'm kind of proud that I was one of your original clients."

"Yeah. Well, I couldn't do it alone. Deek has been a big help. And the new location has brought in a lot of people."

"Deek is great, but you're the real talent in there. Word travels fast when someone is good at their job. I know I've recommended you to more than a few people."

I stared down at the full sleeve I'd inked on him. "Well, I really appreciate that, Eddie. You're a good egg."

My phone chimed. When I looked down, I saw a text from Colby.

Nice to know you're actually capable of going out on a real date. Hope you're having a nice time.

Adrenaline coursed through me as I looked around the room. *What the hell is he doing here?* It was a weeknight, so I would've thought he'd be home with Saylor.

I typed.

Billie: Where are you?

A few seconds later came his response.

Colby: Does it matter?

Billie: I want to know how you know where I am.

Colby: Maybe you should pay attention to your date and stop worrying about such things.

"Is everything okay?" Eddie asked.

"Yeah. Just a…personal issue." I stood from my chair. "Will you excuse me for a moment? I need to use the restroom."

"Of course," he said, looking concerned.

I went to the bathroom to text Colby in peace. Leaning against the sink, I typed lightning fast.

Billie: Have you been watching me all night?

Colby: Yeah. Because I have SO much time on my hands that I've now taken to stalking you. Really, Billie?

Billie: Are you here, though?

He dodged the question.

Colby: I just wish you were fucking honest with me.

Billie: What do you mean?

Colby: All this time you've been acting like you're afraid of anything serious, not wanting to date. But apparently you're just hesitant to date ME. Why not say that and be done with it?

He had no clue. He wanted me to be honest? Honest would have meant admitting that I'd never been more scared of anything in my life than my feelings for him. They were the very reason I was on this date.

Billie: It's not that simple, Colby.

Colby: Love the royal blue corset, by the way. I hadn't seen that one before. You must reserve that one for real dates.

Ouch.

I walked back out and surveyed the place. There was no sign of him.

Billie: Why won't you tell me where you are?

Colby: Because it doesn't matter.

Billie: It matters to me.

After about a minute, he texted back.

Colby: You think I like coming across as a jealous bastard? This is not a good look, and I know it. I debated whether I should text you. But people do stupid things when they like someone. And I truly like you, Billie. I like you so much that I can't even think straight right now. I put fucking hot sauce in my daughter's spaghetti, thinking it was mine. Thank God I caught it before I burned her mouth off.

I just stood there staring down at my phone. My heart hurt.

Colby: Don't text back. This was a mistake. I shouldn't have interrupted your night. You don't owe me anything.

Then one more.

Colby: Goodnight.

My legs were wobbly as I forced myself back to the table. Then I looked to my left and spotted Holden at the bar. His eyes locked with mine, and he lifted his beer in salute. He was the one sending information to Colby. I waved, though I really wanted to give him the finger.

❤CHAPTER 11

Billie

"**B**illie?"

I heard Deek call my name but was only sort of half listening. "Hmmm?"

"I'm going to run out and get a smoothie. You want one?"

I continued to sterilize the equipment I'd been cleaning for a while until a high-pitched whistle grabbed my attention. I looked up to find Deek with his brows raised.

"You want one or not?"

My nose wrinkled. "Want what?"

Deek folded his arms over his chest. "Alright, that's it. Sit your ass down."

"What? Why?"

"Because you and me, we're going to have a talk."

"Why do you sound like you're in dad mode?"

"Just sit, Billie."

I rolled my eyes but tossed the paper towel in my hand into the garbage before planting my butt in my hydraulic chair. "What's up?"

Deek pointed at me. "You're fucking miserable."

"I *am not.*"

"You've been cleaning crap for almost two weeks now. You're the person who spills shit and leaves it long enough that you yell at someone else to clean it up because you no longer remember you did it."

I squinted at him. "I do not."

Deek turned his head toward the front of the store. "Hey, Justine!"

"Yeah?"

"Who spilled the purple juice that sat on the floor for six months?"

"Billie. Why?"

"And does Billie ever clean?"

"Only when she's pissed off or sad."

Deek turned back to me. "So, like I was saying, you're so miserable that even our customers are feeling it."

I took offense to that. "I don't give bad tattoos, even when I'm in a bad mood."

"Didn't say you gave a bad tattoo. But the poor girl who walked in here the other night wanting a butterfly walked out with the Grim Reaper on her arm, Billie."

I shrugged. "So? The Grim Reaper is way better than a butterfly."

"I agree. But the girl wanted a *fucking butterfly.* It went with her annoyingly chipper personality. But when she asked your opinion, you told her most people who get butterflies are shallow ex-cheerleaders who live empty lives and wind up marrying for money that they blow on bad Botox."

Had I really said that? *Oh God.* I guess I had. Yet I shrugged. "Well…it's the truth."

Deek smiled. "Of course it is. Who the fuck wants that shit on their body? But my point is, you're usually good at vibing with a client and giving them what they want, even if it is unoriginal and boring."

I sighed. "I went out with Eddie last week."

"I knew that. Figured you'd tell me about it when you were ready." He paused. "Wait, that fucker didn't do something to you, did he? I'll stick a dumbbell up his 'roid-riding ass…"

That made me smile. "No, Eddie was a perfect gentleman. He didn't even complain at the end of the night when he went in for a kiss and I stopped him."

"So what's bugging you?"

"Well, while I was on my date, Colby texted me. Holden was at the same place Eddie and I were, and he told Colby I was on a date. Colby was really hurt."

Deek frowned. "Why don't you just go out with him already?"

I hesitated for a moment before speaking quietly. "Because I'm scared, Deek."

A giant smile spread across my friend's face. "It's about fucking time you admitted it."

I flipped him the bird and shook my head. "Every damn time I've put myself out there, I've gotten hurt."

Deek walked over and put his hands on my knees. "I get it, sweetheart. It's not just guys you dated who have screwed you over. Your mother and that deadbeat father of yours didn't exactly instill trust through their actions either."

I shook my head. "Colby makes me feel things, Deek."

"I know. Why do you think I've been pushing for him so hard? I see it in your eyes, babe."

"I'm so afraid I'll get hurt again."

"Aren't you hurting now, though?"

"Yeah, but it will be easier to get over him if we never get involved at the next level. Plus, he's got a daughter. I don't even know if I want kids."

Deek smiled sadly. "The kid thing is just an excuse, and you know it. I'm kinda tired of hearing it. But it's your life, so I won't keep bugging you about it. Though I'm gonna say one last thing."

"What?"

"I don't think we ever get over *the one*. I'd rather try and get hurt than spend the rest of my life wondering what I might've lost."

A couple of hours later, Deek and Justine were getting ready to leave for the day. Deek went into the back to use the bathroom, and when he came out, he thumbed toward the rear of the studio.

"I think the AC is broken again."

Oh crap. I was warm, but I'd thought it was just me. There was a vent in the ceiling above the station next to mine, so I hopped up on a chair and held my hand to feel if anything was blowing. "Ugh. Nothing's coming out."

Deek shrugged. "I turned it off and on when I was back there. No luck."

I sighed. "By tomorrow when we open, it will feel like ninety in here with this humidity. And we have a packed Saturday and Sunday schedule."

"You want to call the super, and I'll stay and wait for him?"

I shook my head. "No, it's fine. I don't have any plans anyway. I'll do it and stick around."

Deek nodded. "I'll lock the door and set the alarm behind me. Call me if you need anything."

"Thanks, Deek. Goodnight, Justine."

After they left, I debated texting Colby. He'd told me to let him know if the unit gave me any more trouble. Though of course, he wasn't the super and probably didn't want to speak to me. I should probably call Holden, who was in charge of maintenance. Then again, Colby was already familiar with the unit, so it made more sense to call him. Plus, he was my landlord, so we were going to have to learn to co-exist. He couldn't ignore me forever.

I dug out my phone, scrolled to his name, and hit call. On the second ring, he picked up.

"Hello?"

"Hey. Um, I'm sorry to bug you, but the AC at the shop stopped working again."

He was quiet for a solid ten seconds. "Are you there now?"

"Yeah."

He took so long to speak again, I was starting to think he'd hung up. "Fine. I'll be there in ten minutes."

For someone who was not interested in moving things out of the friend zone with Colby, I sure ran to the bathroom to clean myself up fast enough. It was the first time in a while I'd felt excited, too.

Great, I'm so desperate to see this guy that broken air conditioning thrills me.

A few minutes later, Colby knocked. I turned off the alarm and opened the front door with a hesitant smile. "Hey."

"Hey."

He stepped inside. As he passed, I got a whiff of his delicious cologne. Wasn't it bad enough that he was dressed in a form-fitting dress shirt and a pair of slacks while carrying a toolbox? That stupid red box was like catnip to me. Did he have to smell good, too? But while I was busy trying to put a fire extinguisher on all my feels, Colby seemed all business.

"Is the unit running?" he asked.

"I don't think so. Air isn't coming out."

He nodded and headed to the back to double-check the vents before resetting the system.

"Deek already tried that."

He nodded and bent to his toolbox, pulling out a screwdriver. "Was it blowing cool all day, then just stopped, or was it warm for a while first?"

"I think it just stopped. It was fine in here most of the afternoon."

He didn't say another word as he unscrewed the unit's cover and pulled it off.

"Is…everything okay with you?" I asked.

"Sure."

Colby's cell phone rang, so he dug it out of his pocket and swiped to answer. I only heard one side of the conversation.

"I'm downstairs," he said. "The commercial tenant on the ground floor has a problem with the AC that I needed to take a look at before we go."

Quiet…and then…

"Well, do you mind coming here and getting the keys? It's a tattoo parlor called Billie's Ink. It's right downstairs from my place."

Pause again.

"Alright, see you in a few."

Colby tucked his phone into his pocket and went back to working on the AC unit in silence. But I just couldn't help myself. "I, uh, hope I didn't interrupt anything?"

His eyes slanted to me. "You did."

I blinked a few times. "Oh. I'm sorry. I should've just called Holden."

"It's fine. I'm here already."

Talk about the cold shoulder…

A few minutes later, the front door opened and an absolutely gorgeous woman walked in. She had on a little black dress and looked classy. But for some stupid reason—maybe I was in denial or something—even though he'd just told someone on the phone to meet him here, I didn't put two and two together until Colby walked over to the woman. *Oh my God. She's his date.* I felt like I wanted to throw up.

The woman smiled and waved to me as he approached. "Hi! Don't mind me. I'm just picking up a key."

Colby dug into his pocket and pulled out a set of keys, placing them in her hand. "I'll meet you upstairs as soon as I'm done."

She smiled. "Okay…but don't be too long. Le Coucou is all the way down on Lafayette, and we're still going to hit traffic. I don't want to be late."

"I won't. If I can't fix it pretty quick, I'll call Holden to take over."

The woman wiggled her fingers at me and flashed a pageant-worthy smile. "Bye. Sorry I interrupted things."

I felt my cheeks heat with jealousy—or maybe it was anger. I wasn't sure which one surged through my veins faster.

If Colby noticed, he didn't say anything. He went right back to working on the AC unit like I wasn't even here.

I lasted all of three minutes in silence this time. "So…Le Coucou. Sounds overpriced. Oh, and I guess I'm not the only one going on dates?"

Colby looked over at me. He held my eyes for a few seconds but didn't respond. Again, he just turned his attention back to the damn AC unit.

"She's beautiful, if you like the plastic, beauty-pageant type…"

Colby stopped working and turned to give me his full attention. "You're jealous."

I lifted my hand to inspect my nails. "I am not."

"Can't even admit that, huh?"

"Well, there's nothing to admit. Because I'm not jealous. I was just stating the obvious about her looks and the restaurant."

He nodded. "Riiiight."

"I *am* right."

Colby took a step closer. "So it wouldn't bother you if I told you I was going to *fuck* some other woman?"

I gritted my teeth. "Not at all."

He took another step toward me. "What about the thought of me wrapping another woman's hair around my fist while she's down on her knees and I'm fucking her mouth?"

I closed my eyes at the visual. "You don't have to be a pig about it."

"Apparently I do." He raised his voice. "Because it's the only goddamn way I can get a reaction out of you, Billie!"

My eyes sprung open. Colby took another step forward, causing me to take one back. Then he did it again. Eventually my back hit the wall. He placed one arm on either side of my head and lowered his so we were eye to eye.

"You know what I wanted to do to that guy you were on a date with the other night, Billie? I wanted to rip his head off and fuck you against a wall so hard you'd have no choice but to remember who you belong to."

My heart raced out of control. Colby moved his head closer. We were practically nose to nose. "You know what I think? I think you're just as jealous as I am."

"I am not."

The heat between us sparked so hot, it felt like my entire body was on fire.

"*Liar.*"

"I'm not lying."

"Bullshit, Billie! All I'd have to do right now is move two inches closer. Once we touched, you'd be begging me to fuck you, and you know it. Maybe I should do it. We'd both get our rocks off and feel a hell of a lot better. But I won't do that to you. Do you know why?" He moved still closer and spoke into my eyes. "Because I don't want your body without your heart."

That did it. I could take jealous and angry, but that jab hit me hard. Tears welled in my eyes. Seeing them, Colby's face immediately fell. He took two steps back, put his hands up, and shook his head.

"Fuck. I'm sorry. I shouldn't have done that. It's just... I don't know how else to get through to you, and it's so goddamn frustrating." He raked a hand through his hair. "I'm sorry I got in your face and said those things, Billie."

I stayed quiet, still trying to fight back tears.

Colby blew out an audible breath and shook his head. "The woman who was just here? Her name is Caroline, and she's my sister. She's married with two kids and lives in Jersey. My dad is throwing my mom a small surprise party tonight. Caroline bought Saylor a special dress to wear. It matches her daughter's. She came by to help her get ready and do her hair." He closed his eyes and spoke softly. "There's no way I could go on a date or be with another woman. You're all I think about, Billie."

I felt the wall around my heart crumbling, so I excused myself and went to the bathroom. I stayed inside for at least ten minutes, trying to get a hold of my emotions. When I heard people talking in the studio, I figured I couldn't hide anymore.

The beautiful woman—who was apparently Colby's sister—was back, holding Saylor's hand. I hoped neither of them would notice how red my face was as I tried to act as normal as possible. "Hey, Saylor." I bent down. "Wow, that's a beautiful dress. I bet it flairs out really pretty when you spin around."

Saylor was thrilled to demonstrate. She twirled, making the tulle bottom of her dress puff out like an umbrella. I smiled.

Colby looked at his sister. "Would you mind giving us a minute, sis?"

Caroline looked between us. "Of course. Saylor and I should go call the Uber anyway."

Once the two of them were out of earshot, Colby stroked my cheek. "I have to go to the party before I ruin the surprise. Could we have breakfast tomorrow? Please?"

When I didn't respond, he continued.

"It won't be a date. But we need to talk. We can't leave things fucked up like this. I've been going crazy the last two weeks."

I nodded. "Okay."

He kept his hand on my cheek as he moved in and kissed the other one. "About nine at the diner down the block?"

"Okay."

He packed up his toolbox and headed for the door. "Oh, and I fixed your AC. Apparently the new fuse I put in last time somehow came loose." He winked as if he thought I'd done it.

"I did *not* unscrew anything."

He grinned. "Whatever you say."

I rolled my eyes. "You're so full of yourself."

He went to leave again but only made it one step more before stopping. "One other thing…"

"What?"

His eyes raked up and down my body. "Don't wear a corset tomorrow. I'd like to be able to think straight."

The next morning my train got stuck on the way to meet Colby for breakfast, so I was a few minutes late. He stood from the table when I walked through the front door of the diner, and relief washed over his face. But then his eyes dropped to my outfit, and that face changed to something entirely different. Of course I'd worn my favorite lace corset—one that left very little to the imagination.

"Hey." I smiled as I walked over.

Colby shook his head. "You're evil."

I pretended I had no idea what he was talking about. "My train got stuck."

His eyes were glued to my cleavage. "I might need to yank the tablecloth from the table and wrap it around your top half."

I winked. "But if you do that, you won't get to enjoy my corset."

He pointed to the chair across from him. "Have a seat please, so I can sit. Otherwise, we might need the tablecloth to put over my lower half to keep me from embarrassing myself."

I chuckled. The waiter immediately came over and handed us menus, and we both asked for coffee.

Colby looked at his watch. "I only have about forty-five minutes, unfortunately. Brayden's watching Saylor, but he needs to leave by ten."

"It's fine. I have to get to work anyway."

The waiter returned with our coffees and asked if we knew what we wanted. I'd been sitting for all of thirty seconds, so I hadn't even opened the menu he'd handed me. I lifted my chin to Colby. "Do you know what you're having?"

"I think I'm going to get eggs benedict."

I offered my menu to the waiter. "Make that two, please."

"You got it," he said.

Once we were alone, Colby took a deep breath. "Before we talk, I just want to apologize again for last night. I should never have gotten in your face and made you upset."

"It's fine, Colby. It wasn't a big deal."

His face was serious. "It was to me. It'll never happen again."

I smiled coyly. "Really? Because it was kind of hot."

His brows shot up, and then he grinned. "Oh yeah? Can I take back that commitment to never let it happen again?"

I laughed.

"Anyway…" he said. "On that note, I'm going to get straight to the point. I got upset because I like you a lot. I'm extremely attracted to you, which I think is pretty obvious, but it's more than that. I freaking think about you all the time, Billie. Like, it might border on unhealthy."

My heart fluttered, and my belly felt warm and mushy. "I like you too, Colby." I paused. "But you scare me. Plus, I have major trust issues, and I don't want to put that on you."

He reached across the table and laced his fingers with mine. "We're only scared of the things that mean something to us."

I sighed and nodded. "I know."

"I've given this a lot of thought. I can tell you I'm not going to hurt you and you should trust me a million times, but that's not what you need. You've heard that song and dance too often from people who didn't keep their word. The only way you and I are going to work is if I can earn your trust."

"How can you do that?"

"By spending time together. Not dating, because you need to be sure before you jump into that, so more undating. Except this time, we commit to each other that we also won't be dating anyone else."

I chewed on my bottom lip as I thought it over. "So we'll be, what, exclusively undating?"

Colby leaned back in his seat and smiled. "Exactly."

The reality of my situation was that I either needed to completely disconnect from this man, or take the baby steps he was suggesting. Considering how miserable I'd been for the two weeks we didn't see each other, I didn't want to run away anymore. So I took a deep breath and nodded. "Okay."

"Really?"

"Yeah. I think that's a good idea. We were doing well undating until I thought you were with someone else and then I stupidly went out with Eddie."

Colby groaned. "Don't even say that guy's name, please."

I smiled. "Okay, but you have to promise never to mention the threesome you missed out on."

He lifted my hand to his lips, dropping a sweet kiss on the top. "Deal."

Too soon, we were back at my shop. I was the first one to arrive, so we stood in the doorway, just the two of us. Colby weaved his fingers with mine and swung our joined hands back and forth. "I wish undating ended with a kiss," he said. "But unfortunately, that's not the tradition."

"No?"

He shook his head. "Nope. Undating ends with a sniff, not a kiss."

I giggled. "What kind of a sniff?"

"Ah, I'm glad you asked. Let me demonstrate." He leaned in and buried his face in my hair, brushing his nose slowly up my neck as he inhaled until he got to my ear. Then he let out a warm breath with a groan. "God, you smell so fucking good."

Every hair on my body stood at attention. I was about five seconds away from breaking the undating no-kissing rule already... until a voice blinked me out of my stupor.

"Get a room," Deek grumbled. "Some of us have to get to work."

I pulled back like someone had splashed a bucket of cold water over my head. "Oh, sorry."

Deek chuckled. "Let me through, and I'll open up instead of watching you two. Besides, hetero voyeurism isn't my thing."

Colby chuckled. "I gotta get going before Brayden kicks my ass, anyway." He looked to me. "Undate tomorrow night?"

"Okay." I smiled.

"I'll call you later once I figure out the details."

I waved as he went down to the building's residential entrance. Deek had his key out already, so he stepped in front of me and unlocked the door. "So I guess my air-conditioning trick worked?"

"I *knew* you did that!" We walked inside. "You're such a jerk. Colby thinks *I* did it so I'd have an excuse to see him."

Deek grinned. "You're welcome, sweetheart. I'm glad everything worked out and you guys are going to give dating a shot."

I shook my head. "Oh, we're not dating. We're doing something he calls undating—kind of spending time with each other without the pressures of dating. But we're not going to see other people while we do that."

Deek bent his head back in laughter.

"What's so funny?"

"The fact that you're dating this dude and don't even know it."

CHAPTER 12

Colby

On Saturday night, I picked up Billie from the shop after work for our undate. I hadn't told her what our plans were, but we wouldn't have to go far because it was right upstairs.

"Where are we going?" she asked.

I tickled her side. "Wouldn't you like to know?"

"I would." She tickled me back.

"Why? You worried I'm tricking you into a date? Far from it."

Billie poked me with her finger. "Considering you seem to be taking me back to your apartment, I *am* suspicious. Is Saylor at your parents' or something?" She snapped her fingers. "Wait, is this another laundry night?"

I chuckled. "Not going to my apartment. Although, considering the mountain of clothes I have back there, another laundry night can certainly be arranged."

"Where else could we be going?"

"You'll find out."

"Is it a rooftop picnic?" she asked.

"Wouldn't that be like a date?"

"Yup. Just testing you." She winked.

"What we're doing is far from a rooftop picnic, my dear."

Excitement filled her eyes. "Well, now I'm intrigued."

I feared she might be sorely disappointed. We continued down the hall and into the elevator. I pressed the number-two button for the second floor. She leaned against the wall as the elevator rose. I stood just inches away and leaned in to take a whiff of her delicious scent, momentarily feeling like I didn't want to share her tonight. But instead of getting her all to myself, I was about to throw her to the wolves.

The doors opened, and she followed me down the hall. When we got to Owen's place, I knocked.

Brayden answered the door. "Hey, dude." His mouth curved into a smile as he got a look at Billie. He hadn't met her yet. "Who's this?"

"This is Billie. She owns the tattoo shop downstairs. She's joining us tonight." I placed my hand at the small of her back. "Billie, this is Brayden—amigo number three, the one I believe you haven't met yet."

"Nice to meet you, Brayden." She held out her hand.

He took it and flashed a shit-eating grin. "Likewise."

The smell of cigar hit me as we entered the apartment. Smoke billowed in the air, and the table was all set up with cards and poker chips. I didn't love cigars like the other guys did, but I always had one anyway if they were all smoking around me.

I spoke into Billie's ear. "Welcome to our quarterly poker night. Tonight you're one of the guys. Undatelike enough for you?"

She nodded. "I love poker. This is the perfect undate."

"You play?"

"I have played, yeah." She jabbed me in the chest with her index finger. "You scared now?"

"Excited is more like it." I turned to Owen. "Owen, you know Billie…"

He nodded. "Good to see you."

I noticed his eyes briefly drop to her chest. That made me want to strangle him, though I couldn't blame him for sneaking a peek. Billie had once again decided to torment me with a corset, this time the infamous royal blue one Holden had snapped photos of when she was out with that guy. She was definitely trying to kill me, and now she was making me want to kill my friend.

In typical Owen fashion, he was still dressed in his work clothes, a crisp, collared shirt rolled up at the sleeves and black dress pants—even on Saturday. We rotated hosting the poker night, and usually Owen was the last one to show up, even if it was at his apartment, since he's constantly working late. I was surprised to see him on time tonight. If you looked up *workaholic* in the dictionary, I was pretty sure you'd see a picture of Owen.

Billie took a seat next to Brayden, and I sat next to Owen across from them. She helped herself to a cigar, and Brayden reached out with a match to light it.

"We have a cigar girl in the house. I like her already," he said.

"Thank you, sir," she said before taking the first puff. I could definitely get used to watching her beautiful mouth wrapped around that. I took one of the cigars and lit it.

Holden emerged from the kitchen, carrying three boxes of pizza. He nodded toward Billie. "How's it going, my friend?"

"Good, and you?" She blew out some smoke. "Long time no see. Spy on anyone interesting lately?"

"You still mad at me about that?" He laughed. "You know I love you. I was only looking out for my boy. I figured he'd be interested in knowing what you were up to, having dinner with that gigantic dude. I didn't mean any harm."

Did he have to point out how gigantic the dude was?

"No harm taken," she said.

"Who was that guy anyway?" he asked.

My pulse raced as the memory of that night came flooding back. My jaw tensed around the cigar, my teeth digging into it a little too much. *Still jealous as fuck, apparently.*

"Eddie is a client. It was just a dinner. Not a date."

Brayden looked between Billie and me. "Wait…back up. She was out with another guy and Holden did what?"

Billie blew out some smoke. "I thought Colby was somewhere in the bar stalking me at first. But it was Holden."

"I was at the bar that night and texted Colby a play-by-play," Holden explained. "Got him pretty worked up. And he made an ass of himself by texting her."

I shrugged. "I did. Because I like her. Had no right to be jealous though, since she and I aren't dating. Have I mentioned this is an undate?" I smiled over at her.

Owen narrowed his eyes. "I don't know about you guys, but I'm confused."

"You're not the only one," Billie cracked. "Even *we're* confused about what's going on with us."

Owen began dealing the cards. "Colby hasn't brought a girl around in ages. So say what you want. I'm a little suspicious of this *undate* thing."

Brayden turned to Owen. "At least Colby is undating. You're working yourself into the ground. Holden is whoring around—"

"And what are you doing?" Holden snapped.

"Me?" Brayden leaned back in his seat. "I'm just chillin'."

Holden rolled his eyes. The funny thing was, the guys were holding back in front of Billie. Usually, it was expletive after expletive by now. All in good fun, but they were definitely keeping things PG on account of our guest.

"So, what has Colby told you about us?" Brayden asked her. "I'm shocked he had the guts to bring you here, considering we like to bust balls."

"Actually, Holden has told me more about you guys than Colby has. He's very talkative during our tattoo appointments." She winked. "I know Owen is a workaholic. I know you, Brayden, are sort of a mediator among the group, never allowing anyone to stay mad at each other for too long. Holden… Well, Holden is a little wild and crazy, from my observations. And I know from Colby that you're all very good uncles to Saylor."

"Pretty accurate assessment." Brayden smiled.

"You know about Ryan?" Owen asked.

The room grew silent.

"Yes." Billie nodded. "I'm sorry for your loss."

Owen blew out some smoke. "The reason there's a fifth chair already set up at this table is for him."

Her expression fell. "Oh crap. And I'm sitting in it?"

Brayden placed his hand on her shoulder. "No, no, no. It's all good."

"He'd be happy if you were sitting on him." Holden laughed.

Seriously, fuckhead? I glared at him. "And here I was thinking we'd get through this night without me having to smack you."

Holden shrugged. "Relax. It was a joke."

I gritted my teeth. "Yeah. I got that."

Billie looked around the table. "You guys don't have to tread lightly around me. My best friend, Deek, never holds back. I'm used to it. I have thick skin."

Once the game got started, much of the talking stopped. I found myself alternating between fumbling with my cards and staring at Billie's beautiful poker face.

A few hours later, I was out of the game.

We'd reached the final betting round, and it was down to Billie and Holden. In a showdown, they each displayed their cards. Billie had the best hand with four of a kind and won.

"Well, damn," Holden said. "Great game, everyone."

"Congratulations, Billie," Owen added.

Brayden laughed. "I guess that's what happens when you bring a badass girl to poker night. She beats all of us, and we can't even swear at the winner like we normally do because we don't want to seem like the assholes we are."

"Swear away. I can take it," she said.

I walked around the table and gave her a celebratory kiss on the cheek.

"Hey, no kissing, remember?" she teased.

"Oh, yeah. Forgot…" I said as I took a long sniff of her neck.

"What the fuck?" Holden drew in his brows. "Does he always sniff you like that?"

"It's what we do instead of kiss," she said.

"Y'all are weird," Holden said, getting up from his seat and heading to the bathroom.

I chuckled and took our trash to the kitchen. Owen followed.

He spoke in a low voice. "You've been holding out on me. What's really going on between you and that vixen? I ain't buying that not-dating crap."

"Could you maybe try a little harder not to stare at her chest, so I don't have the urge to murder my best friend?"

"Was I?" His eyes widened. "Shit. Sorry. I didn't even realize. Maybe I need to get laid."

I arched a brow. "What's going on there? Dry spell?"

"Work's been too damn busy. I haven't gone out in ages." He shook his head. "Wait. I see what you did there. Don't change the subject. I asked *you* a question. What's the deal with Billie?"

I sighed. "The deal with Billie is that…we seem to like each other…a lot. But she doesn't want to date me. So we're pretending like we're not dating so we can spend time together."

"So, you're essentially dating."

"Undating," I corrected.

"Believe what you want." He shook his head. "Anyway, why doesn't she want to date you?"

"I think she's scared. Wouldn't you be? I mean, any woman in my life has to consider the possibility of being a mother to a child who's not hers. That would be enough to make me run away."

"Has she met Saylor?"

"She has. Saylor freaking adores her."

Owen smirked. "Saylor isn't the only one. You really like her. I can tell by the way you look at her."

I smiled. "Remember when your dad took us on that fishing trip when we were twelve? You caught that big, beautiful bass? We were all so damn envious of you. None of us had been able to catch anything all day. That thing was wiggling like crazy to get away from you. And it won. It broke away from the hook somehow, and you lost it after all that. Remember?"

He grinned. "Yeah. I sure do."

"Well, that bass reminds me of Billie."

"Because she's a great catch?"

"No."

He crushed a pizza box. "Not seeing where you're going with this, then."

"I haven't finished yet," I said.

"Well, don't forget what happened after I lost the bass, by the way. I caught it again."

"Yeah. That's getting to my point. The second time *you* threw it back—after all that work. We didn't even get to take it home and eat it. So, Billie is like the bass. I want her. And she's struggling to get away—because she wants me, too, I think, but I scare her. Ultimately, though, I'm not even sure if I'm right for her long term. So, the thought is always there that even if I *did* catch her, I might—"

"Throw her back in the ocean for her own good?"

"Figuratively. Yeah." I rubbed my temples.

"Well, since we're talking fish metaphors," he said. "There are a lot of fish in the sea, but a bass like that is worth fighting for, if it's what you really want."

"I wasn't expecting this, man. You know? I'd written off the possibility of finding someone I could connect with, at least until Saylor was older. But she just came out of nowhere."

"Life has a way of surprising us when we least expect it. Good and bad." He opened the garbage and put in some of the trash we'd piled on the counter. "I envy you, though."

"Why?" I crossed my arms. "You want blue balls, too?"

"You've found someone you're passionate about. I haven't experienced that in…well, ever. I'd rather be alone than waste my time with someone I'm not that into. That's part of why I haven't dated a lot lately. But if you can find that passion? Shit! Don't let it go."

Owen worked with a lot of attractive women who were constantly throwing themselves at him. But he found that to be a turnoff. He wanted to be the chaser. And he was picky. He deserved to be.

"You'll find her someday," I said.

"Find who?" Brayden asked as he entered the kitchen. "If you guys don't come back out soon, I'm gonna start flirting with that smokeshow you brought tonight, Colby. Can't believe she kicked all our asses. I also can't believe I never saw her downstairs before. If I had, I might've gotten to her first."

He must have noticed the pissed expression on my face.

"Damn. I'm just kidding." He shook his head. "You really like this chick."

"I think we've established that," I said.

"Does she have any friends?" Brayden asked.

"Since when have you needed help meeting people?"

"Well, there's nothing wrong with referrals. Hot chicks like that usually have hot friends."

"Well, the only friend I've met so far is a hot gay dude."

He nodded. "She seems to have a lot of guy *friends*. Like the guy she was on a date with when Holden spotted her."

"Are you looking to get smacked, Brayden?"

He laughed. "Give me some credit. I've had to be on my best behavior all night. Just letting it out."

Owen whacked Brayden on the back. "We'd better go back out there. We've left her alone with Holden too long, which is never a good idea."

"You know he had her fix the tattoo that's all the way down by his groin?" I said.

Owen gaped. "What a dick."

After Billie and I left Owen's, we waited in the lobby for the car I'd called for her.

She rubbed her arms. "It was really nice getting to spend time with you and your friends."

"They all liked hanging out with you, too."

"I feel honored that you let me crash your tradition. Am I the only girl to ever play with you guys?"

"The very first. Yup. And the way you beat our asses, probably the last." I ran my fingers through her long, black hair.

"You know, you're all really lucky to have each other. I have girlfriends, but none of them really know one another. It's cool to be part of a group—like a second family."

"Well, we vowed to stick together after Ryan died. His death taught us not to take anything for granted, friendships included. So, yeah, we have each other's backs. That said, I am not beyond punching one of them if they get on my nerves. I almost did that to Owen tonight when I caught him checking out your corset."

She looked down at herself. "Whoops."

"Why do you keep wearing them around me when I asked you not to?"

She flashed a mischievous grin. "Are you mad at me?"

"More like riled up." I inched closer.

"I like getting a rise out of you."

"You have no idea the rise you give me." I tugged at the material of her corset. "I especially hate this one, though. It reminds me of the fool I made of myself while you were wearing it out on that date you're not admitting was a date. Because that's what you do."

"I like you when you're jealous," she whispered.

"You like driving me crazy, yeah. It's working, Billie. It's all working."

I leaned in and buried my face in her neck, taking advantage of my license to smell her. She threaded her fingers through my hair, and I noticed her breathing had sped up.

"Did I miss the memo that said touching like that is allowed?" I groaned against her neck. "Because your hands in my hair feel really fucking good."

"I love your hair. It's so thick and silky," she said, dodging my question. "I love the way you smell, too."

I got the notification that her car had arrived. *Fuck.* Hard as a rock, I reluctantly pulled away.

"Well…goodnight," she said, a little out of breath.

"'Night."

I watched as she sauntered away. After she was gone, I could see my reflection in the glass by the door. My hair was sticking up in all different directions. I patted it down and knew I needed to calm this dick down, too, before I faced the babysitter.

As I went up to my apartment, I knew if I was ever lucky enough to catch Billie, I wouldn't be throwing her back in the ocean. I'd definitely be eating her for dinner instead.

❤CHAPTER 13

Billie

By Thursday the following week, I figured it was my turn to initiate the next undate with Colby. He'd texted a few times since poker night, keeping in touch, but I had a feeling he was trying to hold back and give me some space. He'd hinted at a few things he thought would make good undates but hadn't attempted to nail down any concrete plans. It seemed the ball was in my court, so I started to text him to ask if he wanted to go to an art show with me this weekend. Then decided it would be more *undatelike* to bust his balls a little first.

> Billie: Hey. I'm going to an art show Saturday night. One of the exhibitors paints songs. It's actually pretty cool. Once a month, he has his fans tell him their favorite songs from the indie top 100 charts. Whichever one gets mentioned the most, he creates a painting about. It's not a literal interpretation, but just the feeling the song evokes when he listens to it. You view each painting with a headset that plays the song that inspired it. It's pretty amazing how he nails the emotion every time.
>
> Colby: Wow, that does sound cool. I love art shows.

I smiled. *Yep, he's definitely hinting.*

Billie: I have an extra ticket. I was thinking I'd ask Holden if he wanted to go. You know, the musician connection and all. Of course, it wouldn't be a date.

The evil side of me couldn't help myself. Then I added:

Billie: It would be more like an undate. ;)

The dots started to jump around and then stopped, then started again and stopped. I might've cackled a little. Eventually, my phone vibrated.

Colby: You want to undate Holden?

Billie: Sure, why not? Of course, it would be platonic like you and I are.

I watched as the message went from delivered to read. A full minute went by and then my phone rang. Colby. Good thing he hadn't FaceTimed me since I couldn't wipe the huge grin from my lips.

"Hey," I said.

"I don't think that's a good idea."

"What?"

A few heartbeats passed. "Wait. Are you screwing with me?"

I laughed. "Why would I do that?"

"You are. You're screwing with me."

My laughter rolled into a snort. "Jealous much?"

"I'm going to kick your ass. I don't even know if you have tickets to an art show. But for that little stunt you just pulled, you'd better find some. Because you're taking *me* to one Saturday night."

I bit down on my bottom lip. "I kind of like bossy Colby."

"Oh yeah? Well I'm happy to boss you around, sweetheart. Just get your ass over here to my bedroom, and I'll show you."

Oh God. That sounded so damn good. But how the hell did we go from me busting his balls to me having blue balls so quickly?

I needed to redirect this conversation before I told him to keep talking while I slipped my hand into my pants. I cleared my throat. "So…anyway. Would you like to join me at an art show, Colby? Of course, it would be an undate."

"It took you long enough to ask."

I laughed. "I have to go a little early. How is six?"

"Sounds good. I'll pick you up."

"I'll meet you at the shop," I told him.

"Are you working?"

"No, I'm off all day on Saturday this week."

"Then let me come to you. I want to see where you live."

"Umm…"

"Seriously? You don't trust me yet? I'm not going to maul you, Billie."

The funny thing was, not trusting Colby was never even a thought. It was *me* I didn't trust alone with him in private anymore, especially not in a place with a big bed. But I was the one who was keeping things platonic, so I'd have to suck it up. "Of course, I trust you. I'll see you when you get here.."

"You're early…"

Colby's eyes dropped down to my bare legs. I'd just finished doing my makeup and drying my hair and was dressed in a short, silk robe that skimmed the tops of my thighs.

He rocked back and forth on his heels. "It looks to me like I came at the perfect time."

I chuckled and stepped aside for him to enter. "Come on in. Make yourself at home. I'm going to go get dressed."

In my bedroom, I slipped out of my robe and into the sundress I'd picked out.

Colby yelled from the other room. "I was trying to imagine what your apartment would look like."

I yelled back. "Well, what's the verdict? Is it what you expected?"

"It totally is. It's feminine and girly, yet also kind of funky. By the way, is the handle on this mug *a dick*?"

I laughed as I put on my shoes. "Indeed it is. Deek made it for me for my birthday. He and his boyfriend took a pottery class, and everything they made had a dick or balls on it."

I looked in the full-length mirror on the back of my bedroom door and didn't recognize the woman staring back at me. It had been a long time since I'd worn an outfit like this, but I knew walking into my mother's gallery in my regular duds would give her a heart attack. So I gave a little, hoping she would do the same tonight.

Out in the living room, Colby was busy checking out the dozens of framed art pieces I had along one wall.

"Did you draw th—" He stopped mid-sentence when he turned and blinked a few times. "Wow. You look…"

"Like I'm on my way to church?"

"Church is the opposite of what I think of when I see you in that dress. I'm going to hell for what I'm thinking…"

I looked down. "Really? This does it for you? But you love my corsets so much."

"Oh, I love those, too. But that dress…something about the innocent look of it mixed with your sleeve of tattoos… It makes me want to—" He dragged his eyes up and down my body again and shook his head. "Forget it. We should probably go."

God, this man was killing me. My body tingled at the frustration in his voice. I wasn't a stranger to men wanting me, but Colby made me feel like he wanted so much more than my body.

I nodded. "That's probably a good idea. My mother loathes lateness."

Colby's brows pulled together. "Your mother?"

I grabbed my purse. "Oh, did I forget to mention that the art show is at my mother's gallery?"

"I think you did."

"Did I mention that I wasn't technically a guest, but that I was exhibiting some of my work? The show is called *The Edge* because the artists are all supposed to be—" I made air quotes with my fingers. "—Edgy."

"You definitely didn't mention that either."

"Welp, then let me wish you luck with my mother. Because you're probably going to need it."

"So, Colby. Tell me about yourself." My mother lifted her wine to her perfectly painted red lips and sipped. "What do you do for a living?"

"I'm an architect."

"Oh, that's a wonderful profession. It affords you an outlet for your creativity while still providing stability. I so wish I could have talked Billie into something along those lines."

I spoke through gritted teeth. "My tattoo parlor is thriving, Mother."

She shook her head. "Yes, but the clientele you work with—"

"Are a lot more fun than the clientele you work with."

Mom smiled and turned her attention back to Colby. "How did you two meet? It's such a rarity that my daughter brings anyone around. I hope you don't mind so many questions."

Colby was gracious. "Not at all, ask away. Billie and I met at her tattoo shop. I'm actually her landlord, and I came down to introduce myself." He looked at me with a sparkle in his eyes. "She was throwing a little party when I walked in."

I raised my glass of champagne to cover my smirk. "Yes, I even gave the guest of honor a special gift."

My mother seemed oblivious to our exchange. She was too busy focusing on one word Colby had said.

"Landlord!" Her eyes lit up. "Manhattan real estate at your age? That's impressive."

"It's not as exciting as it sounds," Colby said. "I have three partners."

"It sounds to me like you're being modest. Half the battle is getting your life on track." She looked over at me. "Maybe some of your levelheadedness will rub off on my daughter, and she'll stop rebelling against me by mutilating her body with ink and hanging out with a seedy crowd."

The muscle in Colby's jaw flexed, and I could see his face turning red. "I doubt that. Because I believe in encouraging people to do what they love. I've also met some of the people she spends her time with, and there's nothing seedy about them. They're loyal and protective of your daughter, exactly the type of people I'd want around someone I cared about."

My mother sighed. "She's living a lifestyle beneath her."

Colby shook his head. "I hope you'll excuse me for saying so, but we've been here for five minutes, and you've insulted Billie four times. In my experience, when someone judges others because of what they look like or do for a living, it's rarely about the person being judged. It's about the judgmental person's own insecurities."

My mother blinked a few times, clearly shocked at being spoken to like that. But then she recovered and plastered on her best fake smile. "Enjoy the show. It was lovely to meet you, Carter."

My jaw hung open as she strutted away.

Colby shook his head. "I'm so sorry. I shouldn't have said that."

"Are you kidding me? That was *fucking awesome!*"

"You're not mad?"

"Mad? I could kiss you right now."

He grinned. "You should really go with your instincts."

I laughed. "Seriously, that was perfect, Colby. She didn't see it coming, and you said it without raising your voice or making a scene."

"Honestly, I'd thought you were exaggerating the few times you've mentioned your mother."

"I wish." I linked my arm with Colby's. "But let's try to forget about her. Come on, I see Devin, my mentor. He just walked in. I told you about him. He was the one who first got me interested in tattooing, and I apprenticed under him. I want to introduce you."

After we spent a little time talking to Devin, I took Colby around the room to see the art. We walked the perimeter, stopping at each exhibit. As we approached my section, I felt a little nervous. Colby had seen my tattoos, but not the type of art I was showing today. I took a deep breath as we stood in front of the first painting—a nude woman lying down with her back arched. Her face was tense and muscles taut. The entire painting was done in black and white, except for a piece of bright red silk fabric strewn over her breasts.

"This is one of mine," I said. "My mother made me rename it for the show."

"Wow. It's incredible." Colby glanced over to the little sign hanging under the artwork. "Unto Eve," he read. "What does that mean?"

I laughed. "I have no idea. I'm guessing it's some biblical reference to Eve from Adam and Eve."

"What was it originally called?"

"I refer to it as *The Peak Before Pleasure*. In my head, the pose encapsulates the moment before an orgasm hits."

Colby looked back at the painting. He studied the woman for a long time, and then he swallowed. "It's really beautiful, Billie. It causes a stir inside when I look at it."

I bumped my shoulder with his and lowered my voice. "A stir, huh? You want to know a secret?"

"Absolutely."

"I took a naked photo of myself in that position to use as a reference for the arch of the woman's back. I used the self-timer on my iPhone."

Colby's eyes dropped to my lips. "You still got that photo on your phone?"

I flashed an evil grin. "Maybe…"

He groaned. "You're killing me, woman."

It took us an hour to finish looking at all the art. When we were done, I needed to use the restroom, so I excused myself.

I found Colby studying *Unto Eve* again when I returned. He had two glasses of champagne in his hands and a piece of thick cardstock.

"A woman came by and asked if I wanted another glass of champagne," he said. "So I got us each one."

"Oh great. Thanks."

He held up the card. "She gave me this, too. What is it? The ID numbers of all the paintings or something?"

I smiled. "That's the price list."

He'd just sipped his champagne and started to cough. "The price list?" He lifted the card closer to his face and scanned it. "Are they missing the decimal point that separates the dollars from the change?"

I chuckled. "No. My mother would never use change. She finds using a dollar sign tacky and appalling. That's why there are only numbers printed."

Colby pointed to the painting in front of us. "So that's eleven-thousand-five-hundred dollars if I want to buy it?"

I shook my head. "Actually, you can't buy it." I pointed to the small colored sticker on the placard. "It looks like it sold already."

"For eleven grand?"

He glanced around at my other pieces nearby. Most of them had stickers now as well. "Holy shit. You just made half my annual salary in an hour."

I smiled, feeling a little embarrassed. "It's not always this way. But now you probably think I'm an idiot for not following the path my mother would prefer."

"That's not what I was thinking at all." He looked around. "I was just wondering if the guy who bought this piece is still here. I feel like kicking his ass because he's going to have a painting on his wall that's based on your nude body. And my other thought was…" He grinned. "I got me a sugar momma."

I snort-laughed. "You're demented, Lennon."

After the show ended, Colby asked if I wanted to take a walk. My mother's gallery was downtown, and it was a nice night, so he suggested we go over to the pedestrian entrance to the Brooklyn Bridge.

I looked up as we started across. "You know, I've lived here my entire life and never walked on this thing."

"Really? How come?"

I shrugged. "I don't know. I guess I never paid any attention to bridges before. They were just kind of a means to get off the island of Manhattan."

Colby gripped his chest. "Oh, that hurts. These things are works of art."

I looked up at all the suspension wires and the twinkling lights at the top. "It is really pretty."

Colby slipped his hand next to mine and casually weaved our fingers together. When I looked over, he held up his other hand. "I hold Saylor's hand when we walk all the time. So don't read into it too much. I'm well aware it's not a date."

I laughed. "It's fine."

"Good, because it felt wrong to be walking next to you right now and not be holding your hand."

I smiled. Holding his hand actually did feel right. And I tried not to let that thought freak me out by changing the subject. "So, what random trivia do you have for me about this architectural splendor, Mr. Bridge Aficionado?"

He held up a finger. "Ah. I thought you'd never ask."

For the next hour, as we walked from one borough to the next and back, Colby told me story after story about the Brooklyn Bridge—how PT Barnum once walked twenty-one elephants across to show the people of New York that it was safe, and every name the bridge had been called since it was built. If someone had asked if I found bridge facts interesting a month ago, I would have thought they were nuts. Yet I hung on Colby's every word. However, I think that had less to do with the bridges and more to do with the man.

It was almost midnight by the time we got back to my apartment. We'd been together nearly six hours, yet I still wasn't ready for the night to end. As we walked to the elevator, I debated whether I'd be sending the wrong signal by inviting him up. In the end, I decided I was being silly. I'd spent enough time in his apartment—it wouldn't seem out of bounds. "Do you…want to come up for a little while?"

He thought a moment. "I probably shouldn't. I don't want to push my luck and break one of the rules of undating. Plus, the sitter has work in the morning, so I shouldn't keep her too much longer."

I tried to hide my disappointment. "Oh…yeah, of course. I'm sorry. I wasn't even thinking."

He took my hand again. "I had a really good time tonight."

I smiled. "I did, too."

"You know how when we do certain things it just feels wrong or unnatural? Like turning around after you throw a bowling ball down the alley and not watching to see what happens?"

I chuckled. "Yeah?"

Colby looked down at his feet. "That's what leaving without kissing you feels like."

My insides felt all warm and mushy.

"I think I'm going to skip the traditional end-of-undate ritual. No sniffing for me. I don't trust myself to get that close right now."

I smiled sadly. "Alright."

Colby pushed the button for the elevator. It must've been waiting because the doors slid open immediately. I had to force myself to step inside the car and leave him. Colby was one-hundred-percent right. It felt wrong to walk away like this. Once I was in the elevator, I put my hand on the doorframe to stop them from closing.

"Thank you for sticking up for me with my mother tonight. It means a lot to me."

He smiled. "*You* mean a lot to me."

I let go of the door and stepped back. "Goodnight, Colby."

"Goodnight, beautiful."

The second the doors began to slide closed, panic washed over me. My heart raced, my palms began to sweat, and it felt like I was having a panic attack. It was so bad that I stuck my hand out between the doors at the very last second, and the old elevator crushed it before begrudgingly bouncing open again.

"Shit!" I screamed.

Colby ran back. "What happened? Are you okay?"

"Nothing…" I shook out my wrist. "I stuck my hand between the doors to stop it from closing, but it's fine. It scared me more than it hurt."

He took my hand and examined it. It wasn't even red. "Are you sure?"

I nodded. "Yeah, I'm positive."

"Open your fingers and close them."

I did as he said without any pain. "They're fine."

"Why did you stick your hand in the doors anyway?"

"I, uh, I just felt like I needed to get off."

Colby's eyes looked back and forth between mine, and then a cocky smile spread across his face. "It feels weird for you to walk away without kissing me, too, doesn't it?"

"No," I said a little too fast.

146

"Admit it. You want to kiss me."

"No, I don't."

His smile widened. "*Liar*." Colby cupped my face and guided me to take a few steps back, until I hit the elevator doors. He leaned down so our heads were aligned and our noses were practically touching.

"We're going to be standing here a long time if you're waiting for me to initiate it. I'm not breaking the rules."

My heart beat even faster with him so close. Did he have to smell so damn good, too? Who still smells so delicious after six hours out in New York City? I had the strongest urge to press myself against him, feel his warm, hard body up against my soft.

Colby ran his nose along my throat, his hot breath leaving a trail of goose bumps in its wake. My resolve was quickly crumbling. How could it not with my body zapping like I'd touched a live wire? He moved his mouth to my ear, and his voice was gruff and needy. "*You know you want me as much as I want you*."

He was right. The ache for him was unbearable. When he pulled his head back and I saw the desire swimming in his eyes, I was done for.

So, so done. "Fuck it," I said as I launched myself at him. I wrapped my arms around his neck and jumped into his arms, pressing my lips to his. Our mouths opened, and our tongues collided. I might've started the kiss, but there was no mistaking that Colby took it over. His hands slid into my hair, grabbing a handful in the back and tugging my head where he wanted it. He pushed up against me, and I could feel his hard-on pressing against my stomach. My eyes rolled into the back of my head. We stayed like that for a long time, grabbing and groping, pulling and pushing. When the kiss finally broke, we were both panting.

"Holy shit." I shook my head. "That was…" I couldn't find the right word to describe it.

But Colby did. "Just the beginning, sweetheart. That's what it was."

♥CHAPTER 14

Colby

My phone rang Sunday afternoon, and I smiled to see it was Billie. She was scheduled to meet us here in about an hour for our next undate.

"Colby is unavailable right now," I said when I answered. "He's still in recovery from the best damn kiss of his life."

She laughed. "Yeah, it was pretty darn good, I have to admit."

Just hearing her voice got me all revved up again. I fell back on my bed and bounced on the mattress, still so turned on from last night. "How the hell am I supposed to adhere to our rules now that I know what kissing you is like?"

"I guess you'll have to forget."

"Do you want me to forget, Billie? Because you sure as fuck didn't seem like you wanted to be following the rules the way you came at me."

"I lost control. It happens to the best of us. What can I say?"

"Feel free to lose control anytime. I'll be waiting and ready."

"Anyway..." She cleared her throat. "What's the plan for today?"

As much as I was teasing her just now, I needed to cool my ass down a little before being alone with her again. The way I was feeling, I was likely to cross the line, move too fast, or fuck things up. So I decided that since I was in charge of this undate, I'd take the liberty of putting a very big buffer in between us. The biggest buffer I knew.

"So, good news and bad news," I said.

"Okay?"

"The bad news is I couldn't find a sitter today. But the good news is, we get to spend the day with a little girl who loves your presence almost as much as her father does. I hope that's okay."

"Aw... Of course, it is. That'll be fun to hang out with her."

"And with my daughter around, I'll be on my best behavior. So that's a win for you, right?"

She chuckled. "Where are you thinking we'll take her?"

"She's been asking to go to the carousel. I thought maybe we could go there and then grab lunch somewhere fun? What do you think?"

"Sounds good. I'm easy."

I pulled on my hair. "My dear, you're far from easy."

Unfortunately, our plans to visit the carousel were shot. It wasn't very smart of me to promise my daughter something without having checked the forecast. By the time Billie was supposed to arrive, it was pouring rain.

When I opened the door after she knocked, her hair was drenched. My eyes were glued to her, but hers went straight to my daughter.

Billie opened her arms. "Hey, pretty girl!"

Saylor ran to her. "Billie!"

"Long time no see!" Billie bent to hug her. "How are you?"

"I'm good!" She pointed. "You're wet."

"I am."

"I like you wet," I whispered.

"Get your mind out of the gutter, Lennon. I thought today was supposed to be rated G."

"If G stands for gutter, then yeah."

She slapped my arm.

"I deserved that." I touched her hair. "I'm sorry you got caught in the rain."

"Are we still going to the carousel? As you can see by my new style—drowned-rat chic—that may not be the best idea."

"Nah. We'd better not." I broke the news to my daughter. "Daddy's an idiot, Saylor. We're gonna have to pick another time to go to the carousel because it won't be any fun in the rain."

"It's okay, Daddy."

Billie smiled. "You're such a sweetheart, Saylor."

"I guess maybe we can hang out here? Are you okay with that, Billie?"

"I love cozy days inside when it's raining." Billie snapped her fingers. "You know what? I have an idea. Would you be opposed to an arts-and-crafts day?"

"Unlike you, I'm easy." I wriggled my brows. "And I mean that."

She smacked my arm again and turned to my daughter. "Saylor, have you ever had your face painted?"

She nodded. "Yes!"

"I have some paints that are made for skin downstairs. I'm gonna bring them up so we can have a painting party. Does that sound fun?"

My daughter squealed. Not only did she love art, but any opportunity to make a mess with paint as well.

Billie turned to me. "Is that okay with you? I should've asked first. The paints I have are non-toxic, though."

"That's perfectly cool with me." I pulled lightly on Saylor's ponytail. "Whatever makes this little girl happy, right? That's my life's purpose."

"I'll be right back," Billie said.

"Hey, what do you want for takeout? I'll order something while you're down there."

"Surprise me."

I leaned in. "Like you surprised me last night?"

She rolled her eyes and headed out the door.

While Billie went down to the shop, I placed an order at this Japanese restaurant I remember her saying she liked. Since Saylor loved California rolls, I figured that place would be a safe choice for everyone.

When the food arrived, the three of us ate lunch and sat around the table for a while. After that, I cleared our plates to make space for the mess this paint party would likely create.

Billie arranged the paint and brushes. She had a bottle for every color of the rainbow. I gave her a roll of paper towels in case she needed it, and she had me throw an old zip-up hoodie over Saylor so we didn't get any paint on her dress.

"What do you want me to turn you into, Saylor?"

Saylor spun around. "I don't know!"

"I can make you a butterfly princess, a unicorn—anything you want."

My daughter scrunched her nose for a moment, then yelled, "A tiger!"

Billie's eyes widened. "A tiger? And here I was thinking you were a girly girl. You're more my speed, apparently. Because I would have totally picked something like a tiger! In fact, I almost once got a tiger skin tattoo."

For the next hour, I sat and watched as Billie painted Saylor's face. I guess I was used to Saylor being in control of the paint, because the mess I was expecting didn't materialize with Billie in charge. She was meticulous as she painted the tiger face onto my daughter. It was a joy to watch, between Saylor's anticipatory excitement and Billie's adorable look of concentration. She did this thing where she slid her tongue slowly back and forth across her lower lip when she was focusing.

It took a full hour before she was done. But in the end, my daughter looked like something out of the Broadway show *Cats*. Billie had done an amazing job, and Saylor was over the moon. Billie had taken a rainy afternoon and turned it into gold. I hoped Saylor would always remember this day.

Saylor wanted to FaceTime with my mother to show off her new look, so I set up the laptop in the kitchen. Saylor was busy talking to her grandmother when I walked over to Billie in the living room. "Why did you have all this paint at the ready downstairs anyway? I didn't think body painting was a service the shop provided."

She wiped off one of the brushes. "It's not. But I once threw a bodypainting party for one of my girlfriends as part of her bachelorette party. We closed the shop and had it there."

"So, like, you painted each other?"

"Yup…naked."

I gulped. "Naked."

"Yup. Naked." She laughed.

"Were there men at this party?" I had to ask.

"Are you gonna get all jealous if I tell you there were?"

"Me?" I snorted. "Jealous?"

She chuckled. "It was just us girls, actually."

That brought me relief. Always the jealous bastard. I scratched my chin. "Would you…happen to have any pictures of this event? Not interested in seeing anyone else. Just you."

"Yeah. Actually, I do. Lots of them. On my phone."

"Really. And, uh, what does one have to do to get the opportunity to view such photos?"

"They're not for public consumption."

"I'm not the public, though. I'm a friend. You got naked in front of your friends, right?"

Saylor popped off her phone call with my mother and ran into the living room, interrupting our conversation.

"Is Grandma still online?" I asked.

She shook her head.

Billie took out her phone. "You wanna take some pictures, Saylor?"

I held out my hand and winked. "I'll be happy to take your phone and snap them."

"You won't be going anywhere near my phone, Lennon."

I loved messing with her. I hoped she knew I was kidding about the naked photos. *Okay, maybe I'm not. I definitely want to see them.*

Billie spent the next several minutes taking photo after photo of Saylor and her tiger face. My daughter insisted on changing in and out of several of her dresses for this photo shoot. It was adorable to watch. I also couldn't ignore the fact that Billie seemed so comfortable around Saylor. My kid was generally an easy sell, but not everyone had this kind of spark with my daughter. It took patience to keep up with her—patience that sometimes even the most well-intentioned people didn't have. Billie might not have been sure she wanted kids, but she was a natural.

After their photoshoot ended, I asked, "Who wants dessert?"

"Me!" Saylor yelled.

"I made brownies."

Billie arched a brow. "Oooh…spinach brownies?"

"Shh…" I winked. "Yeah."

"She still doesn't know?" Billie whispered.

"Nope." I laughed. "That's the beauty of it."

"Whoops."

Billie and Saylor each noshed on one of my brownies while I sat back with a beer and kicked up my feet.

Billie ended up hanging out with us all afternoon. Since we were still pretty full from lunch, I cut up some fruit and cheese and got out crackers as a light dinner.

After we ate, Billie gave me yet another surprise.

"Saylor, why don't you go pick out your jammies?" she suggested. "I'll help you get all this paint washed off. I have a special soap for it."

With Saylor out of the room, Billie sauntered over to me. "You wanna know something, Colby Lennon?"

"What?"

"You are such a great father. I hope you know that. I've watched you all day, and you don't miss a beat with her. She's very lucky to have you."

"Why, thank you. I appreciate the kind words, beautiful."

"And you know what else I think?"

I caressed her cheek. "What?"

"I think you deserve some daddy alone time. Self-care."

"I don't need to be alone when you're around."

"I think you'll prefer *this* alone time."

I narrowed my eyes. "What are you up to?"

She whispered in my ear, "I'll handle getting Saylor ready for bed. You stay here and relax."

Billie walked over to the refrigerator, grabbed another beer, and popped it open before handing it to me. She then took out her phone and scrolled through her photos.

After a moment, she handed it to me. "When I went to the bathroom earlier, I created a special album just for you. Enjoy."

Then she ran off with Saylor, leaving me alone.

My heart pounded as I looked down to find photo after photo of Billie's stark-naked body, painted in a mixture of red, white, and blue. Everything, and I mean *everything*, was visible. Her tits, her nipples...and my eyes moved farther south. Damn. Damn. *Damn.* My pants grew snug.

Her body was just as gorgeous as I'd imagined it, although with all of the paint covering her, I still had the urge to see her bare skin. But this was a huge gift. One I certainly didn't think I'd be receiving tonight.

Fuck. Me. How was I supposed to sleep with these images in my head?

I was tempted to text them to myself, but I wouldn't do that without her permission. I'd definitely be asking for it, though.

Wow, Billie. You are so goddamn beautiful. My gawking was interrupted by the sound of giggling coming from down the hall. I'd been so into looking at Billie's naked body that I'd been missing out on the fact that Billie and Saylor were having a blast together.

I walked down the hall and peeked into the bathroom. The tub was full of suds, and Saylor's face was already tiger-free.

Billie turned to me. "What are you doing in here? I thought I told you to relax."

"Relax? I think you were trying to rev me up."

Saylor slapped her hands against the water, causing a big dollop of suds to land on Billie's head. I tried to ignore the pang of longing in my chest. Because as awesome as it was to witness Billie bonding with my daughter, I realized there was a huge difference between one day of fun and a lifetime of responsibility. Billie's hesitation with me all this time proved that.

"Alright. Heading back to my relaxation den. You sure you have everything you need?"

"Yup. Got it covered. Found the towels and everything."

I sat back down in the living room, but to my dismay, Billie's phone screen had locked, so I couldn't look at the images again since I didn't know her password. So, I experienced the withdrawal that went along with that and finished off my beer listening to the sounds of laughter coming from down the hall. I realized it was the first time I'd ever heard such a thing, the first time this apartment had been so full of life. Billie was still here, and I was already starting to miss the feeling.

Saylor came running out to me in her pajamas. "All clean, Daddy!"

I lifted her onto my lap. "I don't know how Billie managed to get every bit of that makeup off. There was so much of it."

"Yeah, it wasn't easy," Billie said. "But it was worth the work."

I looked up at her. "I'm finding a lot of things are like that."

She blushed.

We got Saylor in bed, and when she asked Billie to read her a bedtime story, my first inclination was to intervene and suggest Billie was probably tired. As fun as today had been, a part of me also worried about Saylor becoming attached to Billie. But then I remembered how strong my little girl was. We would deal if I ever had to tell her Billie wouldn't be coming around anymore someday. For now, she should get to enjoy the moment with her new friend.

After about twenty minutes, Billie emerged from Saylor's room.

I patted the spot next to me on the couch. "C'mere. I won't bite. I promise."

"Who says I'd be opposed to that?" She raised an eyebrow.

"Be careful when you say things like that."

She sat down next to me. "Did you enjoy the photos?"

"Yeah. Until your phone locked me out when I got up to check on things in the bathroom."

She snickered. "Why didn't you say something?"

"Say what? 'I'm sorry to interrupt your bonding time with my daughter, but can you unlock your phone screen so I can continue getting off on your naked body?'"

She chuckled and slapped my knee. "What did you think of the photos?"

"What did I think?" I sighed. "I think I might not sleep tonight because I'll be replaying those images in my head. I think I'm even more screwed than I was before. And I think I'd give my left nut to paint your body right now."

She got up and went over to the table where the paints were still lined up. My eyes widened. At first, I thought maybe she was going to grant me my wish and let me paint her, but that was probably dumb, given that Saylor wasn't even asleep yet.

"Take off your shirt," she said.

"Are you gonna paint me? Wait—is this just an excuse to see me shirtless?"

"Well, an eye for an eye, right?"

"You don't have to ask me twice," I said, slipping my shirt over my head.

She laughed. "Lie back and relax."

For the next few minutes, I did just that—closed my eyes while Billie painted something up by my neck. Even when I opened my eyes to look at her beautiful face and the way her tongue slid across her lip when she concentrated, I couldn't make out the design.

"There. All done. Perfect," she said.

"Should I be afraid to look?"

"I think you're gonna like it."

I walked over to the mirror, and my jaw dropped. Billie had painted a white collar and black bow tie on my neck. I looked like one of those Chippendale's dancers—or something straight out of *Magic Mike*.

"You turned me into a male stripper."

"I might have played off a little fantasy of mine."

"To see me strip? Because that can be arranged."

"I figured you'd say that. But I'd never exploit you in such a way."

"You don't know by now that I want to be exploited by you?"

She smiled. "You're crazy, Colby."

"Crazy for you, yeah." I sat back down next to her. "Today was…amazing. Truly. Thank you for everything—for winging it with me on a rainy day, for bringing my daughter joy, for letting me look at your beautiful body."

After a long moment of silence, she asked, "Do you think she's asleep by now?"

"Probably. But I'll check."

I figured there was a reason she was asking me that, and let's just say, I was intrigued. I got up to peek in on my daughter, who was indeed out like a light, as I'd suspected she would be, given the exciting day she'd had.

"Would you like to paint something on me? On my chest?" Billie asked when I returned to the couch.

Adrenaline rushed through me. But even though I wanted to leap out of my seat and rush toward the paints, I kept calm. I cleared my throat. "I might be interested in that, yeah."

She chuckled and collected the paints before taking my hand and dragging me to my bedroom. I locked the door.

The mood turned serious as she started to undo her corset. It felt like my heart was about to leap out of my chest. And my dick was about to leap out of my pants.

Billie stopped. "Actually, can you find me a hoodie or something in case she wakes up and I have to cover myself?"

"Yeah, of course." Filled with anticipation, I found a black hoodie in my closet. "Here you go."

"Thanks." She loosened the ties at the back of her corset before removing it. Her beautiful, round boobs popped out, and I couldn't believe this was actually happening. She pulled on my hoodie, leaving it open at the front.

I grew completely hard as I stared at her gorgeous breasts, milky skin with mauve nipples. "I hope you don't mind me looking at you for a moment."

"No."

"You're so beautiful," I murmured. I wanted to touch her but wasn't about to assume that was okay. Instead, I grabbed the black and white paints she'd used to make my bow tie. "Anything in particular you'd like me to paint on you?" I asked.

"No. I'd like to see what you come up with."

Great. This is going to be a disaster.

As I continued to stare at her beautiful tits, only one thing came to mind. I couldn't see anything else. And all I could think was...*she's going to hate it.*

But I proceeded to do it anyway. "You can't look down until I'm done, okay?"

"That's fair." She smiled.

Billie lay back as I carefully began creating my masterful artwork. Considering I had the artistic talent of a five-year-old, she had a lot to look forward to. I figured I would spare her and only paint one of her breasts. I'd decided on the left.

I enjoyed every second of brushing over her skin with the white paint, taking longer than I probably should've because I wasn't sure if I'd get this opportunity again. After her whole breast was covered, I opened the black ink to finish the details of my design. My erection wouldn't let up, and I hoped she'd understand that I had no control over it if she looked down and noticed how aroused I was.

My amateur design work didn't take all that long, and when I finished, all I could think to say was, "Don't kill me."

Her cheeks reddened. "What did you do?"

"Go look."

Billie got up, walked over to the mirror, and her mouth dropped. "You did not just turn my boob into Snoopy!"

I'd painted her nipple black to form Snoopy's nose along with two black slits above it for his eyes. Along the sides I painted black ears. It wasn't a masterpiece, but I felt like I'd pulled it off.

"It was the only thing I could think of."

She started to crack up. Her boobs shook in the mirror, and it looked like Snoopy was cracking up, too. "Colby Lennon, you are insane. But I love it."

"Yeah?"

She walked over and wrapped her arms around my neck. Our eyes locked, and this time it was me who couldn't help making the first move. I leaned in and took her lips with mine, feeling the entire day of pent-up frustration come barreling out as I exhaled into her mouth. Our tongues collided, and it was every bit as amazing as the first time. I couldn't wait to get inside of this woman, even if it took me forever to get there.

She pulled back, panting. This was the moment she normally stopped things, before they went too far. And that was probably a good thing, because any longer and I would've leaned down to take Snoopy's nose into my mouth.

"I'd better get going," she said.

Right on cue. "Are you sure?"

"Yeah. I think today was fun overload, and we need to pace ourselves."

"Okay, sweetheart. Whatever you want." I took out my phone and called her a car.

"I don't want to get paint on my corset. Is it okay if I borrow this hoodie?"

"Of course. Keep the damn thing if you want. Better yet, bring it back the next time you let me paint you."

"I'm afraid of what you'd paint next."

"I already have a great idea for the yellow paint."

"Let me guess. Woodstock?"

"Not telling." I winked. "I don't want to ruin it."

"Say goodbye to Snoopy," she said as she zipped up my hoodie, covering her breasts.

"Damn. I'm gonna miss him."

We both laughed as we left my room and walked to the door. I looped my arm around her waist and brought her into me one last time, savoring every second of her delicious mouth on mine.

"I love the way you taste."

She moaned over my mouth before stepping back. "The car's waiting. I'd better go."

As I watched her walk down the hall, I called, "Hey, I got a story idea for the next time you read to Saylor."

"What is it?"

"Snoopy and the Chippendale."

She shook her head and kept on walking.

♥CHAPTER 15

Billie

"**W**hat the hell are you doing?"

My brows pulled together when Deek interrupted my thoughts. "I'm sitting in a chair. What does it look like I'm doing?"

"You're smiling weird."

"I am?"

Deek was working on one of our regulars. He turned off his machine and swiveled the chair so the customer faced me. "I'm all done, Remy. But does she look funny to you?"

Remy squinted. "I don't think so. What am I looking for?"

Deek rubbed the scruff on his jaw. "I don't know. But something is off." He swiveled the chair back to its normal position and lifted a handheld mirror, offering it to Remy so he could see his back. "Take a look. Let me know what you think."

Remy spent a few minutes checking out his new tattoo from all different angles and then shook Deek's hand. "Superb as usual, man."

"Thanks. Give me a call when you figure out what you want next. It was good to see you."

After Deek walked Remy up to the front and closed out the sale, it was just the two of us. I had started sketching a Medusa head for a first-time customer coming in next week. Deek looked over my shoulder before leaning one hip against the counter at my workstation.

"Did you watch a scary movie before coming in today?"

I shook my head. "No, why?"

"Pet a litter of puppies?"

I chuckled. "No."

"How about insult your mother, and she had no comeback?"

I set down my drawing pencil. "What are you getting at?"

"Four things make you smile like that." He lifted his fingers and counted off. "One, puppies. Two, winning a fight with your mother. Three, movies that scare the crap out of you, and four, getting laid."

I rolled my eyes. "Well, none of those have happened."

"No? So nothing happened with Colby then?"

I shrugged. "Well, maybe *a little* something happened. But we didn't have sex."

Deek shook his head. "So you're telling me you're smiling because of *feelings*? I'm going to have to have a chat with this dude."

"What are you talking about? You're the one who's been pushing me to give him a chance."

"I know. But I didn't realize you were going to fall for him so quick. I need to make sure his intentions are good."

I smiled. "Thanks, *Dad*. But I think I got this."

Fifteen minutes later, none other than Colby walked through the door. Deek rubbed his hands together.

"Oh crap," I mumbled.

Colby strolled into the studio with a smile. "What's up, Deek? Hey, Billie."

I knew better than to try to talk Deek out of whatever he had planned. So instead, I kissed Colby on the cheek. "I'm going to apologize for this in advance."

"For what?"

I motioned to Deek, who pointed to the empty chair next to him. "Have a seat, Colby. I'd like to have a word with you."

Colby looked between me and Deek a few times, but eventually shrugged and sat down. "What's up?"

Deek folded his arms across his chest. "Where do you see yourself in five years?"

Colby's forehead wrinkled. He looked to me for help, and I shrugged. "It will be worse not to go along with it," I said. "Trust me."

Colby looked wary but returned his attention to Deek. "I don't know. I guess in five years I'd like to buy some land and start building a summer place. I can't afford the Hamptons or anywhere trendy, but that's okay. I like the Hudson Valley better, anyway. Maybe let Saylor get a dog." He glanced to me and back. "A wife and another kid, maybe. I'm not sure. I don't really have a timeline for things. I guess I'd just like to be happy and to have my life progress somewhat."

Deek considered his answer with an unreadable face. "What kind of a dog?"

"Lab maybe?"

"Buy or adopt?"

"Definitely adopt from a shelter."

Deek nodded. "What kind of porn do you like?"

"I don't know. Any, I guess?"

"So child pornography is okay?"

"What? No! Of course not."

"A little more specifics in your answer would be helpful then."

Colby shook his head. "I don't know. What kind of porn is there? I guess I like straight, hetero porn. Intercourse, oral, the occasional anal movie."

"How about an orgy?"

Colby shrugged. "Yeah, sure. I'm down for an orgy."

Deek looked at me. "Does this concern you?"

I smirked. "No, I'm good with orgies in movies, too."

Colby wrinkled his entire face. "What the heck is this all about? I mean, don't get me wrong, I'm stoked that Billie's into orgy porn. But where is this all leading?"

Deek held up a finger. "Just one more question. What's your apartment number?"

"Two-eighteen. Why?"

"So I know exactly where to go if my girl gets hurt."

I chuckled and jumped down from my chair, walking over to stand next to Colby. "Are you finished, Deek?"

He glared at Colby. "For now…"

"Okay, great. Why don't you go take your lunch break then?"

Colby waited until Deek was out of earshot before turning to me. "What just happened?"

I pushed up and pressed my lips to his. "He knows things have moved out of the friend zone, so he wants to make sure you're a decent guy."

"Maybe I should invite him and his boyfriend to dinner one night."

I pulled back. "Really? You'd do that?"

"Of course. Why not? He's a good friend of yours, right?"

"One who just interrogated you…"

Colby brushed my hair from my shoulder. "It's okay. I'd want my daughter to have protective friends like that. And I hope she'd pick the kind of guy who would have her friends over to put their minds at ease."

My stomach felt all squishy. "Awww… That's really sweet, Colby."

"Well, I'm glad you think so. Because *sweet* doesn't exactly describe the thoughts I've been having about you since our painting party."

I bit my lip. "I might've had a not-so-sweet thought or two about you over the last few days."

Colby trailed his knuckles up and down my arm. "Oh yeah? Tell me more..."

I was considering it when Colby's phone started to chime. It sounded like an alarm. "Shoot. I have to go. Saylor has dance class. I need to relieve the babysitter and get her to the studio."

I smiled. "I didn't know she took dance lessons. Does she wear a little pink tutu?"

"She does. But for some reason, she won't wear her sneakers for the walk over to the studio. Instead, she pairs the pink tutu with these green rubber rain boots my mother bought her. They have a frog's face molded into the toes."

I chuckled. "Definitely a girl after my own heart."

"I gotta run. But I stopped by to see if you wanted to have dinner Saturday night?"

"That sounds good."

"To be clear. I'm asking you on a <u>date</u>—not an *un*date."

"I thought the breast painting might have moved us past the platonic undate." I laughed. "But yeah, I'd like to have a dinner date with you."

"My place, okay? Saylor is staying at my parents' house." He held up his hand. "No pressure. I know you want to go slow. I just would love to not share you with anyone for once."

I smiled. "Sure. That sounds good."

"Okay." He leaned down and brushed his lips over mine once more. "I'll see you Saturday."

"I can't believe you make sauce from scratch." I was perched up on Colby's kitchen counter next to the stove, watching him stir a pot of tomato sauce.

"When Saylor first came into my life, I had no idea what to do with a baby. My mom spent a lot of time at my apartment because

I was a nervous wreck. I thought I was going to fuck something up and hurt her. Every time Mom came over, she brought an index card with a recipe written down and a bag of groceries. When Saylor would nap, she'd teach me how to cook. I owe a lot to her for making me a better dad." Colby scooped up a spoonful of sauce and blew on it before lifting it to my lips.

"Oh, wow. That's really good. Nice and garlicy, the way I like it."

A tiny drip from the underside of the spoon fell and landed on my collarbone. Colby leaned in and licked it off before running his tongue up my neck and sucking along my pulse line.

"You had some sauce." He grinned. "I don't have any paper towels."

I pointed to the full roll next to me and raised a brow.

"I meant, I'm environmentally conscious and don't like to use too many paper towels."

"Uh-huh." I smiled. Plucking the spoon from his hand, I turned it over and ran the saucy back side along his neck.

Colby's eyes darkened as I leaned up and returned the favor, dragging my tongue over the sauce and sucking along his throat.

He groaned when I pulled back. "I'm going to pour that pot all over our bodies in a minute."

I giggled. "What's with us and painting each other? Do you have a fetish or something?"

"I never knew I did, but it's definitely become an issue for me. The other day I walked past a kid's store. There was a Snoopy backpack in the window, and I started to get hard thinking about your tits. I don't know if I'm going to be able to take my kid shopping anymore because of you."

I couldn't stop smiling. "Why don't you turn that sauce off for a little while? We could go into the living room. I want to sit on your lap and suck your neck some more."

In two seconds flat, Colby had twisted the knobs on the stove, hoisted me into the air, and carried me to the couch. I laughed the entire way. "Anxious much?"

"Sweetheart, you have no damn idea."

It didn't take long before our laughing and fooling around turned into some serious heavy petting. I felt Colby's hard-on straining through two layers of clothes. It hit against just the right spot between my open legs and felt so damn good. I was seconds away from grinding myself up and down when my cell rang. The ringtone was pretty much the only thing that could have stopped me.

Colby wrenched his mouth from mine. "What is that?"

"It's from the *Wizard of Oz*, when the wicked witch is riding her bike in the tornado."

"Why?"

I sighed. "It's my mother. Can we pretend my pocket isn't ringing?"

Colby grinned and squeezed my neck, pulling me back to him without another word. Fifteen seconds later, I was ready to start grinding again when my phone restarted its music. I tried to ignore it, but I really couldn't.

I pulled away. "I'm sorry. She never calls back when I don't answer. I should probably get it."

He nodded. "Yeah, of course."

I dug the phone from my pocket and swiped. "It's not a good time, Mom."

"I was just robbed…" She gasped. "At gunpoint."

I sat up straight and blinked myself out of the haze of lust I'd been in. "What? Where are you? Are you okay?"

"I'm at the gallery. And no, I'm not okay! He put a gun to my head!"

I jumped off Colby's lap and looked around for my purse. "Did you call the police?"

"Yes, they're already here."

I breathed a small sigh of relief and nodded. "Okay, great."

"Can you come to the gallery, please? I can use your help."

"Yeah, of course. I'm leaving right now."

I hadn't even swiped my phone off, and Colby already had my purse in his hand and was opening the door to his apartment. "Where are we going?"

"To my mother's gallery. She was just robbed."

"So your mother said you recently had a showing here at the gallery?" the detective said. He had a small leather flip-up notebook in his hand.

I nodded. "Last weekend."

Colby and I had arrived at the gallery fifteen minutes ago. My mother seemed to have already shifted from scared to bitchy, which actually brought me some comfort. The masked thief had made off with her wallet, which had less than a hundred bucks cash, but she was currently on the phone canceling all of her credit cards.

The police officer nodded. "And some of the people who came to that show were suspicious?"

My nose wrinkled. "What? No. Why would you say that?"

He pointed over his shoulder with his pencil. "Your mom said that particular night brought a different kind of clientele than she normally has. She seemed pretty certain that the man who came in tonight was also here that evening."

My eyes widened. "Really? I thought she didn't get a look at the guy?"

"She didn't. But she mentioned there were some people with gang affiliations present." He flipped a page back in his notepad. "One of them named Devin something?"

My jaw hung open. "Are you kidding me?"

168

"No, why?"

I felt the burn of anger traveling up my face. "Devin is *not* affiliated with a gang. He's a well-known tattoo artist and was my mentor for years. I'm sure the people at Bowery Mission, over in Tribeca, will vouch for him since he volunteers there cooking for the homeless three days a week."

The police officer's forehead creased as he looked down at his pad again. "What about someone named Lenny Prince?"

I felt like there was fire in my veins. "Lenny is a street artist who was exhibiting the same night Devin was here. The same night I exhibited. His wife is a traffic court judge in Brooklyn. I'm sure she keeps him from breaking into galleries to steal wallets. I hate to tell you, but the only crime either of those men committed was thinking my mother supported their work. You see, my dear mother thinks anyone with tattoos and a lifestyle that doesn't mimic hers is a hoodlum." I took a deep breath. "If you really want to know who might want to harm my mother, I'm afraid you're going to have to interview half of New York City. I'm pretty sure she insults most humans."

The police officer and I looked over at my mother. She was talking on her cell as she fingered the strand of pearls around her neck. He turned back and folded his notepad. "Thanks for the info."

"Is there anything else you need from me?" I asked.

He shook his head. "I don't think so."

"Then I'm leaving. Good luck with *her*…"

Colby had been waiting by the door, playing with his phone. He stood when I approached.

I put my hands on my hips. "I want to go back to your apartment and grind myself against your erection until I get myself off while fully clothed. Are you good with that?"

His brows shot up, but he got over the shock really quickly. "Absofuckinglutely."

"Good, let's go."

Unfortunately, my gusto didn't last. My anger morphed into disappointment during the Uber ride back to Colby's. But Colby was really good at reading me and gave me the space I needed until we walked into his apartment.

"How about I finish dinner?" he said.

I smiled. "That would be great."

He moved around the kitchen, taking the things he needed from the refrigerator and putting his sauce and a pot of water back on the stove. When he was done, he lifted me back onto the counter where I'd been sitting earlier and spread my legs so he could stand between them.

"Talk to me."

I shook my head. "I fell for her shit again. I thought she was scared and needed my help. But really she just wanted me to give the police details on some of my friends who'd been at the gallery so they could investigate them as suspects."

Colby frowned. "I'm sorry."

"I don't know when I'll ever learn with her." I sighed. "I'm sorry I ruined our date. I know you have very little time without Saylor."

"You didn't ruin anything. In fact, I'm a little relieved to find your life can be chaotic once in a while. I feel like it's always me—having to bring my daughter when we spend time together because the sitter cancels, having to get home before I turn into a pumpkin…" He shrugged. "This is life, and it's not always easy. In fact, mine is usually a big, fat mess. But I want to share that mess with you, and I want you to share whatever mess you have with me."

I looked into Colby's eyes. "You really mean that, don't you?"

He smiled and gently tapped two of his fingers to my temple. "Well, what do you know? This thick skull is penetrable after all."

I smiled back. This man had opened up his world for me to come in, and it finally felt like time to do the same. I took a deep breath. "I'm crazy about you, Colby."

Colby's face turned serious. "The feeling is mutual. And I'm not going to let you down, Billie."

I nodded. "I think I've always known that. But I was afraid to let myself believe it."

"Believe it. Believe in *me*."

The moment just felt right in my soul. "I want you, Colby."

His eyes jumped back and forth between mine. "You mean you want to straddle me on the couch and dry-hump me?"

I smiled. "No. I want you inside of me."

"You sure?"

"I'm absolutely positive."

Colby lifted me off the countertop and carried me to his bedroom. He set me down in the middle of his bed with my head on his pillow. "There are so many things I want to do to you. Remember a few weeks ago, you said you liked me bossy?"

I nodded.

His lips curved into the sexiest smile. "Raise your arms. Hold onto the headboard and don't let go."

Oh God. The air in the room seemed to crackle as I did what he asked.

Colby unbuckled my jeans and slid them down my legs. He hooked a finger into one side of my panties and yanked, causing them to snap.

I gasped and white-knuckled the headboard. Colby licked his lips from the foot of the bed as he looked down at me. "Open your legs."

He hadn't laid a finger on me, yet I could feel my orgasm building. I did as he asked and spread my legs on the bed. Colby's eyes were fixed on my pussy.

"*Wider*. I want to see how wet you are for me."

Everything tightened as I spread my legs as wide as possible.

Colby shook his head. "You're gorgeous everywhere. I'm going to lick you until you *beg* for my cock."

I wasn't sure where this side of Colby had come from, but I fucking *loved* it. I was about ten seconds away from begging already.

Colby lifted his shirt over his head and climbed onto the bed. He stopped, hovering over me. "Don't let go of that headboard. Not for any reason."

I couldn't form words, so I gave the faintest nod. But it was apparently enough to satisfy Colby, and he buried his face between my legs. There were no teasing licks, or fluttering foreplay; he *dove* in. His tongue lapped at my wetness, nose pushed against my clit, and he moved his head from side to side while he devoured me. My hips churned as the muscles in my thighs began to tremble.

"Oh, God," I whimpered. I had the strongest urge to dig my hands into his hair and pull violently. But I continued gripping the headboard, for fear he might stop. Never in my life had an orgasm built so voraciously. Colby's tongue moved up to torment my clit, lashing and flicking before he sucked it into his mouth. Two fingers slid inside of me and pumped in and out.

My back arched off the bed. "Colby!"

He pumped harder, using his other hand to press against my stomach and hold me down. The sounds of his fingers pushing in and out of my wetness was the most erotic thing I'd ever heard. There was no slow build to the edge of the cliff, I flew over—crying out his name as my body clamped down hard around his fingers.

After, I was in a complete daze, barely aware of Colby standing and stripping out of the rest of his clothes. He opened and shut a nightstand drawer, and when I looked up, he was leaning back on his haunches with a condom raised to his mouth. He used his teeth to tear it open and flashed a cocky grin.

"You can let go of the headboard now."

"Oh..." I laughed. "I didn't realize I was still holding it."

Colby removed the condom from the wrapper and spit out the packaging. My gaze followed his hand as it lowered. "Oh my God." My eyes widened. "Seriously?"

Colby sheathed himself, fisting the base of his cock once the condom was on. "I'm hoping that wasn't a disappointed *seriously*?" He grinned.

I rolled my eyes. "You know it's not. You're...huge."

He chuckled as he lowered onto my body, lining up the wide head of his crown at my entrance. Colby weaved our fingers together and kissed my lips gently before pulling his head back to look into my eyes. Our gazes stayed locked as he pushed inside.

"Fuck." His eyes briefly closed. "You're so wet and tight, I'm not gonna last long, sweetheart."

I smiled. "It's okay. You already took care of me, and we have all night."

He eased in and out, gently at first, but pushing farther down with each thrust. Once I was fully ready for him, his movements intensified. I wrapped my legs around his waist, and together we moved back and forth rhythmically. Normally, I was a one-trick pony, only able to orgasm once a day, if I was lucky. But it didn't take long before I felt the build coming again.

My fingers dug into Colby's hair, and our mouths fused together in a kiss. My heart raced, feeling so much more than physical pleasure. I was consumed by this man, and it seemed like I wasn't the only one caught up in the moment. Colby pulled back again to look in my eyes. His jaw was taut, and the veins in his neck bulged. The intensity of the moment pushed me over the edge once again. "I'm gonna..." I didn't get to complete the sentence before my body was pulsing all around him. "*Oh, God...*"

Colby quickened his pace, never taking his eyes from mine as he watched my orgasm play out on my face. Once my muscles went slack, he ground down one last time and buried himself deeply as he released. "Fuck," he roared. "*Fuck. Fuck. Fuck!*"

He kissed me gently as we came down from the high. We smiled at each other while Colby continued to glide in and out for a long time, until he finally had to get up and deal with the condom. When he returned from the bathroom, he brought a warm towel and gently washed between my legs before climbing back into bed and scooping me up. He positioned me so my head rested on his chest.

He stroked my hair. "That was amazing."

I smiled. "Yeah, it was. I don't think I could lift my head if I tried."

Colby chuckled. "Get some sleep. I'll wake you with breakfast in bed."

I snuggled closer. "That's so sweet."

"Not really. You didn't ask what I'll be feeding you."

I slapped his abs and yawned, feeling groggy. "You know how some people say a burp is a compliment to the chef? Well, I conk right out after a good orgasm."

He kissed the top of my head. "Good. Then you'll be getting lots of sleep from now on."

❤CHAPTER 16

Colby

I'd thought I had a good life before Billie came along. I'd convinced myself I was totally fulfilled just being a dad to Saylor, that I didn't need anything else for the time being. I'd probably needed to tell myself that in order to get through those difficult early days.

But since Billie and I had decided to give it a go, I'd realized how much I'd been missing: how much my sexual appetite had needed to be satisfied, how much I'd needed mental stimulation. And boy, did Billie satisfy all my needs. *Intoxicated* wasn't strong enough of a word to describe how I felt when it came to her. I only hoped it wasn't temporary. Trying not to analyze that had become my biggest challenge. But it was human nature to wait for the other shoe to drop when everything was going perfectly, right? All too often, when you let your guard down, life stepped in and ripped you a new asshole.

Lately, Billie had been sneaking upstairs in the middle of the day to meet me when I came home for a quick "lunch break." We had sex any chance we got during the day because Billie hadn't been spending the nights at my place yet. We'd both agreed it was too soon, treading lightly because of my daughter. During one particular afternoon tryst, we'd rocked my damn bed so hard that the headboard had banged against the wall. There was now a significant hole in the spot.

Thus the reason for Holden's maintenance visit Thursday afternoon. I'd asked him where in the supply room he kept the plaster and other materials to fix the hole because I'd wanted to patch it myself. But he'd insisted on coming by. And I just knew he was going to have a field day with this.

When he knocked, I opened, attempting one last effort to send him away. "Hey, man. You really don't need to do this. Why don't you just give me the materials?"

Holden ignored me, looking around the apartment. "So where is it?"

"My bedroom," I said, bracing for the reaction as he followed me in there.

"What are you doing home today anyway?" he asked.

"The nanny has the day off, so I worked from home. I have to pick up Saylor from school in an hour."

As soon as he got to my room, he asked, "Where's the hole again?"

"Behind the bed." I moved it out to show him.

He smirked. "You dirty dog. Right behind the headboard. No wonder you were so shady about it. You fucked your way to a hole in the wall."

I rolled my eyes.

"I thought I was the only one who'd done that type of thing around here." He laughed. "But apparently not."

"This is why I wanted to do it myself—to avoid your ridicule."

"No ridicule, my dude. Just admiration." He set his supplies on the floor. "And a little bit of jealousy. Don't kill me for saying that. I know how possessive you are of Billie." He laughed. "So, I take it things are *banging* between you and her. No pun intended."

"You could say that."

"I'm happy for you, man."

"Thank you. I'm happy, too. Truly happy in every way for the first time in a long time."

"Billie is amazing." He moved my bed out farther and placed a drop cloth below where he'd be working. "So, you think this is it? Is she the one?"

I let out a long breath. "It feels like it, but you know what? There's still some stuff up in the air, so I'm just trying to enjoy it, take it day by day."

"By some stuff, you mean the fact that you have Saylor, right?"

I really didn't want to get into this today. But I should've known nosy-ass Holden would want the full scoop on everything, including what was going on inside my head.

I sighed. "I'm not the one with a decision to make, you know? Being with Billie is a no-brainer for me. But it's not that simple for her. Staying with me means she has to decide if she wants to be a mother to Saylor. I'm sure that question is always in the back of her mind."

"I get it." He nodded. "Not to make you feel bad, but I'd probably run the other way if I were her."

"Thanks." I rolled my eyes. "I can always count on you for brutal honesty."

"Anytime." He smirked. "But you know…you do have one thing going for you."

"What's that?"

"You have a massive dick."

"That's going to make her want to be a parent?"

"Possibly. Big dicks have a way of working miracles."

"Thanks. Then I shall rub mine and chant after you leave."

He cackled. "I do that every night. Doesn't work for me. I haven't found the one yet."

"I don't think you're looking for the one. You're looking for the *three*," I taunted. "Am I right?"

He shrugged. "Perhaps. For now."

It would be interesting to see if Holden ever settled on one person. I used to wonder the same about myself, and look at me now. So anything was possible, I suppose. But if I had to guess, I would still say Holden would be the last of us guys to settle down, if ever.

We shot the shit for almost an hour while he worked to patch the wall.

"I'll try to be more careful with the wall next time," I said as I helped him clean up.

"Are you kidding?" He flashed a mischievous grin. "I'll be disappointed if I don't have to come back to fix it again."

That night, I asked Billie to come have dinner with Saylor and me. Billie suggested buying stuff to make our own pizzas because she thought Saylor would have fun with that. And she insisted on picking up all the ingredients after her shop closed for the day.

She texted me from the grocery store.

Billie: What kind of toppings does Saylor like?

Colby: She likes pineapple, actually. You can just buy the canned kind. And bacon. That combo.

Billie: Interesting combination for an interesting girl. Okay. What do you like?

Colby: What do I like? That's a loaded question.

Billie: LOL. No need to hold back.

Colby: Quickies in the laundry room with you after Saylor goes to sleep. My cock in your mouth. My dick buried deep inside you anywhere, anytime I have the chance. My cum on your tits. The list is endless.

Billie: You have a one-track mind.

Colby: You know it. I'm addicted. To answer your original question, I'll eat anything—but I do have a favorite thing to eat. Can you guess what that might be?

She responded with a photo of a can of pineapple up against her chest. Her corset today was a burnt orange color I didn't remember ever seeing before. As usual, I was paying more attention to what was inside of it though.

Billie: This can okay?

I couldn't help messing with her, because who's looking at the damn pineapple can when it's up against her heaving chest?

Colby: Can or cans? Those cans are fucking perfect. God, hurry up and come home so I can nuzzle your neck when Saylor isn't looking. (That brand is fine.)

My use of the word *home* wasn't lost on me. We were far from living together, but I still felt like her place was with me, that somehow my home was hers now, even if she didn't sleep here. *Have I mentioned that this woman makes me deliriously happy?*

Billie: Not done yet! Still have to find the sausage. And don't you DARE make a sausage innuendo.

Colby: Why you rainin' on my parade?

Billie: Get it over with then.

I laughed as I typed.

Colby: I've got a sausage for ya. ;-)

Billie: Feel better now?

Colby: Much.

Billie: Okay, in all seriousness: sausage and pepperoni for us. Pineapple and bacon for my girl. Gonna get some fresh basil to sprinkle on top, too. I'm excited!

Colby: I'm excited, too.

Billie: Why do I think you're not talking about the pizza?

Colby: I am most definitely not talking about the pizza. Get your ass back here, beautiful.

After Billie arrived at my apartment, she got to work straight away, pulling things out of bags and laying all the pizza ingredients on the counter. Saylor sat atop one of the stools and watched as Billie got everything ready.

Unfortunately, I didn't have a rolling pin, so Billie improvised with a wine bottle to spread out the dough.

I leaned against the counter. "I'm impressed with your ingenuity."

"Why, thank you." She winked.

I wished I could have reached over and kissed her, but we weren't going there in front of Saylor.

Flour flew through the air as the two girls kneaded and rolled the dough. Soon both of their outfits were covered in white. I loved that Billie wasn't afraid to get messy—especially when we fucked.

Once the dough was ready, it was time to start assembling the pizzas. Billie cooked the sausage with some onions in a pan and put that aside. She opened up all of the other packages and placed the toppings in bowls. This kitchen was gonna be a bitch to clean up, but it was well worth it to see the continuous smile on my daughter's face.

I watched how patient Billie was as they made the pizzas together. For someone who claimed to have little experience with children, Billie was a pro.

By the time the pizzas were in the oven, as expected, the kitchen was a total mess: drippings of pineapple juice, scattered shredded cheese, bacon grease. But it was a beautiful mess. It was life—an example of the life that had been breathed into this place since Billie joined us.

After dinner, Billie surprised Saylor with a princess cupcake she'd picked up from the supermarket bakery. My daughter clearly enjoyed it, because by the time she was finished, she had frosting in her hair and somehow in her eyes.

Billie took Saylor to the bathroom to wash up as I got started cleaning the kitchen so it no longer looked like the Pillsbury Doughboy had exploded up in here. I stopped what I was doing from time to time to listen to the sounds of laughter coming from down the hall.

I want this. Every night. But I knew it would be stupid to assume Billie would want the full-time responsibility that came along with it. Time would tell, and I just had to be patient.

Before bed, Saylor asked Billie for a bedtime story. "No book!" She squealed.

Billie looked over at me for guidance.

"That means she wants you to make up something off the top of your head," I told her. "She likes to challenge me all the time."

She tickled Saylor. "You're so silly. You're not gonna make this easy, huh?"

Saylor giggled.

Billie sat at the edge of the bed and took a moment to think as Saylor settled under the covers.

"Okay, this story is called The Tattooed Witch," she said.

My daughter curled into her as I stood at the doorway, listening in.

"Once upon a time, there was a tattooed witch. She lived in New York and owned her own tattoo shop where she drew tattoos on people all day long." She paused. "One day, a prince walked in and asked her for a tattoo. But the tattooed witch was having a very bad day, so she sent him away."

"This story sounds familiar," I said.

"It might be a bit autobiographical." Billie winked.

"What happened to put the witch in a bad mood?" I teased.

"She had an encounter with the evil Sir Tinder that left her in a bad way."

"Ah. Okay. Go ahead with the story." I laughed.

She turned to Saylor and continued, "The witch felt very bad about being rude. The next time she saw the prince, she cast a spell on him in the hopes that she could have a second chance."

Saylor looked up at her. "Magic?"

"Yup. A magical spell."

"What happened?" Saylor asked.

"It worked! The prince kept coming back. And he even took her on a date once to the magical island of IKEA."

I chuckled.

Saylor grinned. "What else happened?"

"The witch's cold heart started to melt. After a while, the tattooed witch didn't feel like a witch anymore. She felt like a princess—not because she was an actual princess, but because the prince made her feel like one. The witch cast the spell on the prince, but in the end, she was the one who'd been transformed." Billie looked over at me and smiled. "The end."

Saylor's eyes widened. "Did they live happily ever after?"

She hesitated. "I like to think so."

Good answer. I sure as fuck hoped the witch and the prince ended up together, and had lots of amazing sex along the way.

After we put Saylor to bed, Billie looked deep in thought as she sat next to me in the living room.

"Saylor is really happy when you're around," I said, interrupting whatever she'd been ruminating about.

"Yeah, it surprises me how much I love being around her, too."

I traced the tattoos on her arm and decided to open up. "Probably the only thing I've worried about when it comes to you and me is whether you would want this life for the long haul. I never want to pressure you to think about it, but I also feel like we're at the point where I'd like to know if you could possibly see a future with…both of us."

She didn't immediately say anything. I felt like I might come out of my skin as I waited for her to speak.

"I'm not gonna lie…" she finally said. "In the beginning, I was worried about my ability to fit into this equation, to care for a child the way I would need to. But I want you to know, I no longer see things that way. If things don't work out between us, it won't be because of my fears about Saylor. Anyone would be lucky to have her in their life."

"Wow." I kissed the side of her head. "Thank you. I feel like I can breathe a little easier."

"That's been on your mind tonight?"

"Yeah. It's hard not to think about it when I watch you with her."

"I still think we need to take things slowly, though," she said.

"Agreed…but…"

She raised her brow. "What?"

"Does that mean I can convince you to stay the night?"

Billie squeezed my knee and sighed. "I don't know…"

"Saylor always sleeps through. We can get up early and get you out of here. Even though I had that fantasy about taking you in the laundry room, I'd much rather take my time and do it in my bed. We just have to be quiet. No holes in the wall tonight." I wasn't above begging. "Please…" I said, sounding like Saylor when she'd asked me for a second helping of dessert. Except I wanted way more than two helpings of Billie.

"What if she gets up and sees me?" Billie whispered.

"I'll lock my door. I still have a baby monitor, and I can hook it up so we can hear her if she gets up. Even in the worst-case scenario, if she saw you here, she's young enough that she doesn't understand sex. So I think we'll be fine. She'll just think you're sleeping over. She'd probably be thrilled."

Billie's expression softened to an impish grin. "Can I think about it while you pour me a glass of wine?"

I inwardly did a victory dance and stood up to fetch my girl's wine. "It would be my pleasure."

Just as I was opening the bottle, there was a knock at the door. The only people who'd knock on my door at this time of the evening on a weeknight were the guys.

"Are you expecting someone?" Billie asked.

I put the bottle down and headed for the door. "No. It's probably Brayden or Holden."

I should've checked the peephole. Then maybe I wouldn't have nearly had a heart attack the moment I saw her. It took a few seconds because it had been a long while. Her dark hair was a bit longer, and she was thinner than I remembered. But the cold eyes were the very same.

The words wouldn't come to me, so I stood there speechless for several seconds as panic started to seep in.

What the hell does she want?

The woman I knew only as Raven was the first to speak. "Hi, Colby."

Still nothing. I didn't know what to say. All I could think was, *What the fuck is she doing here, and how the hell do I make her magically disappear before Billie catches on?*

"Who the hell is she?" I heard Billie say. My eyes were still firmly on the woman standing at the door.

Remember when I was talking about how the other shoe always drops when things are going well? Well, the other fucking shoe had just landed at my door.

I finally managed the words to answer Billie's question.

"This is Saylor's egg donor."

♥CHAPTER 17

Colby

Slam.

"Colby, what the hell?" Billie looked at my front door, horrified.

"Whatever she wants, I don't want to hear it." I walked back into the living room, filled my wine glass, and chugged half of it down.

"So you just slam the door in Saylor's mother's face? What does she even want?"

"First of all, she's *not* Saylor's mother. Biology doesn't make you a damn parent. And second of all, I don't give two shits what the hell she wants. Third of all—" My rant was cut short.

Knock. Knock. Knock.

Billie and I both turned and looked at the door.

"You need to answer that," she said.

I shook my head. "No, I don't."

My eyes locked with Billie's, and we stared at each other. I hadn't thought there was anything I could say no to this woman about, until this moment.

Fifteen seconds later, the knock on the door grew louder.

Bang. Bang. Bang.

Billie sighed. "Colby…"

I stayed rooted firmly in place while I lifted my wine to my lips and guzzled the remainder of the glass.

"Open the door, Colby! I need to talk to you!"

I felt anger rising inside my body. It started in my toes, traveled up through my legs and torso, and settled in to heat my face.

"Colby, she's going to wake Saylor. And then what?"

I still hadn't moved. Not until my daughter padded out from her bedroom, rubbing her eyes. "Billie, were you just yelling?"

Billie immediately walked over and bent down to Saylor. "No, sweetheart. There's someone outside. Umm…a woman got locked out of her apartment, so Daddy is going to go outside and help her." She turned and gave me a look. "*Right*, Colby?"

I still didn't respond. Billie shook her head at me and frowned, then lifted Saylor to her hip. "How about if I tell you another story while Daddy goes out and helps the woman?" She glanced back at me. "I have another one about the witch who flies away on her broom because the handsome prince turned out to be a frog after all…"

My daughter smiled, none the wiser. "I want to hear about the frog!"

"Okay. Let's go, girlfriend." She carried Saylor to the bedroom, stopping once more to look back and motion with her head toward the door, silently telling me to go deal with things.

The minute Saylor's door shut, Maya started again.

Bang. Bang. Bang.

"I'm not leaving, Colby! So you might as well open the damn door before I wake up all the tenants in this building!"

I closed my eyes and took a deep breath. It did nothing to calm my nerves or quell my anger, yet what choice did I have? I did *not* want Saylor asking questions. I didn't want her to see the woman's face or hear her voice.

Maya straightened her posture when I stepped out into the hall. This woman really had some balls. I pulled the door shut behind me and folded my arms across my chest.

"What the fuck do you want?"

"I need your help."

I bent my head back in maniacal laughter. "You need *my* help? That's a good one. What about your *fucking kid*? Do you think *she* might've needed your help in the last four years? You've got a lot of balls showing up at our door and saying you need anything from me."

Maya looked away. "I never planned to have a child. When I found out I was pregnant, I thought I could handle it. But I couldn't. The child is better off without me."

I leaned forward and put my face in hers. "*Saylor.* The child has a goddamned name. And you better believe she's better off without a woman who thinks nothing of handing her flesh and blood off to a guy she's only met *once*. You never even called to check on her, for Christ's sake. Where the fuck have you been for four years? I had a private investigator search for you."

"You are her *father*. Not a stranger."

"So what? The Green River Serial Killer murdered forty-nine women. He had a child, too." I shook my head. "Though right about now I'm starting to understand how someone can be a parent *and* murder a woman."

Maya frowned. "I planned on coming back. I just needed a break, and I had no one to turn to. The baby wouldn't stop crying, and I thought one night away would help. But one day led to two, and two led to a week. And then I started to get my life back."

"How nice for you…"

She shook her head. "Listen, Colby. There's a lot about me you don't know. First of all, my name isn't Raven. That was just my stage name."

"Yes, I know. Raven wasn't much help when the private investigator tried to find you, *Maya Moreno*."

"Oh. Well, do you know I'm not here legally? I came on a summer visa from Ecuador when I was seventeen and never went back."

"I knew that, too. Anything else you want to tell me about your life?" I shrugged, giving her no time to actually answer before continuing. "No? Good. It's been great catching up, but why don't you go back to wherever you came from and forget I exist? Enjoy the rest of your life as much as you have the last four years." I turned and reached for the door handle, but Maya put a hand on my arm.

"Wait!"

I glared at her. "Don't you goddamn touch me."

Maya held up both hands. "Fine. I won't. But I need a favor from you. I can see you're upset right now. So why don't we meet for coffee in the morning to talk after you've had some time to cool off? I can explain everything then."

My face twisted. "*I'm not meeting you for coffee.*"

Maya raised her voice. "Listen, Colby. You're going to have to get over your problem with me for the sake of our daughter."

I spoke through gritted teeth. "*My* daughter."

Maya sighed. "I didn't want to do it like this." She lifted a flap on her purse and pulled out a thick, manila envelope, holding it out to me.

I continued to glare at her with my arms folded across my chest, making no attempt to take it.

She rolled her eyes. "I'll be at the coffee shop on the corner tomorrow morning by eight AM. If you're not there..." She dropped the envelope to the ground between us. "I'll be filing those papers at nine."

♥

I sat at the kitchen table with a bottle of whiskey and a now-empty glass, staring at the envelope. Billie walked out from Saylor's room and quietly took the seat across from me.

"I got her back to sleep."

"Thank you."

She nodded. "Talk to me. What's going on, Colby? I thought Saylor's mom wasn't in the picture."

"She wasn't. You know the entire story. I met her at a strip club on Halloween a few years back. She came home with me. We had a one-night stand, and she skipped out the next morning, leaving me a wrong number. Next time I saw her was when she showed up at my door with a baby, saying it was mine, and I needed to watch her for a little while because she had an important job interview. She ran out my door as fast as she'd showed up." I shook my head. "Haven't seen or heard one word since. I tried looking for her after she disappeared, but she was here illegally, so it was easy to vanish without a trace."

"What did she say outside?"

I refilled my glass with whiskey and shook my head. "Not much. Just said she wanted a favor. I went off on her. Then she threatened that if I don't meet her tomorrow at eight AM at the diner down the block, she'll file those papers." I motioned to the envelope with my eyes, then lifted the whiskey glass and chugged back a heaping gulp. It burned, but not enough.

"What's in the envelope?"

I looked at it again. "Take a look for yourself. I can't say the words…"

Billie slipped the packet of papers out. Her head moved slightly from side to side as she scanned the typed print. I knew the second she read the caption. Her eyes flared wide and her head snapped up. "A motion for petition of custody?"

I felt like throwing up, hearing the words out loud.

"Colby, oh my God, is she serious?"

I shook my head. "Looks that way. I only skimmed the papers, but she's got affidavits from doctors saying she suffered from postpartum depression and that's why she left. Some bullshit about her being worried for the safety of her baby. There's even a certificate in there saying she took some sort of a parenting class. As if they can teach you to love someone and protect them with your life, or stay up all night watching them when they come down with a fever. Or teach you to forget you once had a life of your own." I shook my head. "A fucking class."

"Oh, Colby…" Billie reached across the table and took my hand.

I'd been so damn angry the last fifteen minutes, yet that one little touch made a chink in my armor. I felt all my nerves start to flood out through that crack.

I just kept looking down and shaking my head. "They can't do that, right? Give my daughter to a woman who walked away from her child and never even called to check on her?" I swallowed and tasted salt. "They can't, right?"

Billie shook her head. Her face was so sad. "I don't know, Colby. But I do have a friend whose baby daddy didn't see his kid for five years, and they gave him visitation. He was an addict and sobered up though, so it's a little different."

"Different than what? A woman who has a letter from a doctor swearing she had postpartum depression? Both are diseases, right?"

Billie squeezed my hand. "Let's slow down for a minute. I think we're getting ahead of ourselves by trying to guess what a judge might do. It may not even come to that. You said she didn't file the papers yet, right?"

"I don't think so. She said if I didn't meet her at eight, she'd be filing them at nine tomorrow."

"What does she want you to meet her at eight for?"

"I have no damn idea."

"Well, I think you need to find out…"

I barely slept all night.

Billie had gone home after all. She'd said she wanted to give me time to think, and I didn't fight her too hard on it. I wouldn't have been good company anyway. Talk about a quick turn of events. One minute, I'm the happiest I can remember being, maybe ever— my girl's going to stay over, Saylor and Billie clearly adore each other, and the woman I'd thought might run away when she saw what my day-to-day life was really like wound up running *to me* because of it. And then there was the knock.

The fucking knock.

With the same woman standing on the other side of the door who had turned my life upside down four years ago. And she was trying to do it a second time.

Maya.

Isn't there a limit on how many times you can sucker punch a guy you've spent the sum total of less than eight hours of your life with? If not, there goddamned should be.

"Daddy…" Saylor padded into the kitchen where I was drinking coffee and held up a pair of my socks. "Are you being silly?"

My brows dipped together. "Why do you have my socks, honey?"

She grinned. "Because you left them for me to put on when you laid my outfit on the bed." She pulled something from behind her back. "And these!"

I blinked a few times. Had I really done that? Left my underwear and socks for her to wear instead of her own? I guess I had.

Saylor tilted her head. "Are you sad, Daddy?"

Shoot. "No, honey, I'm not sad. Just a little tired, that's all." The last thing I wanted was to worry my little girl before I dropped her at school. So I scooped her off the floor as I stood and put on my best fake smile. She giggled.

"I was *wondering* why my underwear were so tight that they were going up my butt. I guess it's because they're yours…"

Saylor's eyes widened with a sparkle. "You're not really wearing *my* underwear are you, Daddy?"

"I don't know. Do you have pink ones with little purple butterflies on them?"

She nodded fast.

"Hmm. Okay, well, good thing then. Because the ones I have on are black and don't have any butterflies on them." I rubbed my nose with hers. "You don't really think I can fit into your undies, do you?"

She giggled again, and it felt like a salve had been rubbed on the gaping wound in my heart. I carried her into her room and opened her dresser drawer, pulling out a pair of her underwear and socks. "Here you go. But you better get a move on. We only have ten minutes before we have to leave for preschool."

"Okay, Daddy."

A half hour later, I rounded the corner back onto my block after dropping Saylor at school. I felt angry and bitter, but also a whole lot scared as I opened the door to the diner and looked around.

Maya held up her hand and smiled and waved like we were besties having a friendly breakfast. *Is she serious?* I took a deep breath before marching to the table. My face was anything but friendly.

"Hello, Colby."

The first thing I noticed is that she was dressed differently than last night. Today she had on a business suit, while last night she'd worn jeans and a top I couldn't even remember. I only knew she'd been casual, and now it looked like she was all business. Her dark hair was tied up, and she had on a pair of thick-rimmed glasses. I had no idea she even wore fucking glasses.

I nodded and sat down. "What do you want?"

The waitress walked over. "Can I get you some coffee or juice?"

I waved her off. "Nothing for me, thank you. I won't be staying long."

Maya smiled at the woman. "I'll take a coffee, with milk and sugar, please."

I barely waited until the waitress disappeared. "So what do you want from me?"

Maya folded her hands in front of her on the table. "I need you to marry me. They're trying to deport me."

My brows jumped. "Are you freaking high?"

"No. I'm very sober."

"Then just mentally insane? I'm not fucking *marrying you*. I can't stand the sight of you."

"If you do it, I will sign over full custody of Saylor. My attorney has advised me that I have two ways to stay in the country at this point: either file for custody of my daughter and apply for a green card as the primary caretaker of my child, or marry an American citizen. You're the most logical choice, and I'm told we would likely sail through the immigration process if we say we've been together since Saylor was conceived."

I stared at her for the longest time before speaking again. "Saylor's doing great. Thanks for asking."

Maya took a deep breath and exhaled. "I'm trying to keep emotions out of this, Colby."

"Well, isn't that grand of you? It must be nice to be able to see your child as nothing more than a business transaction you can barter."

The waitress returned with coffee and poured a cup for Maya. She looked back and forth between us. "Are you guys ready to place an order?"

Maya shook her head. "We need a few more minutes, please."

"No problem."

I leaned forward. "You don't even *want* custody of her, do you?"

"Like I said, I think it's best if we keep emotions out of this conversation. Let's just make it simple. I need something from you. You need something from me. Marry me, and as soon as I get my green card, we'll divorce, and you will forever not have to worry about custody."

I glared at her. "I'm not worried about it now. No judge in the world is going to give you custody."

"You're speaking from an emotional place because I've made you feel threatened."

I lifted my chin. "Go fuck yourself."

"Do your homework, Colby. Consult a family law attorney. Whoever you pick is going to tell you that I *will* get visitation once I file that paperwork. It may be limited at first. But courts like mothers in their children's lives, especially a little girl. Eventually, when I do everything correctly and a little time passes, I'll be awarded shared custody."

"You'd uproot a little girl's life to serve your own purposes without blinking twice? You already walked out on her, isn't that enough damage?"

Maya picked imaginary lint off her pants.

I couldn't take it anymore. Her nonchalance had my blood boiling. I stood, the bottom of the chair scraping loudly against the tile floor. "I'm done here."

When I turned, Maya grabbed my wrist. "Go see a lawyer," she said. "Confirm what I've told you. Then meet me back here one week from today at the same time. I'll hold off filing the paperwork until then. I realize this is a lot for you to digest."

I pulled my wrist from her grip and looked her in the eye. "Go fuck yourself."

"Same time next week, Colby. I'll see you then."

♥CHAPTER 18

Billie

It was one of those days where it was so rainy that it almost looked like nighttime. The weather was an exact match for my mood. I'd also been dropping things all morning. Deek looked over at me curiously every time. It would be great if I could get through this workday without losing my mind. Thankfully, I hadn't screwed up any tattoos yet, but the day was still young. All morning, I hadn't been able to think of anything except Colby's meeting with Saylor's mother.

Maya. She now had a name and a face. A face I wanted to punch.

Things had been so much better when she was just a blurry ghost, someone I could pretend didn't exist. Everything had happened so fast last night that I'd barely gotten a look at her. My priorities were elsewhere. Namely, protecting Saylor so she would never catch wind of what a terrible person her mother was.

Finally, Deek and I had a break between clients, which gave him the opportunity to corner me about my strange behavior. I'd yet to tell him what was going on.

He came up behind me and shook my shoulders. "What the hell is up with you today? Something going on with you and Colby?"

I let out a long sigh. "You could say that…"

"I knew I shouldn't have trusted a guy without tats." His eyes narrowed. "Do I need to go fuck him up?"

"Believe me, there is *nothing* you could do to make him more fucked up than he is right now."

A look of concern crossed his face. "Uh-oh. That sounds ominous. Spill."

I explained what had happened. Deek always had something to say about everything. But this time? He stood with his mouth hanging open for a long while.

"What do you think she wants?" he finally asked.

"I don't know. She dangled the custody thing in his face to get him to meet with her. So there's obviously more. He's coming here later to fill me in."

"Wow." Deek stared off. "What an asshole this chick is… To be out of the picture this entire time and then come back out of the blue like this?"

I exhaled. "We'd had the best night together before she showed up. The three of us. It was like the first time I could really see…" My words trailed off.

"See yourself as part of their family?"

I nodded, feeling my eyes well up. I didn't want to cry, but better now than in front of Colby. He needed me to be strong and not make things harder. Colby didn't need to be worrying about me and my feelings at a time like this.

"Are you worried this could affect your relationship with him?" he asked.

I shook my head. "I haven't been worried about Colby and me at all. Saylor's well-being is the only thing that's been on my mind. I can't imagine a scenario where she would be forced to spend time with this virtual stranger—or God forbid, be taken away from Colby. Those two are like extensions of each other. That can't happen. Not even part of the time. It's not an option, Deek!"

Deek shook his head slowly. "I don't like the sound of this. Any person who would come out of nowhere and threaten Colby like that is probably capable of anything."

"Exactly. Who does that?"

"An evil bitch," he answered.

I rubbed my temples. "I would give anything to make this go away right now."

"Well, I know a guy…" He teased.

"Last resort." I chuckled.

"But listen," he said. "Don't freak out until you have a chance to hear what happened."

I suspected Colby's "breakfast" with Maya would only make things worse, not better. "You know sometimes you just have a bad feeling you can't shake?"

"Yeah…"

"That's how I feel about their meeting today. I know he's gonna walk in here and tell me something I don't want to hear. I can feel it in my bones."

"The way this is affecting you? I can see how much you care about that little girl, and how lucky she'd be to have you in her life."

"I would be the lucky one, Deek. I really would."

Deek gave me a hug. "Maybe you do want kids after all, huh?"

I would adopt Saylor this minute if it meant making that woman disappear.

"Maybe." I smiled. "I don't know about giving birth. But being a mom to that sweet little thing?" I sighed. "That would be a pleasure."

"She sure as hell deserves a better mother than the one she was born to."

I thought back to my brief first impression of Maya.

"It's hard to believe that strange woman gave birth to Saylor. I think until now, I'd sort of pictured her like a snowy television screen. Nothing clear. Just white noise."

"What was she like?"

"I didn't spend all that much time in the room with them when she was there." I shrugged. "She was pretty. I mean, I always knew she would be, because it wasn't like Colby was going to hook up with someone who wasn't. She had dark hair, long like mine but not as dark. She doesn't look much like Saylor. It made me realize how much Saylor takes after Colby." I shrugged. "I might have gotten a better look at the woman if I hadn't been so damn focused on making sure Saylor didn't notice anything was off."

"Understandable, yeah. In that sense, it's really good you were there."

I rubbed my eyes. "God, I can't imagine if I wasn't."

Justine returned from her break, interrupting our conversation. I was close with her, but I didn't want to rehash everything, and Deek knew to keep his mouth shut without me having to tell him.

Within a few minutes, our next clients arrived, ironically a mother and daughter getting matching tattoos. The universe definitely had a way of fucking with you sometimes. I nearly cried while tattooing the same sentence onto each of them: *I love you more*. The mother-daughter relationship was like no other. For someone like me, who didn't have the best mother, I'd always longed for more. Maybe the only way I would get to experience that would be to become a mother myself.

The day dragged on as I waited for Colby to stop by after work. I'd specifically not texted him because I didn't want him to feel obligated to explain everything in a message or on the phone when I knew his plan was to lay it on me in person.

After the shop closed, Deek hung out with me until Colby arrived.

When my man finally walked through the door, his eyes looked sunken and bloodshot. His tie was crooked and his hair mussed, probably because he'd been pulling on it. This was definitely bad.

I ran to Colby and pulled him into my arms. I knew he needed that first and foremost. For once, Deek remained quiet. Now was not the time for words, and he knew it.

I was looking over Colby's shoulder when Deek said, "I'm gonna lock the door behind me."

I nodded and mouthed, "Thank you."

After Deek left, I stepped back and wrapped my hands around Colby's cheeks, bringing his face to mine and kissing his forehead.

"Whatever it is, it's going to be okay," I whispered.

It took Colby a few minutes to even start speaking. I'd wanted so badly for him to tell me what happened. But once he opened his mouth, I wished I'd never heard the words.

"She wants me to marry her."

I paced nonstop. After Colby told me the story, all I could do was walk back and forth. If I didn't do that, I might do something rash, like toss a chair through the window. I'd never been angrier in my life.

While I continued to pace, Colby sat down with his head in his hands.

"I can't believe the nerve of that fucking woman," I spewed.

He looked up at me. "I'm not marrying her."

If only it were that simple, and that statement could have made her disappear.

"Except that she said if you did enter this sham marriage, she'd sign full rights over to you, Colby. That's something to at least consider, as hard as this is to stomach."

He gritted his teeth. "I can't fucking marry her."

"You'd rather have to deal with fighting her for custody?"

"Are you trying to convince me to give in to her?"

"I don't know." I pulled on my hair. "I don't know what I'm doing. I feel like I'm in the middle of a nightmare." I stopped pacing for a moment. "Look, I am the last person who wants you anywhere near that woman. The idea of it makes my skin crawl like you wouldn't believe. Which is why making her go away permanently is so enticing. A little pain for major gain—never having to worry about her threatening you again."

Colby's hands trembled. I ran over, grabbed them, and brought them to my mouth, showering them with kisses. I'd never seen him like this. I worried about his mental health in the weeks to come. No matter which direction we went, this wasn't going to be an easy road. "We're gonna figure this out," I whispered. "She said you have a week to decide, right?"

His voice was barely audible. "Yeah."

"Okay…" I lifted his chin. "Look at me, Colby. We're gonna decide this together, okay? We don't have to make any decisions now. There's no sense in overreacting until you've had a chance to speak to a family lawyer, right? Maybe there's something we don't know that will sway things one way or the other."

Colby just kept nodding. It was like he heard me, but nothing registered. I needed to step it up, be even stronger for both of us. Basically, I needed to put on a major act since I was feeling anything but strong right now.

I hopped up and clapped my hands together. "Okay! Here's what we're gonna do, Mr. Lennon."

He looked up.

"The two of us are going to go upstairs, relieve the nanny, hug Miss Saylor, and begin the process of decompressing from this horrible day. You're gonna spend time with your daughter, and I'm gonna handle dinner."

"You don't have to—"

"Shh…" I put my finger to his mouth. "Yes, I do. I want you to relax tonight, and then the three of us will have a nice dinner together. And after she goes to sleep, I'm gonna let you take me to your room and do whatever you want with me."

His eyes came to life for the first time. "I just had the worst day of my entire life, and you're telling me anal sex is gonna solve it?" His mouth curved into a smile. "You might just be right."

"That's my boy." I laughed. "That's the smile I love."

I knew nothing would solve this dilemma tonight, but if I could get him to smile for even a moment, I was doing my job.

I wasn't the best cook, but I didn't want to mess up this dinner. It was important to me that our meal be homecooked to offset the coldness of this day. There was something inherently comforting about a homecooked meal. So to be on the safe side, I opted for a simple dinner of spaghetti, salad, and grilled artichoke, a combination I often made for myself when I was having a night in alone and felt like comfort food.

I was standing at the counter, stirring the tomato sauce, and Saylor was coloring at the table when Colby came up behind me, wrapping his arms around my waist. "Thank you for this." He pressed his mouth to my ear. "There's something I want to say right now, but I don't want it to be marred by this day. I don't want today to be the first time I say it."

Chills ran through my body. *I love you, too, Colby.* I never realized how much until this shit happened.

He returned to the table to draw animals with his daughter. They had about five minutes before I would make them clear the crayons and paper so we could prepare for dinner.

After Colby helped me set the table, we all took our seats for a nice, peaceful pasta supper. Colby and I stared at Saylor a little more than usual as she slurped her noodles—as if that simple act was the most fascinating thing we'd ever seen. Soon her face was covered in tomato sauce. I caught his eyes glistening, and it broke my heart. Nothing could lessen the weight of my heart tonight.

Dinner was interrupted by a knock on the door.

My stomach sank. "Who's that?"

"I don't know. But I'm damn well checking the peephole this time," Colby said as he stood up.

Relief washed over me at the sight of the guys standing there. Jesus, it was like I had PTSD from last night. Would I ever hear a knock on his door and not be reminded of it?

"Holden told us," Owen said as he stepped inside.

He held a bag of chicken wings. I laughed a little—as if chicken wings could make this mess disappear.

"We can't talk about it right now," Colby said, nodding toward Saylor. "If you know what I mean."

"We'll talk in code," Holden said.

"How are you doing, Billie?" Brayden asked.

Shrugging, I sighed. "You know..."

"Yeah, I know," he muttered with a sympathetic look.

"I brought you some of your favorite beer," Holden said as he handed it to Colby.

"Thanks, man. I appreciate it." Colby took the beer to the fridge before returning to the table.

"And donuts for Saylor!" Brayden lifted a box that he'd been holding.

She jumped in her seat. "Yay! Donuts!"

Despite their best efforts to cheer us up, the mood still felt somber.

Holden pulled up a chair and cleared his throat. "So anyway, we really have to do something about the trash problem around here lately."

Brayden crossed his arms. "Yeah, we need to take out the trash."

I guessed the talking in code had commenced.

"We've decided not to talk tonight about whether we're taking the trash in or throwing it out," Colby said. "We're trying to let the dust settle a bit first."

Owen, who was still dressed in his work clothes per usual, chimed in. "Okay. But I just want to say this. Sometimes when you let the trash in, it really starts to stink. My opinion is not to let the trash in at all. To light a match to the garbage and fight it with everything you have. Let it burn. We also have some money left over for sanitation emergencies such as this."

"I hear you," Colby said. "And I appreciate that. I really do. But there's also risk in fighting garbage with fire." He took a long breath. "It can explode."

"That's very true." Holden nodded. "And I just want to put this out there. If you need any help seducing and manipulating said garbage, just say the word."

Brayden cackled. "You think you can solve every situation with your—"

"Smile!" Colby interrupted before glaring at him. "Brayden, careful with your language."

Brayden chuckled. "I was gonna say trash compactor."

Colby actually laughed, which was nice to see. He was lucky to have these guys in his life. As difficult as this was, it would be far worse if Colby had no support system.

"I love garbage trucks!" Saylor announced, clearly trying to figure out what her crazy uncles were talking about.

Holden poked her side. "You do?"

She twisted her fork around the last of her pasta and nodded. "Yup."

Colby looked over at her adoringly. "Saylor likes to watch the garbage trucks come and take the garbage away, don't you, sweetie?"

She nodded. "We can see it out the window!"

Owen feigned excitement. "That's so cool, Saylor. I remember liking to watch that too when I was your age."

Holden smacked the table. "Okay, no more trash talking. Let's pop open the beers."

The guys stuck around for a half hour before leaving together at the same time. I insisted on cleaning up while Colby took Saylor in for a bath. I could hear the sounds of splashing and giggling in the distance. Ah, the blissful ignorance of having no idea that your so-called mother was trying to destroy your father's life. I hoped Saylor never had to find out what was going on.

After they came out, I watched as Colby joined her on the floor with her Barbie dolls. He had the Ken in his hand and, per Saylor's request, was pretending to be Barbie's boss at the zoo. Her Barbie was a zookeeper from Mars.

At one point, Colby suddenly put the Ken doll down and pulled Saylor into a tight hug. This little girl had no idea how many different emotions must have been swirling around in her dad tonight. Frightening thoughts flooded my own mind. There were so many unanswered questions. Would Maya be able to take Saylor out of the country? That would absolutely kill him.

Colby closed his eyes, and I somehow knew he was saying a silent prayer. I said one of my own. It was more like a vow. *Billie, you're going to do whatever it takes to make sure this man never loses his daughter.* Whatever it takes.

It was a hard truth to swallow. Because in that moment, I knew I wasn't going to stand in his way if he had no choice but to marry that bitch, even if it killed me.

CHAPTER 19

Colby

Phillip Dikeman, my family law attorney, frowned and shook his head. "I wish you'd come in sooner, Colby."

"Maya just showed up four days ago, and this is the first appointment I could get to see you."

He tossed the petition she'd given me on his desk. "I meant before Saylor's mother waltzed back into your life."

"Why would I have come in before she reappeared?"

"Because we could have terminated her parental rights by abandonment. New York only requires six months of absence to file a claim for involuntary termination of rights."

I dragged a hand through my hair. "Fuck. I had no idea. When everything first went down, I met with my parents' attorney. He told me I should file and get legal custody right away, but I guess I kept expecting Saylor's mother to come back. When it eventually became clear that wasn't going to happen, our life just sort of fell into place. No one ever asked me to prove I had custody of my daughter, and I don't know… One day passed and then a week and suddenly my daughter was four."

Phillip smiled and pointed to a framed picture on a shelf behind his desk. "Tell me about it. Mine just went to the movies with a boy last night. I swear she was four just yesterday."

I shook my head. "How screwed am I?"

"I'm going to be straight with you. If she's able to prove everything that's in this petition, which I'm going to assume she can for a moment, there's a good chance the court will give her some visitation. It will be limited and supervised, at least at first. But any judge we get is going to weigh what's in the best interest of the child versus penalizing a parent for mistakes they've made. And barring a mother from seeing her daughter because she sought treatment for mental health issues—especially one who stayed away from the child out of fear she was not fit to parent—is not something a judge wants to do unless it's absolutely necessary."

"But it's all bullshit! She didn't keep away from Saylor because of any mental health issues! She admitted that to me. She kept away because she liked her life better without a kid. The only damn reason she came back is because *she* needs something. This has nothing to do with my daughter being better off with her mother in her life. Honestly, as much as I despise Maya, if she had come back with a true desire to see her daughter—really had some mental health issues and regretted leaving her the way she did—I'm not sure I would try to keep them apart. Saylor *deserves* a mother. But this woman—she doesn't deserve Saylor. She's doing this for the wrong reasons, and I need to do everything in my power to protect my daughter from that evil."

Phillip nodded. "I get it. I really do. And I'm absolutely on board with fighting this every step of the way. I don't want you to think I'm not, Colby. But the paperwork she's got here paints a different story than the one you're telling me. She has independent professionals swearing she suffered from a mental condition and has worked hard to get to a better place for the sake of her child. What do you have to prove your story is the one the judge should believe? Unfortunately, more often than not, it's what you can *prove* is true and not what is *actually* true."

I felt like throwing up. "So are you saying I should've recorded what Maya said to me? Unlike her, my mind doesn't work that way. The last thing I was thinking about when she knocked on my door was building a legal defense."

He shook his head. "Of course. And I'm not saying you needed to record her. In fact, even though New York is a one-party consent state—so only one person needs to consent to being recorded—it's still inadmissible in court unless we can find an exception. Not much is black or white in the law, unfortunately. I'm just laying things out the way a judge is going to see them. We can absolutely have you testify that Maya has an ulterior motive, but it may come down to our word against hers."

I dropped my head into my hands and yanked at my hair. "Jesus Christ. This is insane. What am I supposed to do? Marry her?"

"It wouldn't be ethical for me to advise you to enter into a sham marriage for the sole purpose of securing a green card. But since the subject of marriage has been raised, and immigration is not an area I'm too familiar with, I took the liberty of reaching out to an immigration attorney in this building. Adam's a friend of mine, and he'll give you a free consultation. At least that way, you'll have all the information you need to make an informed decision on how you'd like to proceed."

An hour and a half later, my head was spinning as I walked out of the second attorney's office. I wanted to run straight to the liquor store and drink until I couldn't think anymore, but my little girl was at my parents', and I knew Billie was anxious to hear how my appointment had gone, too. So I sucked it up and went to pick up my daughter.

"Hi. How did it go?" My mom opened the door looking almost as stressed as I felt. I probably shouldn't have filled her in on everything when I dropped off Saylor earlier today, but she'd taken one look at me and been convinced I was hiding a terminal disease.

I walked inside and looked around. "Is Saylor taking a nap?"

Mom shook her head. "Your father took her out to the park."

I nodded and pulled out a seat at the kitchen table, heaving a big sigh.

"I'm going to make us some tea," Mom said.

"Thanks."

A few minutes later, she set two mugs on the table and slid into the chair across from me. "Do you want to talk about it?"

I frowned. "I want to rewind time and make it stay four days ago forever."

"Not good news?"

I stared down into my tea. "I just can't believe this is happening. My choices are basically to take my chances in a custody fight or marry a woman I loathe and chance up to five years in prison if I get caught attempting to marry someone for the sole purpose of evading immigration laws."

My mother covered her heart with her hand. "Oh my."

"Tell me about it…"

"Does the attorney think you would have a good chance at winning full custody?"

I shook my head. "He thinks Maya will get some sort of visitation. Which means I'd have to explain who she is to Saylor and risk Maya disappearing again once she got what she really wanted out of things. I can't trust this woman with Saylor's heart, Mom."

"I never thought I'd tell my son to keep a mother from a child. But the reasons Maya has come back scare me, too. Any person who would use a child as a pawn to get what they want can't be trusted with our Saylor's well-being. I hate to say not to fight for what's right, but sometimes it doesn't matter who wins. The war itself does all the damage."

My eyes welled up. "I don't know what to do. But I can't risk Saylor getting hurt in all this."

My mother reached out and covered my hand with hers. "It sounds like you've already made a choice, son."

I closed my eyes.

"How long would you have to stay married?" she asked.

"I met with an immigration attorney, and he said the process averages about nine months from the time the application is made. We'd have to go through interviews and stuff, which is where the risk of getting caught comes in. But the attorney didn't seem too concerned with that since Maya and I have a four-year-old. I guess it helps to look like we've been together a while."

Mom nodded. "Well, at least it wouldn't interrupt your life for too long." She forced a smile. "I guess the bright side is that you're single, so there won't be a third party involved to get hurt."

Heaviness settled into my chest as I caught my mom's eye. "I met someone, Mom. I was going to tell you about her."

"Oh, Colby…"

"Her name is Billie, and she's absolutely amazing. We've been circling around things for a while because she wanted to be sure before she got involved with someone who has a child. But I really think she could be the one."

My mom smiled sadly. "I'm so happy to hear that. Though obviously the timing isn't ideal."

"Yeah…"

"What does Billie think about all of this?"

"I haven't spoken to her about what the attorneys said today yet. But since the moment Maya knocked on my door, Billie's priority seems to have been looking out for Saylor. Though I'm not sure she could handle things if I wind up marrying this psycho. I'm hoping to talk to her after Saylor goes to sleep tonight."

Mom and I were both quiet for a moment before she squeezed my hand. "It sounds like this Billie has her priorities right. Why don't you let Saylor stay over here tonight? We love having her, and I think you could use some time."

I nodded. "That would be great, Mom. I'll ask her when she and Dad get back, but I'm sure she'd love to spend the night."

An hour later, I headed home without my daughter. Saylor had jumped up and down with excitement when I'd mentioned sleeping at my parents'. It was probably for the best, seeing as my little girl was already an expert at reading her old man. Since I had the entire evening to myself, I decided to walk the mile and a half home to my apartment. It was a nice night, and I hoped the fresh air would help clear my head. On my way, I stopped at a florist and picked up a bouquet of wildflowers for Billie, then took a leap of faith and picked up some fresh ravioli and bread, thinking maybe I could make her dinner and get her to spend the night. By the time I arrived at Billie's Ink, I hadn't worked out any of my problems, but I did figure out what I needed for the next twelve hours—a quiet night at home with my girl.

Justine greeted me as I walked into the shop. She took one look at the big bouquet in my hands and smiled. "She's with a client. But any man who comes in looking like you do right now gets a free pass to the back." She tilted her head toward the door. "Go make my boss's day, cutie pie."

I smiled. "Thanks, Justine."

But my smile wilted damn fast when I got one look at what Billie was doing—tattooing some dude's *ass*. Though her face lit up when she saw me standing there.

"Hey, you." She took her foot from the pedal and lifted the needle from the guy's skin. "I didn't know you were stopping by."

Deek winked at me. "You didn't have to bring me flowers, big boy. I'm easy. Wine and lube is more my brand of romance."

I chuckled and lifted my chin. "What's up, Deek?"

The guy lying on his belly across Billie's hydraulic chair looked up at her. "Can we take a piss break?"

"Yeah, sure. Just give me a second to cover your cheek with some plastic so the area stays sterile."

When she was done, she told the guy not to pull up his underwear in the back. So I watched some man's hairy ass walk to the bathroom with three quarters of a rose tattooed on it. Well, the left cheek was hairy, anyway. The right had been shaved.

Billie snapped off her gloves and sauntered over. "Are those for me?"

I leaned down and brushed my lips with hers. "There're only two women in my life, and the other one prefers I bring unicorn-shaped bath bombs that shit glitter when they get wet."

Billie grinned. "Shit glitter? I didn't know that was a choice. I think you might be returning these beautiful flowers."

I wrapped one arm around her back and pulled her close. "Will you have dinner with me?"

"That depends. What are you feeding me?"

"That's a very loaded question..." I smiled and lifted the bag in my other hand. "But I'll be good. How does fresh ravioli and semolina bread sound?"

"Mmmm...that sounds yummy."

I brushed a lock of hair from her face. "My parents are keeping Saylor for the night. I was hoping maybe you could stay over."

"I think that could be arranged..." Her client walked back from the bathroom, so she lowered her voice. "You want to step outside for a minute to talk about how things went at the lawyer's office?"

I shook my head. "Let's put off talking about that until morning. Maybe we spend the night pretending it never happened since it's so rare that I get a whole night alone. I don't want to waste a minute of it doing anything but focusing on you."

Billie smiled. "That sounds amazing."

"Great. What time are you done here?"

"Tex is my last customer. I should be done in about forty-five minutes."

I looked over her shoulder. Tex was positioning himself ass up on her chair once again. "By the way, why does he get a rose tattooed on his ass, yet you wouldn't put one on my chest when I asked you?"

"Because I don't have to look at his ass all the time."

"I asked you to ink a rose on me the first time we met. You didn't know you were going to be looking at my bare chest all the time back then, either."

Billie tilted her head with a devilish grin. "Are you sure about that?"

"Good answer." I grinned. "You go finish up and enjoy that ass. But get yours upstairs as soon as you're done."

She pushed to her toes and gave me a quick peck on the lips. "Yes, sir."

I pulled out all the stops to set tonight's mood. By the time Billie knocked, I had two burners going, bread warming in the oven, soft music playing, and the table set with lit candles.

When I opened the door, she held out the flowers I'd given her down at the shop. "I brought you these."

I smirked. "How thoughtful of you."

Billie chuckled. "I didn't want to leave them downstairs since I'm off tomorrow. Do you have a vase? I realized on the way up here that you might not. It's usually men who are giving flowers, not getting."

"I think I do. My mom sends me flowers for Father's Day."

"Awww... That's so sweet."

I took the bouquet from Billie's hands, set it on the kitchen counter, and wrapped her in my arms. "Thank you for giving me this."

"The flowers? I'll let you in on a little secret... I sort of got them for free." She smiled.

"I meant the night off from everything going on. The way I was feeling this afternoon, I didn't think I'd be able to change my mood. But the idea of spending a night alone with you made it easier than I thought."

Billie's face softened. "I'm glad I can help."

I rubbed my nose with hers. "You do. A lot."

I poured us each a glass of wine, and Billie sat on the counter next to the stove while I finished cooking. "I brought us a game in case your mood needed some cheering up."

"Oh yeah? What kind of game?"

She pointed to her purse on the chair. "Grab my bag, and I'll show you."

Billie dug out an oversized deck of cards from her purse and held them up, showing me the name on the front of the package.

I arched a brow. "Sex Trivia?"

"I bought them at that little bodega down the block that sells bongs and dirty magazines. They're behind the counter at eye level, and I've been curious about them for a while."

I grinned. "You shop in that place? I've only ever seen the stuff they sell from the outside."

She gave me a look. "Don't be so judgy. They have the best coffee, and it's only a buck."

I took the cards from her hand. "I'll have to check it out. We have a little time before dinner is ready. What do you say we wager on this trivia game?"

"You haven't even seen the first question yet, and you want to bet you're going to win?"

I shrugged. "If I lose, I'll eat you out for dessert. If you lose, I'll eat you for an appetizer."

"Umm… That sounds like I win even if I lose."

"Do we have a deal?"

Billie smirked. "I'm never one to turn down a wager."

I smiled. "That's my girl."

The first card out of the pack was an interesting one. I cleared my throat and read it aloud. "What position is the most likely to bring a woman to orgasm? A. Doggy style, B. Missionary, C. Reverse cowgirl, or D. Woman on top?"

Billie's lips twisted as she thought about it. "Hmm… I'm going to go with D. Woman on top, because the woman has more control then."

"Control, huh? Is that what you like?"

She nodded. "It usually is. But I really like it when you get all bossy. I think my trust issues have kept me from being able to enjoy giving a man control."

I looked back and forth between her eyes. "That means a lot to me."

"So what's the correct answer?"

"You called it. Woman on top is the position that can most commonly bring women to orgasm." I grinned. "Also, I can't wait to have you ride me."

Billie chuckled and plucked the card pack from my hands. "I believe the score is one to zero. Let's see what we have here." She scanned the next card. "A woman would rather A. Clean the house, B. Eat dinner, C. Play a trivia game, or D. Get fucked on the kitchen counter next to a pot of boiling ravioli."

My brows pulled together for a half second before I caught on. Then I yanked the card from her hands and tossed it over my shoulder. "I'm gonna go with D."

Billie wrapped her arms around my neck. "Solid guess. I like D."

"That's good, sweetheart. Because that's exactly what you're about to get."

The ravioli would have to wait. I shut off the water that was just starting to boil and lifted Billie up onto the countertop, wrapping her legs around my waist. This was the first time we'd had free rein to do whatever we wanted in this apartment for an entire night, and I was here for it.

"I'm gonna have you for dinner first, okay?" I murmured.

Billie nodded as she lifted my shirt and I worked to undo the ties of her corset. Her beautiful, milky mounds popped out simultaneously, and I wasted no time taking her nipple into my mouth. I sucked so hard that she winced. Billie dug her long nails into my back before sliding her hands upward and pulling on my hair.

Hard as a rock, I couldn't wait another second to be inside of her. I undid her jeans, and she wriggled out of them before kicking them to the floor. I unbuckled my belt and lowered my pants just enough to take my dick out. I couldn't even wait the amount of time it would have taken to fully remove my pants. That's how much I needed her right now.

Letting out an unintelligible sound, I buried myself inside of her. Her pussy felt like pure ecstasy. Billie's muscles tightened around my cock as I thrust hard into her. I continued to hold her up as she bucked her hips. I must have been damn wound up today because it was as if I couldn't fuck her hard enough. Billie didn't seem to mind as she writhed under me, matching the rhythm of my thrusts.

She'd never felt tighter, wetter, or more ready for me. We'd both been under an incredible amount of stress this week, and this was just what the doctor ordered. We were so into it, that it took a moment to realize I'd never stopped to put a condom on. Billie had mentioned that she'd gone on the pill recently, but I needed to double-check that she was ready for this.

"Is this okay?" I asked. "I don't have anything on."

"Yes," she panted. "I'm good."

I groaned. "I didn't think it could feel any better with you, but holy shit."

"I know. I've never had sex without a condom."

I stopped moving inside her for a moment. "Are you serious?" She nodded.

"Wait…" I blinked. "I'm gonna be the first guy to come inside you?"

She bit her lip and nodded again.

"Damn. You have no idea what that does to me." I pushed inside again.

She yanked on my hair. "Don't stop again, please."

"Yes, ma'am." I pumped harder.

You could hear the slick sounds of our wetness as I moved in and out. When I felt her muscles contract, I couldn't wait a second longer. I grunted, burying myself deep as I came. She continued to tighten around me as her head bent back, and her voice echoed throughout the kitchen as she orgasmed. I kept moving in and out until there was nothing left, then stayed inside her for a while as her ass rested against the counter.

She panted. "We'd better clean this countertop."

"Never mind the countertop, but I should go get you a towel. I kind of like the idea of my cum inside you, though."

She spoke into my skin. "We can arrange for a refill later."

"I love the sound of that." I reached over to pull a towel from the drawer, gently placing it under her as I showered her neck with kisses.

"I have an idea," I said.

"What?"

"You go take a relaxing bath. I'll finish making dinner. Then we'll take it into my room and eat naked in bed. How does that sound?"

"That sounds like the perfect night."

Rather than rush to the bathroom, Billie lingered, her arms still wrapped around my neck as she gazed into my eyes. I realized that there had been few moments in my life as special as this one: standing here half-naked in the kitchen with this beautiful woman I'd just made love to, who trusted me to come inside of her beautiful body.

This might have not been a classically romantic moment, but it felt like the right time to tell her. "I'm falling for you, Billie."

My heart was in my mouth as she stared at me for several seconds. *What if she doesn't feel the same? Or what if she's afraid to love me given everything that's going on lately?*

She finally said, "You're not alone, Colby. I just didn't want to be the first to express what I've been feeling. I think I've been hesitant because I'm afraid if I fall, you might not be there to catch me. Which is dumb, I know. I've let my past experiences interfere with what's going on between us. I should've told you before you went to have breakfast with that witch because that was the day it really hit me how much my feelings had grown. I knew because the thought of you hurting made me physically ill. Anyway, I'm sorry to bring all that up right now. I know we're supposed to be forgetting about it for one night."

I pulled her into a kiss and whispered over her mouth, "I'll be here to catch you always, Billie."

"I believe you, Colby."

I refrained from saying the other thing I wanted to: *I wish it were you who needed me to marry you.*

CHAPTER 20

Billie

Last night was raw in every sense of the word—the way we'd had sex, the way we'd expressed our feelings for each other. And now that I'd opened my eyes, I felt the rawness of our present reality creeping back in.

The morning was bittersweet. Colby filled me in on his meeting with the attorney and all of the new insecurities and regrets that had resulted from it. The attorney felt Maya's case was stronger than we'd hoped. That upset me, but I had to remain strong for Colby. He still hadn't made a decision on what to do yet.

Our talk about the Maya situation was the bad part of the morning. The good part was that we'd spent the entire time prior to that conversation having amazing sex.

Colby asked me to go to his parents' with him to pick up Saylor. I planned to return to my apartment after that.

When we arrived at his parents' house, his mom seemed to know exactly who I was.

"You must be Billie."

I looked at Colby, then back at her. "I am."

"It's wonderful to meet you."

"Likewise."

"She's quite beautiful. You're a lucky guy, Colby," Mrs. Lennon said to her son.

He squeezed my side. "Don't I know it."

Saylor came running toward us. "Billie!"

I knelt down to receive her hug. "Hey! Did you have a good time?"

She nodded eagerly.

"Would you guys like to stay for a bit?" Colby's mom asked. "I made some of that split-pea soup you like, Colby. Saylor already had some, so she probably won't be hungry for a while."

Colby looked at me. "I think we'd better get Saylor home and out of your hair. But thank you for the offer."

I smiled. "Maybe another time, Mrs. Lennon. That soup sounds great."

"Please, call me Yvonne."

Outside on the sidewalk, Colby held Saylor's hand as he asked, "Do you have to be somewhere?"

"I figured I'd head home. I'll let you have some catch-up time with Saylor."

"Are you kidding?" He pulled me toward him. "I'm not ready to let you go."

"Oh really?" I grinned.

"Yeah. Will you stay with us?"

Honestly, how many more uncomplicated days did we have? There was no way I could say no. With no clients booked today, I'd only be home ruminating about Colby. So I might as well just stay with him. "There's nothing I'd rather do than stay with you guys."

"Cool." He looked down at Saylor. "This one needs peanut butter, and I have to get cold cuts for the week. Mind if we stop at the market? I can pick up something for us for dinner, too."

"Lead the way." I smiled.

When we got to the market, Colby went one direction to get the things he needed, while us girls took off in another direction.

We were having fun just browsing. I put Saylor in the cart and might have raced down a couple of the aisles. I also might have snuck some Cap'n Crunch, Pop-Tarts, and Goldfish into the cart. You can't take me to the market, apparently. I'm an unsupervised kid with an adult budget.

We ended up in the bakery aisle—of course, because I was in charge—so I could spoil Saylor with a cookie. There was a bit of a line. At one point, the woman next to me looked down at Saylor and said, "She's adorable. Such a pretty little girl."

"Thank you." I smiled.

I realized the woman had very likely assumed Saylor was my daughter. And I'd essentially taken credit for Saylor's beauty. I took a few seconds to marinate in that feeling. In this stranger's eyes, I was a mother. Saylor was my daughter, safe with me. Life was simple. And I truly wished that were the case, that we could go home tonight and sleep soundly without a worry in the world. An overwhelming feeling of longing came over me.

The moment was interrupted when we finally reached the front of the line.

"What can I get you?" the attendant asked.

I let Saylor choose what she wanted. She pointed to the last giant chocolate chip cookie left in the display case.

"We'll take the gargantuan cookie," I said.

It had to have been at least six inches in diameter. After the woman wrapped it in tissue paper and handed it to Saylor, the toddler behind us suddenly started crying.

Saylor's joyous expression faded as she looked over at the girl.

"Is she okay?" I asked the girl's mother.

"I'm sorry. Unfortunately, she's not. She had been waiting for that cookie. She always gets it when we come here, which thankfully isn't all that often. She calls it 'big cookie'. It's the reason we came to the market today. I'd promised her if she tolerated her haircut, I'd get it for her."

Aw, damn. I turned to Saylor. "Sweetie, do you think you might be able to share half of your cookie with this little girl? She's sad because we got the last one."

To my surprise, Saylor handed over the entire cookie. "Here you go. Don't cry."

My heart clenched, not just because of how cute that was, but because Saylor's eyes were also watering. What a little empath. An amazing human.

"That's very nice of you," the woman said. "But you should take half."

Saylor shook her head. "She can have it."

"Wow. Thank you," she said. She smiled over at me. "That's some kid you have there."

"I know," I said without hesitation.

She turned to her daughter. "Say thank you, Elena."

"Thank you!" The sniffling girl grinned, her cheeks still wet with tears.

Saylor waved goodbye, and the girl waved back.

After they left, we got back in line to get Saylor a cupcake. I kept thinking about how sweet she was to insist on giving the girl not half, but her entire cookie. Saylor's generosity was a testament to her kind spirit, and certainly a result of having a father who raised her right because he set his own good example. Colby, too, was the kind of man who would give the shirt off his back to a stranger. He'd also go to the ends of the Earth for the people he loved.

We got to the front of the line again, and I ordered Saylor's new treat.

Saylor took a giant bite of the cupcake and got pink frosting all over her nose. I couldn't get enough of her cuteness.

I knew my attachment to Saylor was in direct correlation to my falling in love with her father. After all, Saylor was an extension of Colby. I truly cared for them both.

And then my handsome man appeared, wheeling a cart filled to the top. So much for coming to grab a few things. "There you are." He grinned. "I thought I'd lost you."

"Never." I winked.

He kissed me on the cheek and looked down at my cart. "Some nice healthy choices there."

"Well, my boyfriend is due to make me some spinach brownies so I can eat better." I wrapped my arm around his waist. "Wait until I tell you what your little sweetie pie did."

I recounted the cookie story for Colby as we walked to the checkout line. He was very proud of his daughter.

We returned to Colby's apartment and hung out together until dinnertime. Even though we ended up enjoying the fajitas he prepared, the mood had definitely darkened. My feeling from earlier that reality was seeping in felt stronger than ever. Colby, in particular, looked lost in thought as we finished our meal.

I offered to give Saylor a bath while he cleaned up.

When Saylor went to her room afterward to play for a bit before bedtime, I found Colby in the kitchen and wrapped my arms around him from the back. "Talk to me. I can tell you're drowning in your head tonight."

He leaned both of his arms against the counter and exhaled. After a few seconds of silence, he finally turned to look at me.

"What if she gets deported and can somehow take Saylor out of the country with her? I'd die, Billie."

"That's not gonna happen," I assured him, though I'd found myself worrying about the same thing lately. There were many possible catastrophic scenarios.

"How do you know that's not gonna happen?" he asked.

"Okay, I don't. I don't really know anything. But I will pray that doesn't ever happen. And I have faith that good will prevail in the end."

Colby stared off. "I had a nightmare about it last night. I woke up in the middle of the night sweating. You were asleep. I was glad you didn't see me like that. But I guess you're seeing me freaking out about it now anyway."

I wrapped my hands around his face. "You have every right to freak out, and don't ever feel like you have to hide anything from me. I'll take the good, the bad, and the ugly."

Saylor ran into the room, interrupting our conversation.

"Billie, can we have a story before bed?"

I looked at the clock. Her bedtime was 8:30, and neither of us had realized it was 9 PM already.

"Of course," I said.

"No book!" she insisted.

"No book again? I'm not that creative, Saylor."

"No book!" She giggled.

"Okay, no book." I lifted her up and tickled her. "Let's go."

I looked back at Colby who had a smile on his face, despite the lingering fear in his eyes.

Saylor cuddled next to me in her bed. I loved her room at night with the lights off. She had glow-in-the-dark decals on the ceiling that lit up in purple. It was a relaxing place to hang. I had no idea what story to tell her, so I started with a simple sentence. "Once upon a time, there was a beautiful little bird." Then I just started making shit up as I went along. "The little bird lived safely in a nest atop a tree with her family."

Saylor's eyes were like saucers as she looked up at me, eager for the next line. She was so stinking cute.

"One day, a big hawk came and tried to take the baby bird away."

Jesus. Art imitating life anyone? Apparently, I had a one-track mind.

"Why?" she asked.

Because she's an opportunistic bitch. "Because the hawk wanted the nest. She was using the baby bird as a way to get the bird family to give their home to her, even though she had no right to it."

"That's so mean."

"I know. But the story has a happy ending." *I just don't know how they get there yet.*

"What happened?" she asked.

"Well, the hawk took the baby bird, but when she came back to try to get the nest, the big birds got together and flapped their wings so hard and fast that it scared the hawk. The hawk realized she couldn't bully the birds. So the hawk gave the baby bird back and left."

"He never came back?"

"She. The hawk was a girl." *Of course, she was.* "But no, she never came back, and they all lived happily ever after."

Saylor yawned and rested her head against me. She was asleep within minutes. That was how riveting my boring story had been.

I decided to stay here for a while and just look at her while she slept. It occurred to me that right now I was the only female in her life besides Colby's mom and sister. That gave me a sense of responsibility. It felt like my job to protect her, even if that meant protecting her from her own mother.

The impending doom of what I knew had to happen overwhelmed me. A sudden rush of nausea hit, and I removed myself from the bed as swiftly as I could without waking her.

I headed straight for the bathroom and leaned over the toilet, trying not to throw up. I focused on the tattoo of my grandmother's key on my arm, silently praying to her for strength right now. But a few seconds later, I succumbed to the sick feeling in my stomach, vomiting into the bowl. *Well, this day is certainly full of surprises.* I could hear Colby's footsteps coming down the hall.

"Are you okay?" he said, looking panicked and grabbing my hair to hold it back.

I nodded, praying that was the end of it. I didn't want to puke again in front of him. Because what's more attractive than that?

"I think it was one and done," I said, panting into the toilet.

I knew this was the physical manifestation of everything that had been building up inside me today. The love. The fear. The dread. Ultimately, it was the conclusion I'd drawn that had forced the vomit. Because it was literally sickening.

I turned to him and vocalized it. "You need to do it. You need to marry Maya and get it over with. The sooner you do, the sooner we can be done with this."

♥CHAPTER 21

Colby

"So tomorrow is the big day, right?" Holden twisted the cap off a beer and slid it across his kitchen table to me. "You have to give Maya your decision?"

I frowned. "Don't remind me."

"You know what you're going to do?"

Over the last week, I'd flip-flopped a half dozen times. The problem was, my head thought one thing was right, and my heart had a different idea. I sighed. "I'm pretty sure I'm going to change my mind twenty times between now and eight AM tomorrow."

Holden nodded. "I get it. I can't even decide which sneakers to put on most days, much less the shit you're dealing with. What does Billie think of all this?"

"She's been pretty damn amazing. Not sure I would be as supportive as she's been if the shoe were on the other foot and she was considering marrying some other dude. But Billie's been adamant that she thinks I should marry Maya."

Holden eyebrows jumped. "Really?"

"She doesn't want me to put Saylor at risk in any way. She said neither of our feelings matter, only protecting my little girl."

"Wow."

I drank some of the beer in front of me. "I know. She's the most amazing woman I've ever met. You wanna know something fucked up?"

Holden smirked. "Fucked up is my middle name, my friend."

"Last night I had a dream that Billie was pregnant with our baby. She was like six months along and had this big, round belly, and I couldn't keep my damn hands off of her."

My buddy smiled. "Have you told her you're in love with her yet?"

I shook my head. "Not in so many words. To be honest, I sort of chickened out and told her I was falling for her instead of already *in love* with her."

"How come?"

I shrugged. "It doesn't feel fair to lay that on her with everything going on. I don't want to make it harder for her to walk away if that's what she needs to do."

"You've been talking, but have you listened to what you've said the last few minutes? You're both putting each other first, over your own happiness. She'd rather you marry some other broad to protect Saylor, and you don't want to tell her you love her so it makes it easier for her to dump your ass. Do you really think not saying the words makes them any less true for either of you?"

I ran my finger over the condensation on the beer bottle's label. "I guess not. But it feels selfish to put that on her right now."

Holden caught my eyes. "I've been there. But you know what *failing to speak your truth* gets you?"

"What?"

"A night of watching the girl you're crazy about hold hands with her fiancé years later. Which in turn makes you get shitfaced drunk and go home with a random woman who yells out the wrong name when she orgasms and then hands you your pants ten minutes later as she tells you she needs to get up early the next morning."

My brows drew together. "You saw Lala?"

Holden nodded. "Played a gig in Philly the other night. She came in with her fiancé, Dr. Douchebag."

"What did he do that makes him a douchebag?"

My friend looked me square in the eyes. "He was holding Lala's hand."

It was the first time Holden had spoken about Lala—what we called Ryan's little sister Laney—since the week after Ryan's funeral, when he'd gotten drunk and admitted to me that he'd had feelings for her for a very long time. I'd suspected as much, but I'd kept my mouth shut because it was none of my business. Besides, Lala could handle herself. She was smarter than all of us boneheads put together.

"How is she?"

"All grown up…" Holden looked away for a moment. "My point is, if you think she's the one, tell her. Don't beat around the bush or feel guilty for the way you feel. Take it from me, there's a reason love and lose are only one letter apart. It's so damn easy to miss the boat and wind up with the wrong one."

Damn. And here I'd thought his crush on Lala had long passed. Holden was the last person I would've thought could give insightful advice on love, yet he'd gotten his point across loud and clear. I nodded. "Thanks, buddy. You're right. I'm going to nut up and make sure Billie knows I'm more than falling for her."

He nodded. "So how does it work if you marry Maya? Do you move in with her and shit?"

"No fucking way. It would be a piece of paper only. I wouldn't have any contact with her at all other than the interview required for immigration. I've been reading up. My lawyer had said the process usually takes about nine months, but I've also read that sometimes shit slows down, and it can take a few years. The only possible way I could do it is if I could forget Maya exists during that time. I wouldn't even want to know where she lives."

"Not to make things more complicated, but what happens if Billie gets pregnant during that time? Something unplanned pops up? Could you get out of the sham marriage if you needed to? Like, get a quickie divorce or an annulment? I mean, shit like that happens every day in real life, right? Is there an escape clause of any sort?"

I dragged a hand through my hair. "I have no damn idea. But the lawyer I met with said sometimes cases can be fast tracked when someone is in jeopardy of being deported and has a child who's a US citizen. He said we could request that, but there's no guarantee."

"Would Saylor meet her?"

"Definitely not. Maya only came back into our lives to use her as a bargaining chip. This isn't a woman who realized she'd made a big mistake and truly wants to get to know her daughter. I see nothing but hurt if Saylor got to know her as her biological mother—or in any capacity, for that matter."

"Will you put her on your health insurance at work and tell people and stuff? What about if, God forbid, something happens to you? Does that mean Maya gets custody? And do you have a will? I had an uncle who was married for six months. His wife was cheating on him for their entire short-lived marriage, but he dropped dead of a heart attack before they were legally divorced, and she got his house and stuff. Is there a way around that, just in case?"

I blew out two cheeks full of hot air and shook my head. "You're making my damn head spin, Holden."

"Sorry, man. I'm just trying to help."

I nodded. "I know you are, buddy. And I appreciate that more than you know. If I do decide to go through with it, I'm going to have to sit with my attorney and ask all those questions before anything happens, to make sure Saylor and I are adequately protected. Right now, though, I just need to not talk about it anymore."

"No problem. Why don't we talk about my favorite subject…" Holden grinned and sipped his beer. "*Me.*"

I chuckled. "That sounds perfect. Tell me what's going on with you lately. Aside from seeing Lala and her fiancé. I'm sure you've amassed at least a dozen new stories you can amuse me with since we last spoke."

Holden guzzled the rest of his beer. "Well, I did almost get a Prince Albert the other day."

My brows shot up. "You were going to get your dick pierced?"

"Not on purpose. But it almost happened accidentally."

I shook my head with a smile. This was exactly what I needed right now—Holden's crazy life. "I'll bite. How exactly do you *almost accidentally* pierce your dick?"

Holden wagged his finger at me. "That's a very good question. But before I explain, let me preface by saying that I sort of went on a tear after seeing Lala and Dr. Douchebag. I know now that I was trying to fill a void by spending too much time talking to women on Tinder, so I don't need a lecture. Plus, I already got one from Owen when I told him this story. Anyway, I found this one woman who made it clear she was looking for a good time and nothing more. We met at a bar and had one drink, and then she suggested we take an Uber somewhere so she could go down on me in the backseat. She was into the driver watching through the rearview mirror as he drove."

I shook my head. "Only you, my friend."

"She was really cute, too. Redhead with a tatted arm—sort of a Billie vibe." He winked. "Probably why I was into her."

"Don't even joke, buddy."

He laughed. "Just teasing. Her name was Ryland, and she had one of those small, hoop nose rings. We get into the Uber, and she wastes no time dropping her head into my lap. After, I suggested we go back to her place, so I could return the favor—you know, because I'm a gentleman and all. But she tells me it's that time of the month and suggests we meet up next week at a different bar. She wants me to go down on her in the ladies' room while she's sitting on the sink without the door locked."

"Is she an exhibitionist or something?"

Holden shrugged. "I think so, but I'm game. Whatever floats your boat as long as no one gets hurt in the process, right? Anyway, we call it a night, and I take the train back to the bar where we'd met. It was a nice day, so I'd ridden my motorcycle and needed to pick it up. But when I hopped on, the damn battery was dead. I had to push seven-hundred pounds to a hill so I could roll it down an incline and jump on to bump start it. When I did that, I felt a sharp pinch at the base of my dick. It hurt like a motherfucker and wouldn't let up. I actually had to turn the bike off and go back into the bar to use the men's room to see what the hell was going on. Turns out, my redheaded exhibitionist lost her little hoop nose ring while blowing me. The thing was damn sharp, and it somehow wound up in my underwear. It had pierced the skin at the base of my dick. Hence, an almost accidental Prince Albert."

"Jesus Christ, you're a train wreck." I laughed my ass off. "But thanks, man. I really needed that."

"Anytime. I'm here for whatever I can give."

The following morning, I still had no idea what I was going to do as I walked to the coffee shop to meet Maya. The sight of her as I opened the door physically repulsed me—my stomach lurched into my throat and I tasted bile. I hated that this woman had anything to do with my sweet, innocent daughter.

She smiled as I took the seat across from her. "I ordered you coffee and breakfast. If I recall correctly, you made me pancakes the morning after we spent the night together, so I figured that was a safe choice."

If only eyes could *actually* shoot daggers. "I'm not hungry."

Maya sighed and folded her hands on the table. "Fine. I was trying to be friendly. Why don't we just cut to the chase then, shall we? Are we getting married or not?"

Fuck. I don't want to make this decision.

Yet she sat with zero emotion on her face, waiting for an answer.

I couldn't help myself. Leaning forward, I glared at her. "How the hell can you do this? Use your own child? Were you abused as a kid? Tortured? Neglected by your own parents so badly that you no longer have a basic respect for humanity? Molested? There's got to be a fucking reason."

She looked down at her watch like I was boring her. "Is that a yes or a no?"

Nothing I said or did knocked this woman off her game. She had a one-track mind, and that scared the living shit out of me. It meant she would stop at nothing to get what she needed, regardless of who got hurt. I closed my eyes and prayed for strength before opening them again.

"I want everything filed by my attorney, not yours. I don't trust anyone associated with you. I'm only marrying you so you can stay in this country and will leave my daughter alone. After it's done, don't contact me. I'm pretending this sham of a marriage never happened."

"Fine. What's your attorney's name?"

"Adam Altman," I said through gritted teeth.

Maya reached to the back of her chair and dug into her purse, pulling out a cell phone. She typed for a minute and then looked up. "On Fifty-Third?"

I nodded.

She clicked around a few more times before lifting her cell to her ear. Her eyes never left my face as she spoke. "Hello, I'd like to make an appointment with Mr. Altman, please."

She was quiet for a moment, then... "Yes, a rather urgent immigration issue. Would he have anything available right away? Tomorrow, perhaps? I know it's a Saturday, but we really need to speak to someone as soon as possible."

Quiet again. She covered the phone and leaned forward. "Tomorrow at three PM?"

"Fine."

I vaguely paid attention as she spoke for the next few minutes, giving both our names and other information to make the appointment. When she hung up, she looked pleased with herself. "All set. I'll meet you there."

"Can't wait," I grumbled.

"So tell me, how is Marisol doing? Is she healthy and thriving?" Maya shook her head. "I mean Saylor? That's what you call her now, correct?"

"Do you even really give a shit?"

"Of course. She was named after my grandmother, you know."

"Oh yeah? Did your grandmother raise your mother?"

Maya's forehead wrinkled. "Yes."

"Well, I'm glad her original name was from a good mother and not you, at least." I pushed away from the table and stood. "By the way, she's Saylor because you left without even telling me her name. I had to call her something. I'll be there tomorrow at three."

Maya showed up the next afternoon with her attorney. Xavier Hess was as crooked as his client.

"I have someone on the inside at the local immigration office," he said. "I'll get the case pulled and fast tracked as soon as the paperwork is filed."

My attorney shook his head. "I don't want any part of anything illegal."

"Nothing illegal about having friends. Don't tell me you've never schmoozed a judge's clerk to get your case called first because you had a packed day?"

"As long as that's all it is."

"How long will it take if we get it fast tracked?" I asked.

"Probably only a few months," Xavier said.

"Good. I'd like to be divorced by year's end."

My attorney frowned. "Colby, you're going to have to keep those kinds of comments to yourself. I can't represent you if I believe your marriage to Maya is a sham."

For the first time since the evil witch walked back into my life, Maya looked a little nervous. She reached into my lap and took my hand. "It's not a sham marriage. Colby just has a dark sense of humor, *right, sweetheart?*"

I yanked my hand away.

My attorney looked between us before speaking. "You'll need to know each other very well. The interview process is not always simple. They sometimes ask invasive questions that a husband and wife should know about each other."

My brows pulled together. "Like what?"

"Anything they want. How quickly did you have sex for the first time? How many siblings do you each have? What was the proposal like? Your answers need to be in sync, or you'll be referred for a fraud interview. Like I told you the other day, the penalty for attempting to defraud the government by marrying someone for immigration status is up to five years in prison and a two-hundred-and-fifty-thousand-dollar fine."

Maya's attorney spoke up. "Let's not get ahead of ourselves. These two have a four-year-old child together. This isn't a mail-order-bride situation."

I was about to say it was worse, I was being *fucking blackmailed*. But I stopped myself, knowing my attorney had some scruples. Instead, I swallowed the information. Besides, we hadn't done anything illegal yet anyway, so there was still time for me to pull out. After another half hour, I told my attorney I'd be in touch *if and when* we wanted to file an application for citizenship. But I still had a few questions about things I could do to protect myself before entering into a marriage, and I didn't want to ask those in front of Maya. So I told her and her attorney I needed a few minutes alone with my lawyer. Maya said she'd wait outside for me.

I really wished she would have just left—today had been draining enough—but of course she didn't. She and the shyster attorney were waiting outside on the street when I walked out of the building.

"Are we all set?" she asked.

"I don't know if we could even pull this off. We don't know anything about each other. How the hell can we pass an interview with intrusive questions like my attorney mentioned?"

"There are businesses that will prep you," Xavier said. "I'll give Maya a few numbers she can call."

"Prep you? What does that mean?"

"Immigration interview preparation services. They maintain a database of commonly asked interview questions. You both answer them and swap answers, so you can memorize how you'll need to respond. A few are even pretty high-tech these days and can be done right online."

I frowned and shook my head. "People make a living off helping other people defraud the government. *Great.* God bless America."

"Think of it as test prep, Colby," Xavier said. "When you want to be a lawyer, you take a Kaplan review course and study practice questions from previous bar exams. It doesn't mean you still can't fail, but the more you practice, the more likely it is that you'll be well prepared and there won't be any surprises."

The entire thing was gross, but what choice did I have? I shook my head. "Whatever. Fine."

Maya's shoulders relaxed. "Okay, good. Now that we have things squared away, why don't we meet Monday morning?"

"For what?"

"To get our marriage license, of course. Then we can have the ceremony Tuesday."

❤CHAPTER 22

Billie

Tick-tock. Tick-tock.

I checked my phone for the hundredth time on Tuesday morning. Apparently, I was counting down the minutes until the hour of doom.

Colby's sham ceremony was scheduled for just before 4 PM this afternoon. Five hours left until my boyfriend would marry someone else. I knew it wasn't as simple as that—it wasn't a "real" wedding—but it still hurt like a motherfucker. As much as I hated that it had come to this, I was happy he'd decided to bite the bullet. This meant one step closer to the nightmare being over.

Saylor.

Saylor.

Saylor.

This is all for Saylor, I reminded myself.

I kept trying to dive into work today because I had no choice. But my brain and hands just couldn't communicate with one another. I'd had one other bad workday like this—right after Maya showed up. But today took the cake. And to make matters worse, I was fully booked, so I'd have multiple opportunities to fuck something up.

Deek had been watching me crash and burn all morning: dropping tools, forgetting where things were, asking a client to repeat the details of the ink they wanted more than once. The only thing I hadn't done was screw up a design. That was one thing I'd *never* done, and I didn't want to start today.

After my second client left, Deek went to the front of the shop, changed the sign on the door from open to closed, and pulled down the shades on the windows.

"What the hell are you doing?"

"I'm shutting us down for the day," he explained.

"Why?"

"You're not in your right mind. I've got Justine calling all of the remaining clients to reschedule."

I looked over at Justine, who had the phone to her ear. She waved at me. This felt like an ambush.

"Clients are counting on me." I looked around frantically. "You can't just make that call to close down. This is my shop!"

"What are you gonna do? Fire me?" He laughed as he walked over to the door. "Come on, butterfingers. Let's get out of here."

After a few seconds of standing in a huff with my arms crossed, I conceded and grabbed my purse. I waved to Justine, who still had the phone to her ear. "You'll lock up?" I asked her.

She nodded and gave me a thumbs up.

"Where are we going?" I asked Deek.

"Anywhere and everywhere, my friend. I am going to occupy every second of this day so you're not suffering, thinking about you know what. We are going to make the time pass in the least painful ways possible."

We headed out the door together, and I followed Deek down the sidewalks of New York, secretly relieved that he'd absolved me of the struggle to remain professional today.

For our first stop, Deek led me into a candy store, of all places—the kind where you grab a bag and fill it to your heart's content.

"Why are we going here?" I asked.

He shrugged. "Because I'm making this up as I go along? You once told me that when you were younger, you'd fill up one of these bags and go to town when you were sad about something. I thought it'd be nostalgic. Plus, I had a hankering for some chocolate."

I'd never been one to turn down candy. I grabbed a bag and went after all of my favorites—Sour Patch Kids, Skittles, gummy worms, and SweeTARTS. Deek filled his mostly with chocolate.

Ten minutes of picking out junk had definitely managed to take my mind off things, until I got to one of the last bins.

The sign atop the Jordan Almonds read: *Perfect for wedding favors!* Suddenly all of my thoughts about the impending ceremony came flooding back.

Deek must have noticed me frozen in front of the white almonds. "Aw, shit," he said behind me.

"Perfect day for a wedding, isn't it, Deek?" I rolled my eyes.

"Those candy-coated almonds suck. Nearly broke my tooth on one when I was a kid." He dragged me by the arm. "Come on. Let's check out."

After he paid for our candy, we once again roamed the streets.

"Where are we going now?" I asked, chewing on a blue-and-red gummy worm.

"If I tell you, you're gonna nix it. So just go with the flow."

He hailed a cab and directed the driver to take us to Times Square. The next thing I knew, we were in front of Madame Tussauds. My jaw dropped. "You're taking me to the wax museum?"

"You said you'd never been."

"That's true. But there's a reason for that. I have no interest."

"Come on. It'll be fun," he said, helping me out of the cab.

Honestly? He was right. Deek and I had a blast posing for pictures with the wax figures and chatting them up. We discussed politics with Barack Obama and let Britney Spears know how relieved we were for the end of her conservatorship. We inserted ourselves as additional members of the British royal family and the Kardashians. I blended in pretty well with the latter. With my long, black hair, I was like the long-lost tattooed sister. We also danced with Beyoncé—that had to be my favorite part.

The fun ended, however, when we came upon a display featuring The Beatles. There was nothing wrong with it per se, aside from the fact that John Lennon made me think of Colby Lennon, which sent me down the rabbit hole. *Ugh.*

My eyes were fixed on John when Deek came up behind me. "What's going on in that head of yours, Yoko?"

I continued to stare at the figure. "You know Colby's last name is Lennon, right? After today it's going to be Maya's last name, too."

"For fuck's sake." Deek sighed. "Another change of pace needed, stat! Let's get the hell outta here and find something to eat."

We left Madame Tussauds and hit Katz's Deli for my favorite pastrami sandwich. Then we hopped on the subway and went to Central Park to have our lunch on a bench. We'd just finished eating when I spotted a couple approaching. She wore a wedding gown and held up the bottom of her veil so it didn't drag on the ground. They were about to say their vows in the middle of the park. Then a horse and carriage appeared, waiting to whisk them away after.

When Deek saw them, he hung his head in defeat. The poor guy had tried like hell to distract me, and the universe dealt him quite a blow.

"Someone up there just doesn't want me to forget, Deek."

"First of all, look at her dress. It's horrendous. And not a tat on her. Boring as hell." He sighed and stood up. "Okay, you know what? I was thinking we could get through this day without alcohol, but doesn't look like that's going to be the case. Let's find a bar."

"It's five o'clock somewhere." I hopped up from the bench. "Lead the way."

We went back out to the street, and Deek searched down the block for the nearest bar. Once he found it, we headed inside, took a corner seat, and settled in to spend the afternoon.

I was already on my second beer when my phone rang. *Colby.* It was nearly 3 PM, which meant "it" hadn't happened yet. I picked up and tried to sound cheery. "Hey."

He, on the other hand, sounded out of breath. "Where are you? I'm at the shop, and it's closed."

Oh no. "Crap, really? I'm at a bar with Deek."

"Why?"

I didn't want to lie. "Okay…I might have had some trouble focusing this morning. And Deek made the executive decision to close down after the first couple of clients today. We've been wandering around the city."

"Which bar are you at?"

I didn't even know. "What's the name of this place?" I asked Deek.

"Sammie's."

"Sammie's. It's somewhere near the Park."

"Shit. That's far. I needed to see you and figured maybe you'd have time for a quick visit if I stopped by before I had to head to the courthouse."

I felt terrible. "That wasn't the plan, Colby. You said you were going there straight from work. I wish I'd known."

"I know." He sighed. "I just…needed to make sure you were okay. I didn't feel like I could go through with this if you weren't. And admittedly, I wanted to see you. I just…" His words trailed off. "I don't know. I'm not okay right now."

My chest constricted. "I'm not really okay, either. But that doesn't matter. Because you marrying her will never feel okay. Feeling okay is not what it's about. Nothing is going to make it feel okay for either of us, you know? We just have to accept that."

"I don't have to go through with it," he said in an urgent tone.

"Yes, you do." I sighed deeply. "You know you do."

There was a long pause where all I could hear was his breathing. I wished I didn't have alcohol in me because it made me more emotional than I wanted to be at this moment. Tears stung my eyes.

"Let me talk to Deek," he finally said.

I handed the phone to my friend. "Colby wants to talk to you."

"Yo," Deek said as he took the call. He listened, and then he nodded. "Yeah. No worries." He paused. "Take care of yourself, man. I've got it covered." Deek handed the phone back to me.

"Hey," I said.

"I'm sorry I didn't get to see you," Colby said. "But I'm glad you're with Deek."

"It's probably better that we missed each other. Seeing me would bring out all the emotions. You shouldn't be emotional going into this. It's a business transaction."

"Of the worst kind, yeah. Pretty sure I'd rather be meeting with the mafia right now."

I looked at the time. He had less than an hour. "You'd better go. The courthouse is on the other side of town. You don't want to be late."

"Yes, I *do* want to be late. I'd like to get married to her at a half past never."

I put on my big-girl panties for a moment. "Colby, it'll be okay. You got this." Exhaling, I said, "Call me when it's over, okay?"

"Okay."

Then I hung up before he could say anything else. I could tell he wasn't going to be the first to hang up. I immediately regretted ending the call, but I couldn't bear it if he'd said something that made me cry. I didn't want to turn into a blubbering mess in this bar. That wouldn't have been good for him or me.

"What did he say to you?" I asked Deek.

"He thanked me for looking out for you today. That's all. He's really worried about you."

I ran my finger along the condensation on the beer bottle and became lost in my thoughts. A few minutes later, I looked up and noticed someone waving as he walked toward us. It was…Owen?

"Fancy meeting you here." He grinned.

He was dressed in a navy three-piece suit. His shiny watch gleamed. Everything was on point.

"What are you doing here?" I asked.

He clasped hands with Deek. "This bar is not far from my office. Figured I'd come for a little happy hour."

I narrowed my eyes. "Really…"

Owen sat down with us and signaled for the waitress before ordering a beer. "What's new with you guys?" he asked.

"Nothing much. Just trying to forget the fact that Colby is getting married in the next hour." I took a long sip.

Owen played dumb. "Oh, is that today?"

"Come on, Owen. You knew it was today."

His expression darkened. "Yeah, I did. He just texted me to come by and check on you. He knew Deek was with you, but I think Colby wanted some representation from his side to make sure you were okay. If he couldn't be here, I was the next best thing."

"Well…thank you. But that's totally unnecessary," I said.

"Anything I can do to make this day easier for Colby, I'm gonna do it."

"This is a rarity, though. You left the office before four PM?" I teased.

"I honestly couldn't tell you the last time I left work early."

A little while later, Brayden walked toward our table in the corner with a big smile on his face.

"Not you, too?" I said.

"What?" He shrugged. "I'm just here for a drink." He winked and looked over at Deek. "'Sup, man?" Then Brayden gave me a look like he felt sorry for me. "How are you doing?"

"Jesus Christ. Nobody died," I shouted. "Why is everyone acting like someone died?"

Brayden patted my shoulder. "If you're okay, then we're okay."

"I heard there was a party!" another voice yelled.

Holden. I shook my head and laughed. "I should've known this was going to be a trifecta."

Holden bent to kiss my cheek. "Hey, Billie. Looking amazing as always." He nodded toward Deek. "Hey, man. I saw your Instagram. What the hell were you guys doing with the Kardashians today?"

"You're not serious, are you?" Deek cackled.

Holden winked as he sat down. "So what are we drinkin'?"

I lifted my bottle. "Beer."

"Sounds good to me." He grabbed a menu. "Let me see what they have on tap." Holden lifted his hand to flag down the server.

"How is it that all three of you have the time to babysit me today?"

"It's simple," Holden said. "When one of us needs something, we drop everything. And there's nothing more important to Colby today than making sure you're okay. So of course, I had to come look out for you. I'm his best friend."

Brayden and Owen whipped their heads toward Holden at the same time.

"Who the fuck crowned *you* Colby's best friend?" Owen snapped.

"Yeah." Brayden agreed. "Who died and made you the best friend?"

"Who died? Uh, Ryan, dumbass," Holden answered.

The table went quiet.

Then Holden pointed at them. "Anyway, did you offer to marry Maya last night so Colby didn't have to?"

"No," Brayden squinted.

Holden flashed a smug grin. "That's right. You didn't. Cuz you're not the *best friend*. I am. A best friend would have offered to marry her."

I blinked. "Wait… Come again, Holden? What did you do?"

"That's what all the chicks say to me." He winked. "*Come* again."

"Seriously, Holden," Deek interjected. "You offered to marry Maya?"

Holden took a long swig of his beer and shrugged. "Yeah. I mean…I went to Colby's late last night and offered to do the deed so he wouldn't have to, so she would leave him alone. I was dead serious. I would've absolutely married her."

"That was really sweet of you, Holden, but totally nuts," I said. "Nuts only because I know it was more than just an offer. You would have gone through with it."

"That's right. Why is that so crazy? I don't have a girlfriend like Colby does. No skin off my back. Nobody's gonna be hurt. But he thought it would be too complicated because of Saylor and the attorneys and stuff. Wish I had thought of it sooner. I was totally willing to pretend to be in love with the bitch just to get her out of his hair. There's nothing I wouldn't do for that guy. If there's one thing Ryan's death taught me, it's that your true friends are the most important thing in your life. Even more important than family sometimes, depending on who your family is."

Deek placed his hand on my shoulder. "Don't I know it. This chick is my lifeline. When times are tough, I know I can count on her. And her on me. That's why I've been dragging her ass around the city today to try to get her mind off shit." He lifted his finger. "I didn't, however, agree to marry Maya. So, Holden, you're a better man than I am."

Everyone laughed.

I was one lucky girl to have all these guys by my side today.

"Billie, are you ready to laugh your ass off?" Owen asked.

"Sure. Lay it on me."

He looked over at Holden. "Have you ever heard of someone accidentally getting a Prince Albert?"

Owen then proceeded with a dramatic retelling of Holden's crazy story of the blowjob that nearly gave him a cock piercing. They actually managed to make me laugh. But at a certain point, my attention drifted away as they continued to joke around. Everything at our table faded into the background once I glanced over at the clock.

Quarter to 4 PM. Colby was marrying Maya at this very moment, or close to it. At that point, I totally zoned out.

Then my phone chimed. It was a simple message. But a profound one.

Colby: I love you.

My heart broke. Because I just knew. He'd texted me that because it was about to happen. *And he loved me.*

❤CHAPTER 23

Colby

"**H**ow many of those have you had?"

I tossed the tiny tequila bottle into the hallway trash can and reached into my pocket for another. "Apparently not enough, because I can still make out your face."

Maya scowled. "You act like it's the end of the world marrying a beautiful woman. Many men would be thanking their lucky stars to marry me."

I scoffed and twisted off the cap to the tequila. "First off, beauty comes from the inside, so you're as ugly as they come. And second, if so many men would be lucky to marry you, why aren't you here with one of them?"

Maya looked around. "Lower your voice. And you know the answer to that. Because a marriage that occurs right when the government is trying to deport you is questionable. It's more believable if I've been with someone for a few years, and we have a child together."

"*We* don't have a child. A child is someone you put first in your life, someone you love and protect. *I* have a child. You have a fucking chess piece."

She rolled her eyes. "Whatever. But you need to slow down on the drinking, because if the officiant thinks you're drunk, he might deem you to not have the capacity to marry."

I snorted. "The capacity to marry… When did you go to law school?"

"Just because I was a stripper doesn't mean I'm not educated."

"My judgment of you has nothing to do with your profession, sweetheart. It has everything to do with your actions. Only a dumb bitch would take off on her kid with no warning. *Newsflash: I'm an adult who doesn't shun my responsibilities.* I would've taken her if you were struggling, and we could have worked something out for you to visit once in a while."

For the first time since she walked back into my life, Maya's face fell. At that moment, a man opened the door we were sitting outside of.

"Lennon and Moreno!" he yelled.

I chugged the tequila in one gulp and held my hand up. "Is it our time to go before the firing squad?"

"He's joking," Maya said. She turned and flashed me a warning glare. "*Right, honey?*"

The guy didn't look like he gave two shits one way or the other. He looked right, then left, and spoke in a monotone voice. "Where's your witness?"

"Witness?" Maya said. "I thought you supplied them."

He shook his head. "That's not how it works. It's clearly printed in the brochure you receive when you come in to apply for your marriage license. No witness, no wedding."

"Ummm… Can you just give me one minute?" Maya asked.

"That's about all I can give you. You're the last ceremony of the day, and they cut our budget again, so no more overtime. We close at four sharp; that's why the last appointment is three forty-five."

"I'll just be one minute. I promise."

The man shrugged and went back into the clerk's office.

I cackled. "Guess you didn't think of everything."

Maya narrowed her eyes. "Wait here and *don't drink anything else.*"

I responded by taking yet another bottle of tequila from inside my jacket pocket and twisting the cap with a smile.

Maya shook her head before storming off.

She came strolling back down the hall three minutes later with a guy who looked like he might be homeless. He didn't even have shoes on. "Let's go," she said. "Frank is our witness."

I reached into my pocket and offered Frank a mini bottle of tequila. "Want one?"

He snatched it out of my hand and looked at Maya. "You're still paying me the hundred bucks."

I wobbled a little. "You might want to get it from her now. She can't be trusted."

Maya glared, but Frank was smart enough to heed my warning. He held out his hand, palm up. "Give me the hundred or I'm leaving."

She dug into her purse. "You better have the ID you say you have."

A few minutes later, our lovely threesome was standing in the clerk's office. I'd expected we were going in to sign some papers before going into some sort of courtroom, but apparently a New York City *courthouse* wedding didn't actually happen in court. The clerk didn't even come out from behind the counter.

"Would you like to join hands?" he asked.

Maya went to take my hands, but I yanked them from her grip. "Is that necessary?"

The clerk frowned. "No, it's not."

I shoved my hands into my pants pockets. "Then let's get this over with."

The clerk looked between us. "Is there a problem?"

The alcohol had started to hit me, and that always brought out my sense of humor. At least, I thought so. I shrugged. "Nah, my religion just prohibits me from touching her before we're married." I snort-laughed again. "Too bad it doesn't prohibit sleeping with strippers, huh, Father?"

"Umm…I'm not a priest. I'm a city employee, a clerk of the court."

"I was wondering why you didn't have one of those collars on. Those things are probably hot as balls in the summer, huh? Like wearing a turtleneck."

Maya's eyes drilled into me. "Why don't we let the man do his job and marry us?" She plastered on a pageant-worthy smile and looked at the clerk. "He tells jokes when he's nervous. I'm sorry."

The clerk shrugged and went on with the ceremony. A whopping seven minutes later, he said, "Congratulations, you are now husband and wife. You may kiss the bride."

A wave of nausea hit me, and I actually had to cover my mouth. "I don't feel so good. Can we leave now?"

Maya offered the clerk an apologetic smile. "Bad sushi for lunch."

The guy couldn't care less. He just wanted us out of here before four. He stamped a bunch of papers and pointed to lines for each of us to sign before offering us a certificate. "Good luck. I think you might need it."

I made it as far as the garbage can in the hall outside the clerk's office before everything really did come up. I wasn't sure if it was what I'd had to drink, or what I'd just done to my life. But my new bride didn't seem to give a fuck.

She put her hands on her hips while my face was still hovering over the top of the garbage. "This behavior isn't going to fly with the investigator, Colby. You'd better learn to act like I'm your loving wife."

I spit the bad taste in my mouth into the garbage. "De Niro isn't good enough to pull off that shit."

Maya shook her head. "I'll be in touch about prepping for the interview soon."

I lifted my head. "Go fuck yourself."

"What can I get you?" The bartender put a napkin out in front of me.

"Tequila."

"A shot or a drink?"

"Both."

"Any particular type of tequila?"

"Whatever."

The guy shrugged. "Coming right up."

A few minutes later, he came back and set down a shot glass, a whiskey glass filled with ice, some limes, and a can of Coke. He poured Don Julio from a bottle with a tapered spout. "This stuff is a little more expensive, but you'll appreciate it the next day. I also brought you a choice of chasers. I don't suggest chasing tequila with tequila."

"Thanks."

I knocked back the tequila shot and made a face that probably looked like I'd just sucked on a lemon.

The bartender snickered. "I thought so."

"What?"

"This isn't a regular thing for you, is it?"

"Definitely not."

He leaned an elbow on the bar. "You want to talk about it?"

I looked him over. He was probably in his early sixties, wearing a tucked-in plaid shirt and a pair of jeans with a towel slung over his shoulder. "You married?"

He held up three fingers. "Third time's a charm."

It hit me for the first time that if I married Billie, she wouldn't be my first wife. She'd always be number two, and she didn't deserve anything but being a one and only.

I lifted the glass of tequila and sipped. "What happened to the first two?"

"I've been sober for six years. Can't really tell you what went wrong the first couple times because I don't remember most of those years. But I'm guessing it had something to do with me being a raging alcoholic. I'm not a happy drunk."

"You're in recovery and you work at a bar?"

"Own it. Not much else I know how to do except run a bar." I nodded.

The bartender held out his hand. "Name's Stan Fumey. Nice to meet you."

"Colby Lennon." I shook.

"So what's your story?" Stan asked. "Wife giving you a hard time so you're in here trying to forget she exists?"

"Something like that…"

"How long you been married?"

"What time is it now?"

Stan looked over his shoulder at a Budweiser clock on the wall. "It's just about five o'clock."

I nodded. "About an hour then."

His brows pulled together. "You're shittin' me."

I sipped more tequila. "Wish I was. Got married at four o'clock."

"Where's your bride?"

"Getting run over by a bus, hopefully."

The bartender chuckled. "I have two words of advice for you."

"What's that?"

"*Walter Potter*."

My forehead wrinkled.

Stan took a few steps away and grabbed something from next to the cash register. Then he tossed a business card toward me.

I squinted to read it.

Walter Potter

Attorney at Law

Divorce Specialist

"He's good and cheap. Maybe he can get you one of those annulments or something."

I shook my head. "I wish it were that easy."

Stan studied me for a minute. "You get the girl pregnant or something?"

I finished off my glass of tequila and shrugged. "Yeah, I guess I did."

"That's tough. When is she due?"

"Four years ago."

Stan's entire face wrinkled. "Sounds complicated."

"It is."

"Well, you already know I'm no expert on marriage, so I can't give you any advice on making that work. But I can tell you one thing—sometimes staying together for the kids is more damaging than the effect of a separation. I give you credit for trying to make a go of it. But never forget that kids learn by watching, not by you telling them how to act. So if you haven't already, start living by example."

As if I didn't already feel like shit. The last thing I'd want is for my daughter to get herself into a predicament like this. I was sure Stan meant well, but he wasn't helping. So I pushed my glass forward. "Think I can get a refill?"

He nodded. "Sure thing."

A few hours later, I was so shitfaced that my new buddy Stan cut off my alcohol supply. I tossed whatever bills I had left in my pocket on the bar and grumbled that I was going somewhere else before staggering out. But when I hit the street and attempted to walk, I wasn't so sure I could keep upright without some assistance. So I held one hand against the brick on the outside of the bar and skooched along the street, leaning my weight one step at a time. It probably took me ten minutes to go all of four buildings and get to the corner, only to realize I was fucked because I wouldn't have a building to lean against while I crossed. Rather than get run over by a cab, I thought maybe I should sit down for a few minutes, which is exactly what I did. I slid my back down the last building on the block and sat on the disgusting New York City street.

Just as I got comfortable, my phone buzzed in my pants pocket. But my inebriated state kept me from being coordinated enough to dig it out before I'd missed the call. Reading the name of the missed caller, the nausea I'd experienced earlier today came flooding back. *Billie.* I fucking hated what I'd dumped in her lap. Nevertheless, I didn't want her to worry, so I hit the button to call her back.

"Hey." She sighed. "How are you?"

"I'm *gucking freight.*" No, wait…that's not right. "I mean I'm gucking freight."

"Oh boy. You don't sound like you're doing too well. Or should I say not *wooing dell.*" She paused. "So…I guess it happened?"

"You mean, did I sell my soul to the devil?" I frowned. "Yeah, I did."

Billie was quiet for a few moments. "It's going to be okay, Colby."

Her voice was so tender that tears streamed down my face. "It's not going to be okay. You know why? Because you don't deserve this shit."

"Neither do you, Colby. Neither do you." The line went silent again, until I heard her sniffle.

Fuck. "Please don't cry. I can't fucking take hurting you like this."

"I'm sorry. I should be the least of your worries right now."

"Can I see you?" I asked. "Saylor is staying at my parents' house tonight."

"I don't think that's a good idea, Colby. Not tonight anyway. But maybe tomorrow? I just know I'd be even more emotional if I were to see you right now, and you need a good night's sleep."

Heaviness weighed inside my chest. "Okay."

"Where are you?"

"Not far from the courthouse. I went straight to the nearest bar."

"Will you do something for me?"

"Anything…"

"Will you go home now? Don't drink anymore. Get in an Uber and get some sleep."

I nodded. "Yeah, I can do that."

"Thank you." She paused. "I'm going to go now, but everything is going to be okay. We'll get through this, Colby."

I wasn't sure how, but I knew she meant well. "Goodnight, sweetheart."

After I hung up, I did exactly what she asked. I pulled up the Uber app and ordered a ride home. At least I thought I did… Until a voice woke me sometime later.

"Colby?"

I blinked my eyes open. "Billie? You're here…"

"Of course I'm here. Why wouldn't I be at my apartment at three in the morning?"

Her apartment? I glanced around. I was lying on the floor in a hallway, so I pushed up onto one elbow. "How long have I been sleeping?"

"I don't know. I was sleeping myself and had no idea you were out here. My neighbor works late. She called to ask if the man outside my door belonged to me or if I wanted her to call the cops."

I raked a hand through my hair. "*Fuck.* I'm sorry. I thought I went home." I shook my head and tried to remember how I got here, but everything was fuzzy. "I remember being in an Uber and shutting my eyes. But after that, I'm drawing a blank."

She held out a hand to help me up. "Come on. Come inside."

I took it and climbed up from the floor, following her in.

Billie shut the door behind us and started texting. "I just need to tell Amber everything is fine so she doesn't actually call the cops."

I nodded and waited until she set her cell on the counter. "What time did you call me earlier?" I asked.

"It was about nine o'clock, I guess."

"Shit. I guess I was out there for a while. Sorry." I thumbed toward the door. "Do you want me to go?"

Billie shook her head and held out her hand. "Why don't you come to bed with me?"

I nodded and followed her into the bedroom. Normally, I wouldn't think twice about undressing, at least down to my boxer briefs, but it felt wrong to do more than take off my shoes before getting under the covers. The room was dark, but there was a window open, and the streetlights illuminated enough for me to see once my eyes adjusted. I rolled onto my side, and Billie did the same.

"Are you okay?" she whispered.

A giant lump formed in my throat. It felt like if I spoke, it might move and then all the feelings stuck behind it would rush to the surface. So I shook my head.

"Oh, Colby. I'm so sorry you're going through this."

I couldn't believe *she* was trying to console *me*. It should've been the other way around. Instead, it was yet another testament to the fact that I'd fallen for the kindest, most beautiful soul on the planet. I tried to swallow, but it was no use. I couldn't hold back anymore. Tears streamed down my face as I took her cheeks into my hands. "I am so fucking in love with you that it hurts, Billie. I hate that I'm causing you pain. And I hate that I just told you I loved you for the first time today, when this day has been so ugly.

I wanted it to be a day you could look back on, filled with nothing but good memories."

Matching tears formed in Billie's eyes. "It's three thirty AM, Colby. Yesterday was filled with bad memories, but we still have time to fill today with good ones. Let's not look back anymore and just move forward and choose to be happy, because I love you, too."

I shook my head. "I have no idea what I did to deserve you."

She smiled. "That's how I know this is real. Because true love is when you *both* feel like you've found someone you don't deserve."

♥CHAPTER 24

Billie

One early morning a few weeks later, when Colby was still sleeping, I lay in bed next to him, thinking how lucky we were that things had been quiet lately.

How was any peace possible, given the sham wedding? Well, Maya had disappeared from sight for a while. And that was a blessing.

Knock on wood.

Several times.

I didn't want to jinx this. But I hoped she stayed away as long as possible.

We'd had nearly three weeks of this ignorant bliss. It was almost possible to pretend the nightmare had never happened. Almost. I'd had a dream the other night that she'd walked in on Colby and me having sex, demanding that I get off her "husband." I'd woken up in a cold sweat. That was one of several dreams I'd had about her. In another, she'd told Saylor she was her mother, and Saylor burst into tears. In the dream, I couldn't tell if they were happy tears or sad ones, and I woke up before I figured it out. So while Maya remained out of sight for the time being, I wished I could say she was totally out of mind, too. I'd take out of sight over nothing, though.

Until this whole thing was over, there would be a dark cloud hanging over us. And I knew the current reprieve could end at any moment, since Colby would be scrutinized soon by the immigration people. But their lag in action was our gain. And I wasn't going to take a second of this break for granted.

It was 6 AM when I felt Colby rubbing my back. I rolled over to meet his handsome face.

"I want you before we have to get up," he said groggily.

I swear, this man got horny in his sleep. He couldn't have been awake more than two seconds before he'd decided he wanted sex. And even though I wasn't totally awake yet, I was *always* up for sex with him. Lately he'd been more insatiable than ever. Ever since I'd started spending a few nights a week at his place, the situation had gotten more intense. We always made sure we got up before Saylor did, though, so she'd find us in the kitchen instead of the bedroom. She always seemed happy to see me, and so far, nothing awkward or damaging had happened during my sleepovers. She appeared to want me here just as much as I did.

Earlier this week, Colby had spent several hours in his room fixing his squeaky bed to make it quieter. Dude took the assignment very seriously. He wouldn't let up until the bed no longer made any sound when pressure was applied to the mattress—all because he didn't want me making excuses for why we couldn't have sex in his bed. The noise factor had been one of the reasons I'd been hesitant to start spending the night at his apartment in the first place. Operation Kill Squeak involved replacing his mattress with one made of quieter memory foam that didn't bounce. He also tightened a bunch of bolts on the bedframe. Needless to say, we'd tested it multiple times, and it was a *banging* success.

I curled into him. "What did you have in mind this morning?"

"I was thinking you could ride me. You know…if you felt so inclined."

"I'm inclined to think you'd take me any way I'd give it to you right now."

"Your inclination would be correct." He smiled mischievously.

"But you're in luck because I'm really in the mood to ride you. I'm no starfish, Lennon. You know that."

"No. You're like a fucking shark, and I love it." He winked.

"A shark and sometimes a blowfish." I shrugged.

Colby laughed as I lifted myself up. My long hair covered my breasts as I straddled him, and when I sank onto his beautifully rigid cock, his eyes momentarily closed. I loved being on top, especially because it gave me such a clear view of his gorgeous face.

"Damn, did you wake up wet like this?" he rasped. "You're so fucking ready."

"I'm always ready for you." I dug my nails into his chest and swayed my hips as I rode him. His eyes bore into mine in a way that made me feel like nothing else existed for him right now. I was sure I looked at him the same way.

He squeezed my ass. "Jesus, woman. You ride me so good."

I thrust my hips harder and faster, at times lifting myself off of him before bearing down hard. Colby took my breasts in his hands, massaging my nipples with his thumbs.

"Damn it!" His eyes closed as his body shook. "Sorry...fuck, I'm coming. You're too good. Couldn't hold it in, baby."

He was lucky I'd been holding back my own orgasm, or I would've had to give him shit about blowing his load before I went. I let go as my muscles contracted around him and he came inside of me. I loved feeling the heat of his cum.

After we settled down, I lifted myself off and lay down to face him.

"That was damn incredible." He panted. "I can't get enough of you."

I looked over at the clock. "We'd better get up soon."

"Okay. Five more minutes." He pulled me close, nuzzling his nose in my neck. "I have to meet with some contractors today to talk about renovations on the building's roof, which means I can't take Saylor to her Mommy class this morning. She's gonna be sad."

"I can take her." I offered without even having to think about it.

"You sure? Don't you have clients today?"

I massaged his hair. "Only one early appointment. I've been trying to book my Saturdays a bit lighter. I know this client, though. I bet he'd be okay with Deek doing the job. Deek's worked on him before."

"Are you sure? I don't want to put you out."

"I'm absolutely positive. I've actually been curious about this Mommy class. I think it'll be fun."

"Saylor will be super excited that you're taking her."

I smiled. "I hope so."

Mommy class was held in a brownstone on the Upper West Side.

As expected, Saylor was thrilled to have me accompany her. But you know who *didn't* seem too thrilled? The Mommies, AKA The Stepford Wives—they all looked the same in their pastel clothing and perfectly coiffed blond hair. Not a tattoo in sight. Deek would get a kick out of this. He'd definitely deem them all untrustworthy and lame.

Based on the strange looks I got when I walked in there with Saylor, they didn't appreciate a new face joining their little club. Either that or they were sorely disappointed that they wouldn't get to flirt with my boyfriend today. Colby had once told me how many of these women, some of them married, hit on him. I couldn't blame them, but I still wanted to punch them all.

"Oh, you must be Saylor's new nanny?" some bitch asked.

Nanny? No, she didn't. "No," I said.

Not that there was anything wrong with being a nanny. But she'd found it inconceivable that I could be anything more because I didn't look prim and proper like the rest of them.

She tilted her head. "Oh. Sorry. I just assumed…"

I wanted to follow my "no" with an explanation that I was Colby's girlfriend, but I concluded that I didn't owe her any explanation. It was kind of fun to just enjoy her confusion.

They'd set up tables where the girls were supposed to get their faces painted by the moms. I was relieved, because this kind of thing was my jam. Colby had mentioned that you never really knew what activity was planned. Sometimes it was a tea party, other times they all walked to the playground together. But messing with paints I could handle.

"We're gonna paint!" I told Saylor. "This reminds me of the time we turned you into a tiger. Remember?"

She nodded eagerly before running over to join some of her little friends in a corner. I had to admit, despite the fact that the women all annoyed me right off the bat, every single one of their spawn was absolutely adorable.

One of the women appeared next to me. "I'm Lara," she said.

Looking out toward the kids, I nodded once. "Billie."

"Where's Colby today?" she asked.

That's all she has to say to me? "He had some business to attend to."

She finally asked the question she really wanted to. "I heard you say you're not the nanny. What is your relation to Saylor, if you don't mind me asking?"

At that moment, Saylor came running toward me. I pulled gently on one of her pigtails. "Who am I to you, Saylor?"

"You're Billie!"

"I know, but besides my name. Who do you think I am?"

She bounced a couple of times. "You're the girl my daddy loves. You're his Princess Jasmine!"

Lara's mouth fell open slightly, and I loved it.

"Where did you get that idea?" I asked Saylor.

"Daddy told me."

Wow. While Colby had definitely become more affectionate with me in front of her, I hadn't realized he'd told her he loved me. "When did he tell you that?"

"We were watching *Aladdin*. He told me he loves you like Aladdin loves Princess Jasmine."

"Well, isn't that *lovely*?" Lara chimed in.

I hadn't even remembered Lara was standing there. The way she'd said *lovely* made me think she was taunting me, though. I squinted. "You serious?"

She blinked in confusion.

While I couldn't help calling her out, I left it at that, reminding myself that Saylor was next to me. But I wanted to tell that fake-ass bitch where she could put her *lovely*.

Once everyone sat down to do the face painting, I assumed that Saylor would want an animal on her face like last time. Instead, she had a different request.

"I wanna paint my arm like yours, Billie."

"Really?"

She nodded.

Gosh, that was sweet.

So I gave Saylor her very own sleeve, painting lots of colorful animals and other designs on her arm. The paint didn't exactly look like ink, but her arm was covered just the same. The best part, though? All the dirty looks these women gave me for trying to make her more like me. I'm sure they all thought that was a terrible mistake.

But she *wanted* to be like me. And I considered that a huge compliment, so they could all go fuck themselves.

The entire way home, I couldn't wait to tell Colby all about my experience with the Momsters. I'd probably keep what Saylor admitted to me about *Aladdin* to myself, though. That was a private moment between them, even if it had involved me. So I'd just keep it close to my heart.

Saylor and I went back to the apartment, and when I knocked on the door, I almost wondered if Colby wasn't home since it took a bit longer than usual for him to answer.

When the door finally opened, it wasn't Colby in front of me. It was…*everyone*. Literally everyone—well, everyone who meant anything to us. Deek and his boyfriend, Martin. Justine and her husband. And of course, Holden, Brayden, and Owen.

"Surprise!" they all yelled.

Then I turned to my left and saw my beautiful man handing me a gigantic black balloon with gold speckles.

"Happy birthday, beautiful."

"Yay! A party!" Saylor squealed.

"What the…" My hands shook. "My birthday isn't until Monday."

"I know. But I wanted to surprise you on the weekend when everyone could make it."

When he wrapped his arms around me, I felt enveloped by love. "I can't believe you managed to surprise me. This was the entire reason you wanted me to take Saylor to Mommy class?"

"Guilty."

Saylor jumped up and down. "Happy birthday, Billie!"

"Thank you, sweetie. Did you know about this?"

She shook her head no.

"I kept Saylor in the dark," he said. "I don't think she would've been able to hold it in. She would've been too excited."

Saylor held out her arm. "Daddy, look!"

"She requested that specifically," I felt compelled to say.

"That's awesome, honey. You look just like Billie now."

"I know!"

I handed her my balloon so she could play with it and made my way around the room to hug everyone. After, I looked around at all their smiling faces. "This was an awesome surprise. Thank you all for being here."

"Are you kidding? We wouldn't have missed it for the world," Justine gushed.

Colby had ordered a huge array of my favorite sushi. It was all laid out on the table in a gigantic wooden boat. We all sat down to an amazing lunch. After the meal, Holden insisted we do tequila shots, with each person toasting in honor of me first.

He began as he lifted his glass. "To Billie, the best tattoo artist in the land."

Then Brayden spoke. "To Billie, the woman who makes my best bud here happy."

"To Billie, for indirectly getting me to leave work early two times now." Owen smiled.

Deek was next. "To Billie, the person I can truly count on. You make my world a better place."

"To Billie, for putting up with Deek's shit half the time, so I don't have to," Martin teased.

Justine then lifted her glass and said, "To Billie, someone who will always tell it like it is."

"What about you, Saylor?" Colby said, handing his daughter a plastic cup of lemonade. "Can you say something nice about Billie?"

She turned a little red, looking bashful, then finally said, "Billie is my best friend."

Everyone collectively *aww*ed.

I walked over to give her a big hug. "Thank you, sweetie. That means so much to me."

"Your turn, Colby." Deek smiled.

Colby lifted his tequila. "To Billie…" After a pause, he looked into my eyes and said, "The love of my life."

Short.

Sweet.

Everything.

We kissed, and I'd never felt more cherished.

A few minutes later, when I blew the candles out on my cake, Justine told me to make a wish. I had only one wish this year—to be rid of Maya. I'd somehow managed not to think about her the entire day, until now. When I looked up, Colby's expression fell a little. It was as though he'd guessed my deepest wish. It was likely the same one he had.

After I finished my slice of cake, I went to throw out my paper plate, and Deek followed me into the kitchen. "Hey, I just wanted to see how you're doing," he said.

"I'm fine. Why do you ask?"

"You seemed a little sad after you blew out the candles."

"It was that obvious, huh? I think Colby noticed, too."

"Yeah. Of course, he did. Because anyone who loves you—myself included—has the same wish right now."

"Yeah." I looked down at my toes. "Thanks again for covering for me today."

"I love that you had no idea why he sent you uptown."

"I was totally surprised."

"He was all tense, thinking he wasn't gonna have enough time to set everything up before you guys got back. He really loves you."

"I know." I smiled.

"How was the Mommy class thing?"

"The Stepford Wives, you mean? They looked at me like I was Elvira walking in there." I shook my head. "Bunch of dumb bitches. But it was all worth it when Saylor asked me to paint that sleeve on her arm."

"Yeah. I saw that. That's the cutest thing. You'd think she was my daughter and not Colby's." He winked.

Later that night, after everyone left and I'd put Saylor to bed, I told Colby I'd help him clean up. But he refused, saying the birthday girl shouldn't have to clean up after her party.

So, I reluctantly watched as he put everything away. As I leaned against the counter, I spotted an envelope lying there. As soon as I noticed the return address, I felt like I was hyperventilating. Picking it up, I asked, "What's this, Colby?"

He put down the glass he was drying and exhaled. "I was gonna mention it. But I didn't want to ruin today."

I opened it to find a letter announcing a date for the first hearing Colby had to attend with Maya. Our reprieve was about to end. In six days.

CHAPTER 25

Colby

"**D**id Saylor give you that to sleep with?" I lifted my chin, pointing at the stuffed animal Billie had just set on the coffee table.

"Nope." Billie plopped down on the couch next to me. "I asked her if I could borrow it. I figured if we literally had one in the room, we wouldn't be able to ignore it anymore."

My brows drew together before I realized what she meant: *A stuffed elephant.*

I frowned. "I guess we have been avoiding a certain subject, haven't we?"

"If the elephant in the room gets any bigger, there isn't going to be room for me."

I sighed. "I'm sorry. I should've talked to you sooner. I just hate to spend a single minute of our time together discussing anything to do with…*her.*"

"I know. And so do I. But when I don't know what's going on, my brain fills in the blanks, usually while I'm sleeping. The other night I had a dream that immigration officers busted down my door and deported me to Guam." Billie shook her head. "I don't even know where Guam is on a map."

I smiled sadly. "I get it. Our subconscious mind doesn't take a rest. So we should talk about it. But first let me do something." I picked up my phone from the coffee table and set a timer for five minutes, along with unlimited snoozes. Billie watched me do it.

"Are we limiting our talk to five minutes?" she asked.

"Nope. We'll talk however long you need to. But every five minutes, I'm going to stop and tell you something I love about you. I think it's important to remind ourselves that what we have is real, and what we're talking about is nothing but fake."

Billie smiled. "I like that idea."

I took a deep breath and shifted to give her my full attention. "Okay, so you know the hearing is the day after tomorrow. But what I haven't mentioned is that Maya called me last night."

The smile on Billie's face wilted. "What did she want?"

"We need to prep for the interview with immigration. You and I haven't really talked about what happens during that, but the officers assigned to our case can basically ask us any questions they want to determine if our marriage is real."

"What kind of questions?"

"Personal ones. Like, what color toothbrush does your wife have?"

Billie's eyes bulged. "Oh my God, Colby. How are you supposed to know that?"

"That's why Maya called. She wanted my email address to send me a questionnaire to fill out. The damn thing is thirty pages, typed. The plan is that we will both fill out the parts that apply to us individually, and I fill out the questions that relate to our relationship so we can swap and memorize each other's answers." I rubbed the back of my neck. "I'm supposed to have it back to her by tomorrow morning, and I haven't gotten past page one. Every time I start to work on it, I feel physically sick."

"Can I see the questions? Maybe I can help you get it done."

I met Billie's eyes. "You sure you want to do that? Some of them are pretty personal, and it might be hard to read."

She nodded. "I'll do whatever I can to help because the sooner you pass the interview, the sooner she's out of our lives."

I wasn't sure this was such a good idea, but I got up and got the papers from the drawer in the kitchen anyway. Handing them to Billie, I watched her face closely as she read. The first page was somewhat innocuous. It asked questions like my favorite color, if I slept on my back or stomach, my favorite foods, and how many cups of coffee I drank in the morning. But when she flipped to the next page, I knew those questions would give her pause. And they did. Billie's eyes grew wide before she began to read out loud.

"Do you come inside your wife or wear a condom? Oh, God, Colby. This is really personal stuff." She scanned the page a little more. "Your wife's favorite sexual position?" She shook her head, but kept reading. "Holy shit. Does your wife *swallow*? Can they really ask things like this? It sounds like the damn officer is planning on getting his rocks off listening to you two answer these questions. How are you supposed to know all this when you only spent one night together years ago?"

I shook my head. "I know. That's why I haven't gotten very far."

Billie was still flipping through the rest of the pages when the alarm I'd set went off. I hit snooze and waited for her to look up at me before taking her hand. "I love that you treat my little girl like she's your own."

Her face softened. "You don't know how badly I wish she were right now, Colby."

I leaned in and brushed my lips with hers. "I love you, Billie."

"I love you, too."

When I pulled back, she sat up taller. "Okay, we need to get this done. Can you grab us a pen, so we can get started?"

"You sure?"

"Very."

I got a pen from the kitchen, and Billie flipped back to page two. "Here's what we're going to do," she said. "We're going to answer all of these questions as if they apply to you and me."

I shook my head vehemently. "No fucking way. I'm not giving that woman or anyone insight into our life."

"No one is going to know the responses apply to us. And it will be easier for you to remember all the answers if they're true. Besides, I sort of like that you'll be thinking of us during the interview, and that Maya is going to unknowingly be pretending to be me."

I grinned. "That's a little twisted, but I fucking love it."

Billie chuckled. "Okay, so let's run through these. I'll ask the questions, you answer as if it applies to us, and I'll write down the answer."

"Okay, if you say so."

"Do you come inside your wife or wear a condom?"

"I come inside her because she turns me on so much a condom can't hold all my jizz. Plus, she trusts me, and she's on the pill."

Billie smiled. "I think I'll skip the jizz part."

After she finished writing, she looked up again. "What is your wife's favorite position?"

"Easy. On top."

"I do like riding you." She bit her lip. "I was actually thinking maybe next time I can face the other way and you can watch my ass go up and down."

I closed my eyes and conjured up that visual with a groan. "You're killing me, woman."

She giggled. "Next question, does your wife swallow?"

That was it. The thought of Billie on her knees with my cock down her throat was too much to handle. We were going to have to take a quick intermission. I plucked the packet of papers and pen from Billie's hands and tossed them over my shoulder before scooping her off the couch and into my arms.

"What are you doing?"

"Making sure I get the questions right. How am I supposed to answer your favorite position if you haven't ridden me reverse cowgirl? You wouldn't want me to risk failing this test, would you?"

Billie's smile stretched from ear to ear. "Definitely not."

"Mr. and Mrs. Lennon?"

Two days later, a man with a handlebar mustache called our names. We'd been waiting for the better part of an hour in uncomfortable plastic seats. I stood and held my hand out for Maya to walk first, and we followed the guy down a dimly lit hall toward a conference room with no windows.

"I'm Officer Richard Weber." He slid a business card across the table to us. "I'm the officer assigned to your immigration application. Can I have some picture ID from both of you, please?"

I dug into my wallet and pulled out my driver's license, while Maya took out an expired passport from Ecuador. The officer examined them both carefully, looking between the photo IDs and our faces a few times before handing them back and taking his seat.

"You should have received some papers that contain a notice of your rights during this hearing," he said. "Twice actually. Once in the mail with your appointment letter, and again today from the receptionist when you signed in. Have you received these notices?"

Maya and I looked at each other and nodded. "We have," she said.

"Any questions about your rights?"

We both shook our heads.

"Good. Then let's get started." The officer picked up a pen and clicked the top, then looked directly at me. "Mr. Lennon, how do you normally greet your wife when you see her?"

My forehead wrinkled. "I'm sorry. I'm not sure I understand the question."

"It's pretty straightforward. When you see your wife, perhaps when you get home from work or whatever, do you give her a hug, a kiss on the lips, kiss on the cheek, maybe? Shake her hand?" He shrugged. "Or perhaps no physical greeting is exchanged?"

Fuck. That definitely hadn't been a question on the sheets Maya made me fill out. But I decided to stick to the method Billie and I had used to come up with thirty pages of answers and responded as if the question applied to my relationship with her. "I kiss her on the lips."

He held my eyes. "Yet when you arrived today, you didn't kiss your wife hello. Is that correct?"

My face must've asked the question I was thinking because the officer shrugged. "I happened to be coming in from my break when you walked up, and I saw you greet Mrs. Lennon."

Maya jumped in. "We…had a bit of an argument last night."

The officer kept his focus solely on me. "What was the fight about, Mr. Lennon?"

I was suddenly nervous as shit and drawing a complete blank. So I said the first thing that popped into my head. "Maya ran up the cell phone bill, and I was upset about it."

"How much was the bill?"

"Uh, I think about three-hundred dollars."

"And what is it normally?"

I shrugged. "I don't know. Maybe a hundred."

"Do you two have the same cell phone provider?"

I shook my head. "No."

He jotted something down on his yellow notepad. "As a follow up, after this hearing, I'd like a copy of both of your cell phone bills for the last sixty days."

Fuck.

Maya flashed a plastic smile. Even I could tell it was fake. "Sure," *she said. "I'll make sure you receive that."*

"Mr. Lennon, which hand does your wife write with?"

Jesus Christ. None of these questions were in the papers we'd filled out. Since I had no goddamn clue if she was a righty or lefty, my first reaction was to stay consistent and answer as if it applied to Billie. But Billie was a lefty, and there were definitely more righties than lefties in the world, so I decided at the last second to go with the odds. "She writes with her right hand," I said.

The officer set his pen down on top of the pad he'd been writing on and slid them both over to the other side of the table in front of Maya. "Can you please print your name and then sign in script, Mrs. Lennon?"

Maya looked at me. "Sure. But I think my husband might be a little nervous today. He knows I'm a lefty. *Right, sweetheart?*"

Things didn't get much better after that. Even when our answers were in sync, I couldn't stop sweating. I had to blot my forehead several times just to keep droplets from falling on the damn table. My attorney had said the average interview lasted about twenty minutes, but it was well over an hour before Officer Weber put us out of our misery. By then, I had to be careful not to lift my arms because I was pretty sure if I did, I'd have giant sweat rings in my suit jacket.

We left with a lackluster goodbye after being told we'd receive a letter in the mail in a few weeks.

Maya was silent the entire elevator ride down to the street level, even though it was only the two of us in the car. But the minute we stepped out onto the street, her hands flew to her hips and she got in my face. "*You did that on purpose!*"

"Are you out of your *fucking mind*? The last thing I want to do is be stuck with you one minute longer."

"If my application gets denied, this is all your fault!"

"All my fault? You're the one who gave me the dumb packet of questions to fill out. *Nothing he asked was in there*!"

"You couldn't tell by my handwriting that I'm a lefty?"

"I was too busy memorizing thirty pages of answers to questions that *no one asked*. Your favorite color is black, which matches your heart, and you usually go to bed around three in the morning and wake up at eleven. What are you, a *fucking vampire*?"

We glared at each other. Every second that ticked by just made me hate her more. I needed to get the hell out of here before I did something I'd regret. I shook my head in disgust. "I gotta go."

"How are we going to fix this?"

"That's a *you* problem. *You* dragged me into this mess. *You* need to find a way to get us out of it."

"Daddy, are you sad?" Saylor asked as I dried her off from a bath that night.

I froze. "No, honey. Why?"

She pointed to her head. "Because I still have shampoo in my hair."

I looked to find my daughter's hair was indeed still full of suds. I'd taken her out of the bath and started drying her off without even noticing. Worse, I didn't even remember sudsing her up.

I forced a smile. "I was just testing to see if you were paying attention."

My little girl might've only been four, but she already knew how to see right through bullshit. She wagged her pointer. "Did you get in trouble at work?"

That made me chuckle. "No, sweetheart, I didn't get in trouble at work."

"So why aren't you smiling?"

"I'm sorry. I guess I was just thinking about something."

"It's okay, Daddy. But maybe you should call Billie."

"Why would I call Billie?"

Saylor shrugged. "Because you always smile when you're around her."

God, this kid doesn't miss a thing. I lifted her up and set her back in the bathtub so I could rinse her hair. "You know who else makes me smile?"

"Who?"

I swiped my finger through her hair, grabbing a dollop of suds, and tapped them onto her nose. "*You.*"

She smiled, and I felt it in my chest. There wasn't anything in this world I wouldn't do to keep my little girl happy. I needed to remember *she* was the reason I had to get through this shit with Maya.

After Saylor's bath, I read her a story and tucked her into bed. As I walked out of her room, I heard my phone buzzing from the kitchen counter. I frowned as I read the name flashing. *Adam.* My immigration lawyer. I took a deep breath before answering. "Hello?"

"Hi, Colby, it's Adam Altman. Sorry to call so late, but I just spoke to Xavier Hess, Maya's attorney."

"Oh?"

"Did things not go well this afternoon?"

I sighed. "It was a shitshow. Apparently the officer had been coming back from his break at the same time I arrived at the building, and he saw me walk up to Maya. He noticed my frosty greeting, and that put him on the offensive from the minute we started. Then I was wrong about which hand she wrote with, and things went downhill from there."

"Well, Xavier claims he's friendly with a clerk in the office you went to, and your file was marked for a Stokes hearing after you left."

"What's that?"

"It's a second interview that takes place when the officer suspects the marriage is fraudulent."

"*Shit.* How screwed am I?"

"Well, it's not good. But it's essentially a second chance for you two to prove you have a real marriage. So you can get this back

276

on track. Though a Stokes hearing is way harder than whatever you went through today. You and Maya will be interviewed separately and recorded. The officer will then compare the videoed answers for any discrepancies. And these interviews are notoriously long and detailed, sometimes running up to eight hours."

I dragged a hand through my hair. "I was soaked with sweat after five minutes today. How the hell am I going to handle eight hours of interrogation?"

"It's not easy. But if it's any consolation, I can attend this one with you, if you'd like, and I should also represent Maya so we present with a united front."

Nothing could console me at the moment. "When will this all take place?"

"We'll have to wait until we get the formal notice in the mail to find out the date. But usually it's a few weeks after the letter arrives."

"*Great.*" I sighed.

"I should probably also warn you, this particular officer has been known to make unannounced house calls bright and early in the morning and late at night. He also likes to stop by people's jobs to speak to coworkers."

"*What?* How can he do that?"

"It's an investigation. He has a lot of leeway."

"What am I supposed to do if he shows up here?"

"Let's just take this step by step. That doesn't usually happen until the officer sees how things go at the Stokes hearing. I only wanted to give you a heads up about what might happen down the road. Try to hold off on the panic. Nothing is even official yet."

I was long past panic. But what could I do about it? *Nothing.* So I shook my head. "Yeah, okay. I'll try."

"I'm sorry I'm not calling with better news, Colby. But these things can get back on track. I've had cases go to a Stokes hearing, and then subsequently a green card is issued. It's not over yet."

No? Then why does it feel like someone just nailed my coffin shut?

Fifteen minutes later, I was pouring my second glass of whiskey when there was a knock at the door. I froze, thinking it was Officer Weber, before realizing it was probably only Billie. She'd said she was coming over tonight after her last appointment.

This was the first time since I'd walked into her tattoo shop to introduce myself as her landlord that I really didn't want to see her. I'd let us down today, and I dreaded hurting her any more than I already had. But it was obviously too late to cancel, so I walked to the door and tried to put on my best face to greet her.

Though she was apparently as perceptive as my daughter. Billie took one look at me, and the smile fell from her face. "*Shit.* What happened?"

CHAPTER 26

Billie

Just when we'd started bracing for the worst, nothing happened—for weeks. We'd had a three-week break from any action as we waited for the next step in the hearing process. Every single day that went by felt like borrowed time, so once again, Colby and I cherished each minute. And just as this latest stretch of peace had been unexpected, so was the moment it all came to a screeching halt one Friday afternoon.

It was the start of the weekend, and Colby had gone to pick up some takeout. I'd closed the shop down early, and we'd planned to have an early dinner and watch a kid-friendly movie with Saylor.

There was a knock at the door, and I assumed it was Colby returning earlier than expected with our food: sushi for us and Panda Express for Saylor. She loved their orange chicken. I figured maybe he'd knocked because he'd forgotten his key or was carrying too many things.

I opened the door with a smile, which quickly faded when I realized it wasn't Colby standing before me. It was a strange-looking man with a handlebar mustache I didn't recognize.

"Can I help you?"

"I'm looking for Colby and Maya Lennon," he said.

My stomach sank. "They're not home. Who are you?"

"I'm Officer Richard Weber, an investigator on Mrs. Lennon's immigration case. I've been assigned to do a home visit today."

Shit. Even though I figured it was legit, I needed all the time I could get, so I asked, "Do you have identification?"

"Of course," he said before taking out his official badge and showing it to me.

Saylor was playing on the ground. I looked over my shoulder at her, then back at him. "Like I said…they're not home at the moment."

"And you are who exactly?" he asked.

"I'm the babysitter. My name is Billie."

"Good to meet you." He nodded. "Are they due back anytime soon?"

"At some point, yeah. We didn't discuss an exact time."

He took a step inside. "Do you mind if I stay here until they return?"

Ugh. I paused to think about this before answering him. My first inclination was to ask him to leave. But then what? Sending him away would make things seem more suspicious. No matter what decision I made right now, I knew one thing: he was not getting anywhere near Saylor.

"I was just about to put her down for a nap." Quickly realizing late afternoon was an odd time for that, I added, "She's not feeling well. They told me she didn't sleep last night. So she needs to lie down."

"Her parents went out despite the fact that their daughter is sick?"

Adrenaline rushed through me. "Well, that's judgmental of you," I said. "They called to cancel, but honestly, I told them I didn't mind taking the risk in getting sick. Quite frankly, if you must know… I really need the money." I huffed. "So, if you could just wait here, please."

Crap. I might've botched that one. I walked over to where Saylor was playing with her toys. "Come with me for a moment, sweetie."

She dropped the baton in her hand and obediently followed me into her bedroom without question.

I knelt down so I was eye level with her and whispered, "Saylor, I need you to listen to me, okay? I need you to do me a really big favor. Alright?"

Her eyes widened. "Okay."

"Everything is okay. But I have to have a grown-up talk with that man out there, so I need you to stay in your room and not come out until I tell you to."

"How long?"

"I don't know yet, sweetie pie. But I need you to play with your toys in here until I tell you to come out."

A look of fear crossed her face. "Is he a bad man?"

Shit. What have I done? I don't want to scare her. Squeezing her shoulders, I said, "No, not at all, honey. Not at all. He's a nice man. But there's just some grown-up stuff he and I need to talk about. You don't have anything to worry about, though. Okay?"

She blinked several times. "Okay, Billie."

I hugged her tightly. "Thank you so much, pumpkin. I'll come back in as soon as I can."

I realized telling her to stay in her room was not ideal. But all I needed was for the investigator to start questioning her. Or Saylor to innocently offer him information. Then what? It would all be over.

I have to warn Colby.

Before I left the room, I shot out a text. My hands shook as I typed.

Billie: There's an investigator here.

The dots moved as he responded.

Colby: OMG. What?

Billie: I told him I was babysitting.

Colby: Fuck! I thought they didn't do drop-ins until after the hearing!

Billie: Apparently, they do.

Colby: He's not talking to Saylor, is he?

Billie: I made up a story that she wasn't feeling well and asked her to do me a big favor and stay in her room. I explained that I needed to talk to the man about grown-up stuff. I'm texting you from her room. I feel sick right now.

Colby: You did the right thing.

Billie: He asked if he could hang out here until you got back. I was afraid to send him away because this might be a good opportunity to deal with it head on, since I'm able to warn you. One less visit where you're unprepared. If you can get back here with Maya...it might work out.

In what universe was I actually asking him to bring that bitch back here?

Colby: Good thinking. I'm gonna try to track her down.

Billie: If not, don't come back here at all because he thinks you're out together. You'd better get your stories straight about where you went, too. I need to go back out there. Just get here if you can.

I put the phone in my pocket and headed back out to where the man was still standing by the door.

"Sorry… She wanted me to read her a story," I said.

He crossed his arms. "So, how long have you worked here?"

"I don't recall exactly when I started, but it's been a while now."

"Years or…"

"Months," I answered.

His eyes wandered down to my chest and back up. *Lovely.* A perv in disguise.

He cleared his throat. "Do you mind if I ask you some questions about the household?"

If I refused, would that only add suspicion to the whole situation? "Sure…" I forced a smile.

"What's it like to work here?"

"Oh, I love it. Saylor is the sweetest. And Colby and Maya are great parents. They mainly call me over when they need a break. I'm not the main nanny or anything. Just an occasional babysitter."

"What do you know about their relationship?"

"They're very loving toward each other. But given that I'm mainly here with Saylor, I can't say I spend a lot of time with them."

Richard scratched his chin. "I suppose that's a good point."

"Their lives aren't really any of my business," I added.

He wrote something down. "Where did they go today?"

"I don't typically ask them where they're going. But it was a day-date…for leisure."

He arched a brow. "You said it's okay if I wait for them to return?"

"Sure. I don't mind," I said, feigning a lax attitude. "Can I get you anything to drink? A juice box? Some Goldfish?"

He laughed. "I'm good, thanks. Although if my ten-year-old were here, he'd be champing at the bit for some Goldfish."

Richard began wandering the space. There weren't any photos out. Nothing incriminating one way or the other that I could see. I prayed he didn't ask to go into Colby's bedroom. When he finally stopped walking around and took a seat on the couch, I used the opportunity to go check on Saylor.

"If you'll excuse me, I'm just going to check on her again— make sure she's okay and doesn't need anything."

"Go right on ahead." He smiled.

I slowly opened her bedroom door and closed it behind me. "How's it going, Saylor?"

She waved her little hand. "Hi."

She was being so good, with her dolls seated at the little table. I wanted to cry. Such an innocent scene in the midst of this horrid drama.

She looked so proud. "We're having a tea party."

"Wow. I can see that. What a nice spread you have set up."

"Can I come out now?"

My heart felt like it was breaking. "No, honey. Not yet. I just wanted to check on you and let you know I really appreciate you being such a good girl. If you need anything, just yell for me, okay?"

Her tone was morose. "Okay."

I fucking hate this.

A few seconds after I returned to the living room, the front door opened and Colby walked in—with Maya. As much as I hated having to see her, I breathed out a sigh of relief.

Maya promptly put her arm around him. And now I felt like I was going to be sick.

"What's going on here? Can I help you?" Colby asked the guy, playing dumb.

I answered before Richard could get the words out. "Mr. Lennon, this is Officer Richard Weber with Immigration? I told him he could wait here for you guys."

"I'm just here for a routine visit," the officer said. "I was hoping we could talk for a bit."

"Of course." Maya put on her best fake smile. She then turned to me. "How's Saylor feeling?"

"She's still not feeling great. But no worse than when you left."

She pouted. "Poor baby."

I shot quick daggers at Maya. Hopefully the man didn't notice.

"Where were you two coming from?" he asked them.

"We just had a little mommy-and-daddy time," Colby answered. He looked over at me. "Since she was nice enough to babysit for us."

"We went to a movie and lunch," Maya added.

Richard tilted his head curiously. "What movie did you see?"

"The new Tom Cruise one," she said.

"Ah, yes. I saw it last weekend. It was very good." He turned to Colby. "What was your favorite part?"

Colby scratched his chin. "That's a tough one. I really like the whole dynamic between Goose's son, Rooster, and Maverick."

"Oh yeah. I loved that whole plotline." He smiled, seeming to buy it.

Maya clung to Colby tighter. "We don't get to the movies very often, so it was nice."

My blood felt ready to boil.

"I have a ten-year-old, so I can relate to the need to get out." Richard nodded.

Colby must have noticed my eyes fixed on Maya's arm around him. I suspected he wanted to put me out of my misery. "Do you mind looking after Saylor while we talk to Officer Weber in private?" he asked me.

"Of course not." I thumbed back toward her bedroom. "I'll just go join her."

I went back to Saylor's room and found her still at the table she'd set up.

"I'm back, honey. Thank you for being such a good girl."

"I heard Daddy. I wanted to run out to see him, but you told me to stay in here."

"Yes!" I smiled. "Thank you for listening. It's Daddy's turn to talk to the man now. And as soon as he's done, we can both go back out there. But the good news is, I'm done talking to the man and can play tea party with you now."

As I sat down with Saylor and began pretending to drink some of the imaginary tea, I tried to make out what they were saying behind the door in the living area, but it was all faint and jumbled.

"Is there a lady out there, too?" Saylor asked.

Crap. "Yes. She's an associate of Daddy's who also came to talk to the man."

"What's her name?"

Hesitating, I answered, "Maya."

"That's a pretty name."

I cringed. "Yeah, it is." It was unsettling to appear jovial around Saylor when that bullshit was happening in the next room.

A few minutes later, the door burst open. "How's my baby?" Colby headed straight to Saylor. It was like he couldn't get to her fast enough.

"Daddy!" She ran to him.

Colby looked exhausted as he glanced at me and murmured, "He's gone."

He knelt and pulled her into a tight hug. "Were you the best girl ever while we were out there talking? Thank you so much, sweetheart."

"I was, Daddy. Can I have orange chicken now?"

His shoulders sank. "Baby, I didn't have a chance to pick up the food after all. I'm so sorry. But how about I make you your favorite homemade cheesy macaroni? You haven't had that in a while."

Her eyes lit up. "Okay."

He stood up and whispered in my ear. "Maya insists on saying hello to her. I didn't want to make a scene. I'm too damn spent. She promises to leave right after."

Ugh. She's still here? I let out a long sigh. "Okay."

"You wanna come say hello to someone, Saylor?"

"Is it Maya?" she asked.

He looked to me, confused.

"Saylor heard a woman's voice and had asked me who was talking. I told her she was an associate of yours named Maya."

He nodded and looked down at Saylor. "Yes. Her name is Maya." He exhaled. "Let's go say hello."

Saylor followed him out. "Okay."

Maya was sitting on the couch. She stood up as soon as she saw Saylor enter the room.

Saylor was the first to speak. "Hi, Maya."

Maya bent to meet her. "Well, hello, beautiful girl. How are you?"

"I'm good. Who are you again?" Saylor asked.

"I'm your daddy's friend."

"Oh."

"Were you playing with Billie?" Maya asked.

The sound of my name coming out of her mouth was grating.

"Yup. We had a tea party."

"That's so much fun. I used to love to do that when I was young."

Several awkward seconds of silence passed as Maya just stared at Saylor's face. Poor little girl had no clue what was really happening.

"Well…" Maya's eyes started to water. "I just wanted to say hello to you before I left."

"Hello," Saylor said innocently. She apparently hadn't picked up on the fact that Maya was about to cry; I knew Saylor would have said something if she'd noticed.

Then Maya pulled Saylor in for a hug. Colby's face was beet red. He looked like he was ready to lose it. She finally let Saylor go and turned to us. "Well, goodnight."

Colby nor I said anything as she left.

Don't let the door hit you on the way out.

Thankfully, Saylor didn't question us any further about Maya or anything else that had happened. She was just happy to have her daddy home and cooking her favorite meal.

Colby ended up making a huge batch of that mac and cheese for all three of us. It wasn't the dinner we'd imagined, but then again, this entire evening had been flipped on its axis. I only hoped it had been worth it.

Because we ate later than expected, we opted to let Saylor pick an episode of a Disney show on demand instead of watching a full movie. Colby and I mostly stared at each other, still in disbelief as Saylor watched TV.

After the show ended, I offered to put her to bed.

When Colby and I were finally alone for the first time since this ordeal began, he wrapped his arms around me and let out a long breath into my neck. "You were a fucking rockstar today. I can't thank you enough for putting up with that and for saving the whole situation. It could have been a huge disaster."

"I didn't do much."

"Are you kidding? You handled it like a champ. You could've sent him away, but you knew facing the fire would be best. And it worked, I think. She and I didn't fuck up because we'd had a chance to talk about what we were going to say."

"I wasn't sure if you were going to come back."

"I probably wouldn't have come back if I hadn't located her in time."

"How did you know that detail about the Tom Cruise movie?" I asked.

"I Googled spoilers on the way here."

"Smart."

He shook his head. "This whole thing is like a mind game, isn't it? Like how fast can you absorb information?"

Colby's phone rang, and he picked it up immediately. "Hello?" He turned to me and whispered, "It's the attorney."

Once again on edge, I watched as Colby spoke to him.

He pulled his hair in frustration as he listened. "Okay. Well, it's unavoidable, so at least it's set." He stood up and paced. "Yup. Okay. That sounds good. I'll see you next week on Thursday then. Thank you."

After he hung up, he let out a long breath. "They set a date for the Stokes hearing. The attorney wants Maya and me to come in and meet with him this week so we can discuss a strategic plan."

"Well, at least it's progress."

"Exactly. It's like we have to go through hell to get to the other side," he said.

"That's a good way to describe it."

A dark expression suddenly came over his face.

"What's wrong?" I asked.

"I feel like today is hitting me in waves," he said. "I'm so ashamed to have put you through that."

I shook my head. "Don't worry about me. I'm fine. Truly."

"Well, I'm not. You're the most important thing in my life besides Saylor, and to have to reduce you to a babysitter? That just felt so damn wrong."

"Please don't expend any more energy worrying about my feelings. It was all an act. I know that. I handled it. It's all good, Colby. Get out of your head tonight and come back to me instead."

I tried my best to reassure him, but I knew with the hearing looming, the coming weeks were going to be the beginning of a new and very difficult chapter in our lives. For tonight, I just wanted to make him feel good again. Make *us* feel good again.

There was only one thing I could think of that might make that happen. "Hey, I have an idea," I said.

"What?"

"Let's go to bed early and play Mr. Lennon fucks the babysitter."

CHAPTER 27

Colby

"I spoke to Richard Weber a little while ago," my attorney told Maya and me as we sat in his office the following week. "I usually give the investigator a courtesy call to let them know if I'll be joining a client at a Stokes hearing."

"How'd that go?" I asked.

He frowned. "Unfortunately, he didn't think the home visit went as well as you guys did."

Shit. I looked over at Maya. "Did he mention why?"

"Something about a drawing on the refrigerator that showed you holding hands with the babysitter."

I closed my eyes. I'd noticed Saylor's artwork the morning after the investigator's surprise visit when I'd grabbed the milk out of the fridge. But I'd chosen to allow myself to believe he hadn't seen it, since both Billie and I thought the visit had gone well. I also didn't have the heart to take away the positivity Billie was feeling after she'd jumped into the role of babysitter without even a warning.

Maya glared at me. "Your *stupid little girlfriend* is going to ruin this for both of us."

The hair on the back of my neck rose. "First of all, don't call Billie *my stupid little girlfriend*. She deserves a hell of a lot more respect than that, especially from you, considering she's taken on the responsibility of being the woman in Saylor's life when you shrugged your role off like it was nothing. And second of all, the only one capable of ruining anything here is *you*, because you dragged us all into this mess."

"Well, if you wouldn't have—" Maya began, but my attorney interrupted her.

"Alright, alright." He motioned with his hands for us to lower our voices. "Why don't we settle down. Pointing fingers isn't going to help this situation at all." He looked back and forth between us and sighed. "You two need to be on the same page and find a way to get along. Things have become serious now. The investigator also mentioned that he plans to seek criminal charges if the Stokes hearing doesn't convince him your marriage is legitimate."

I got up from my chair to pace back and forth in front of Adam's desk. "Jesus Christ. I can't go to prison." I buried my hands in my hair and pulled as I walked. "I have a four-year-old who needs me. What the hell are we going to do? Can we withdraw the petition, maybe tell the investigator we're getting a divorce because Maya cheated on me or something?"

Maya calmly examined her manicure and rolled her eyes. "Men are far more likely to cheat than women…"

Adam shook his head. "We can withdraw the petition, but that won't necessarily stop a prosecution. I've had cases where the couple didn't attend the Stokes hearing, yet the investigator still went after them."

"*Fuck*. What do we do now?"

"You don't have much of a choice here, Colby. You need to pass the Stokes with flying colors."

"We couldn't even pass a joint interview that lasted *an hour*, and now this guy is out for blood. How the hell are we going to pass an eight-hour interrogation?"

"You want my advice?"

"Of course."

"You have two weeks before the hearing. Move in together. You'll learn everything about each other and then some. Trust me, I've been married for twelve years and didn't live with my wife before the wedding. There's a lot of truth to the old adage that *you don't really know someone until you live with them.*"

I shook my head. "No fucking way."

"Don't be a stubborn mule," Maya said. "We don't have a choice, Colby."

"I'd rather rot in prison than spend two weeks cooped up with you."

Maya rolled her eyes again.

I stopped pacing and stood with my hands on my hips as I spoke to my attorney. "Is there anything else we need to discuss?"

Adam shook his head. "I don't think so. You know what you're in for at the hearing."

"Fine. Then I'm leaving." I walked toward the door.

"Where do you think you're going?" Maya shouted.

"As far as possible away from *you.*"

The office was two blocks away from my subway line. But just as I was about to descend the stairs, I noticed a bar a few doors down. My heart felt like it was going to explode in my chest, so I decided to have a quick shot or two to take the edge off. Inside, the bar was dark, with only a few old men sitting around. I sidled up to an empty spot near the door and ordered a double shot of tequila. Luckily the bartender didn't want to talk and just took my money in exchange for the alcohol and a lime. I knocked it back and skipped the fruit, wanting the burn to last for as long as possible. Then I raised my hand to call the bartender back. "One more, please."

He nodded. "You got it."

The second double shot went down easier than the first, and I probably could have kept going. But I didn't want to get shitfaced.

So I tossed two twenties on the bar to close out my bill. As I did, my phone buzzed with an incoming text. Maya's name flashed in preview, making my teeth clench. I was just about to stuff my cell back in my pocket and ignore the message, but then I remembered Billie was coming over later, and I didn't want Maya blowing up my phone. So I swiped to read the text, never loosening my jaw.

Maya: We need to move in together or you will go to jail.

I immediately typed back.

Colby: Go fuck yourself.

A few seconds later, another text came in. Except this time, it was a voice text. I hit play, expecting to hear Maya's righteous tone, but instead my own voice came through.

"I'm only marrying you so you can stay in this country and will leave my daughter alone. After it's done, don't contact me. I'm pretending this sham of a marriage never happened."

That bitch must've recorded me at our second meeting at the coffee shop. Before I could figure out what the hell she was trying to prove by sending it to me now, another text arrived.

Maya: I'll be at your apartment with my stuff Saturday morning. If you don't let me in, this recording is going to the investigator.

"Oh no." Billie frowned the second she caught a glimpse of me, even though I'd forced a smile.

I shook my head as I stepped aside to let her in. "How do you always know when I had a shitty day before I say a word?"

Billie stopped in front of me as she passed and pushed up on her tiptoes. She pressed her lips to mine and mussed my hair. "This. It's a dead giveaway."

"My hair?"

She smiled and nodded. "You yank at it when you're stressed, and then it sticks up in a thousand directions."

I closed the door. "No wonder I'm going to prison; I can't hide anything. I didn't even know I did that."

Billie pointed to the half-empty bottle of wine on the dining room table. "I get the feeling I'm going to need one of those."

I nodded and motioned to the living room. "Go sit down. I'll pour you one and refill mine. Or maybe I'll just chug from the bottle."

After I fixed us each a full glass, we settled onto the couch.

"What happened?" she asked.

"The investigator saw the picture Saylor drew of you and me holding hands."

"The one on the refrigerator? I didn't think he went into the kitchen." Her shoulders slumped. "I guess it must've been when I went into Saylor's room with her. I'm so sorry I didn't hide that, Colby."

"You have zero to apologize for. You handled that surprise visit like a champ. I definitely would have fucked it up if I'd answered."

Billie sipped her wine. "So what happens next?"

"We're supposed to go to the hearing in two weeks. If we don't pass, the investigator plans on filing criminal charges."

Billie's eyes widened. "You said *we're supposed to*. Does that mean you're not planning on attending?"

"I'm thinking about going to the investigator and telling him the truth, that the marriage was a fraud, but I was blackmailed into it." I shrugged. "He mentioned he has a kid. Maybe he'll have compassion when I tell him why I did it and just let me pay a big fine."

Billie shook her head. "I don't know, Colby. What if he doesn't care that you're the sole caretaker of your daughter and you did it to protect her? Then you've just admitted you committed fraud to an immigration investigator. Maybe you should take your chances at the hearing and see how it goes?"

I shook my head. "We're never going to pass that interview. He already knows it's a fraud, and he's going to be all over us with every question."

"But at least you have a chance. If you go to him and admit what you've done, you have *zero chance*."

I gulped my wine. "I have zero chance anyway. Maya recorded me saying I'm only marrying her so she can stay in this country and the entire marriage is a sham. She says if I don't do exactly what she wants, she's turning the recording over to the investigator."

Billie's forehead wrinkled. "I don't understand. You're already doing exactly what she wants."

I shook my head. "It's never enough with her. Now she's demanding we move in together until the hearing. My attorney suggested it so we could get to know each other and have a better shot at answering questions."

Billie blinked a few times. "Oh…wow. I guess if you live like a married couple, it would give you a chance to get to know each other on a different level."

"It doesn't matter. I'm not doing it."

"Well, then let's go back to your plan and play it out. Let's say you go to the investigator and admit what you did and he's sympathetic and only hits you with a fine and doesn't press for jail time. What happens then? Even if that works, the only other way for Maya to stay in this country is to apply as the mother of her child who is a US citizen, right? So you're back to square one."

I shook my head. "Not if she's locked up for immigration fraud."

"Okay, let's say she gets some jail time. We have to assume when she gets out she's going to want to stay in the US. Might you just be prolonging the inevitable? Or what if she also gets fined and then applies for custody immediately?"

"Jesus, Billie. Whose side are you on?"

"I'm on your side, Colby, of course. That's why I don't want you to make any rash decisions. You need to think this through, look at it from all angles, and play out all possible outcomes."

My head felt like it was spinning. "I don't feel so great. Would you mind if we talked about this later? Right now, I just really need to hold you."

Billie's face softened. "Sure."

For the next half hour, I sat with my arms wrapped around my girl. She leaned her back to my chest, and I rested my chin on the top of her head. It felt good, but even that wasn't enough to shake the feeling of impending doom. Since she'd come after her late night at work, it was soon almost ten o'clock.

"You want to watch some TV before we go to bed?" I asked.

Billie turned to face me. She put a hand on my chest. "Actually, I think I'm going to head home."

"What? Why?"

"You need some time to think, and I do too."

I didn't like it one bit, but I couldn't argue if space was something Billie needed. So I nodded and tried not to pout. "Okay. Whatever you want. But I'm calling you an Uber."

Unfortunately, when I hit confirm on the app, the car was only three minutes away, and she still had to get downstairs on the slow-as-shit elevator. "It's going to be here by the time you get outside."

Billie nodded, and I walked her to the door. Before I opened it, I took her face in my hands. "I love you. I'm so sorry I'm putting you through this shit."

"I love you, too."

"Can I see you tomorrow night?"

"I have a busy afternoon at the shop. Can I let you know?"

A heaviness settled into my chest, yet I nodded. "Sure. Get some sleep."

"You, too."

The following day, it took every bit of my willpower not to text Billie until the afternoon. I managed to make it until three o'clock.

Colby: Hey, beautiful. Can I make you dinner tonight?

It took almost an hour for her to text back.

Billie: My last appointment is at five. Could we talk for a bit right after I get off, before the babysitter goes home?

I got the feeling that meant she wasn't planning on staying over again, but I was desperate and would take whatever I could get.

Colby: Sure. I'll see if she can stay a little later, too.

Billie: See you soon.

When I walked into the shop after work, Deek's face told me I hadn't been the only one unable to stop thinking about things today. He laid a hand on my shoulder. "Keep strong, man."

I nodded and walked over to Billie, who was in the back stocking her portable cart.

"Hey." I brushed my lips with hers.

Her smile was sad. "I'll be done in a few minutes."

"Take your time. The sitter can stay until whenever I need her to."

"Okay."

We were both silent until she finished and grabbed her purse. "Do you want to go for a walk, maybe?"

"Sure." I shrugged. "Whatever you want."

We walked to a park a few blocks from the shop and got hot dogs from the truck that was always parked at the entrance. Then we sat down on a bench inside and made awkward small talk while we ate. After, I wiped my mouth and lifted a knee up on the bench so I could look at her while I spoke.

"I would give anything for an easy way to fix this so we could go back to the way things are supposed to be, Billie."

She touched my cheek. "I know you would, Colby, and that's part of what makes you a special person. You're willing to sacrifice whatever it takes for the people you love, including your own happiness." She paused and took a deep breath. "And that's why I also know that when I ask you to do something for me, you will."

My brows drew together. "Of course. Whatever you need."

Billie held my eyes. "I need you to let Maya move in."

"You're kidding, right?"

She shook her head. "I'm very serious, Colby. I was up all night thinking about things. It's the only real solution we have. You need to redeem yourself as a married couple during this second interview, and the only chance you have to do that is if you spend time with each other. You need to know things you can't study for, like your morning routines and habits, and you only have two weeks to learn it all."

I shook my head. "I can't do that, Billie. I can't do that to us."

"You wouldn't be doing it *to* us. You'd be doing it *for* us. I see you, me, and Saylor as a team, and this team needs to do what is best for Saylor, regardless of how we personally feel." Billie's eyes filled with tears. "I love Saylor, too. I'll never be able to live with myself if my selfishness—not wanting you to live with another woman for a few weeks—got her hurt. So I'm not taking no for an answer. Maya is moving in, and you two are going to spend every waking moment together getting to know each other."

I had to swallow the giant lump in my throat to be able to speak. "It means the world to me how much you care about Saylor."

She sniffled. "Well, that's good, because that's what we both need to focus on for the next couple of weeks."

I leaned my forehead to Billie's and lost the battle to hold back my own tears. "You are the best thing that's ever happened in my life."

Tears began to stream down her face, too. "So it's settled, then. Maya is moving in."

It felt wrong in my heart, but my head couldn't deny it was probably the best shot I had at getting through the hearing. So I nodded.

Billie took a deep breath. "There's just one more thing I need you to do for me."

"Anything."

"I can't see you for a while."

I froze. "What do you mean?"

"My heart will be with you, but it will be too painful to deal with seeing you when you'll be going home to another woman. And you need to spend all of your spare time on getting to know Maya, not hanging out with me."

"But…"

Billie held her finger to my lips and shook her head. "I need you to do this for me,

Colby. Please."

♥CHAPTER 28

Colby

A few days later, my life had turned upside down: Maya had moved into my apartment, but thankfully, so far she hadn't been around a whole lot. That was the good news. The bad news was that my separation from Billie had begun, and not being able to see or talk to her every day absolutely blew. What also blew was having to lie to my daughter and tell her Maya was a friend who needed a place to stay.

Maya wasn't home early Monday morning when I invited Holden over to help me with a little project before I had to get to work.

He peeked his head in the spare room. "That's her stuff?"

Maya had a leather jacket and some other clothing piled on the bed.

"Yeah."

Holden looked around. "She's not here right now, is she?"

"No. She moved her things in and spent last night here, but she's been pretty MIA overall. I heard her get up and leave at like five this morning. I have no clue where the fuck she went that early, nor do I care."

"Is she still stripping?"

"No clue."

"Do you need me to go investigate?" He winked. "Haven't been to the strip clubs in a while."

"Do whatever you want, man." I chuckled.

"Seriously, though, you don't even know if she's still stripping? Do you know anything about her life at all?"

"I don't need to know the real Maya, only the fake one who's married to me."

"Fair enough," he said, lifting his tool chest. "So what am I putting a lock on?"

"My bedroom. I need to be able to lock it from the outside, so she can't get in while I'm at work."

He arched a brow. "You think she's gonna steal from you or something?"

"She's already stolen my life, why not my watch and the cash I keep around? I don't trust her."

"How's Billie handling all this?"

I sighed. "I wish I knew."

"What do you mean?"

"We agreed not to see each other while Maya's living here. That includes talking."

Holden gaped. "Fuck… You broke up?"

"No!" I said adamantly. "We're just taking a break because it's too difficult for her. A *break*. Not a breakup."

"But why no talking?"

"Because Billie and I can't be in each other's lives in a half-assed way. It's all or nothing. But we're able to handle this because we know it's temporary. That's the only way it would be doable. It's not what I want, but it's for Billie's mental health. I know not talking at all sounds extreme. But I get it. The whole thing is hurtful. And I'm willing to do anything I need to in order to make sure she's still around when this is over."

"Damn. I wish you would've just let me marry that bitch."

I rolled my eyes.

I might've been making myself out to be more confident about the situation with Billie than I actually was. Lord knows how long Maya would be living here. For all I knew, she could extort me again to buy herself more time to live here rent free. If this little living arrangement exceeded a few weeks, it was going to be very difficult to maintain my agreement not to see Billie. The other thing I worried about was whether Billie would come to her senses while we were apart and realize she didn't need to be putting up with this shit at all. She could easily find a man who didn't come with a fuck ton of baggage and an illegal "wife." I couldn't even think about that right now.

"All set," Holden said a little while later as he tested the lock he'd installed.

"Thanks, dude. I wish I could have you change the locks on the front door, too, so she can't get in again." *If only.*

That evening, after I read Saylor her bedtime story, she had questions. I knew this would be coming.

"Why did Maya move in with us again?"

I'd already lied to my daughter once, which I hated, but she clearly didn't understand. Nor should she, since the whole thing made no rational sense.

"She needed a place to live for a while…" I once again told her. "So, since she's my…friend…I agreed to let her stay with us."

"When is Billie coming back?"

Billie had had a talk with Saylor to let her know she'd be gone for a little while, but that she'd be coming back. She didn't want my daughter to worry or think anything was wrong. But that hadn't stopped Saylor from asking me for updates. Who could blame her?

"Hopefully soon, sweetie."

She hesitated then asked, "Do you love Maya?"

Why would she ask that? My daughter was way too smart. She was starting to put two and two together—that Billie's departure coincided exactly with Maya moving in.

"No. I don't love Maya. I need you to understand that, okay? Maya is just a friend." I hugged her. "I love Billie. And you, of course."

Saylor pouted. "I want Billie to come over. I miss her."

That broke my heart. "I know you do, honey. Believe me, I miss her, too. More than anything."

From behind the door, I could hear that Maya was home now, based on some clanking out in the kitchen. Not wanting to go out there and face her, I told Saylor another bedtime story. And then another. But before I went for a third, I realized avoiding Maya totally defeated the purpose of this torturous living situation. If I had to live with her, I might as well study up on the information I needed to nail this hearing.

So, I tucked my daughter in and kissed her goodnight. When I emerged from Saylor's room, Maya was standing at the stove, frying something.

She turned to me. "Hey."

I groaned and pulled up a chair.

Before I had a chance to blink, flames flew everywhere. Maya freaked out, flailing her hands.

I jumped up. "What the fuck?"

I immediately grabbed a baking tray from the drawer and covered the flames with it. Somehow a brown paper bag had caught on fire. I managed to put it out before it got out of control and burned my damn apartment down. Wouldn't that have been fitting symbolism? Everything just burned to hell like my life at the moment...

Maya continued shaking uncontrollably.

"Relax. It's out."

She covered her mouth with trembling hands. "I'm so sorry, Colby."

"You need to be more careful." I looked closer at what she'd been cooking. "Why the hell did you have a paper bag near the flames anyway?"

"I was making French fries. I put the fries in a bag to shake off the grease."

"Can't you just buy fries like everyone else?"

"It's not the same." She kept shaking her head, and then she leaned against the counter and started to cry.

I had no time for her crocodile tears. But as the seconds went on, I realized she was truly shaken. So, I took it upon myself to discard the burned fries sitting in the grease and clean up the mess she'd made. I looked over at her as I was dumping grease-soaked paper towels in the trash. "Did you have a plan B?"

"Huh?"

"For dinner."

She shook her head in a daze. "I don't have anything else to make. All I bought was potatoes."

I rolled my eyes. "Sit down. Try to calm yourself." Begrudgingly, I offered, "There's some leftover casserole, if you're hungry."

Her eyes widened. "Really? That would be great. I'm so hungry, and it's late."

I heated up a plate, placed it in front of her, and took a seat across the table. I crossed my arms and watched her as she ate. Every so often, she'd take a bite and wipe more tears. She still seemed broken up over the grease fire, and I didn't quite understand it.

I forced myself to ask, "Why are you still upset? It's done."

Maya sniffled. "You can't possibly care why I'm crying. You don't have to pretend to."

Was she trying to make *me* out to be the heartless one in this equation? "While I may not care about your feelings—because you sure as hell don't care about mine—I *do* care about getting through these days with you. We need to get our shit together and figure out how to relate to one another if this is going to work. Sitting here in front of me, crying and not telling me what the hell is wrong with you right now isn't helping."

She wiped her eyes. "I'm not proud of the way I've handled the situation with you. I've taken things too far in my desperation to stay, but it's too late to go back now. I knew forcing you would be the only way to get you to help me. I don't expect you to ever forgive me or understand. But I have my reasons for needing to stay here." She blew her nose into a napkin. "I can't go back to Ecuador, Colby. It's a nightmare."

I narrowed my eyes. "Why is it a nightmare? Isn't all your family there?"

She looked down into her plate. "It's a very long story."

I leaned in. "Well, if you haven't noticed, I've put my entire life on hold for you. I think at the very least, I deserve to know why your nightmare has now become *my* nightmare."

She exhaled and nodded. "You're right." She wiped her eyes. "You do deserve to know."

I leaned back and folded my arms. "So…what is it?"

Maya buried her face in her hands. "I shouldn't be here, Colby."

"Well, that's for damn sure. I'm counting the days until we're done with this arrangement."

She looked up at me. "No…I mean, I should be dead."

My jaw dropped. *What the hell is she talking about?*

"I tried to kill myself back in Ecuador." She shook her head slowly. "But I'm such a failure, I couldn't even do that correctly. So I'm still here. But I shouldn't be."

I sat with my mouth hanging open. I might have hated her, but I certainly didn't wish her dead. "What happened?" I finally asked.

She stared off for a moment. "Six years ago, I was working as a nanny back home. Ironically, I was taking care of a little girl around Saylor's age." She paused. "One day, while I was watching her, I got absorbed by something on my phone. It couldn't have been more than a minute that I was checking Facebook. Rocio was in her room, so I figured it was safe to take a break. I had no idea that she'd snuck out. She'd gone out the back door that led to the pool."

I gulped. I had a feeling I knew where this was going, and as the parent of a little girl, it made me absolutely sick.

With tears in her eyes, Maya went on. "She fell in, and I never even knew. When I went to her room to check on her, she was gone. I went crazy, searching the entire house, but while I was inside looking, she was outside in the pool, drowning. Finally, I noticed the back door open and realized she had fallen into the pool. I found her lying face down in the water. I tried to save her, but she was already dead when I got to her. I called for help, but it was too late."

Oh man. "Shit." I then muttered words I never thought she'd hear from me. "I'm sorry."

"Her parents told my family they'd better never see me again. They made sure everyone in our town knew what had happened. My family couldn't handle the negative talk and the gossip. My father lost his job over it, and my family alienated me." She stared at the ceiling as she began to cry again. "Everyone hated me. But they couldn't hate me more than I hated myself. I tried to take pills one night to end it all, but I didn't take enough. Someone found me lying in the street and took me to the hospital where they pumped my stomach."

This is so sad and fucked up. "God…" I whispered.

"In the hospital," she said, "I met a sweet nurse, the first person to ask me what was wrong and truly listen to my side of things. She found me a doctor to talk to. They got me help. I started to believe maybe I deserved forgiveness and a second chance. But I knew I needed to get away from my family and the people in my town because they would only have me believing I deserved to be dead. So I started saving money for a ticket, and took off to the US, vowing to leave my family behind and never look back. When my visa expired, I stayed here illegally. I have nothing back in Ecuador but shame. I feel like I'll die if I ever have to go back there."

"So you got here and started dancing right away?"

She nodded. "Yes. It was the only job I could get. And the owners of that club didn't care that I wasn't here legally, only that I took my clothes off and made them money."

"Are you still stripping?"

"Yes. For a different club." She smiled slightly. "I'll never forget the night I met you. I'd never had a more handsome client— someone who actually made me nervous. Your friends paid for a private dance for you, and we went to the back room together. You probably assumed that because of what I did with you, I slept with everyone. But that wasn't true. You were the first client I ever had sex with. You don't have to believe me, but it's the truth, Colby. You were drunk. I was a little, too, but I knew what I was doing. I wanted to feel good for one night, forget about all the miserable memories. I never imagined I'd get pregnant. We used a condom. And I was on the pill. But looking back, I hadn't been good about always remembering to take it. From the moment I found out I was pregnant, I knew it was yours. Because there had been no one else. But I also knew I couldn't keep the baby. I would never allow myself to take care of another child after what happened to Rocio. I wasn't capable of being a mother. And I didn't deserve to bring life into this world when I was responsible for the loss of another." She breathed out. "But I didn't want to have an abortion. I didn't know what to do, and I didn't know how to tell you. I kept putting it off until I finally just…had her. After she came out, she was so perfect. I was even more sure I needed to give her up so I wouldn't ruin her." She looked over at me. "She looked just like you. I knew that was the sign I needed to give her to you. She was yours. Always yours. And that's when I dropped her off. I hated myself for giving her up, but I knew it was best for her. Clearly, I was right."

I pulled on my hair. I'd never had any idea what the hell she'd been thinking back then. "I'm sorry about what happened to you back home," I said after a moment. "And I'm glad you weren't successful in your attempt to end your life."

"I suppose Saylor wouldn't be here if it had worked, huh?"

She'd sort of read my mind. As much as I despised Maya, without her, there would be no Saylor. But while I did feel a bit sorry for her tragic past, it wasn't enough to make me sympathize with her actions toward me. There was still no excuse for what she'd pulled.

"Look…" I said. "Let's just get through this, okay? We've come this far. Let's learn enough about each other so we're not wasting our time here." I stood from the table. "I'm gonna get paper and pens so we can take some notes. We need to ace this hearing."

She wiped her tears and smiled. "Okay."

The following day, I found myself unable to focus on anything but how much I missed Billie. It had been several days now since I'd last seen her face. I knew the agreement was to not see each other, but it was killing me to be apart from her.

After work, I decided to walk by her shop. My plan was just to peek in, get a look at her for a quick fix, and head upstairs without her seeing me.

But for some reason I hadn't realized how late it was when I got there. Lately, I seemed to have no concept of time—every day was just a miserable Groundhog Day. I'd been expecting to look in Billie's shop window and catch her in action, busy at work. But that wasn't what I saw.

She was alone.

I hadn't been expecting that.

I also hadn't been expecting to see her looking so sad as she swept the floor after closing. Her expression was morose, and she seemed lost in thought. How could I just walk away now? My heart pounded as I debated whether to knock and get her attention.

Before I had a chance to decide, Billie looked up and noticed me standing there. I must've looked like a sad puppy dog staring in the window. She rushed to the door to let me in. "How long have you been out here?"

I simply shook my head.

She exhaled. "Colby…"

I interrupted her. "I just…need to hold you. I know this is against the rules."

"We were never any good at sticking to rules, were we?" she said.

I took her into my arms and held her tightly, drowning in her vanilla scent. My heart pummeled my chest as our bodies rocked back and forth. I'd yearned for this so damn much.

When we finally stepped back and looked at each other, I needed just one taste and couldn't help but press my lips against hers for a slow and painful kiss.

"You should go," she whispered over my lips before pulling away.

It was damn hard to stop, but I did.

"Thank you," I said.

Billie stood at the door and watched me as I left. I knew she didn't want to let me go, but I knew why she'd told me to leave. My being there was a violation of our deal—but it was worth it.

Upstairs, I was surprised to find Maya in the living room coloring with Saylor while the nanny watched. I didn't know whether to be mad about it, but I supposed if she were living under our roof, I had to expect that she'd have some interaction with my daughter.

"What's going on here?" I asked as I entered the apartment.

Saylor ran to me. "Daddy! You're home!"

"What are you up to, sweetie?"

"Coloring with Maya."

"That's…fun."

Saylor pointed. "You have red all over your lips!"

Billie's lipstick.

I rubbed the corner of my mouth. "Do I?"

No fucking way am I washing it off.

"I guess we know why you were late," Maya chided.

I glared at her.

That night, Maya joined us for dinner. While things still weren't great between us, I felt a bit more tolerant of her now. We'd spent some time after our talk getting our fake stories straight in preparation for the Stokes hearing.

In bed that night, I couldn't stop thinking about Billie. Holding and kissing her earlier had put me over the edge. It made me realize I couldn't live without her.

Next to my bed, I had a pen and paper laid out with notes I'd taken about Maya. I ripped off a new sheet and began pouring out my thoughts and my heart to Billie, all the things I wished I could say to her tonight. I'd probably never send it to her, but I needed to put these feelings somewhere.

❤CHAPTER 29

Colby

It was the third time I'd caught Maya watching me tonight. Saylor and I were sitting on the floor in the living room playing Candy Land, and Maya had been cleaning up after eating her dinner. I probably could've ignored it or chalked it up to her studying me to prepare for tomorrow's interview, but after nearly two weeks of living together, I'd learned to read her. Tonight, the look in her eyes made me think she wanted something.

She smiled as we locked eyes, and I immediately forced my gaze back to the game board without returning the sentiment. The last thing I wanted was to give her the impression I was interested in anything more than getting us out of this mess. I guess she took the hint, because she disappeared into the guest room and didn't come out until after I'd put Saylor to bed.

"Is she asleep?" Maya came into the living room where I was watching TV. Well, at least the television was on, and I'd been staring in that direction.

I nodded. "The sitter took her to the park after school. She's become obsessed with going back and forth on the monkey bars, and that always seems to knock her out."

Maya smiled. "I think I'm going to have a glass of wine. I'm a bit on edge about tomorrow. Would you like one?"

"No, thanks." Even though things between Maya and I had become more cordial over the last week, I wasn't about to do anything that felt the slightest bit *coupley*. It would be too disrespectful to Billie.

Maya poured herself a glass of merlot and sat down at the other end of the couch. "I have an implant in my arm for birth control." She pointed to the triceps area. "On my right side."

Maybe it was the way I'd thought she was looking at me earlier, or the fact that she wore only a skimpy pair of sleeping shorts and a tank top now, but I jumped to the wrong conclusion. "There's no way in hell I'm sleeping with you."

Maya sighed. "I'm telling you because I realized earlier that a husband would know that type of thing about his wife. The investigator could ask what type of protection we use."

"Oh. Okay."

"Also, I usually sleep naked. How about you?"

"I have a daughter, so no, I don't usually sleep naked. Sometimes she gets up before me, and I wouldn't want to scar her for life."

Maya frowned. "Yeah, of course. That makes sense. I guess I should say the same thing if I'm asked then, huh?"

I shrugged. "If you want."

She nodded. "Why don't we say I sleep in a tank top and shorts like this? No bra, of course."

"Fine."

"And what about you? What should I say you sleep in?"

"Just my underwear is fine."

"Do we lock the bedroom door when we have sex?"

"Sure."

"Maybe we should say we usually do, but there's been a few times where things got heated fast and we didn't get a chance to. It sounds more believable since we're supposed to be newlyweds."

This entire conversation made me very uncomfortable. "Fine."

Maya sipped her wine. "Do you remember the night we met? We couldn't keep our hands off each other. We barely made it to your apartment before we had sex against the wall in the entryway. I would imagine if we were a real couple, our passion would still be that way. Don't you think?"

My jaw tightened. "I *don't* think about it. But if you want to say we missed locking the door a few times, I'll say something similar if asked." I aimed the remote at the TV and pressed the button to turn it off. "I'm going to bed. We have to leave here by eight thirty for our appointment. Will you be around or are you meeting me there?"

"I'll be here. I wouldn't put it past the investigator to be watching how we walk up again. So I think we should arrive together."

I nodded and stood. "I'll come back after I drop Saylor at school."

"Or…we could take her together?"

I shook my head. "I'll come back."

In my room, I got changed and was about to walk into my bathroom to brush my teeth when there was a light knock on the door. I opened it to find Maya standing there. She thumbed behind her. "I was getting ready for bed, and I realized we don't know each other's bathroom routine."

I held my hand on the top of the door, not budging to allow her to enter. "I brush my teeth and wash my face."

Maya held up her cell phone. "Every night I read a different article about what questions people have been asked during a Stokes hearing. The one I read tonight said the investigator focused on the small details of their bedtime routine. He asked if they put the toothpaste away or just leave it on the counter, and if they used mouthwash and flossed and stuff."

I glanced at her phone, which showed a website with a bunch of questions, and then looked back to her.

"I really want to pass this so I can get out of your hair," she said. "I promise it won't take long. I'll just stand in the background quietly and watch you do your routine, in case we're asked about it."

I took a deep breath before stepping aside to let her in. "Fine."

Maya leaned against the doorway of the bathroom as I went about brushing my teeth and then took out floss.

"Oh, you use the old-school string stuff?" she said. "I use those Pluckers, the plastic things with a piece of floss attached on the end."

I looked at her reflection in the mirror as I threaded between my teeth. I'd already taken off my shirt for bed, and I watched as Maya's eyes dropped down to check out my chest. It made me *really* fucking uncomfortable. So I did a half-assed job on my teeth and finished up as quickly as possible before turning to face her. "Happy?"

"Do you want to come watch me now?"

I shook my head. "How about you just say your routine is exactly like the one you saw me do, if we're asked?"

"Oh. Okay. I guess I can do that."

I motioned behind her, into my bedroom. "Think I can go to bed now?"

Maya stepped aside for me to exit the bathroom, then slowly walked toward the door. As she passed the bed, she ran her finger along the top of the comforter until she reached the end, then stopped and looked over her shoulder at me.

"Maybe we should spend the night together. You know, to pick up any last-minute details. I don't even know if you're a snuggler or if you sleep on your stomach." She looked up at me from under her lashes and bit on her lower lip shyly. "It could be our little secret. I wouldn't mention it to Billie or anything."

I clenched my jaw so hard, I was surprised I didn't crack a pearly white. "Get *the fuck* out of my room."

Maya blinked a few times. I'm guessing not too many men declined an offer for her to join them in bed. She had the balls to pout. "You don't have to be so rude about it."

I pointed to the door. "*Rude* would be telling you to get the fuck out of my apartment and go sleep on the street. Which I'm about two seconds away from doing if you don't get out of my bedroom right now."

She huffed and stomped toward the door, slamming it shut behind her.

The following morning, Maya and I barely said two sentences to each other while we took the train downtown to the interview. I was a nervous wreck and had reached a point that I jumped if a car so much as honked its horn. The only thing that was going to settle my nerves was having today finally over with. My lawyer, Adam, met us out front of the federal building, and we talked for a few minutes before going inside together. He'd told us the questioning could last up to eight hours long and be conducted separately, or it could be less than an hour with us being interrogated together in one room. So I had no idea what to expect, until Officer Weber walked in.

"Mrs. Lennon can wait here," he said with no preamble. "The video equipment is set up down the hall. I'd like to meet with Mr. Lennon first."

Adam nodded and spoke to Maya. "I'll be back as soon as we're done."

"Okay."

Maya stepped to me and opened her arms for a hug. "I'll see you in a little bit."

Through my peripheral vision I caught the investigator watching, so I had no choice but to follow through with the embrace she offered. Maya kissed my cheek before I could pull away and whispered loud enough so everyone could hear. "Love you."

I nodded and couldn't get out of the room fast enough. Facing the firing squad down the hall was more enticing than being in Maya's arms.

Again, the investigator wasted no time jumping in. As soon as he'd turned the recording equipment on, he fired off the first question, asking about the type of birth control Maya used. Thanks to the chat I hadn't even wanted to have last night, I knew the answer. The subsequent ten or so questions were all focused on things we'd either practiced or learned about each other over the last two weeks of living together. He asked how Maya took her coffee and where she put her dirty laundry. Knowing the answers went a long way toward settling my nerves, and it wasn't lost on me that I probably wouldn't have known half of them if she hadn't forced me to let her move in. Everything seemed to be going well, and I started to feel like maybe I actually did know Maya a little bit. Until the first question came that stumped me.

"How many times a week do you and Mrs. Lennon go out to dinner?"

"Umm… Not too often."

Investigator Weber pursed his lips. "I need an actual answer—five times, zero, three?"

"Well, it varies from week to week."

"Okay. Let's be more specific then. How many times did you go out to dinner in the last seven days?"

Shit. I took a few seconds to consider the question. "I think once."

"You think?"

I nodded. "Yeah, it was once."

"And can you tell me if Mrs. Lennon has any scars?"

"Scars?"

"Yes, you do know what a scar is, don't you?"

Oh Jesus. This isn't good.

Over the next three hours, I was grilled like a criminal. There were a few more questions I wasn't sure of, and I tried to answer those as vaguely as possible. After the investigator finished with me, he asked me to wait out in the lobby, and Maya and Adam took their turn. I had the urge to pace as the minutes ticked by at a snail's pace, but I thought it best to stay in my chair and try to not look so terrified, just in case the receptionist reported back to the investigator about my behavior. It was three-and-a-half hours more before Maya and my attorney came walking out from the back.

Officer Weber nodded to Adam. His face was an unreadable mask, just as it had been through most of the interview. "I'll be in touch," he said.

Adam nodded back. "Thank you. Have a good afternoon."

None of us said a word the entire elevator ride down to the street level. I think I might've held my breath until we were outside the building.

"So…" Adam turned to face us. "How do you think it went? Neither one of you seemed to stumble much on anything."

"I felt like it went okay," Maya said.

I nodded. "I'm afraid to say I thought it went okay, too."

Adam smiled and rested a hand on my shoulder. "I get it. But at least it's over now. It will be a few weeks before anything else happens."

After my attorney left, Maya and I compared notes. We walked toward the train station rattling off questions and answers.

"What did you say for how many times a week we go out to dinner?" I asked.

"I said what I've witnessed so far—maybe once, at the most."

I blew out a deep breath and nodded. "Good…good. I said the same thing. How about scars? Do you have any?"

"Just the C-section scar."

I stopped in my tracks. "Saylor was born via C-section?"

"Yes."

"How come?"

"She was breach."

I shook my head, suddenly feeling rattled—though it was less about how the interview went and more that I didn't even know how my daughter had been born.

I ran my hand through my hair. "I had no idea you had a C-section. I said you didn't have any scars."

"That's the only one."

"Do you think we have to get every question right? Is it like high school where a sixty-five is passing, or do we have to score a hundred percent? I mean, I might not have even thought of a C-section scar as a scar. When he asked me, I was trying to remember if you'd told me about any injuries or accidents. So I'm not certain I would have said C-section even if I'd known you had one. People overlook things or forget."

Maya shrugged and shook her head. "I have no idea what it will take for us to pass." She held up a finger. "Oh, another one I wasn't sure about was what color underwear you had on last night."

"What did you say?"

"I guessed gray."

"Good guess, because that's how I answered. Though I wasn't sure."

We continued comparing answers the entire walk to the train, while we waited on the platform, and through almost the entire ride back. In the end, there seemed to be only one other question aside from the scar one that we'd gotten wrong. The investigator had asked what day garbage went out at our apartment, and Maya had said Tuesday, while I'd responded Friday. But she said she'd tried to laugh off the question by admitting she was guessing and saying garbage and repairs were my chores, and laundry and dishwasher duty were hers.

I felt like it wouldn't be uncommon for the person who doesn't take out the garbage to be uncertain of the day it went to the curb. Other than those two questions, it seemed like we'd done pretty well. I just hoped it was enough. Regardless, what was done was done, and by the time we got off the train at our stop, my shoulders were definitely a lot more relaxed than they had been the last few weeks.

I even felt like I could breathe a little easier as we approached the staircase that led up to street level. Just before we hit the landing, my phone buzzed in my pocket. I took it out to see who it was and tripped over something on the floor. I flailed around for a solid thirty seconds trying to regain my balance before ultimately landing flat on my ass. Before I got up, I looked around to see what I'd tripped on, and found a random work boot in the middle of the floor. I shook my head and started to laugh as I got up. "Who the hell loses one boot in the subway?"

Maya's eyes widened as she pointed to my ass. "Oh my God, Colby! You split your pants!"

I twisted to check out the back of my slacks. Sure enough, they were ripped at the seam. And not just a little—the damn things were torn from one end to the other.

"Crap." I laughed.

Maya cracked up. "I guess I know what color underwear you have on today."

The last few weeks had been so stressful; I was pretty sure I hadn't smiled once. So my pants splitting turned into much needed comic relief, and the two of us laughed harder and longer than was probably appropriate for the incident. In fact, we were still laughing when we started up the stairway to the street again. Though my laughter came to an abrupt halt when I looked up and saw the face of the woman coming down the stairs—she was *definitely* not smiling.

Billie.

I froze.

She froze.

Maya, completely oblivious, was still laughing as she climbed the stairs ahead of me.

"Billie, what are you doing here?"

Her face fell. "Apparently not having as good of a time as you two…"

I shook my head. "No, no, no. It's not what it looks like. I swear."

She held up her hands and started to walk down the stairs again. "It's fine, Colby. I need to go so I don't miss my train."

"Billie, wait!" I chased after her.

But she rushed through the turnstile and shook her head. "Just go, Colby. Your *wife* is probably waiting for you on the street."

Hours later, I was sitting alone at my kitchen table with an empty bottle of tequila when Maya walked in. I hadn't seen her since the incident with Billie this afternoon.

"Where were you?" I slurred.

"I saw Billie get upset, so I thought I'd make myself scarce for a while. Is everything okay?"

I drank the last of the alcohol in my glass and guffawed. "Sure. Why wouldn't it be? The woman I love doesn't want to see me because I'm living with another woman, who happens to be my wife, and then today she saw what looked like me having a great time with said wife." I shrugged. "Everything is *just fucking peachy*."

Maya sighed and sat down across from me. "I'm so sorry for all the trouble I've caused you, Colby. I really am."

If I didn't know she had no heart, I might've bought her act and thought she felt bad for me. I got up from the table. "I'm going to bed."

After I brushed my teeth and changed, my mind circled back to where it had been all afternoon. I'd been wanting to text Billie, but I didn't want to upset her any more than I already had, so I'd refrained. Though in my current drunken state, I talked myself into believing it would be *irresponsible* of me not to check on her after she'd been visibly upset. I picked up my phone and laid back on my bed to type.

Colby: Hey. I'm sorry about today. I'd just tripped and split my pants. The hearing was today, and I felt like I was about to lose it. I swear it wasn't what it looked like. Things have definitely not been fun. I want to make sure you're okay and say I love you.

I watched as the message changed from *Sent* to *Delivered*, then a minute later finally showed as *Read*. I stared down at my phone, waiting for her response.

And waited.

And waited.

And waited…

♡CHAPTER 30

Billie

When it rains, it pours.

On top of my already miserable mood, Sunday morning I woke up to a leaky pipe under my kitchen sink that required immediate attention. The first person I thought to call was Holden, being that he was a jack of all trades and handled stuff like this all the time. Even though I didn't live in the building, I knew he'd come over to my place with his tools and help me if I needed him. But that wasn't an option right now. Holden was an extension of Colby. He'd run right back to Colby and tell him everything. Then Colby would think things were alright again with us when they weren't. Things hadn't been okay, in my mind at least, for a few days now—not since I'd run into Colby at the train station.

I did know one other plumber: Eddie Stark, AKA "Eddie Muscle," my client I'd let take me out on a date that one time. I decided to swallow my pride and call him for help.

He agreed to come on one condition: that I join him for lunch after—as friends. He knew by now that I wasn't interested in him romantically, so I trusted his intentions. I agreed to go to lunch as long as I got to treat him as a way to say thank you for helping me out.

Eddie had been in my kitchen for over an hour before he finally figured out what was wrong with my pipes. While I watched him work and listened to all the clanking under the sink, my mind was off in La-La-Land, replaying the scene at the subway station for the umpteenth time and alternating between seething and sad. At this point I couldn't even be sure my memory hadn't distorted everything, exaggerating what I'd seen and heard. I no longer had a clear picture of what had happened. Still, I continued to ruminate.

What were they laughing about?

What changed between them?

Does he like her now or something?

Should I text him back?

I really should text him back.

Hell no, I'm not texting him!

Was I wrong to get so mad?

How is Saylor? Is she laughing with them now, too?

Does she still miss me?

Are she and Maya getting close?

I felt like I was going crazy.

Yes, I knew I could've just contacted Colby for the answers to those questions, but my ego wouldn't seem to let me. It had, instead, paralyzed me into inaction.

Eddie finally came up from under my sink and announced that he believed he'd fixed the issue. We ran the water repeatedly to test things, and there wasn't a leak in sight. He was packing his stuff away when his eyes landed on something lying in my fruit bowl. "What the hell is that?"

Ugh. I meant to discard her. "You weren't supposed to see that," I said.

"Care to explain?"

"Not really."

"Billie…" He lifted it. "There's a fucking naked Barbie doll with her hair hacked off lying amidst a bunch of bananas. I need an explanation; otherwise, I'm gonna have to assume you're into some weird, Barbie-fruit voodoo."

I laughed. "It's nothing like that."

He arched a brow. "So what is it?"

"It's an old habit from childhood." I sighed. "Barbie's hair was sacrificed for my mental well-being."

"Oooh. Okay. That makes total sense." His eyes widened as if to say "this bitch is crazy."

"Okay, let me explain." I took the doll from him and looked down at it. "When I was younger and got upset, I'd take one of my older Barbie dolls and snip away at her hair, strand by strand, until there was nothing left. Something about that process was therapeutic for me. Sort of like one of those resistance balls you squeeze when you're stressed. Or popping bubblewrap."

He crossed his arms and laughed. "Yeah, sort of like that... But batshit crazy. I get it."

I couldn't blame him for thinking it was nuts, but he'd asked for an explanation.

"Something happened a few days ago," I told him. "That night I was so frustrated that I went to the five-dollar-and-under store for candy to stress-eat and picked up a cheap, generic Barbie, too. Hadn't done it in years."

He glared. "Billie..."

"Hmm?"

"You wanna talk about what the hell made you do that?"

My stomach growled. "I'm starving. Let's go to the restaurant, and I'll explain there."

It was the perfect, clear day in New York City for a stroll. Even though Eddie's truck was parked down the street, we walked to a bistro a couple of blocks away.

After we ordered our food, he leaned his arms on the table and said, "Okay, so tell me what's going on. I'd heard you were dating that guy who owns your building. Is he why Barbie got a crew cut?"

Sighing, I nodded. "Not just *dating*, Eddie. I fell hopelessly in love with him—and his little girl." My heart clenched. "And I miss them."

"Miss?" His eyes widened. "You broke up?"

"Not exactly."

He narrowed his eyes. "Sounds complicated."

"You have no idea."

"Do I need to go kick his ass?"

"It's not *his* ass I want to kick," I answered.

"What's going on? Talk to me."

"How much time do you have?" I took a sip of my water. "Seriously, this is a freaking long one."

"How much time do I have? More time than it takes to snip Barbie's hair off strand by strand. How about that?"

I ended up telling Eddie everything about the whole situation, ending with how I'd run into Colby with Maya laughing in the subway and how it really bothered me. Playing with my straw, I looked down into my glass. "I'd been missing him so much that entire day, and it was just…jarring to see him laughing with her. He supposedly hates her, and now they're laughing together like two best buddies? I mean, what the fuck?"

Eddie scratched his chin. "Well, let's break this down to get to the root cause of the issue. Because something tells me it's about more than just the laughter. What was it about him laughing that *really* bothered you?"

"Everything?" I shrugged. "How am I supposed to dissect it?"

"That's what Eddie's for." He grinned. "I'll help you."

I'd take any help I could get at this point. "Okay…"

Our lunch arrived, momentarily interrupting our conversation.

Eddie popped a French fry into his mouth. "So, first ask yourself, would you prefer he be unhappy the entire time he has to go through this living arrangement with her?"

Squirting some ketchup onto my plate, I shook my head. "No, not at all. That's not it. I *do* want him to be happy."

"Okay, so happiness might encompass laughter, correct?"

"This sort of reminds me of being on the stand in court." I chuckled. "Yes, I suppose it would."

"So we know it wasn't the fact that he was being jovial that got to you." He took a bite of his burger and spoke with his mouth full. "Next question. Did you feel like his laughing with her meant that he's developing feelings for her?"

As much as my insecurities wanted to latch onto that, I couldn't. "That doesn't sound right either, knowing how much he detests and resents her. So that's not what I think."

He put his burger down and brushed off his hands. "You know what *I* think?"

"What?"

"I think Eddie's verdict is in."

"What is it?"

"I think you were upset to see him laughing because you somehow applied it to his feelings toward *you*—like how could he possibly be happy when he's supposed to be miserable, missing you. Am I right? Somehow his laughter showed that the world hadn't, in fact, ended for him without you in it."

Wow. My eyes widened. I think Eddie just hit the nail on the head. "That's it, Eddie. That's what bothered me. It felt like a reflection of his feelings toward me, even though he's never given me a reason to doubt them. I think I've been ultrasensitive lately because of the stress of the situation. It must be warping my sense of reality."

I took a deep breath. Somehow having worked this out in my head made me feel a bit better. "Damn, you're good, Eddie Muscle. Wanna trade tattoos for therapy?"

"I like that idea." He bit into his burger. "Just think, Barbie could've been spared a botched haircut if you'd just talked to me sooner about this."

I chuckled. "I guess I'll never live the Barbie thing down, huh?"

"Probably not." He winked.

"Great."

Eddie poured some salt on his fries. "A lot of things make people laugh, Billie. You shouldn't read into it. Sometimes we have to laugh for survival. You probably just caught the dude in one of those moments." He pointed a fry at me. "I'll give you a great example from my own life. You know about my divorce, right?"

"Yeah, of course."

"It wasn't pretty. Very bitter. Lots of resentment. I told you that whole story once."

"Yeah…" I sipped my water.

"She and I weren't speaking for a long while. On the day we went in to finally sign the divorce papers, we were in the conference room with the two attorneys. It was quiet. And I shit you not, her lawyer just ripped one right in the middle of the damn thing."

"What?" I started cracking up.

"I don't think it was intentional, obviously, but still. He sneezed and a huge freaking fart came out. Nicole and I looked at each other as if to say: *did you fucking just hear what I did?*" He smiled at the memory. "Then we both lost it. Totally lost it—two people who'd barely spoken a word to each other in two years. There we were, still hating each other's guts, but we enjoyed that moment together, nevertheless. You know why? Because we're human. That's what humans do. We laugh at sick shit, we laugh with our enemies, and sometimes we laugh when we probably should be crying."

I wiped my eyes, no longer knowing whether I was laughing or crying. "Thank you for the perspective, Eddie. You've helped me see everything differently."

"Good."

"Does it make me selfish that I still want him to know it upset me, and I'm doing that by not responding to his text for three days?" I asked.

"There's nothing wrong with making him sweat because he *does* need to realize how difficult this whole thing is on you."

Poor Eddie let me vent to him that entire lunch. Then he drove us over to the shop since I'd offered to do a quick add-on to his most recent tattoo that he'd mentioned he wanted—on the house, of course.

After we finished, we stood outside the shop. As I did whenever I was out on the street in front of the building lately, I looked around for Colby, on the off chance he was leaving or passing by. I never quite knew if I was wishing to run into him or praying not to, but adrenaline always pumped through me until I was safely back inside.

"I can't thank you enough for taking my mind off things today and for your wise insight," I told Eddie.

"Well, you've done a lot for me over the years, Billie." He lifted his arm. "Each one of these beautiful pieces of art you've inked brings me joy every day. The least I could do is return some of it."

"You really are a great guy, Eddie. You're gonna make someone very happy someday."

"Hopefully not as happy as I made my ex." He guffawed.

"You'll find the one. She's out there. I just know it."

"Spoken like a true friend." He winked. "As much as I've been trying to date you all these years, I'm happy to have you as a friend, Billie. Although if you ever change your mind, I'm totally DTF."

Down to fuck.

"Kidding," he added. "I know that ship has sailed." He winked again. "Unless you bring it back to port."

I laughed, wrapping my arms around Eddie to hug him goodbye. He gave me a peck on the cheek. When I let go, my stomach sank. Brayden was approaching the building. He offered me a slight smile and wave before he headed inside. I assumed he'd seen me embrace Eddie. My first inclination was to run after him and try to explain, but then I concluded that would probably make me look even more guilty. After all, Eddie and I were just two friends sharing a hug; there was nothing to explain.

I suspected Brayden would tell Colby he saw me, though. Maybe now would've been a good time to reach out to Colby and finally respond to his text. But then I caught myself: I was getting too wrapped up in my fears and emotions. Colby and I were supposed to be on a break. So I decided to leave it that way.

After I locked up the shop, I opted to walk home to clear my head. As I did, guilt started to seep in about not having responded to Colby's text and about Brayden seeing me with Eddie. I didn't want to hurt Colby any more than he was already hurting. I decided after I got home, I would take a hot shower and think about what I wanted to say before texting him back tonight.

When I got to my apartment, there was a large envelope sitting outside my door. It was addressed to me. The return address was Colby's.

I took it inside and opened it to find a stack of letters written on yellow legal-pad paper. And a note from Colby.

I'm supposed to be taking notes every day on the woman I'm living with, but when I'm alone at night, all I want to do is write to the one I'm in love with. I wasn't going to show you any of these. They were written for my own therapeutic benefit—for my sanity, as a place for me to put all of these feelings while I am unable to tell you directly. I've written to you almost every night since you disappeared from my day-to-day life. If you want the truth about what's going on inside my head, you can find it here. You know where you cannot find the truth, though? Through one quick snapshot in time, a silly moment of misunderstanding like the other day at the train station.

The first letter really hit me in the feels:

Billie,

Okay. It hasn't even been that long, and I'm already going out of my mind. I'm not gonna make it through without seeing you. This sucks worse than anything I've ever experienced. I miss your laugh. I miss the way your ass feels warm against my dick when I spoon you at night. I miss the way Saylor lights up whenever you walk in the room. I miss your toothbrush. I know that's a strange thing to miss, but the first time you left your toothbrush in the holder in my bathroom, it meant something to me, that you planned to come back time and time again. And now it's gone.

I read each and every letter until I got to the last one, written the day I saw him at the subway.

Billie,

I feel like I'm losing you, and I'm not gonna lie: I'm freaking out about it. I've never felt so damn scared about anything. At the same time, I'm afraid to push you over the edge. I agreed to your request that we wouldn't be in contact for a while, so I suppose my writing to you right now instead of picking up the phone is me keeping my end of the bargain.

Every night before bed, Saylor asks if you're ever coming back. I always assure her that you are. My answer to her tonight was no different. But a small part of me worried that for the first time I was lying to her about you.

As painful as it was running into you a little while ago, it was SO damn good to see you. I was in a better mood earlier today than I had been in a while because we'd just left the Stokes hearing. I was so damn relieved to be out of that torture. And it went better than I thought it would. As we were heading back, I tripped over a random shoe, fell on my ass, and split my pants. Split my fucking pants, Billie. It was freaking ridiculous and hysterical. And so I laughed. I hadn't laughed that hard in a while. Pretty sure it had needed to come out. That's when I saw you. And you know how that went.

What you haven't seen is everything else that's happened since you've been gone—like me lying in bed at night aching for you, praying tomorrow won't be the day you come to your senses and realize this is all too much for you to handle. You deserve so much better, but I'm too selfish to let you go, Billie. I love you too damn much. So I'm gonna fight for you. I'm not giving up on us, even if at the moment you hate me. Hate me if you want. Just don't leave.

All my love,
Colby
AKA Pantless in the City

I smiled at that last part. It took me a long while to figure out my next move. I was mentally exhausted from all of the emotions reading his words had conjured up.

I finally texted him.

Billie: And to think I was so messed up at the train station that I didn't even catch a glimpse of your sexy ass peeking through your pants.

❤CHAPTER 31

Colby

Stepping off the elevator, I found Maya waiting outside my apartment door. She smiled. I frowned. Two-and-a-half weeks had passed since the Stokes hearing, yet I still felt a shock whenever I got home and saw her face and not Billie's. I dug my keys from my pocket. "Are you waiting for me?"

"Yeah, I was hoping we could talk for a few minutes."

"Is everything okay with Saylor?"

She nodded. "I didn't go in because I was waiting for you, but I can hear her laughing with the sitter."

"Okay." I shrugged. "Well, what's up?"

She nodded toward the emergency stairwell door diagonally across from my place. "Do you mind if we talk in there? I don't want them to overhear us."

"Sure."

Maya and I stepped into the stairwell. She took a seat on the top step and patted the empty space next to her. I reluctantly sat down.

"I heard from my lawyer an hour ago…"

I froze. "And?"

She sighed. "He didn't know the outcome, but apparently a decision has been made on our case. The friend he has in that office saw an envelope addressed to us in the outgoing mail. She looked up our names in their database, and the status had changed from *In Review* to *Closed.* But their system records every user who goes in and out of electronic files, so she didn't want to open the case."

"Okay… Well, I guess we only have a day or two until we find out at least."

Maya nodded and looked down. She was quiet for a long time before speaking again. "My lawyer said once a case has a final determination, there's no longer a risk of the investigator coming around. It's against procedure for them to do a home visit or anything like that once a case is closed. So I'll move out tomorrow morning, if that's okay?"

"Oh…yeah. That's fine."

She twisted her body and faced me. "Listen, Colby, I know I've said it before, but I'm really sorry for everything I've put you through. There's no excuse for the things I've done, but it was definitely easier when I didn't know you and Saylor. In my head, I justified my actions. You were just some guy who trolls strip clubs and brings home whatever vulnerable woman is willing to come with him—a user. So why not use you back?" She sighed. "But you are nothing like the person I made up in my head."

I ran a hand through my hair. "Maybe a part of me was that person when we met. But whoever I was changed the minute my daughter came into my life." I shook my head. "You've apologized more than once, yet I never have. It wasn't like I went back to the club where you worked in the weeks after we hooked up to see if you wanted to go out to dinner. So maybe I was a user. And for that, I'm sorry. I would never want a man to treat Saylor that way."

Maya's eyes filled with tears. "The fact that you could apologize to me after everything I've done speaks volumes about who you are. Saylor is so lucky to have you for a father."

"Thank you. That means a lot."

"She's a special little girl, Colby. I don't need to tell you that. And so much of that has to do with the example you set every day. So many parents tell their kids to be kind and then show them something very different with their own behavior. But you don't say empty words—you show your daughter the right way to live. Heck, she's not even here to know how you're acting right now, yet you apologized to me and showed me more kindness than I deserve." A tear rolled down Maya's cheek. "I wish I could have been a mother to her. I really do. But I could never trust myself."

I'd always thought Maya left because she was selfish, but maybe I'd been looking at it wrong. "Over the years, I've thought about what I might say when Saylor eventually asks about her mother. I could never come up with a response that wouldn't hurt her. But I think I have one now."

Maya wiped her tears. "What?"

"When she asks, I'll explain that sometimes walking away isn't a selfish act, but a selfless one, that her mother loved her enough to want a better life for her than she felt she could provide."

"Thank you." She sniffled. "Thank you from the bottom of my heart."

I nodded toward the door. "I should go relieve the sitter."

"Could I…ask you for a big favor?"

I raised a brow with a smirk. "You mean *another* big favor?"

Maya laughed. "Yes, definitely."

I stood and offered a hand to help her up. "What do you need?"

"Could I possibly take Saylor for ice cream tonight? Just the two of us?"

I might've found a way to accept what Maya had done, but I wasn't sure I was ready to trust her that much…

When I didn't immediately answer, she nodded. "I know it's a lot to ask, but it wouldn't take more than an hour. When I was a little girl, my mom worked two jobs. There were four of us kids, and we didn't get to see her that much, but every Sunday afternoon, she took one of us out for ice cream alone. I can't tell you how much I looked forward to those once-a-month dates with her. I always imagined I'd have children of my own someday, and I'd keep up the tradition of taking each of them for ice cream alone."

Fuck, it was hard to say no when she explained it. "Where would you take her?"

"There's that cute little ice cream shop right down the block. I pass it all the time. I think it's called Coyle's?"

Coyle's was only five or six buildings down. She wouldn't even have to cross a street… "And you won't say anything to her about who you are?"

"Oh God, of course not. I wouldn't do anything to confuse or hurt her."

"You'll be back in an hour?"

"I promise."

Even though it freaked me out, I nodded. "Okay. But please be back in an hour."

Maya wanted to wait a few minutes for the blotchiness on her face to fade, so I went into the apartment first. The sitter was gone by the time she came in, and when she appeared, Saylor ran to her.

"Hi, Maya! I'm learning how to line dance at school. You want to see?"

"I'd love to. I've never line danced myself."

"I can teach you!"

For the next ten minutes, Saylor counted steps as she moved side to side, and back and forth. Maya followed along like a good student. Watching them was the first time I second-guessed myself about whether keeping Maya's true identity from my daughter was the right thing to do. But then I remembered Maya hadn't even asked to keep in touch with me after she left tomorrow. She wasn't interested in keeping tabs on how Saylor was doing. Whether she had good reason or not, she didn't plan on being in my daughter's life.

When they were done dancing, Maya knelt down. "That was so much fun. But dancing really made me warm. You know what I think we should do to cool off?"

"What?"

"Go get ice cream after dinner."

Saylor jumped up and down. "Can we, Dad? Can we go get ice cream with Maya?"

"I have some work to do, sweetheart. But how about if Maya takes you?"

"Okay!"

Forty-five minutes later, I was completely tense watching the two of them walk out the door hand in hand. I stepped out into the hall as they headed to the elevator. "It's only going to take an hour, *right*?"

Maya turned and smiled. "Yes. We'll be back in a little while."

I waited until they disappeared from sight before going back into my apartment. I decided to take a hot shower, maybe put the showerhead setting on massage and see if I could get the knot in the back of my neck to loosen up.

It helped a little. But I'd been so preoccupied with letting Saylor go out with Maya that I forgot I'd never restocked the bathroom with towels after doing laundry. So I creaked open the door while I dripped all over the floor.

"Saylor? Are you here?"

No response.

"Maya?"

Silence.

Using the shirt I'd worn to work today, I at least covered my junk before darting to the laundry room. I grabbed a towel out of the dryer and wrapped it around my waist. But as I walked out of the room, I realized something looked different. It took me a minute to figure out what it was.

The top of the dryer is empty.

Maya's big suitcase had been stashed there for weeks, since the first day she'd moved in. An ominous feeling came over me, but I reminded myself she was leaving in the morning. She'd probably come home earlier today and brought it into her room to start packing.

Yeah, that's why it's missing. Still, I ran to the guest room to check.

My heart stopped when I opened the door. All of Maya's shit was gone. She'd had crap piled on top of the dresser for weeks, and now it was completely empty. But I was in denial, so I ran to the drawers and yanked every single one open, praying to God she'd just tidied up. But they were all empty, as were the nightstands and closet. And there was no sign of her suitcase either. Then I noticed something in the middle of the bed. It was a letter, typed and folded. I grabbed it, and my heart sank finding *US Citizenship and Immigration Services* at the top of the paper. The letter was dated last week.

DECISION

Thank you for submitting your Application to Register Permanent Residence or Adjust Status, to US Citizenship and Immigration Services (USCIS) under section 204(c) of the Immigration and Nationality Act (INA).

After a thorough review of your application and supporting documents and testimony, unfortunately, we must inform you that we are denying your application for the following reasons:

1. *Inconsistent testimonies given at interview*
2. *Insufficient evidence of a bona fide relationship*
3. *Adverse information gathered in USCIS' investigation, including home visit*

My head spun so fast that the letters on the rest of the page became jumbled even though my eyes kept scanning—the words *fraud* and *deportation* in the last paragraphs were clear as fucking day.

What the fuck? Why did Maya tell me she didn't know what decision had been made if she already had the letter? When the answer hit me, I ran to the bathroom and lost my lunch in the toilet.

I held open the front door to my fucking apartment so she could walk out with my daughter and never come back.

I yanked on clothes and ran out the door, sprinting down sixteen flights of stairs. The shirt I'd grabbed from the bathroom floor was inside out, my hair was still dripping from the shower, and I hadn't bothered with socks before jamming my feet into my dress shoes. But none of that mattered. Only getting to the ice cream shop did.

Running at full speed down the Manhattan street at the tail end of rush hour wasn't an easy task. I knocked into or shoved a dozen people as I raced my way to the store. Whipping the door open when I arrived, I scanned the room for Saylor.

"Table for one?" The hostess lifted a menu. "Would you like to sit at the counter?"

"Have you seen a little girl with blond hair…about four and a woman with long, dark hair in her mid-twenties?"

The woman's brows pulled together as she glanced around the ice cream parlor. There were a half-a-dozen tables with people, none of which had my little girl.

"I don't see anyone who looks like that."

"Did anyone like I described leave recently?"

She shook her head. "I've been here since three. I don't think so."

Fuck.

Fuck.

Fuuuuuuck!

I ran back out to the street and looked right and left. Where the hell did I go now? This city had eight-million people, and it felt like they were all blocking my view at the moment. Maya could have taken her anywhere! Where the fuck did I even start to look?

Think.

Think.

Think.

If I needed to get out of town undetected, how would I do it?

Maya wouldn't want to fly because she was here illegally. She'd be too afraid of getting caught by security at the airport. She also didn't have a driver's license to rent a car.

Then it hit me. The bus depot was only about three blocks away. So I ran toward it. Of course, just like the rest of the damn city, it was packed. I frantically weaved in and out of people, but there was no sign of either of them anywhere. Unsure what the hell to do next, I whipped out my phone to enlist the help of my friends. We could split up the city and check more places.

Holden didn't answer, so I left a message. "I need your help! Maya took Saylor! Call me back!"

Then I dialed Owen. My damn call went straight to voicemail.

Fuck.

My fingers shook as I searched through my contacts for Brayden's number. But before I could hit enter, my phone buzzed with an incoming call.

Billie.

I swiped to answer.

"I can't talk. Maya took Saylor!"

"I know. She brought her here."

"*What?*"

"She's here with me at the shop, Colby. That's why I'm calling. I thought it was strange. Maya just showed up two minutes ago with her, handed me a letter to give you, and told me to take good care of Saylor."

My heart pounded. "Saylor's okay?"

"Yes, Colby. She's fine. What's going on?"

I leaned over with my hands on my knees to catch my breath. "Holy shit. Thank God."

"You're scaring me. What happened?"

"I'm not sure. But I'll be there in two minutes. Just don't let Saylor out of your sight, please."

"I won't."

Even though Saylor was apparently safe, I ran the entire way to the tattoo shop. When I walked into the back, my little girl's eyes lit up. "Daddy!"

I wrapped her in my arms so tight. "Where did you go, sweetheart?"

"Maya took me for ice cream."

"At Coyle's?"

She shook her head. "No. The ice cream man was parked outside, and I wanted a cone with sprinkles."

I pulled back and looked her up and down. There was a giant brown spot on her shirt. "I guess you got chocolate."

She nodded.

I pulled her to me once again, hugging her tightly.

Saylor laughed. "You're acting weird, Daddy."

I took a deep breath before releasing her. "Sorry. I missed you, that's all."

Deek, whom I hadn't even noticed in the room until now, walked over. "Hey, kiddo. We just got some new glow-in-the-dark paints. How 'bout you paint your name and then we'll turn off the lights in the bathroom and check it out?"

My daughter's eyes grew wide. "Can I, Daddy?"

"Of course, baby."

Billie waited until they were out of earshot. "What the heck happened? You sounded unhinged on the phone."

I took a deep breath. "I was unhinged. I thought Maya took Saylor."

"Why would you think that?"

I explained everything—from talking to Maya in the stairwell to finding her room empty with the determination letter from Immigration on the bed.

"Why did she lie to you, only to bring her here?"

"I have no damn idea."

Billie held up her pointer. "Here, she gave me this. Maybe whatever's inside will make sense of it all."

I stared at the envelope for a moment before ripping it open.

Dear Colby,

The day I showed up at your door with Saylor, I was so worried I couldn't give my little girl a good life. But it turned out I gave her the best life ever with you, where she belongs. I'm so thankful you're her father. If I learned one thing from you over the last few months, it's that words don't mean anything—it's actions. Your example has shown me what sacrifice, family, and love mean, and it's about time I owned up to the mess I've made.

Today I mailed a sworn affidavit to Officer Weber at Immigration. In it, I detailed all of my actions, including blackmailing you into marrying me or risk sharing custody of a child with a woman who had nothing but bad intentions. I hope it clears you of any charges the officer decides to bring. I've also left pre-signed, no-fault divorce papers with my lawyer.

Tonight I'm flying back to Ecuador to accept accountability for my mistakes. I will participate in the open investigation of the drowning since I left before it could be completed. If I'm lucky enough that I'm allowed to keep my freedom, I hope to work on salvaging my relationship with my family.

Take care of our little girl.

Always,
Maya

I blinked a few times.

"What does it say?" Billie asked.

Still shell-shocked, I handed her the letter. She read and shook her head. "So that's it? Maya's gone?"

I shrugged. "I guess so."

"What do we do now?"

I had no idea what was going to happen with Immigration or the divorce, but I absolutely knew what needed to be done in this moment. I wrapped my arms around Billie and pulled her to me.

"This." I pressed my lips to hers. "This is what we do from now on…"

❤CHAPTER 32

Billie

Is it just me or is the sun shining brighter today?

Colby wanted me to spend the night at his place yesterday, but I insisted he take Saylor home alone and decompress. I'd promised we'd get together tonight instead. Giving him space, even if he didn't want it, was the right call. What he'd been through—thinking Saylor had been kidnapped—was traumatic as hell. I wanted him to spend quality time with her and not worry about me. Because if I knew Colby, he would've spent last night trying to make up for lost time and apologizing for everything.

I was grateful that I'd only found out about the false alarm after the fact. Believing Saylor could have been in harm's way would have given me a heart attack. I'd been so confused when Maya had dropped her off at my shop. I still couldn't get over the fact that Colby had to spend those minutes thinking Maya had fled with his precious little girl.

But today was a new day.

With Maya headed back to Ecuador—not far enough, if you ask me—the worst seemed to be over. But I knew there was still a lot looming. We didn't know whether Maya's confession would clear Colby of wrongdoing. He was still responsible for trying to deceive the authorities, even if she *had* been holding a virtual gun to his head. So part of me was still holding my breath.

As I readied to leave the shop and head upstairs after my last client, Deek wished me well.

"Hey," he said. "You finally made it to the other side of that freaking mess. So try to enjoy tonight, alright? Save the heavy discussions for another time. You guys deserve some peace. Just enjoy each other."

"Thank you. I'm gonna try."

"And I called your appointments tomorrow and personally let them know I'm gonna take care of them. Just enjoy the night and sleep in. Take the day off."

Still on cloud nine, I agreed—which was so unlike me. "I'm not even gonna argue with you, Deek."

He winked. "You're learning."

"Thank you, my friend." I hugged him goodbye.

As I took the elevator up to have dinner with Colby and Saylor, I felt oddly jittery. It had been a while since I'd been at their apartment. And Saylor still didn't know the true reason I'd been away. I'd gotten a vibe from her last night that she felt a bit cautious around me, as if she wasn't sure to trust that I wouldn't leave them again. She hadn't been as excited to see me as I'd thought she might have been. It was understandable, but it sucked to have to earn her trust back. Was I supposed to act like nothing had happened? I felt like I owed her more of an explanation for why I'd been gone. But any explanation would be a lie, and I wasn't comfortable with that, either. Maybe less would be more.

I knocked on the door, but it wasn't Colby who answered.

Brayden stood there instead, and my first reaction was panic.

"Brayden, what's going on?"

"Hey, Billie." He smiled. "You look worried to see me. Don't be."

"Is everything okay?"

Before he could answer, Saylor came running toward me. "Billie!"

I knelt and extended my arms wide, so happy that she seemed more excited than yesterday. "Hey, sweetie! How are you?"

She hugged me. "Are you back now?"

"I am, honey."

Saylor squeezed me tighter. "Good!"

"Where's Daddy?" I asked her.

"I don't know." She shrugged, but seemed to be stifling a smile.

I narrowed my eyes. "You don't know?"

She bounced on her feet. "I'm not supposed to tell you we made pizza for you, and Daddy took it with him!"

Now I was even more confused. "Pizza for me?"

"Thanks a lot, Saylor." Brayden laughed.

I looked up at him. "Where's Colby?"

"He's arranged a little private something for the two of you. We already explained to Saylor that she gets to hang out with Uncle Brayden tonight while you and Colby catch up." He pulled on one of her pigtails. "Which of course makes her a very lucky girl."

"Oh… Colby said he and I were going to have dinner with Saylor."

"Yeah, well. Change of plans. He thought you guys should have some alone time." Brayden winked and handed me an envelope.

I opened it and read the piece of paper inside.

You once implied that you'd like to have dinner on the rooftop.
I thought tonight would be nice for that. Take the elevator
to the top floor, then turn right to access the stairwell to the roof.

"Oh my gosh," I murmured.

"Well, you'd better not keep my boy waiting." He winked.

"Thanks, Brayden."

"You guys stay out as long as you need to." He gave me a look.

I hugged Saylor goodbye and headed down the hall. Chills ran down my spine as I got back into the elevator and took it to the top floor. I followed Colby's instructions to get to the roof, and when I opened the door, the most magnificent sight met my eyes.

Colby was waiting for me. He'd been looking out toward the skyline but turned when he heard the door open. His mouth curved into a smile. He'd set up lanterns, white lights, and heaters—since it was the middle of winter. There were burgundy and red flowers on the table and a bucket of champagne. It was wildly romantic.

"Hi, beautiful. You found me."

Found him. It certainly felt like we'd lost each other, and this moment marked finding our way back again. He opened his arms, and I rushed to him. He wrapped himself around me, and I basked in the feeling of safety and love as he held me.

Finally.

We fell into a warm and passionate kiss. I hadn't realized just how hungry I'd been for it until our tongues collided. "You didn't have to do all this…" I breathed after a moment.

He rubbed my bottom lip with his thumb. "It's been way too long since I've been able to be the boyfriend you deserve. I know we have a lot to discuss, a lot to repair in our relationship. But tonight, I want to show you how much you mean to me. I hope it's the first of many more dinners on this rooftop we get to have together."

I noticed a table of hot foods set up in the corner. "What did you do over here?"

"Just a few of your favorite things."

I lifted one of the stainless tops to find little meatballs.

"They're the IKEA ones you love," he said.

The other tray contained square slices of all kinds of homemade pizza.

"Saylor and I made the pizzas together."

"Yeah." I smiled. "She told me."

"Ah. She did? Little blabbermouth."

"She tried to keep it in for all of three seconds." I laughed.

"Do you remember what we ate the night Maya showed up and turned our world upside down?" he asked.

I wracked my brain. "No, I guess I don't."

"That was the night we made the pizzas with Saylor."

"Oh, that's right! Of course. How could I forget?"

He smiled. "I often think about how that pizza dinner with you and Saylor was the last normal memory I had before my world changed. That day, that pizza dinner, was the last night I was able to exist without living in constant fear of losing everything that ever mattered to me. I can't tell you how many times I wished I could go back to that night and take up where we left off, before that knock on the door." He exhaled. "So the pizza is a symbol of picking up the pieces and going back to *exactly* where we left off—to that simple night when we had so much hope for the future."

I looked him in the eyes. "I actually don't wish we could go back, Colby."

His eyes widened. "Really?"

"Really…" I caressed his cheek. "I've learned a lot about myself in the past several weeks. Being apart from you showed me what I value the most in this life: family—not the one I was born into, the one I chose. What bothered me more than anything was that Maya was getting to spend time with the two people I care about the most, the two people who have become my world. It was never about her or what she got to have. My frustration and anger had to do with what *I* was missing."

"I get that, baby." He ran his hand through my hair. "I so get that."

"In the end, we can't definitively say we'd be better off if this whole thing had never happened. We don't know that. Things happen for reasons we sometimes don't understand. All I do know is I might not be here on this rooftop with you right now if everything hadn't happened the way it did. And I'm really grateful for this moment."

Colby's eyes glistened. "This night is different than I imagined it would be."

I tilted my head. "How so? What did you imagine?"

He sighed. "I don't know. I thought you might still be a little mad at me for that day you saw me laughing."

"No." I laughed. "A wise man named Eddie Muscle helped me understand what was bothering me with all that. It was never about the laugh. It was my own insecurities. You deserve to be happy. I just always want to be a *part* of your happiness."

"C'mere." Colby brought me into a tight embrace and spoke into my hair. "I felt like I needed to say so many things to you tonight, but you've just said everything I could ever hope for. How the fuck did I get so lucky?"

I reached up to kiss him and patted his shoulder. "Let's eat before everything gets cold."

We plated our food and sat down under the beautiful Manhattan night sky. We devoured the pizza and meatballs and broke open the champagne, laughing when it exploded all over Colby's sleeve. It felt euphoric. And now also a little tipsy.

"Do you want dessert? I made you some spinach brownies." He smiled.

"Mmm... I'll definitely be having one. But there's something I need even more right now."

His eyes filled with lust. "I wonder if it's the same thing I want."

I looked behind me. "Does that door lock?"

"It sure does. And if it didn't, I'd figure out a way to jury-rig it shut." Colby took out a key and scurried over to lock the door.

He returned, lifting me as I wrapped my legs around him. We kissed like we depended on each other for oxygen. The wind blew our hair. This felt like something out of a movie: we were about to have rooftop sex under the stars surrounded by magnificent lights. It was so intimate and beautiful.

Colby's erection dug into my abdomen. "It feels like it's been forever," he mumbled over my lips.

"I need you now, Colby." I panted. "Right fucking now."

He undid his pants just low enough so his cock sprang out. He lifted my skirt and pushed my panties aside, entering me in one swift movement.

I briefly shut my eyes in ecstasy as he wrapped his hand around the back of my neck. His eyes sparkled under the white lights as he gazed at me while he moved in and out. I threaded my fingers through his thick hair, loving the look on his gorgeous face while he fucked me. I bucked my hips, and my clit rubbed against his lower abs. I could've come at any moment if I'd let myself. It had simply been too damn long.

Still carrying me, he walked over to a leather couch at the far end of the rooftop and sat down with me on top of him. I began to ride him hard and fast—angrily. Angry not at him, but only for the time we'd lost. While everything had ended the way it was meant to, time lost together was one thing we could never get back.

His eyes were hazy as he looked up at me. "I was so fucking scared to lose you," he whispered.

"You own me, Colby," I said, bearing down harder on his cock. "You never lost me."

That seemed to set him off, because almost as soon as I said it, his eyes rolled back.

"I love you so fucking much, Billie." He groaned as his body shook beneath me. He pumped harder as his hot cum filled me.

"I love you, too." I clenched my muscles and let my orgasm rocket through me. "I missed feeling your cum inside me."

"Keep saying stuff like that, and I'll be ready for round two in three, two, one..." He paused. "I'm ready again." He slapped my ass.

He wrapped us in a blanket he'd brought, and we lay together for a long time, sated from that amazing sex, which was fast and furious—exactly what I needed after so much time apart.

As we looked up at the stars, I wasn't sure what compelled me to risk ruining the mood. But I had to ask. "Did she ever try anything on you?"

He took a couple of seconds to process. "Maya, you mean?" He shook his head. "Not directly. There was one night, though, when she asked if she could watch me brush my teeth to get a feel for my nighttime routine, so I went along with it. Then she wouldn't leave and suggested she spend the night in my room… you know, to learn more about my sleeping habits."

Ugh. I stiffened. "What did you say?"

"I told her to get the fuck out."

I smiled. "She listened?"

"Yup. And she never tried anything like that again."

"She probably figured men are weak and she could get you to fall for it."

"I might have been a weak person when she met me, but I'm nothing like that now. You couldn't have paid me all the money in the world to sleep with that woman." He looked at me. "Since we're asking the uncomfortable questions, I should ask you about your *date* with that Eddie guy."

Colby was only half-smiling, so I couldn't tell if he was mad or not.

"It wasn't a date—I promise you that. Eddie's just a friend and always will be. He helped me get over my anger after running into you at the subway."

"He may be your friend…" Colby rolled his eyes. "But there's no way he's not trying to get into your pants. I don't care what you say."

I shrugged. He was probably right. "Anyway, I felt bad that Brayden saw me saying goodbye to him. I was afraid you'd get the wrong idea."

"I knew deep down that you wouldn't cheat on me. But like you said, it reminded me of what I was missing. When Brayden told me he saw you, I punched a hole in my bedroom wall."

I covered my mouth. "Oh my God."

"Yeah. Holden was pissed. He said I'm only allowed to wreck the walls again if it's during sex."

"I'm sorry you got upset."

"It's all good now."

Colby's phone buzzed. He looked down at it for a few seconds. "Jesus," he muttered.

"What's going on? Who is it?"

"Brayden." He turned the phone toward me so I could read it.

Brayden: I know you guys must be "busy," but Saylor keeps asking if she's gonna get to say goodnight to Billie. I think she's still a little paranoid about Billie not coming back. Not sure if you guys want me to keep her up or not so you can say goodnight. Also, everything is fine, but we had a little incident where Saylor grabbed my phone while I was in the bathroom and started looking through my photos. She happened to come across a nude selfie this chick sent me. So, I lied and told her I was taking a medical school class and had been studying anatomy. She didn't question the fact that I am not in medical school. But as a result of our discussion, I am now desperately in need of a stiff drink, so if you feel like putting me out of my misery, I'd be game.

"Oh, Lord." I shook my head.

"Well, it could've been worse. It could've been Holden's phone." Colby laughed.

I sighed. "That's very true."

"What do you think?" he asked. "We should probably go save him, huh?"

"Yeah." I smiled. "I think we should go tuck Saylor in together. I want to read her a story."

"She'll love that so much." He smiled.

"And then I want to tuck you in after that." I winked.

He kissed my neck. "I definitely have something to tuck inside *you*."

❤️CHAPTER 33

Colby

Three weeks had passed since Maya left, and things finally started to return to normal.

True to her word, she'd left signed divorce papers with her attorney and disappeared without a trace, just like she had four years ago. While I didn't wish her any harm, I also hoped this time she stayed gone from my life for good.

Billie and I had spent a lot of time reconnecting. We were pretty solid now, but I knew something that would really help move things to the next level. Billie thought that *something* was out of our hands. But she didn't know the power of Holden's dick…

I stepped off the elevator on my buddy's floor and knocked on his door. As always, it took a while for him to answer. When he did, he looked completely disheveled and blinked at the sunlight like it was an intruder. "What time is it?"

I helped myself inside his apartment. "Nine AM. Sorry to wake you at the time normal people get up, but I couldn't wait anymore. Were you able to get it?"

Holden padded over to his kitchen table and picked up a manila envelope. "Would I let you down?"

I pulled him into a bear hug. "Holy shit! I can't believe you were able to get this done. You're the best. Does that dick of yours have a tickler on the end of it or something? You just take it out of your pants and women do whatever the hell you want?"

One night last week, Holden and I had been hanging out having a beer. He'd asked how things were going between Billie and me. I'd said good, but it would be better if the wait for a judge to sign the no-fault divorce papers I'd submitted wasn't a minimum of three months. Holden had asked what courthouse they'd been filed in. I told him Centre Street, and he said he used to hook up with a clerk who worked there. They hadn't talked in a while, but he offered to reach out to see if she could do anything to expedite the processing. I'd said sure, but didn't really expect anything to come of it—until a few days ago, when Holden texted me that he'd had lunch with the woman, and she'd said she could probably get the file pulled and signed within a few days.

I slipped the papers out of the envelope and read the signed divorce decree. "I don't know how to thank you, man."

Holden grinned. "No thanks needed. Tessa thanked me in a stall in the ladies' room when I stopped into the courthouse to pick up the papers yesterday afternoon."

I shook my head. "Only you can get laid and a divorce finalized in one outing, my friend."

He laughed and put a hand on my shoulder. "Glad I could be of service. Now get the fuck out of my apartment so I can go back to sleep, and go tell your girl the good news."

"I'm gonna give these to her…but not until later. So if you happen to see her at some point today, don't mention this, okay?"

"You got it, buddy."

My next stop was downstairs at Billie's shop. She wasn't in this morning because she'd taken Saylor to her Mommy and Me class today, which worked out perfectly since I needed to check in with Deek without her around.

Justine was on the phone when I walked in. She covered the mouthpiece and smiled. "She's not in this morning, babe."

"I know. I came to see Deek. But do me a favor and don't let her know I stopped by."

Justine's face lit up. "Are you and Deek up to something?"

"Yeah, and I want it to be a surprise."

"Your secret is safe with me." She nodded toward the studio behind her. "Go on back. His first appointment isn't here yet."

Deek was setting up his station when I walked in. He lifted his chin. "What's up, man?"

"Were you able to work on what we talked about?"

He nodded and opened his drawer, taking out a stencil and a photo. "I found this picture of her that shows her forearm, so I used it as my reference. Should be pretty spot-on. What do you think?"

My eyes went back and forth between the stencil and the photo. In the picture, Billie had her hands up in the air, so it perfectly displayed the ornate key tattooed on the inside of her forearm. She'd told me her grandfather had given that key to her grandmother the day they'd met to symbolize what she meant to him. That story had given me hope that underneath the layers of armor, Billie was a woman who believed in true love. Now I was going to get a matching Victorian heart-shaped lock tattooed in the same spot on my arm. It seemed fitting since Billie held the key to my heart.

I smiled. "It's perfect, man."

"Hell of a lot better than a dumb fucking rose, too…"

I chuckled. "I'm glad you approve."

"When are you going to have her ink it on you?"

"Tonight. I booked an appointment under a fictitious name."

"What time is that?"

"Six."

"I have an appointment at six thirty, but I can probably move my guy to tomorrow so you guys have the place to yourself."

"That would be great."

He nodded. "No problem."

"Thanks, Deek." I handed him back the stencil. "I have to run. Would you put it in your drawer so it's safe until later?"

"Sure thing."

"I appreciate it." I waved.

"By the way," Deek yelled after me. "If I find your ass-cheek imprint on my chair tomorrow, we're going to have a problem."

I smiled and tapped two fingers to my forehead in a salute. "Got it, boss."

My next stop was to meet Billie and Saylor after Mommy and Me. Saylor had a check-up at eleven, and I'd promised my parents I'd stop over for lunch after. My mother had subtly reminded me that it had been a while since she'd seen my face. I arrived at the class a few minutes early and watched Saylor and Billie from the window. They were both laughing, shaking tambourines and dancing around like they didn't have a care in the world. It made my heart feel so warm and full. These two little ladies were my entire world. I knew it was too soon to ask Billie to marry me, but she was going to be my wife someday. As corny as it sounded, I'd met my soulmate.

As if to prove she was my other half, Billie turned around and her eyes immediately found me watching through the window. I waved before walking inside to wait by the door until class was over.

"Hey, Daddy!" Saylor skipped to me. "Are the shelves fixed?"

My brows pulled together. "What shelves?"

"Billie said you were fixing the broken shelves in the laundry room."

I looked to Billie who bent to speak to Saylor. "Umm... sweetie, could you go get my purse from the cubby for me, please?"

Billie waited until Saylor was out of earshot. "Two of the ladies inquired where my *boss* was today, assuming I was the sitter

356

again. So I told them he was at home recuperating because he'd spent all morning drilling me. I thought I said it low enough that Saylor wouldn't hear. But apparently, she caught part of it because she asked me what you were drilling. The shelves in the laundry room were the best I could come up with."

I hooked an arm around Billie's waist and yanked her close. "I love it when you get all possessive."

"Oh yeah?" She grinned. "Good because here comes another member of your stupid fan club." Billie grabbed two fistfuls of my shirt and planted her lips on mine.

Yep. I fucking love my girl possessive.

After Billie was done marking her territory, the three of us walked down the block together. We stopped at the corner, where Billie had to go into the subway station to catch the train down to her shop. I gave her a quick peck. "Can I see you later?"

"Sure. But I might be kinda late tonight. My last client of the day is new, and I have a feeling he might be difficult."

It was hard to contain my smile. "What makes you say that?"

"Well, for starters, he made the appointment using a middle initial. Who makes an appointment anywhere using their first name, middle initial, and last name? Someone who is very precise and picky, that's who. And of course, he wants *a rose* tattoo. Not even original art. He told Deek he likes the one on the sample wall."

I couldn't hide my smile this time. "Sounds awful. But maybe he'll surprise you and be cool."

"Doubt it. Anyway, I have to run. I'll text you when I'm done for the day."

At 6 PM precisely, I walked into the shop with a huge bouquet of wildflowers and an envelope tucked in my back pocket. I'd expected to see Justine at the front desk, but I found Billie there instead.

Her lips curved to a smile. "Aren't you a sight for sore eyes? It's a good thing you didn't show up to the Mommy and Me class looking all adorable with those flowers. Your fan club might have trampled me."

I chuckled. "I'm here for my appointment."

"Your appointment? Like for a tattoo?"

I nodded. "Yep. I'm your six o'clock."

Billie's nose wrinkled. "You're my middle initial guy?"

"That's right."

"What's with the fake name?"

"I wanted to surprise you. I'm a little upset you didn't figure out it was me."

"How would I have known?"

I pointed to the open appointment book on the desk. "Read the name out loud."

"Hugh G. Rection." It took her a few seconds to catch on. Then she peered over the counter and eyed my crotch with a smirk. "I don't see any."

"Trust me, you're going to be seeing one *very* soon." I walked to the front door and twisted the lock until it clanked shut, then flicked off the neon OPEN sign.

"I'm guessing Deek was in on this?" Billie closed the appointment book. "Because he rushed out of here a few minutes ago, right after telling Justine she could go home early. He would normally never leave me alone on a Saturday night."

"Yeah, Deek was in on it." I walked behind the counter and pressed my lips to hers. "Remember that fantasy I told you about a long time ago? The one where I fuck you on your hydraulic chair?"

Billie bit down on her bottom lip. "I do."

"That's happening tonight, too. But first…I'm getting the tattoo you owe me."

"The rose?"

"Definitely not the rose. I'm actually really glad you wouldn't ink that on me. You were right that a first tattoo should have meaning."

"So what do you want to get?"

"I'll show you. But first…" I lifted her off her feet. "I'm taking you in the back so I can suck your face without everyone on the street being able to see."

Billie giggled as I carried her into the studio. I got so into the kiss that I almost forgot the big news I'd been dying to tell her all day. When we came up for air, I used my thumb to wipe the lipstick I'd smeared underneath her bottom lip. "I have something for you."

She grinned. "I know. I feel it against my hip bone. I guess maybe you're living up to your fictitious name after all."

I carried her over to her hydraulic chair and set her down before pulling the manila envelope from my back pocket.

"What is it?" she asked.

"Open it up and find out."

Billie tore into the envelope. She pulled the pages out and scanned the top one for a few heartbeats before looking up with wide eyes. "Is this for real? I thought finalizing the divorce was going to take months?"

"Holden knew someone at the courthouse and used his powers of persuasion to get it moved to the top of the pile."

"So you're really not married anymore?"

"I'm all yours, sweetheart."

Billie stared down at the papers for a long time, shaking her head, and when she looked up again, her face was full of emotion. "Oh my God, Colby. I'm so happy. I didn't realize how much it was weighing on me until right now. I feel so much lighter."

I nodded. "Me too. And my lawyer has been talking to the investigator. He's pretty sure we're going to be able to settle on a smallish fine as a penalty for what I did, rather than criminal prosecution. It feels like we can put this all behind us now."

She shook her head. "Today has been the best day. I spent the morning with Saylor, you're officially a free man again, and I'm going to take your ink virginity."

"Hey, don't forget about tattoo-chair sex."

She laughed. "That, too. So what am I inking on you, anyway? Did you bring a picture of what you want?"

"I did better than that..." Walking over to Deek's station, I pulled open his drawer and took out the stencil he'd made. Handing it to her, I pointed to the inside of my forearm. "I want this right here."

I thought I'd need to explain, but when Billie covered her mouth and her eyes welled up with tears, I knew she understood. She turned her arm and showed me her tattoo. "It's the lock that goes with my key."

I nodded. "Deek drew it. He used a photo of your tattoo for reference to make them match. I may not have given you a key on our first date, like your grandfather gave your grandmother, but you've had my heart since the moment I met you. Now you'll always have the key that goes to it."

Tears streamed down Billie's face. "Oh my God, Colby. You are the sweetest, most romantic man in the world. I love you so much."

"I love you, too, babe. But I'm not sure I'm really that sweet. Because while you're thinking how romantic I am, I'm still sitting here with a hard-on, wondering if I could get away with banging you on the chair *before* you start my tattoo."

Billie laugh-cried as she opened her arms. "We definitely can do that. Come here and let me make that dream of yours finally come true."

I cupped her cheeks. "Sweetheart, I can't wait to get you naked, but you've already made all my dreams come true..."

♥EPILOGUE

Colby
One year later

Holden stood at the podium, readying to give his speech. The DJ held his hand up, prompting everyone to quiet down as Holden took the mic. I held my breath, unable to imagine my best man taking this seriously, and wondering whether I was about to get roasted.

Holden smirked at me, ·then began to speak. "Loyal… talented…stunningly handsome—the best friend anyone could ask for." He paused. "But enough about me."

Our guests roared with laughter.

"My name is Holden Catalano, and I'm here for the free food and booze." He grinned as everyone laughed again. "Actually, much to his dismay, I'm Colby's best man." He looked over at me. "While I'd love to be able to say Colby chose me for this role, I'm standing here today because I drew from a hat a piece of paper with the words *best man* written on it. Our buddies Owen and Brayden, on the other hand, drew blanks and were relegated to mere ushers as a result." He turned to me. "I want you to know, Colby, that I take this responsibility very seriously. I've even waited until *after* this speech to get shitfaced because I didn't want to botch this up.

Because let's face it, I'm the worst man, not the best for this job. But alas, you're stuck with me." He sighed. "We all know that if Ryan were here, *he* would be the best man. Instead, he's looking down on you right now, thinking... How the hell did you snag a woman as awesome as Billie?"

Laughter once again erupted throughout the ballroom. When it dissipated, he went on. "Colby and I, along with Owen, Brayden, and our late friend, Ryan, have been friends since childhood. Growing up, we called upon Colby as the oldest in our group to set an example for us." Holden paused. "That explains why we're all idiots."

I clapped. Billie and I looked at each other as we cracked up.

"But honestly, I *am* the wrong man for this job, partly because Colby and I have always been like yin and yang. He went to the fancy schools and got the fancy jobs. Most of the jobs I manage to snag are of the blow variety."

Billie placed her hands over Saylor's ears. Thankfully, my daughter had no idea what that meant and seemed unfazed.

"And you certainly don't need to go to a fancy school to be a drummer like me," Holden continued. "That said, Colby doesn't have a musical bone in his body. We used to take girls we were looking to let down easy to karaoke so they could hear Colby sing—they'd magically disappear."

I rolled my eyes and shook my head.

"And don't even get me started on our styles. Couldn't be more different. Colby wears three-piece suits on the regular. The last time I wore a three-piece suit, I was sitting next to my defense attorney in court after a barroom brawl."

My shoulders shook. "True," I mouthed to him.

"So if we're so non-compatible...why the hell did I agree to this important task? Well, the answer is simple." He paused. "I'm here for Billie."

I looked over at my bride, who wiped a tear of laughter from her eye.

"I knew from the first time Billie worked on my body art that she had amazing taste. I thought she could do no wrong. Then I found out she was in love with Colby and realized…nobody's perfect."

Our guests were once again in stitches.

Holden scratched his chin. "So, yeah, Colby and I…we're yin and yang. And I know this because earlier, I looked up the meaning of yin and yang for the first time in my life—to make sure I had it right." He looked around the room. "It's one of those things you always hear about but don't fully understand. And in learning about it, I realized that even more yin and yang than Colby and me, are Colby and Billie." Holden turned to us. "Listen to this: yin represents an energy that is feminine and dark." He pointed to my bride. "That's totally like badass Billie, right? And yang represents energy that is bright, masculine, and I shit you not…hot. You're welcome, Colby." He laughed. "Doesn't that remind you of the two of them? Opposites that go so damn well together that it's like they were made for each other, like the sun and the moon." He looked over at us. "The most important realization in my research of yin and yang is that even though they're opposites, they rely on each other to exist. Without night, there is no day. Without love, there is no grief—we all learned that the hard way when Ryan passed. And I think it's safe to say, without Colby, there is no Billie. Without Billie, there is no Colby. They've become one today." Holden flashed his megawatt smile. "And yes, I did manage to bring this speech to a sappy ending."

My cheeks hurt from grinning.

He grabbed his champagne flute and lifted it. "So, to Billie and Colby, yin and yang. You inspire me to want to fall in love someday…when I'm sixty-five and can no longer get it up." Amidst the laughter of the audience, he added, "Love you both! And Colby, man, if you didn't like this speech, I suggest choosing someone else to be your best man the next time you get married." He winked at me.

I gave him the finger and got up to give him a huge hug—those two gestures in quick succession pretty much summed up our relationship.

When I returned to my seat, Billie was beaming. "That was freaking awesome."

"Only Holden," I said.

Our wedding was a pretty grand affair held in the ballroom of a hotel downtown. Billie had insisted she wanted a smaller wedding, but I'd convinced her that after everything we'd been through, we deserved a massive party. Since Billie wasn't really into the planning component, we gave my mother the gift of her life, letting her take full charge of making the arrangements. She, of course, met with Billie several times and took my gorgeous bride's taste and style into consideration. We ended up with a colorful motif that was vibrant yet classy. Red and burgundy flowers with black feather accents. You could call it gothic chic.

My wife turned to me as they began to serve the cake. "I can't believe how amazing this day turned out."

I glanced down at her chest. "Almost as amazing as your tits in that corset. I nearly died when I saw you coming down the aisle on Deek's arm."

"Did you really think I'd have any other kind of top for my dress?"

Billie's dress was nothing short of spectacular. It was two pieces: a satiny, white corset top and a massive ballgown bottom. Her black hair was styled half up, half down in loose curls. I'd always imagined I would cry when I saw her coming down the aisle, but my reaction surprised me. Of course, I was filled with emotion, but instead of crying, I wasn't able to stop smiling. In fact, I'd yet to shed a tear at my own wedding, even during my father-daughter dance with Saylor. But the night was still young.

After the meal, everyone hit the dance floor. At one point, the DJ played a slower song, and I happened to look over and notice an interesting sight—Holden dancing with Ryan's little sister, Laney, whom we all affectionately called Lala. Well, I say *little*, but she was definitely all grown up now. She'd been dancing with her fiancé just minutes before. But in this moment, her fiancé was nowhere to be found. Normally, there wouldn't be anything notable about a girl dancing with a so-called friend of the family. Except I knew about Holden's crush on her that went way back. The way he'd swooped in the first chance he got tonight made me wonder if he had an ulterior motive.

When the song ended, he bent to give her a kiss on the cheek. Then he walked away.

My eyes followed as he headed straight for the bar and ordered another drink. Then I looked back over at Laney and noticed her fiancé, Warren, reappearing on the dance floor next to her. It was like that little blip with Holden never even happened. My eyes wandered from Warren and Laney back to Holden, who now watched them from the bar.

Billie was off chatting with guests at one of the tables, so I took the opportunity to go over to where Holden was sitting.

I placed my hand on his shoulder. "Feel like getting some air with me? It's a nice night."

He shrugged. "Sure."

I ordered a beer, and we walked out to the veranda.

"I saw you dancing with Lala."

Holden's longish hair blew in the breeze. "You mean the blink-and-you-missed-it dance?"

I smiled. "You took the opportunity the one moment Warren went to the bathroom, huh?"

He grimaced. "What does she see in him anyway?"

"He seems like a nice guy. Really smart—like her. Maybe that's not what you want to hear."

"Smart?" His eyes widened. "Why? Because he's got some dorky science job?"

I glared at him. "Cancer researcher."

"Details." Holden sipped his beer. "Anyway… He's still a fucking dork."

"Well, so is Lala, sort of." I laughed. "And I mean that in the nicest way. She's a sweet, adorable nerd."

"Yeah, she is," he muttered, staring out.

"We can't help who we're drawn to, Holden. You said it yourself. Opposites attract. But I mean, even if she didn't have the fiancé, do you think you'd be right for her at this stage in your life? Lala's not the type of girl you cheat on." I stared into his eyes. "You know?"

"Fuck no, she isn't." He looked down at the ground.

"So maybe it's better that she's with this guy, if he makes her happy and takes care of her. It's what Ryan would've wanted."

"Right. Ryan would *not* have wanted her with me. We all know that." He laughed bitterly before taking another sip of his beer. He slammed the bottle down on a table. "Can we be done talking about this? It's pointless."

I regretted bringing it up. "Whatever you want, man."

Holden then walked away, brushing past Billie on his way inside.

"There you are," she said, looking over her shoulder. "Everything okay with Holden?"

I shook my head. "Not really. But he'll be alright. I think he's had a little too much to drink."

A look of concern crossed her face. "Is this about Ryan's sister?"

"You know about that? I didn't think I'd ever mentioned it to you."

"Have you ever heard that guy talk during a tattoo appointment? I've heard Holden's entire life story ten times over. Plus, I saw him dancing with her. She's really cute—and nice. Too bad Holden wasn't…"

"Holden?"

"Yeah." She smiled sadly.

I exhaled. "Has anyone seen my daughter lately?"

"Don't worry. My mom is looking after her. Oddly, she actually enjoys my mother's company. At least someone does."

"Saylor loves everyone," I said.

"I think my mom loves what a girly girl Saylor is, since she never got that from me."

I laughed, wrapping my arm around her. "Hey—question. Has anyone ever left their own wedding to fuck in the bushes?"

Billie and I had decided to skip sex for a week before the event to make our wedding night even more intense.

"I said we could wait until the wedding, but I didn't mean *at* the wedding," she said.

I kissed her forehead. "I'd probably never be able to undo all those ties on your dress in time to get us back in there before the reception ended. So I guess I'll have to wait." I sighed, inhaling some of the night air. "It's kind of nice to have this break, just the two of us, huh? I feel like I haven't stopped to breathe all night."

She brushed her fingers through my hair. "I know."

"Listen…I wanted to mention something to you while we have a moment to ourselves."

She tilted her head. "What?"

"After our dance, Saylor whispered in my ear, asking me if I thought she could call you Mom now that you and I were married."

"Oh my God." Billie placed her hand on her chest. "You know that's something I want. I just never wanted to pressure her. I always figured it would happen when she felt ready, you know?"

"Yeah. Of course. I think she's holding back because she needs to know that's what *you* want."

Tears filled her eyes. "I'm so glad you told me. To think she's been afraid to…"

We heard the DJ call out for us, so we returned inside where Billie threw her bouquet. This woman who worked at my firm ended up catching it, nearly falling flat on her ass in the process. Soon after, I was surprised to see Billie head up to the DJ and ask him for the microphone.

She cleared her throat to get everyone's attention. "Thank you, everyone, for coming tonight and celebrating the beginning of the rest of our lives with us. I just wanted to acknowledge how much I appreciate you all. This is the most important day of my life…" Her eyes searched for me on the dance floor. "Not only because I married the man of my dreams, but because of the beautiful little girl I get to spend my life with." She looked down at Saylor standing next to me. "Saylor has accepted me with open arms from the moment we met. We became instant friends, but over time, we have become so much more. There's only one thing I want more than to be Colby's wife, and that's to be Saylor's mom." She waved for Saylor to come join her.

I watched as my daughter walked slowly toward Billie.

Walking toward her mom for the first time.

Billie bent to embrace her. "I love you so much, sweetie."

My daughter broke out into tears. "I love you, too, Mommy."

My heart was fuller than it had ever been. This was the moment that brought everything we'd been through full circle. Because no matter what happened between Billie and me, agreeing to be someone's mother was for life. It was the ultimate commitment, more than any wedding ceremony or legal paper. I knew Billie would always be there for Saylor. As much as I'd tried to be Saylor's entire world, the one thing I could never be was her mother. I was grateful Saylor didn't have to live her entire life without one.

As I looked over at my two angels hugging in their white dresses, for the first time on my wedding day I finally broke down and cried.

GUESS WHAT'S COMING IN 2023!
HOLDEN'S BOOK

Dear Readers,

While we were writing *The Rules of Dating*, we fell so in love with Holden that we immediately had to start writing his book as soon as we finished Colby and Billie's story! Which means, you don't have to wait too long for it…

The Rules of Dating My Best Friend's Sister is coming in April, 2023 and is available for pre-order now!

(https://smarturl.it/TRODAmazon)

ACKNOWLEDGEMENTS

Thank you to all of the amazing bloggers, bookstagrammers and BookTokers who helped spread the news about *The Rules of Dating*. Your excitement keeps us going, and we are forever grateful for all of your support.

To our rocks: Julie, Luna and Cheri – Thank you for your friendship and always being just a click away when we need you.

To our super agent, Kimberly Brower – Thank you for always believing in us and helping to get our books into the hands of readers internationally.

To Jessica – It's always a pleasure working with you as our editor. Thank you for making sure Colby and Billie were ready for the world.

To Elaine – An amazing editor, proofer, formatter, and friend. We so appreciate you!

To Julia – Thank you for being our eagle eye!

To Kylie and Jo at Give Me Books Promotions – Our releases would simply be impossible without your hard work and dedication to helping us promote them.

To Sommer – Thank you for bringing Colby to life on the cover and for creating the perfect backdrop.

To Brooke – Thank you for organizing this release and for taking some of the load off of our endless to-do lists each day.

Last but not least, to our readers – We keep writing because of your hunger for our stories. We are so very excited for our next adventure with Holden and Lala! Thank you as always for your enthusiasm, love and loyalty. We cherish you!

Much love,
Penelope and Vi

OTHER BOOKS BY
Penelope Ward & Vi Keeland

Well Played

Park Avenue Player

Stuck-Up Suit (

Cocky Bastard

Not Pretending Anymore

Happily Letter After

My Favorite Souvenir

Dirty Letters

Hate Notes

Rebel Heir

Rebel Heart

Mister Moneybags

British Bedmate

Playboy Pilot

OTHER BOOKS FROM PENELOPE WARD

Moody

The Assignment

The Aristocrat

The Crush

The Anti-Boyfriend

Just One Year

The Day He Came Back

When August Ends

Love Online

Gentleman Nine

Drunk Dial

Mack Daddy

Stepbrother Dearest

Neighbor Dearest

RoomHate

Sins of Sevin

Jake Undone (Jake #1)

My Skylar (Jake #2)

Jake Understood (Jake #3)

Gemini

OTHER BOOKS FROM VI KEELAND

The Boss Project

The Summer Proposal

The Spark

The Invitation

The Rivals

Inappropriate

All Grown Up

We Shouldn't

The Naked Truth

Sex, Not Love

Beautiful Mistake

Egomaniac

Bossman

The Baller

Left Behind

Beat

Throb

Worth the Fight

Worth the Chance

Worth Forgiving

Belong to You

Made for You

First Thing I See

CONNECT
with the Authors

Enjoy *The Rules of Dating?* Then connect with the authors!

Join Penelope Ward's reading group
https://www.facebook.com/groups/PenelopesPeeps/
Join Vi Keeland's reading group
https://www.facebook.com/groups/ViKeelandFanGroup/

Follow Penelope Ward on Instagram
https://www.instagram.com/PenelopeWardAuthor/
Follow Vi Keeland on Instagram
https://www.instagram.com/vi_keeland/

Check out Penelope Ward's website
https://penelopewardauthor.com/
Check out Vi Keeland's website
https://www.vikeeland.com/

Check out Penelope Ward on TikTok
https://www.tiktok.com/@penelopewardofficial
Check out Vi Keeland on TikTok
https://www.tiktok.com/@vikeeland

Penelope Ward is a *New York Times, USA Today,* and #1 *Wall Street Journal* Bestselling author. With over two-million books sold, she's a 21-time New York Times bestseller. Her novels are published in over a dozen languages and can be found in bookstores around the world. Having grown up in Boston with five older brothers, she spent most of her twenties as a television news anchor, before switching to a more family-friendly career. She is the proud mother of a beautiful 16-year-old girl with autism and a 14-year-old boy. Penelope and her family reside in Rhode Island.

Connect with Penelope Ward
Facebook Private Fan Group:
https://www.facebook.com/groups/PenelopesPeeps/
Facebook: https://www.facebook.com/penelopewardauthor
TikTok: https://www.tiktok.com/@penelopewardofficial
Website: http://www.penelopewardauthor.com
Twitter: https://twitter.com/PenelopeAuthor
Instagram: http://instagram.com/PenelopeWardAuthor/

Vi Keeland is a #1 *New York Times*, #1 *Wall Street Journal*, and *USA Today* Bestselling author. With millions of books sold, her titles are currently translated in twenty-seven languages and have appeared on bestseller lists in the US, Germany, Brazil, Bulgaria, and Hungary. Three of her short stories have been turned into films by Passionflix, and two of her books are currently optioned for movies. She resides in New York with her husband and their three children where she is living out her own happily ever after with the boy she met at age six.

Connect with Vi Keeland
Facebook Fan Group:
https://www.facebook.com/groups/ViKeelandFanGroup/)
Facebook: https://www.facebook.com/pages/Author-
Vi-Keeland/435952616513958
TikTok: https://www.tiktok.com/@vikeeland
Website: http://www.vikeeland.com
Twitter: https://twitter.com/ViKeeland
Instagram: http://instagram.com/Vi_Keeland/

Made in the USA
Las Vegas, NV
21 September 2022

55700584R00225